· TO ·
HATRED
TURNED

OTHER BOOKS BY KEN ENGLADE

▼

BEYOND REASON
A FAMILY BUSINESS
DEADLY LESSONS
MURDER IN BOSTON
CELLAR OF HORROR
HOFFA, A NOVELIZATION

◄ TO ►

HATRED TURNED

A True Story of Love and Death in Texas

▼

KEN ENGLADE

ST. MARTIN'S PRESS
New York

Design by Kathryn Parise

Library of Congress Cataloging-in-Publication Data

Englade, Ken.
    To hatred turned : a true story of love and death in Texas / Ken
Englade.
        p.   cm.
    ISBN 0-312-09924-X
    1. Aylor, Joy.   2. Murderers—Texas—Biography.   3. Murder—Texas—
Case studies.   I. Title.
HV6248.A94E54   1993
364.1′523′097642812—dc20   93-20793
                                                                CIP

10   9   8   7   6   5   4   3   2

For Gary and Shell

ACKNOWLEDGMENTS

Due to circumstances beyond my control, there were times when it seemed that this book would never be published. If any single person was largely responsible for getting it into print, it was my agent and friend Scott Siegel. To him I am especially grateful.

Helping to fill in many of the blanks in this story, which so far has been ten years in development and still is not played out, was Larry Aylor, whose life was changed radically by the events described herein. There are others as well who helped me along the way, many in more ways than they realize. Among those to whom I owe special gratitude are Larry Mitchell and Peter Lesser, who gave generously of their time and expertise, and who provided me with priceless insight into a complicated situation. Also providing valuable material at times when I really needed it were Captain Morris McGowan and Glenna Whitley. To them, I am also indebted.

One tremendous personal benefit that resulted from researching this book was that I got the chance to renew old friendships among current and former journalists in Dallas and Paris, all of whom gave unselfishly of their insight and knowledge. My sincerest appreciation to Steve Reed, Travis Hughs, Paul Freeman, and Arthur Higbee.

Others to whom I owe special thanks for many services en route to the completion of this book include Judge Pat McDowell and his courtroom family—Pat, Ginny, Margie, and King—along with Scot Key, Donna Reed, Heidi Hizel, Rich Gibula, Diana Higbee, Linda Little, Jim Wieck, Nicole Perrier, Michael Byck, and C.C. Risenhoover. Thanks to you all.

DRAMATIS PERSONAE

Joy Jeannine Davis Aylor, homemaker and wife of Larry Aylor. Daughter of Texas multimillionaire Henry Davis, who made his fortune in the construction business. A.k.a. Mary, Mrs. John Storms, Jodi Packer, Jodie Packer, Leigh Curry, Stephenie Grimes, J. Taylor, and Elizabeth May Sharp. Born August 13, 1949.

Larry Wayne Aylor, successful builder of homes in wealthy Dallas suburbs. Husband of Joy. Born January 16, 1948.

Christopher Davis Aylor, Larry and Joy's only child. Born May 8, 1970. Died December 26, 1989, of injuries suffered in a car crash.

Carol Davis Walker Garland, Joy's sister, older by two years.

Elizabeth Davis Goacher, Joy's sister, younger by eleven years.

Dr. Peter Gailiunas, Jr., a respected Dallas kidney specialist. Husband of Rozanne. Born circa 1947.

Rozanne Borghi Gailiunas, a registered nurse and wife of Dr. Peter Gailiunas. Born September 24, 1950. Died October 6, 1983.

Peter Gailiunas III, son of Peter and Rozanne. Born April 19, 1979.

Morris McGowan, an investigator in Richardson, Texas, a Dallas suburb.

Ken McKenzie, also an investigator for the Richardson Police Department.

George Anderson Hopper, auto body shop manager, entrepreneur, free-lance insurance estimator, and one-time student in an Assembly of God seminary. Born October 6, 1955.

William Wesley Garland, a Dallas pest exterminator and later secret spouse of Joy's older sister, Carol. Born December 17, 1942.

John Michael Wilson, former Dallas prosecutor and defense attorney. Joy's lover. Born circa 1945. A.k.a. John Storms.

Jodie Timothy Packer, successful owner of an interior design business in Dallas. Joy's lover. A.k.a. Donald Averille Airhart. Born October 9, 1946.

Douglas Mulder, former Dallas prosecutor and well-known defense attorney specializing in high-profile cases. Joy's lawyer.

Lawrence Mitchell, Dallas defense attorney specializing in appeals. Born July 1, 1947.

Peter Lesser, controversial Dallas defense attorney and unsuccessful politician. Born April 21, 1947.

Patrick McDowell, district judge in Dallas County.

Kevin Chapman, former Dallas prosecutor. Born October 9, 1955.

Daniel Hagood, Dallas prosecutor. Born March 28, 1952.

Buster James, born August 17, 1942, and *William Gary*, born August 9, 1951, *Matthews*, ne'er-do-well brothers from Dallas.

PROLOGUE

▼

Peter Gailiunas was chatting with his mother when the conversation was interrupted by the familiar but irritating click that told him someone else was trying to get through to his number.

"I have to get that, Mother," he said. "Hold on for a minute."

He depressed the plunger to switch to the incoming call and spoke into the mouthpiece.

"Yes," he said sharply, "this is Dr. Gailiunas."

"Hi, Dad," squeaked a familiar voice. "Where are you?"

Gailiunas sighed in relief. It was his four-and-a-half-year-old son, Peter Gailiunas III, commonly called Little Peter.

"I'm at home," Gailiunas said, looking at his watch. It was 6:15 P.M. "You should be here," he scolded. "You're late. Where's Mom?"

"She's sleeping," Little Peter replied.

"*You* didn't call me, did you?" Gailiunas said, doubting that the boy knew how to operate a telephone, much less that he could remember the phone number.

"Yes," Little Peter replied proudly.

"I didn't know you knew how to dial," the doctor said with no little amount of affection. "Go get Mom."

Gailiunas drummed his fingers, waiting for his son to summon his mother.

Little Peter was back on the line in less than two minutes. "I can't wake her up," he said. "She's sleeping."

Gailiunas frowned. "Go back and try again," he said.

For the second time, Little Peter returned and said he still was unable to awaken her.

Gailiunas, annoyed, urged him to try yet again.

"I really can't wake her up, Dad," the boy said after the third attempt. "She's sick."

Gailiunas's exasperation turned to concern. "What do you mean, 'sick'?" he asked.

"She's really sick," Little Peter said. "There's green stuff coming out of her mouth."

Gailiunas tensed. "Are you okay?" he asked abruptly.

"Yes," replied Little Peter.

"Is anyone in the house?"

"No."

"Then lock the door," Gailiunas ordered, "and don't let anyone in. Daddy will be there."

Less than thirty minutes later the phone rang in the house where Little Peter lived with his mother. The boy answered it on the second ring.

"Hello," he whispered uncertainly.

"Hello, Peter," a man's voice replied. "This is Larry Aylor. Let me speak to your mom."

"She's sick," said the boy.

"Where is she?" Aylor asked.

"In bed."

"Go get her," Aylor instructed. "She'll want to talk to me."

"I can't," the boy replied. "She's sick bad."

Aylor opened his mouth, intending to insist, when he heard a man's voice in the background.

"Hang up the goddamn phone!" the man screamed.

Before Aylor could respond, the line went dead.

Heaven has no rage like love to hatred turned,
Nor hell a fury like a woman scorned.

—William Congreve, 1670–1729

PART I

◄ 1983–87 ►

1

Larry Aylor, a wiry, compact man built like a shortstop, had been up since daybreak. The sun had barely cleared the tree-lined horizon before he was out in his pickup truck, making his daily inspection of the houses he was building in the expensive, sprawling neighborhoods of trendy North Dallas.

One of the reasons he was out so early on that steamy, cloudless morning of October 4, 1983, was habit. In the dozen years he had been in business for himself, the thirty-five-year-old contractor had developed the practice of timing his visits so he could arrive at a job site as soon after his subcontractors as possible. That way if there was a problem he would know about it while he still had the whole day to get it fixed. Another reason was because he was too nervous to sleep. In a mere six days, Larry planned to begin a new life. On October 10, his fifteen-year-old marriage to his high school sweetheart, a once-happy union that had turned sour and mutually acrimonious, was scheduled to be dissolved. It was no coincidence that on that same day his new girl-friend's divorce also would become final. Then he and Rozanne Gailiu-nas would be free. As far as Larry was concerned, it could not come too soon.

Since he was in the neighborhood after having inspected one of his houses, Larry drove by the home of his parents, which was not too far from the small apartment he had moved into the previous spring after one too many arguments with his soon to be ex-wife, Joy. As he turned onto their street, Larry was slightly surprised to see Rozanne's brown Cadillac in the driveway. In the six months he and Rozanne had been dating, she had become close to Larry's parents, Clyde and Maxine, and to his three sisters, Karen, Terry, and Cindy. But Rozanne had not told him when they talked the night before that she was planning to visit the Aylors this morning. Shrugging, he turned off the ignition and walked briskly to the back door.

"Hi," he yelled enthusiastically, bursting into the kitchen where Rozanne and his sister Cindy, who was living with their parents, were sitting around a small table drinking coffee. "What are y'all up to?" he asked.

"I was just telling Cindy about my flat," Rozanne said, clipping off her words in a crisp Boston accent that five years in Texas had failed to dull.

"What flat?" Larry asked, frowning.

"Oh, that same old stuff," Rozanne said vaguely. "Someone let the air out of one of my tires."

"Damn," Larry said, his good mood dimming. "I was hoping we were through all that."

"Well," Rozanne said cheerfully, "we will be pretty soon. But let's not talk about that right now."

"Okay," Larry said, forcing a smile. Pulling up a chair and helping himself to some coffee, he joined the women, spending an unremarkable twenty minutes chatting about nothing in particular.

"I'd better go," he said when there was a lull in the conversation. "I've got a ton of paperwork to do." Turning to Rozanne, he asked her if she was coming to his apartment.

"Yes," she said brightly. "You go ahead and I'll be there in a few minutes."

Waving good-bye to his sister, Larry left.

An hour later, he and Rozanne lay peacefully on his bed, sweating freely despite the fact that the air conditioner was turned on high.

"It's going to be a scorcher today," Larry said, as much to himself as to Rozanne.

"Mmmmm," she mumbled drowsily.

Larry raised himself on one elbow and grinned down at her. "You can stay in bed as long as you want," he teased her, "but I wasn't kidding when I said I had some paperwork to do."

Rising, he pulled on his jeans and short-sleeved western shirt and tiptoed into the living room. A half hour later, he was deep in concentration when Rozanne came in fully dressed.

"I have to go," she said softly. "It's time to pick up Little Peter."

Larry glanced at his watch, surprised at how the morning had flown. "I didn't realize it was so late," he said. "You'd better hustle. We still on for tonight?"

"Of course," she said, leaning over to kiss him. "I'll come by as soon as I take Peter to his father's."

"Okay," Larry said, somewhat distractedly, his mind already back on his figures. He turned back to his stack of papers, but when he looked up several minutes later, he noticed that she was still standing at the end of the couch. Tears were rolling down her cheeks.

"What's wrong?" he asked, startled.

"Nothing," she said quietly.

"Then why are you crying?" Larry wanted to know.

"I'll just be glad when this is all over," she sighed.

"So will I," Larry agreed, taking her in his arms.

For several minutes they stood there, neither of them speaking. "Come on," Larry said finally, "I'll walk you to your car."

Seconds later she was smiling and laughing, her earlier concerns apparently forgotten. "Have I told you yet how much I love you?" she said, buckling her seat belt.

"No." He grinned. "How much *do* you love me?"

"The most," she replied, starting the Cadillac with a flick of her wrist.

Larry grinned and waved as she pulled out of the driveway, heading in the direction of the day care center attended by her young son.

As Larry turned to walk back to his apartment, his smile was replaced by a frown as he thought about Rozanne's tears and about how someone had apparently been following her. Over the months since they became lovers there had been one hassle after another for Rozanne, most of them, Rozanne believed, initiated by her husband, Dr. Peter Gailiunas, a Dallas kidney specialist, who opposed his wife's divorce. Almost from their very first date, Rozanne had begun telling him about the troubles between her and her husband. Although Larry's wife, Joy, was scarcely happy about *his* divorce plans, outwardly she was not reacting nearly as badly as Rozanne's spouse. Opening a can of diet Sprite, Larry sank into his couch and thought about how he had first met the Gailiunases.

The association began in December 1982, he remembered, almost a year ago. He was deer hunting on a lease in the Texas Hill Country when Joy tracked him down with a message.

"You need to get back to Dallas," Joy told him when he telephoned. "A doctor called and he wants you to build him a house."

"Did you tell him I was hunting?" Larry asked.

"Yes," Joy said, "but he wants to talk to you *now*."

Larry digested what she had said, then replied, "Well, tell him I'll be back Sunday."

Joy tried to insist that Larry return as soon as possible because the potential customer was impatient to get started.

"He can wait," Larry replied stubbornly. "I'm going to finish my hunt. Then I'll give him a call."

Several days later, just as the sun was setting, Larry drove to the address in north-central Dallas that Dr. Gailiunas had given him over the telephone. Parking at the curb, Larry looked at the house and was surprised to feel himself shiver. Although the Gailiunases lived in a typical Dallas ranch–style brick dwelling, not a New England Gothic, the fact that it was set deep in a stand of pines and all the windows were dark made Larry think of the house depicted in the TV show about the spooky Addams family. Chuckling at his silliness, Larry climbed out of his truck and strode toward the front door. Thumbtacked to the frame was a handwritten placard reading, "Please do not ring the bell. The baby is sleeping."

Shrugging, Larry walked around the back of the house and rapped lightly on the kitchen door. Seconds later, it flew open and Larry found himself gawking at one of the most beautiful women he had ever seen. She had thick, dark hair, eyes the color of Godiva chocolate, and a smile that would thaw Greenland. In her left hand was a chicken leg.

"Oh, God," she said, swallowing a mouthful of fowl, "I thought it was my neighbor. You must be here to see my husband about the house."

"That's right," Larry stammered.

"Well, come on in," she said, waving the drumstick like a wand.

Larry stepped inside and stared at her, their eyes almost on a level.

"Go on in," she said, pointing to a door that led to the den. "Peter will be right with you. I'm still feeding Little Peter," she explained, apologizing for forgetting to remove the "baby sleeping" sign from the door.

The den was a sterile-looking, inhospitable room, Larry noticed, lit only by the light from a television set, which was showing the movie *The Stepford Wives*. Letting his eyes adjust to the gloom, he picked out a chair and nervously plopped down. Twenty minutes later, when the man who had summoned him had not come to greet him, Larry considered saying to hell with it and leaving. Just as he was rising, he heard heavy footsteps coming down the hall.

Looming toward him out of the dark was a tall, gangly figure with broad, bony shoulders and large ears that stuck out from the side of his head. As he watched the man approach, Larry's analogy to the house as that of the Addams family came back to him. This is Lurch, he told himself.

The man, however, introduced himself in a deep voice as Dr. Peter Gailiunas. Without a word of welcome, Gailiunas strode to a wet bar across the room and poured himself a drink. He did not offer to make one for his guest.

Twirling his glass until the ice cubes tinkled, Gailiunas, a slim man of thirty-six, a year older than Larry, with thinning brown hair and sunken cheeks, collapsed ungracefully onto the couch.

Disdaining the small talk that is common when two men are about to discuss a deal in the making, especially in Texas, where strangers go through a complicated social dance before they talk about anything as serious as money, Gailiunas, a Bostonian like Rozanne, jumped immediately to business. He wanted, he said, to build a new house for himself, his wife, and their young son, Peter III, then almost four. He had gotten Larry's name and phone number, he said, off a sign in front of an almost-completed home on the quiet street where Gailiunas wanted to build. It was a well-to-do neighborhood closer to downtown and the city's health-center complex. He had admired the workmanship on the home he had seen, Gailiunas added, and he was interested in having Larry as his contractor. Did he want the job?

"Tell me more about it," Larry said carefully, feeling immediately uncomfortable with this man, whom he had pegged as an impolite snob and a cold fish. But business was business and Larry was not one to reject an opportunity to take on another assignment just because he felt an instinctive dislike for the man with the checkbook.

"Just a minute," Gailiunas said. "I want to get my wife in on this." Walking to the door, he called Rozanne's name loudly. When she appeared, sans drumstick, she sat quietly in the corner, only half-listening as her husband outlined his plans.

Larry, who was studying her carefully through covert glances, got the impression that she was bored.

In the end, despite his feelings about Gailiunas, feelings that would intensify rather than diminish as he got to know him, Larry agreed to build the house, which he priced out at $480,000. Larry had a reputation for building solid if somewhat expensive homes and he did not feel that the figure he quoted Gailiunas was unreasonable. Obviously, neither did Gailiunas because the project moved ahead.

Before leaving the Gailiunas house that evening, Larry explained that he and his wife, Joy, worked as a team in the business. He handled the construction end and his wife designed the interiors. Would Gailiunas have any problem with that? he asked.

No, said the physician, but he had a request as well. He wanted to get his wife, Rozanne, as involved as possible in the new house. She was, Gailiunas confided, unhappy with staying home. Ever since he had talked her into leaving her job as a nurse in the burn unit at Parkland Hospital, the huge, rambling structure off the Stemmons Freeway that drew international attention in 1963 when the wounded President Kennedy was rushed there after he was shot by Lee Harvey Oswald, she had been out of sorts. Would Larry and his wife have any objection to working closely with her?

Larry looked at Rozanne and smiled.

"Of course not," he said.

2

Despite his initial strong attraction to Rozanne, Larry was extraordinarily cautious in beginning an affair. The Gailiunases broke ground on their new house in January 1983 and construction proceeded at a rapid pace. Although Gailiunas had urged Larry to encourage Rozanne's participation in the process, Larry could see that her heart was not really in it. Her lack of interest became unquestionably apparent that spring.

One morning late in April, while Rozanne was on a visit to the site to check on some minor detail that Gailiunas had pushed off on her, Larry thought she looked depressed. He offered to take her to lunch at the Black-eyed Pea, a nearby restaurant that specialized in country cooking. Over meatloaf and iced tea, Larry asked Rozanne what was wrong.

She stared at her plate, pushing her pot roast around with her fork. Finally, she looked up and Larry could see tears brimming in her eyes.

"I just don't want to build this house," she confessed in a hushed voice.

Larry's eyes widened in surprise. "Why not?" he asked. It was going to be a wonderful house and he was doing some of his best work.

"It isn't you and it isn't the house," Rozanne said. "It's just that *I* never wanted to build it!"

Again she grew quiet.

Larry sipped his tea and waited for her to continue.

When she looked at him again, Larry could see more defiance in her eyes than sadness.

"Peter and I are having marital problems," she said, seemingly having decided to unburden herself, "and as soon as this house is finished, I'm out of here."

Larry nodded sympathetically. "I had no idea," he said.

"I know you didn't," she replied. "Maybe I shouldn't have told you."

"No," Larry added hastily. "I'm glad you did because I know what you're going through. Joy and I have been having problems, too. In fact we're talking about getting a divorce."

Rozanne looked at him with new understanding. "I'm sorry," she said.

"Don't be," Larry added. "It happens. But I'm glad you told me about you and Peter because it means we have a lot in common. I'm in the same boat you are."

Rozanne put her hands on top of his. "Tell me about you and Joy," she said softly.

The first time Larry saw Joy was at a football game in October 1964. Hillcrest High, which Larry had attended for two years, was playing W. T. White, the school he was forced to attend in his junior year because of a bureaucratic reshuffling of school districts. Larry had sat through the first half on White's side of the stadium, but at halftime he and a friend walked over to the Hillcrest bleachers so he could visit with some of his former classmates. One of the first people he saw as he climbed the steps was an old acquaintance. Sitting next to him was a slim blonde with large green eyes and a captivating smile. Gosh, she's pretty, Larry remembered saying to himself. I wonder who she is.

The friend did not introduce him, so Larry climbed a few rows higher and sat down, waiting for the second half to start. But he was only half-watching the action on the gridiron. One eye was on the field; the other was on the blonde a few rows below him. He was gratified to note that she also seemed interested in him because she kept turning around and looking in his direction.

A few minutes later, he saw a girl he knew from Hillcrest coming up the steps. She stopped to talk to the blonde, then looked up at Larry, who waved her over. "Who is that?" Larry asked, pointing toward the blonde.

"That's Joy Davis," the girl said. "She's a sophomore."

"Is she going with anyone in particular?" Larry asked.

"Not that I know of," the girl replied.

"Good," Larry replied, "because I'd like to meet her."

"Funny you said that," the girl told him, "because she just told me she'd like to meet you, too."

After the game, he talked briefly to Joy, but did not have a chance to ask her out before her date hurried her away. Larry's opportunity came a few days later.

After school and on Saturdays, Larry had a job as a bag boy at a neighborhood supermarket. A couple of afternoons after the Hillcrest/ White game, Larry and a coworker were talking about girls when the coworker mentioned that he had a date that Saturday night with a Hillcrest girl named Joy Davis. The next day, when the store manager posted the work schedules for the weekend, Larry's coworker groaned in disappointment.

"What's the matter?" Larry asked.

"I have to work Saturday night," the other youth complained.

"So?" Larry asked.

"So that means I can't go out with Joy Davis," the youth replied.

Larry beamed. "In that case," he asked, "do you mind if I call her? Just so she won't have to sit at home all by herself."

The youth studied his friend. "Why the hell not?" he said.

When Larry showed up at Joy's house to pick her up, his knock was answered by another youth whom Larry recognized immediately. Although the youth did not know Larry, Larry knew Michael Walker because he worked in a popular record store that was frequented by neighborhood teens. When Michael opened the door, the first thing Larry noticed was a lot of yelling in the background.

"What do you want?" Michael asked rather abruptly.

"I have a date with Joy," Larry stammered. "Am I at the right house?"

"Yeah," Michael answered, his voice rising above the noise, "come on in."

A few seconds later, Joy rushed up and grabbed Larry by the arm, pulling him into the living room.

"It's kind of wild around here right now," she explained. In the other room, Larry could hear another girl screaming and cursing. He started to ask what was going on when Michael Walker ran through the room. Right behind him was a slim girl with frizzy blond hair. She was waving a shoe in her hand. As Larry watched in amazement, Michael made it almost to the opposite door before the girl threw the shoe, bouncing it neatly and undoubtedly painfully off the back of Michael's head.

"Take that!" she screamed.

Bewildered, Larry turned to Joy. "Who the hell is *that*?" he asked.

Joy grinned meekly and shrugged. "That's my sister Carol," she said.

Later, as Larry and Joy dated regularly and eventually began going steady, Larry discovered that Carol, older than Joy by almost two years, was totally unpredictable. She had a firecracker temper and a nasty mouth that she never tried to govern. In contrast, Joy's younger sister, Elizabeth, usually called Liz, was a sweet-tempered child of five who followed Larry around like puppy. Often, when he and Joy went to the movies or a sporting event, they would take Liz along as well. Carol, however, insisted on going her own way and, despite her frequent fights with Michael Walker, the two persisted in their relationship.

From his position of being slightly removed from the family, Larry was able to stand back and study the dynamics of the Davis household. The patriarch of the clan was Henry Davis, a tall, bony man then in his early forties.

Henry, as so many young men of his generation had done, left the family farm in Ennis, a small community south of Dallas, for the lights of the city. When he left the farm, he often liked to brag, he had only fifty cents in his pocket and no discernible talent other than an amazing capacity for hard, physical labor.

Signing on as laborer in a tile-setting crew, Henry quickly built a reputation as a man of remarkable stamina. While other burlier and seemingly more robust men wilted quickly under the hot Texas sun, Henry was able to continue for hours the back-breaking labor of mixing tubs of the thick cement, called "mud," that was required as base for the tile. The setting of the tile itself was a skilled job that required years of apprenticeship. Eventually, Henry graduated from laborer to tile setter and, while his work was generally regarded as well above average, he was still better known among the area contractors and subcontractors for his physical endurance.

While Henry worked hard, he also played hard. On Saturday nights, after everyone got paid, Henry would often hurry down to lower Greenville Avenue, where Dallas's blue-collar workers liked to gather to drink and play poker and craps. As often as not, Henry would go home the winner.

Still, his Saturday night forays did not sit well with his new wife, Frances, a straitlaced country girl from the community of Alma, which was even smaller than Ennis. Frequently, when Henry returned to their small house early on Sunday, staggering somewhat as a result of the alcohol he had imbibed during the evening, Frances would greet him with a severe tongue lashing. Once, Henry later told Larry, he came home more than a little inebriated and Frances got so furious that she shoved him into the bathtub and turned on the cold water in an attempt to sober him up. As the water rose over the semiconscious Henry, who was sitting uncomplaining in his work clothes in the rising water, a twenty-dollar bill floated to the top. As Frances watched, another twenty floated upward. Then another and another. By the time the surface of the water was covered with bills, Frances had forgotten how angry she had been and threw her arms around Henry with a squeal of delight.

Thanks mainly to his skill at gambling and Frances's careful management of finances, Henry had some money set aside that he could use for investment. Ignorant of stocks and bonds, treasury notes and portfolios, Henry waited instead for an opportunity to invest in the only business he knew: tile setting.

After World War Two, when the housing boom hit Dallas hard, tile became very scarce, so scarce in fact that contractors would pay almost any price for it. Through his contacts, Henry heard of several boxcar loads of tile that had unexpectedly come on the market and were for sale. Using all of his savings, Henry bought the supply and then resold the tile at a handsome profit, which he plowed back into still more tile. In the few years he had been in Dallas, Henry had gone from a helper to a tile setter to a tile dealer.

Shrewdly using the money he made from the tile, Henry expanded his ambitions and opened a contracting business. It did so well that he sent for his brothers, Hugh, Randall, and Sonny, summoning them from the farm to work alongside him in Dallas and eventualiy start their own contracting companies. None of them, however, was as successful as Henry. By the time Larry started dating Joy, Henry was an established high-volume builder who at any one time might have as many as twenty-five houses under construction.

All this time, his bank account was growing. Eventually, after Joy and Larry got married and were raising a child of their own, Henry's worth was estimated to be in excess of $15 million.

But to look at Henry, no one would have thought he was wealthy. Despite his growing bank account, he still preferred khaki pants and work shirts to suits, and rough-cut work boots to fancy Florsheims. Despite his money, he looked rough, acted rough, and talked rough, liberally spicing his conversations with farm-country slang and colorful curses.

His wife, Frances, was totally opposite. She preferred stylish dresses and diamond-studded jewelry. Henry drove a pickup truck; Frances, a Cadillac convertible. Henry liked to associate with working men, while Frances became a patron of the arts and volunteered for civic activities. And just as they themselves were different, their children were different as well.

Carol seemed to be Frances's favorite, while Henry appeared to be more indulgent of Joy. The baby, Liz, came along so late that she seemed to be accepted equally by her parents.

Because they were less than two years apart, a bitter rivalry also developed between Carol and Joy. When Carol was still in high school, she persuaded her parents to give her a 1963 Chevy Supersport convertible, which she used to race through the streets of North Dallas. When Joy got old enough for a car and asked for one just like Carol's, she was given a slightly less luxurious model, a regular convertible.

After Carol graduated from Hillcrest High, her parents willingly plopped down her tuition at Southern Methodist University, a prestigious college located in a fashionable Dallas neighborhood. But when Joy wanted to go to college two years later, her parents refused to send her.

When Carol married Michael Walker soon after she dropped out of SMU well short of graduation, Henry and Frances paid for a large wedding and an expensive reception. But when Joy and Larry married in August 1968, one week after Joy's nineteenth birthday, they were wed in a very small ceremony at a neighborhood Baptist church.

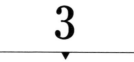

3

While Carol's relationship with Michael Walker had *always* been troubled (it surprised no one who knew them when they were divorced within a few years), Joy and Larry's pairing was relatively tranquil.

A native of Orange, Virginia, a small town in the hill country not far from Charlottesville, Larry had moved to Dallas with his parents and three sisters when he was nine. His father, Clyde, worked in the metal-products industry, selling movable partitions for high-rise office buildings.

Arriving in Dallas at the beginning of the city's expansion period, the Aylors settled in a quiet neighborhood called Lakewood, which was not far from where the Davises had built a home.

For the most part, Larry's early years were uneventful. He adjusted rapidly to Texas ways, forming early attachments to cars, hunting, and horses. To help support his hobbies, he worked at a series of odd jobs, bagging groceries, pumping gas, and selling clothing in an upscale men's shop. He liked girls and dancing and, until he met Joy, he indulged in both fairly heavily. Joy was not particularly fond of dancing, but she was nevertheless popular among her classmates, both male and female.

When Joy and Larry met, she was a sophomore and he was a junior. By the end of that school year they were going steady and dating a couple of nights each week, usually going to football games, concerts, and movies. One of their rituals was to meet every Wednesday night at Joy's and watch "The Beverly Hillbillies" on TV. However, each also maintained other friendships and when they were not with each other, they were likely out with members of their own circle. These extraneous friendships, Larry recalled later, were the cause of the few arguments they had during their courting years. A particular source of disagreement was Joy's friends, many of whom were regarded by Larry as flighty and rather wild.

Like Larry, Joy worked at several part-time jobs during her high school years and soon after graduation. For awhile she worked in the billing department at the telephone company, for instance, and she also sold women's clothes at a boutique.

Like many youths of the period, Larry and Joy had only a hazy view of the future: Neither was sure what to do.

Soon after Larry graduated from high school in 1966, his family moved back to Virginia. At that time, Larry planned to go to college, possibly to become a dentist, but he still needed a summer job. So he joined his parents and went to work with a crew that was building a new library at the University of Virginia. In the fall, he returned to Texas and enrolled at El Centro Junior College.

The following summer he went back to Virginia for an extended visit. A few weeks later, after she graduated from high school, Joy joined him at his parents' house for a few weeks. It was during her stay that they had their first really big argument.

According to Larry, he had met a girl in Texas who had become enamored of him and persisted in writing him. During her visit, Joy found the letters hidden in a drawer in Larry's room and confronted him with the evidence. Although they each did a lot of yelling and hurled accusations back and forth, they managed to patch it up. By the time they returned to Texas, they were again making tentative plans to be married.

It was that summer as well that a strange incident occurred involving a horse. While working at one of his part-time jobs, Larry became friends with a man who had a sideline business dealing in horses. The man would buy animals that were almost wild and break them himself. Then he would then sell them for twice what he had paid for them.

Larry went with his friend on one of his horse-buying trips and became very interested in a partially broken young mare. Intending to buy the horse himself, Larry was extremely disappointed when he discovered that he had only about half the amount of money needed to close the deal. When he told Joy how disappointed he was, she offered to put up the other half of the money. Apparently, however, the degree of her participation in the enterprise became somewhat distorted and a number of people, including Joy's father, believed that Joy had purchased the horse for Larry as a gift.

Larry spent much of the summer gentling the horse and when it came time for him to return to school in the fall, he put it up for sale. However, when the new buyer showed up to take possession of the horse, named Lady, she had disappeared from her pasture. Others who boarded horses at the same location said two men in a red horse trailer had shown up just before Larry and taken the horse away.

Larry reported the animal stolen, but he never expected to see it again. To his surprise, he was wrong. Twelve years later, he was driving through a rural section of South Dallas when he spotted an old horse grazing beside the highway. The horse, although aged and feeble, had the same distinctive markings as the colt that he remembered as Lady.

When he stopped and asked who owned the horse, Larry was directed to an elderly black man, who told him that he had bought the animal sometime earlier for his grandchildren to ride. Asked where he had gotten the horse, the man gave a name that Larry recognized as a friend of Joy's father, Henry Davis.

In the fall after the summer of the horse incident, Larry transferred from El Centro to North Texas in Denton, which was about forty miles north of Dallas and close enough for Joy to make frequent visits in her green convertible. Their relationship continued through that winter, even after Larry dropped out of college due to a severe case of flu that kept him from his classwork.

That August, almost three years after they met, Joy and Larry were married. Some twenty-one months later, on May 8, 1970, Joy gave birth to their only child, a boy they named Christopher Davis Aylor.

According to Larry, that was a major turning point in Joy's life. Just before Chris was born, Joy quit her job, and she didn't work outside the home again until after she and Larry were divorced years later. Instead, Joy devoted herself unselfishly to the baby.

"She was a wonderful mother," Larry said later. "She read to Chris at night. She played with him. She became very protective of him. She organized her life around the child."

At the same time she was moving closer to Chris, she was, according to Larry, moving further away from him, telling him that his sex drive was too strong and that he was making too many demands on her. In desperation, Larry once broached the subject to Joy's father. "What do you think about a woman in her twenties who says she doesn't need sex?" Larry asked Henry.

Henry looked closely at him and delivered some country wisdom, not necessarily reflecting on his daughter: "If you're not scratching it, someone else is," he said.

In a portrait taken late in 1971, when Christopher was nineteen months old, Joy and Larry looked like the typical young Dallas couple of the era. For the photograph, Joy wore a blue and white granny dress, primly buttoned almost to the neck. Her hair was more red than its natural blond, and she wore it in a bouffant, shoulder length with bangs that dipped below her brows. Although possessed of a well-shaped mouth, she was unsmiling, almost grim, for the camera. The picture, too, did little to emphasize her large eyes, which are accented by incredibly long lashes, or her satiny smooth skin. Joy was a woman who would get prettier as she aged.

Larry, on the other hand, was flamboyantly clothed in a sports shirt decorated with red, white, and blue squares. His hair was as long as Joy's, disappearing over his shoulder in the photograph. He, too, wore bangs that dipped sheepdog length—a marked contrast to later years when he would wear his hair in tight curls and sport, in succession, a short beard and then a mustache. Like Joy, Larry was unsmiling. The only one of the three showing any evident emotion was Chris, then a blond toddler, who was perched on Joy's lap wearing a blue and white checked jumper and an uncertain half-smile.

While Joy's attitude bothered Larry, he was too busy to give it his full attention.

After he dropped out of college, Larry continued working at several dead-end jobs, the most profitable of which was the one selling men's clothing. While he claimed to be bringing home $40,000 a year, which was not an inconsiderable amount of money in those days, he realized that he did not want to be a handkerchief and tie salesman for the rest of his life.

Since his father had been peripherally involved in construction and since Larry had worked in the business for a couple of summers, Larry began thinking seriously about going into construction as a future. He also remembered how Henry Davis had brought his brothers into the industry and how his father-in-law had set Michael Walker up in the business soon after he and Carol were married. But the Michael/Carol analogy was a double-edged sword. Michael had never been interested in the construction business in the first place. Besides that, his involvement ceased abruptly when Carol caught him with another woman, someone he met in the business, and divorced him.

Still, soon after Chris was born, Larry went to his father-in-law and told him his plans.

Henry gave him a cold stare. "Michael cost me a bundle," the older man said.

"I'm not Michael," Larry replied.

"I realize that," Henry said, "but you don't know much about construction."

"I can learn," Larry answered.

"Do that and then come back to talk to me," Henry advised.

Larry went from Henry to a man with a reputation as one of the most competent men in the industry and asked for a job. The next day, he began working as a carpenter for $2 an hour. A week later, he got a fifty-cent-an-hour raise.

After a year of working in the grunt end of the business, Larry went back to Henry and asked for some financial backing to help him get started with his own company.

"How much you got on the hip?" Henry asked, meaning how much of his own capital did he propose to put up.

"I've got four or five thousand put aside," Larry said.

Henry shook his head. "You're a little bit light," he said.

Instead of financing his venture, Henry agreed to sell him one of the lots in a subdivision he was developing if Larry could get a loan from a bank for part of the money.

The bank agreed to take a chance, and Larry began his first house late in 1971. A few months later when it was finished, he sold it for $69,500, clearing about $9,000 after he paid off the loan. What really made Larry feel good, though, was the fact that his profit was about twice what the bank expected him to make and that his house sold for some $20,000 more than any of its neighbors'.

That house led to another, and gradually Larry W. Aylor Custom Builders Inc. won a reputation for quality and craftsmanship. As the business grew larger and Chris got older, Joy began working for the company as well, designing the interiors.

The business boomed beyond the Aylors' or the Davises' expectations. Within a relatively few years, Larry and Joy joined the sizable community of the city's young and semi-rich. On her wrist Joy wore an expensive Rolex, and in her parking spot in the garage was a bright red Porsche, right next to Larry's Jaguar. Larry also had bought himself a motorcycle, a pickup truck and trailer, a boat, and several four-wheel-drive vehicles. And, to gratify his need to escape the city once in awhile to indulge a macho self-image, he bought a 140-acre ranch in Kaufman County, an hour's drive to the east.

By all indications, the couple had it made: a prospering business with a good reputation for providing quality and value; a bright, healthy son going into adolescence with doting, financially comfortable parents; and a decade-plus marriage that ostensibly was as solid as the concrete foundation on one of their houses. In actuality, their life was largely a pretense.

The business, indeed, was doing well. But Larry and Joy were having more than a few problems. One of them was Chris, or rather the effect his grandparents Henry and Frances were having on the boy's development.

Joy's parents seemed to thrive on having growing children around the house. Joy's sister Liz was eleven years younger and was almost of another generation. In addition to Liz, Henry and Frances had practically adopted Carol and Michael's daughter, a girl named Michelle, who was a little younger than Liz. And then there was Chris, the only boy-child in the family. No matter how much Larry objected, it seemed as though Frances and Henry were always buying the boy things, or promising to buy him things, if only he would do what they asked of him. As he grew older, the stakes got higher: They each demanded more of the other. While the gifts began with toys and trinkets, they later escalated to sports cars and expensive clothes. In return, Chris was expected to live with them.

But the problems in the two families were not restricted to the relationship between Chris and his maternal grandparents. Larry and Joy's marriage was suffering as well.

According to Joy, Larry had a roving eye and did not go to great lengths to conceal it. At the same time, she said, he hovered over her possessively and often overplayed the part of the jealous husband. According to a neighbor, Larry once ordered Joy to leave a party early because she was spending too much time talking to the hostess's nineteen-year-old son. Neighbors also related how Larry hounded Joy with unimportant calls on his CB radio, tracking her down in her car or in the house, questioning her about who she had seen, where she had been, and where she was going. Joy confided to one friend that she dreaded visiting their construction sites because her trim figure almost always drew whistles from the workers. Although *she* didn't mind the attention, Larry did. As soon as they were alone, Larry would berate her, accusing her of trying to lead on the men.

Joy's friends told *D* magazine that when she was around Larry, Joy appeared intimidated, hardly speaking. But when he was not there, she was outgoing, cheerful, and full of fun. Once, over lunch with a neighbor, Joy asked if her friend thought she was "selfish" or "stupid."

"Of course not, Joy," the friend said, shocked. "Why would you ask such a thing?"

"Because," Joy said, "Larry always says I am."

On the other hand, Larry felt that Joy was becoming increasingly distant from him and closer to her parents, who also were trying to manipulate Chris.

There also were problems with Carol, Joy's older sister.

Beginning in her teens, Carol, a blond, hyperactive adolescent whose weight swung wildly from needle thin to pudgy, had begun demonstrating a mental instability that would worsen as she grew older, eventually leading to treatment in the psychiatric unit at the prestigious Baylor University Hospital when she was in her late twenties. Long before her hospital treatment, however, Carol was engaged in a seesaw love/hate relationship with her parents and siblings, an alliance that on at least one occasion required Henry to summon the police to their house.

Her unhappy marriage to Michael Walker did not help. According to Michael, years after the marriage was over, Carol continued to harass him, forcing him to repeatedly change his telephone number in an effort to dodge her. After she physically threatened him (telling him, Michael said, that she "knew people who make people disappear"), he canceled his utility contracts and reapplied for new ones in the names of friends so she would not be able to trace him.

It was when Carol's instability became undeniably obvious that the elder Davises grew worried that she would not be able to care for her child and took Michelle to raise as their own.

* * *

By 1982, on the eve of Larry's meeting with Rozanne and Peter Gailiunas, Larry and Joy's situation was coming to a head. Strangely, however,
as her marriage moved on rockier ground, Joy seemed to become more
aware of her sexuality. She began taking more pains with how she
dressed, shucking her usual jeans and button-down shirts for more
feminine apparel. She also began paying more attention to her makeup,
which up until then was virtually nonexistent, learning to highlight her
strong features such as her high cheekbones and seductive eyes. She
also took one other major step: She checked into a hospital and surgically
had her breasts enlarged. Larry's response was not enthusiastic.

"Well, you'd better get used to it," Larry recalls Joy telling him,
"because this is the new me."

4

If, by mid-1982, Joy and Larry's marriage could be classified as shaky, so too could Peter and Rozanne's, even though theirs was of much shorter duration.

Rozanne had met her physician husband five years before, in November 1977, when they both worked in the intensive care unit of a Boston hospital. She was a twenty-seven-year-old registered nurse; he was a thirty-year-old nephrologist moonlighting on the weekends in the emergency room so he could, according to one person who knew him in those days, meet more young women. As soon as they met, something clicked; there was an immediate sexual attraction between Peter and Rozanne, a magnetism that soon led to an intense affair.

When he met Rozanne, Gailiunas was dating someone else, but he quickly terminated that arrangement so he could devote more time to the dark-haired nurse. However, for at least several weeks after the beginning of their affair, he was not aware of the fact that Rozanne was already married. By the time she got around to telling him, she added that she had filed for a divorce and would soon be free.

Within a few months they had decided to move to Dallas and get married. It was a decision that Rozanne, at least, would learn to regret.

Rozanne, who had lived all her life in leafy, wet, and chilly New England, was not prepared for the heat, the humidity, the relative barrenness of the North Texas prairie. Dallas's only saving grace, as far as she was concerned, was her job at Parkland. But that did not last long. She had been at the hospital only three months when she got pregnant. After their son was born six weeks prematurely in 1979, Gailiunas encouraged her to quit. She complied, but soon afterward their marriage began a definite downhill slide. The decision to have Larry Aylor build them a grand new house—a dream house—was an attempt to salvage the relationship. The result would be a tragedy.

After the fateful lunch in 1983 when each learned that the other was in the throes of a collapsing marriage, Larry and Rozanne began seeing each other regularly, slipping away for trysts when they could, and making do with hurried telephone conversations when they could not. In no time at all, the relationship evolved from a need for mutual consolation over their individual marital problems to a steamy romance.

Early in June, Larry decided to move out of the Arbor Trail house he shared with Joy into an apartment on Fair Oaks Crossing, less than two miles away. When he told Joy he was leaving, she dashed out of the house in tears and sped away. She drove to White Rock Lake, an oasis in the center of thickly populated East Dallas, and pulled into a parking space along the shore. She was sitting there, she told Larry later, crying like a six-year-old who had just dropped her ice cream cone, when a male jogger stopped and asked her if everything was all right. She replied that it was; that she was only broken up because her husband had just told her he was leaving. The two started chatting and the man asked her to have dinner with him.

"Thanks," Joy said, smiling through her tears, "but I'm not ready for that yet."

"Well," the man told her, "when you think you're in the mood, give me a call." Borrowing a piece of paper from her, he wrote out his name and phone number and handed it back to her.

A couple of days later, when Larry was packing for his move to the apartment, Joy walked by and he noticed something in her hand.

"What's that?" he asked, grabbing her arm.

"Nothing," she said, clenching her fist.

Larry looked at her and smiled. "I think you've got a boyfriend," he said.

Many years later, Larry suspected that the stranger Joy had met on the shore of White Rock Lake was a plumbing contractor named Jodie Packer.

*   *   *

Days after he moved out, Larry filed for a divorce.

Less than a week after that, Rozanne also left Peter Gailiunas. Taking her young son with her, she moved into a three-bedroom rental house at 804 Loganwood Drive in Richardson, a North Dallas bedroom community of about seventy thousand people.

Following Larry's example, Rozanne also filed for divorce, using Larry's lawyer to prepare the papers. And, as soon as she was out from under Gailiunas's spell, she took a part-time job as a nurse in a pediatrician's office.

Although Gailiunas had suspected for some weeks that there was another man in Rozanne's life, he was slower to realize that it was Larry. One day when the two were hunting birds on Larry's Kaufman County ranch, several weeks before Rozanne moved out, Gailiunas confided to the contractor that he thought Rozanne was seeing someone else.

Larry tried to look amazed. "No way," he said as earnestly as he could. "She's not that kind of person."

Soon afterward, Gailiunas began zeroing in on the identity of Rozanne's mystery lover. During one of his infrequent visits to the job site, Gailiunas cornered Larry and told him that he was sure that Rozanne had a boyfriend. "And I have a suspicion about who it is," he added ominously, staring at Larry.

Larry looked him in the eye. "Why are you telling me?" he asked.

"I just wanted you to know," Gailiunas said, turning on his heel.

What may have helped Gailiunas reach that conclusion was the fact that he had hired a private investigator and ordered him to follow his estranged wife to see if she was having an affair and if so, with whom.

The man followed Rozanne diligently and reported to Gailiunas that her secret paramour was Larry Aylor. When he heard the news, Gailiunas nodded in grim satisfaction. According to the investigator, Gailiunas ordered the private detective to continue shadowing Rozanne, keeping close enough to her that she would know she was being watched.

The man refused. "I didn't want to frighten her like that," he said later under oath. "I quit." When asked about it, Gailiunas denied asking the investigator to let Rozanne become aware of his presence.

But from what Larry later said, Gailiunas himself had no qualms about putting pressure on his wife. In fact, a court issued a restraining order prohibiting Gailiunas from confronting or harassing Rozanne.

One day about the middle of the summer, several weeks after Rozanne had moved to Richardson, Rozanne told Larry that she and her estranged husband had a major confrontation—an incident that Gailiunas later denied ever occurred. According to Rozanne, she had gone to his house the night before to pick up Little Peter. But before she could get out the door again, she and Gailiunas got into an argument about her taking the boy home with her.

She grabbed Little Peter by the arm and was leading him outside when Gailiunas grabbed the boy's other arm. Each refused to let go. When she furiously demanded that he release the boy, the doctor ran into another room and returned with a shotgun. "If you try to take my son away I'll shoot you," he allegedly said.

Another time, she related, describing an alleged incident also denied by Gailiunas, she went to pick up Little Peter and walked into the den, where she found Gailiunas sitting on the sofa in semidarkness. He had a paper plate on the coffee table in front of him containing a sandwich and a handful of potato chips. A soft drink stood next to the plate. Gailiunas had his sleeves rolled up, she said, and he was hunched over the table although he was not eating the food.

When she came in, she told Larry, Gailiunas reached for something else at the end of the table and produced a syringe. Allegedly telling her it was filled with a deadly drug, he motioned toward his bare arm, saying that if she did not come back to him he was going to inject the chemical into his veins.

Rozanne remained unmoved by the display. Nodding toward the plate of food, she asked him: "Did you fix the sandwich for me so I would have something to eat while I watched?"

Still one other time, Gailiunas taped a telephone call between Larry and Rozanne in which both made a number of disparaging remarks about their respective spouses. Gailiunas then took the tape to Joy, suggesting it might be something she would be interested in hearing.

According to Larry, Joy was indeed intrigued. Although their marriage was falling apart, Joy had not adjusted to the idea of divorce any better than Gailiunas had. That summer, Larry told his friends, he began getting harassing telephone calls at his apartment. He believed they came from Joy. Joy's friends, however, claim that the actual situation was quite different. It was after Larry moved out, one of them said, that

Joy began getting annoying calls. There was no doubt, her friends said, that Joy was upset about the situation. And not without reason. Before he told Joy he was leaving, Larry closed all of their joint bank accounts, effectively cutting off his wife's financial support. That move sent terror into Joy's heart because she feared she would not be able to care for their son, who was then thirteen, without going to her father and begging for help. And that she was reluctant to do.

There was little doubt, however, that Henry Davis was well aware of the situation. One day he tracked Larry to one of his job sites and cornered him, much as Gailiunas had done.

"Get your ass back home," he told his son-in-law in blunt Texas talk, "and forget that black-haired bitch."

Larry ignored the advice even though he, too, was under pressure from Gailiunas as well as Joy and her father.

One evening early in the summer, Gailiunas and his mother came to Larry's apartment. According to Gailiunas, he knocked on the door and was let in. According to Larry, he was lounging around his apartment, watching TV, when he heard a noise and looked up. As he watched, the knob on his apartment door began turning.

Alarmed, Larry dashed into the other room where he could look out the window and see who was outside. It was Gailiunas and his mother.

After establishing who it was, Larry went back into the living room and opened the door. "What do you want?" he asked Gailiunas angrily.

"Is Rozanne here?" Gailiunas barked.

"No," Larry told him.

When Gailiunas appeared skeptical, Larry invited the two of them inside so they could look for themselves. They went in and sat on the couch. Any belligerence that Gailiunas may have felt initially quickly evaporated. Propping his elbows on his knees and his head between his hands, he looked as though he might break into tears at any moment.

"I want you to quit seeing my wife," Gailiunas pleaded with him while his mother sat rigidly at his side.

"I'm not seeing her," Larry said. Then, he told the doctor in an unsympathetic tone that he was going to have to work out his problems with Rozanne on his own. "In the meantime," he said, "get out of my apartment and don't come back."

Gailiunas and his mother left peacefully.

✻   ✻   ✻

The affair between Larry and Rozanne continued throughout the summer and into a suffocatingly hot fall, interrupted only briefly by flareups the lovers had with their respective spouses. Despite the problems, Larry and Rozanne seemed to be deeply in love. Larry's friends later told investigators that during that period they had never seen him happier.

Rozanne's friends and family said the same thing. During a telephone call with her sister on October 2, Rozanne gushed that she had met a wonderful man who seemed truly to care about her and that she was wild about him.

"Tell me more about him," her sister urged.

"I'm bringing Little Peter up in a little more than a week," Rozanne said, since Larry had given her two airline tickets for her birthday, which was on September 24. "I'll fill you in then."

In an attempt to bring some tranquility to the situation, Rozanne worked out with her estranged husband an arrangement in which he would keep Little Peter on Monday, Wednesday, Friday, and Saturday nights, and she would have him the rest of the time. On the weekday mornings after the boy spent the night with his father—Tuesdays and Thursdays—it was Gailiunas's task to drop Little Peter at day care on his way to work. Rozanne then would pick him up when he got out at noon. In addition, Rozanne also took the boy to have dinner with his father just about every night.

Virtually for the first time in his adult life, Larry was technically free to come and go without any marital responsibility, and Rozanne had no commitments for four nights each week. As a result, they spent considerable time together. And when they were not physically in each other's company, they communicated by telephone, usually chatting at least three times a day. As September drew to a close, Larry and Rozanne's pattern continued, although there were difficulties.

On Wednesday, September 28, while Little Peter was with his father, Rozanne spent the night at Larry's. But the next morning when she returned home, she discovered that someone had broken into her house, shattering a window in the kitchen, which was at the rear and sheltered from the street. The only thing that was missing, as far as she could tell, was a key that had been in the lock on the back door.

Immediately, Rozanne called a glazier, who replaced the broken pane, and a locksmith. When the locksmith arrived, Rozanne was highly agitated, pacing impatiently as he put a new deadbolt on the front door.

"Why do you think nothing was taken?" he asked her, seeking to make conversation in an effort to relieve her anxiety.

"I don't think it was a burglar," Rozanne replied. "I think my husband did it." It would turn out she was wrong.

The next day, Friday, September 30, Rozanne saw Larry only briefly because they both had things that needed to be taken care of. The next time she saw him was Sunday, when she came over in the middle of the afternoon and stayed until about six P.M.

The following day, Monday, October 3, Rozanne and Larry went to dinner; Rozanne went home shortly after six. They talked on the telephone at about eight-thirty and again at about ten, but she was in a foul mood and told him only that she would come see him the next morning before she went to pick up Little Peter.

On Tuesday morning, Rozanne left Larry's apartment at about eleven-fifteen to retrieve Little Peter. Larry went back to work. She told him she would see him that evening at about six, after she took Little Peter to his father's for dinner.

When Larry returned to his apartment at noon, there was a message on his machine from Rozanne saying that she and Little Peter were going to lunch, then she was going to take him to his ice-skating class. She would be back at her house by midafternoon. "Please call," she added, "and remember that I love you."

Larry tried to call her at three, but got no answer. He tried again fifteen minutes later, and again he received no response. At about four-thirty, he called his sister Karen and asked her if she had heard from Rozanne. When she said that she had not, Larry said he was going to go looking for her. "Maybe she's had more car trouble," he said, recalling the flat tire earlier in the day.

"I'll go with you," Karen volunteered.

Larry drove to his parents' house and picked up Karen and the two of them decided to retrace Rozanne's usual routes to see if perhaps she was stuck on the side of the road. But they quickly got jammed in rush-hour traffic on North Central Expressway and decided that the plan was not a good one.

"I'll just go back to my apartment and wait," Larry suggested. "She may be on the way there now."

When he got home, though, he discovered he was too restless to sit. A few days before, he had ordered a new bicycle from a local shop, so he decided to pick it up and take it for a test ride. While he was pedaling down a quiet street in his neighborhood, a large car loomed up behind him and bumped him into a ditch. Larry was unable to get a good look at the driver, but he thought it was an elderly woman.

Cursing and bleeding from a number of minor cuts, Larry limped home and doctored himself with Mercurochrome. Then he picked up the phone and tried calling Rozanne again. But it wasn't Rozanne who answered the phone; it was Little Peter. When the child told Larry that his mother was "sick bad" and a male voice commanded him to hang up the phone, Larry paled. Perhaps influenced by all that Rozanne had told him, Larry believed it was Peter Gailiunas's voice. He would later admit he could not be sure.

Close to panic, he called the attorney who had filed the divorce proceedings for him and Rozanne. He explained the situation to the lawyer's aide, a woman named Sandy Miller, and asked her what she thought he should do.

"Sit tight," she advised him, "and I'll make a couple of phone calls to see what I can find out."

5

With everything that had been happening that day, Larry apparently had failed to note the irony in the fact that Little Peter was occupying himself that afternoon at an ice-skating rink, since ice skating is not a common activity in Texas, especially when the weather is still hot. At about the time he began calling Rozanne, the thermometer at the official weather station in Richardson peaked at ninety-six degrees, which tied the record for the day.

While Rozanne was accustomed to crisp, colorful New England autumns, there is no comparable season on the north Texas prairie. Dallas residents, rather, have come to expect uncomfortably warm temperatures and high humidity for roughly half of every year, often beginning as early as April. Typically, the Dallas "summer" ends abruptly sometime in November with the arrival of a cold front from Canada, usually a rolling, rapidly moving mass of clouds that takes on the characteristics of a weather phenomenon called a "blue norther." It barrels southward across the empty, flat countryside, dyeing the sky a frightening blue-gray and sending the temperature plummeting by thirty degrees or more in less time than it takes to eat a leisurely lunch. To Texans, there is nothing strange or foreboding in this brusque change of seasons. After all, the locals like to say with a certain amount of perverse pride, there is nothing between the North Pole and Texas except a four-strand barbed-wire fence.

But no blue norther was predicted for October 4. The sky that day was a bright, cloudless blue and it emanated a heat that sizzled like a blast from hell.

In the meantime, until Mother Nature did her part, everyone in North Texas would suffer. The lucky ones that evening shut themselves inside their air-conditioned homes, dined in air-conditioned restaurants, or sought relief in an air-conditioned movie house. The unlucky ones had to work out in the elements, unprotected from the heat. Among the latter were Winfred Duggan and Glenn Moore, veteran paramedics for the Richardson Fire Department.

At 6:33 P.M., while others were digging into chicken fried steak and mashed potatoes, washed down with copious amounts of sweet iced tea, Duggan and Moore were in their ambulance, perspiring freely even though the vehicle's air conditioner was cranked to the max. The radio crackled and a bored-sounding dispatcher called their number.

Duggan acknowledged.

"Proceed to Loganwood Drive," the disembodied voice commanded.

"What's the problem?" Duggan asked.

"A sick woman," the dispatcher responded.

Moore shrugged and swung the vehicle around until it was heading north, where Loganwood Drive cut a three-block-long, tree-lined swath through a peaceful residential neighborhood. The dispatcher gave no indication of an emergency, so Moore laid off on the siren and the accelerator.

As Moore drove, Duggan, who had been riding ambulances in Richardson for nine years, began preparing himself mentally for what the two were likely to find when they reached their destination. Probably a little old lady who had slipped and fallen in her living room, he thought, or someone having trouble catching her breath in the heat.

"What number we looking for again?" Duggan asked as Moore turned onto Loganwood.

"Eight oh four," Moore replied.

As Moore drove slowly up the street, Duggan called out the addresses. "Seven ninety-four . . . seven ninety-six . . . seven ninety-eight . . . eight hundred . . . eight oh four . . . here it is!" he said, prompting Moore to brake in front of a house that did not look materially different from its neighbors.

Number 804 was a white, clapboard structure built in an L, with the garage, the short side of the L, protruding outward toward the street. The living area, which made up the longer side, was set farther back, well away from the curb. A pair of mimosa trees, which at that time of the year still had all their leaves, shaded the neatly clipped front lawn and the well-tended flower beds under the windows of what had to be the living room. If either Duggan or Moore had thought to classify it, they would have called it a typical Dallas-style suburban house.

As he always did when he arrived at a scene, Duggan checked his watch. Squinting in the fading light, he noted the time. Then, lifting the clipboard that held the paperwork paramedics were required to keep, Duggan scratched on the pad: "Arrival 6:36 P.M."

"Well," he said to his partner, opening his door and stepping into the furnace, "let's go see what the trouble is."

Striding briskly up the front walk, Duggan saw nothing unusual; the scene appeared placid enough. And why shouldn't it? Richardson was normally sedate despite its close proximity to Dallas, the bustling megalopolis that sprawled to the south and west, threatening to swallow anything within half a hundred miles. Even though the cities were neighbors, the contrast between them was remarkable, particularly as far as statistics on violent crime were concerned. While there might be five hundred murders a year in Dallas, it was unusual to have more than four a year in Richardson. So far, in fact, although 1983 was more than three-fourths done, there had not been a single killing in the smaller city.

As Duggan and Moore reached the front door, they found it slightly ajar. Cautiously nudging it open with his fingertips, Duggan peered inside and blinked in mild surprise. Immediately in his line of sight was a dark-haired boy who seemed to be about four who was sitting on a couch, eating a bowl of cereal and watching television.

Duggan and Moore's arrival startled the child, who swiveled in their direction when Duggan opened the door. Outrage sprang into his eyes.

"What are you doing here?" he demanded. "Get out!" he yelled angrily. "My daddy doesn't want you here. If he finds you here, he'll beat you up. He'll tear your heads off."

The paramedics paused, momentarily shocked by the unexpected vehemence. Duggan glanced around the room. Everything appeared normal. There was no evident disarray, no overturned furniture, or any other indication that something might be amiss, except for one thing: the absence of an adult. Duggan looked appraisingly at the boy.

"Is there anyone else here?" he asked softly. "Where's your mommy and daddy?"

The boy did not answer, but his eyes swung involuntarily to the right, to a hallway that Duggan assumed led to the bedroom area.

"You have to leave," the boy repeated antagonistically. "I want you out of here."

Duggan and Moore exchanged glances. Ignoring the boy, they moved toward the hallway. They had not taken more than four steps when they heard a noise that stopped them in their tracks. At that point, all thought of the day's heat was erased from Duggan's mind. Instead, he felt as if someone had injected ice water into his veins. In an instant, he went as cold as if he had suddenly been thrust into a freezer. What he had heard was a muffled moan, a mixture between a sob and a supplication that sounded like a wet, deep whimper. It was totally unlike anything Duggan had ever heard before and it frightened him to the core. Swallowing the fear that climbed to his throat, Duggan sprinted down the hallway, followed by Moore.

At the door to the master bedroom they reacted in horror to the scene inside. It was one neither would ever forget. A nude young female with long dark hair and an hourglass figure was sprawled on her stomach across a four-poster bed that dominated the room. Her legs and her right arm were tied to three of the bedposts, locking her into a spread-eagled position. A stocking and a piece of cloth were twisted around her throat, and a bloodstained pillow partially covered her head, which dangled over the edge of the bed. On the orange carpet beneath her was a puddle of blood and vomit.

As Duggan stared, momentarily not sure what to do, the woman, trying to draw air into her struggling lungs, emitted a low-pitched, rattling gasp. It was the same blood-curdling sound that Duggan and Moore had heard as they started down the hallway.

Shaking off their astonishment, they leaped into action. Frantically, Duggan grabbed the woman's free wrist, searching for a pulse.

"Anything?" Moore asked hopefully as he struggled to loosen the ligature around her throat.

"Steady and fairly strong," Duggan replied, surprised.

Pushing aside the pillow, Duggan gaped at the sight. The woman's head rested in a large blood stain and her hair was matted into a slick helmet. Gently probing her head, Duggan found two small wounds, one in the rear and one over the temple. He immediately and correctly identified them as bullet entry holes.

"She's been shot," he informed Moore.

"And strangled too," Moore added, grunting as he struggled to unwrap the cord that encircled her neck. The paramedic was puzzled, however, when her breathing did not immediately become less labored once he removed the binding.

"What's wrong?" asked Duggan.

Moore looked closely and saw for the first time a yellow object hanging from the corner of the woman's mouth.

"There's something else," he said, groping for the object.

Prying open her jaws, he found a sizable wad of yellow facial tissue jammed inside. When he tried to remove the tissue, it tore in his fingers. Part of the wad came out, but much of it remained lodged in the woman's throat.

"I need my forceps," he said, reaching for the tool.

Working feverishly, he gripped the tissue and worked it free.

"There," he mumbled in relief. Immediately, the woman's breathing improved.

While Moore was trying to extricate the tissue, Duggan moved to cut the ropes and free the woman's limbs, being careful not to sever the knots, aware that they could be an important piece of evidence in a criminal investigation.

As he worked, a shiny object caught his eye. Lying on the pillow under the woman's head was a casing from a small-caliber shell. He left it where it was for the police to retrieve.

Moore, encouraged by the change for the better that the removal of the tissue had on the woman's breathing, inserted an IV in her arm and started a drip to replenish lost fluid.

Once that was done, the paramedics knew they had gone as far as they could in the house. Their job then was to get her to a hospital as quickly as possible.

Working as a smoothly functioning team, they loaded her onto a gurney that Moore had fetched from the ambulance and wheeled it back up the hallway, across the living room, and out the front door. The boy followed them, looking lost.

As they were loading her into the ambulance, a patrol car from the Richardson Police Department screeched to a halt in the driveway and Officer Jonathan May rushed up. Operating on the assumption that their services would be needed as well, it was routine for the police in Richardson to answer all fire department calls. When Officer May steered toward 804 Loganwood, he had no more idea of the conditions he would find there than had Duggan and Moore. However, he took one look at the scene and knew he had a problem.

"What happened?" he breathlessly asked Duggan.

"Woman's been shot," the paramedic replied tersely.

At that point, May made a command decision. "I'll ride with you," he told Duggan, scrambling into the ambulance.

"What about the kid?" Duggan asked.

"Here comes someone else," May said as another patrol car arrived. "He'll take care of the kid," May said, scrambling into the back of the ambulance. "Let's go."

The vehicle was tearing through Richardson's quiet streets, its siren screaming, when Duggan, who was still trying to administer lifesaving aid to the woman, saw something glowing dully in her hair.

"What's that?" he asked May, pointing with his chin toward the object.

May gingerly removed it. It was a second shell casing.

6

In a matter of minutes other patrol cars began arriving at 804 Loganwood Drive. Already en route, unaware that there was a violent crime involved, was Sergeant Morris "Mo" McGowan, a drawling, slightly built veteran of the Richardson PD, and his partner, Detective Mike Corley. They had been on their way to the scene of a reported robbery when they monitored the "sick or injured person" call. Without knowing exactly what was involved, McGowan decided to go there before chasing down the robbery report.

As soon as he arrived at Rozanne's house, McGowan was told the nature of the incident. Since he was the senior officer present, he assumed command. Without even going inside the house, he began issuing orders dispersing his troops. Some he sent inside to make a search of the house, to make sure there were no additional victims, and to get a quick look before the crime-scene team arrived. Others he ordered onto the streets. Canvass the block, he told them, find out what you can from the neighbors.

As he was giving his orders, a car pulled up in front of the house. A man slid out from behind the wheel and a middle-aged woman got out the other side. Knowing that his officers would check them out, McGowan kept his attention focused on getting the investigation underway. A few minutes later, when he had a breather, he turned to Corley.

"Who were those people?" he asked softly.

"The man says he's the husband of the woman who lives here," Corley replied.

"And the woman?" McGowan asked.

"His mother," Corley said.

McGowan nodded and started toward the man. At the same time, the man began walking in his direction. They met on the driveway and shook hands.

"I'm Dr. Peter Gailiunas," the man said.

After introducing himself, McGowan asked Gailiunas to go with Corley to give him a statement, necessary in view of the situation.

"Okay," Gailiunas said briskly, "but in the meantime, can my mother take my son home?"

McGowan glanced at the boy, who was clearly shaken and confused by the events swirling around him.

"Sure," McGowan said, already advised by his investigators that Little Peter had been asleep in his room at the time of the attack and had seen nothing or no one. "Why not?"

Dismissing Gailiunas to Corley, McGowan turned his attention again toward the scene and what he needed to do to get the investigation quickly and efficiently underway. It was not yet seven P.M. and darkness was a good half hour away. It will probably be daylight again before I get home, he said to himself. He wasn't off by much.

A few minutes after Gailiunas left with Corley, another car pulled up and two men got out, one middle-aged, the other in his mid-thirties.

As Gailiunas had been minutes earlier, they were intercepted by a uniformed officer and asked what they wanted.

"My name is Larry Aylor," the younger man said, "and this is my father. I'm Rozanne Gailiunas's boyfriend."

Before the officer could speak, Larry demanded, "What happened? Did the doctor beat her up or shoot her?"

Faced with the new development, the officer scurried off to find McGowan.

"Sergeant," the uniformed officer said, "there's something you ought to know. That guy over there," he said, pointing at Larry, "claims he's the woman's boyfriend."

McGowan looked at him in surprise. *Boyfriend*, he thought. *What the hell's going on here? I just met her* husband. Shaking his head, he told the officer to take a statement from the man and that he would talk to him later.

The officer reported back to Larry, who was not happy with the news.

"Come this way, sir," the officer said, leading Larry toward a patrol car that was parked nearby. En route, they passed the other patrol car in which Gailiunas was sitting with Corley. As Larry drew abreast, Gailiunas looked up. The two men glared at each other.

After Larry's call, it had taken Sandy Miller only a few minutes to get some information and call him back.

"Larry," she said in a very serious voice, "there's been a problem at Rozanne's."

Her message confirmed Larry's worst fears. "What kind of problem?" he asked.

Miller did not answer him directly. "Did you know that Rozanne and her husband had a big fight last night?" she asked.

"How did you know that?" Larry asked in surprise.

"Rozanne told me when I talked to her earlier today," said Miller, who had become close friends with Rozanne in the weeks since she filed the divorce papers. "Peter went to her house and they really got into it over the settlement."

Larry felt himself go cold. "Is she okay?" he asked in a thin voice, collapsing on the sofa.

"I don't know," Miller said. "But you need to go over there."

Larry said he would leave immediately.

"Oh," Miller added quickly. "One more thing. Do you carry a gun?"

Years before, Larry had formed the habit of keeping a pistol in his truck. In Dallas, as in most large cities, it was not unusual for thieves to break into houses under construction to steal plumbing and lighting fixtures. Since Larry visited his houses at strange hours, he did not want to walk into a theft-in-progress without having something he could use to defend himself. "Yes," he said.

"Well, don't take it with you," Miller advised. "And don't go alone. Can you get someone to go with you?"

Larry said he would call his father, who had moved his family back to Texas after a restless three years in Virginia.

The ambulance with Rozanne in the back pulled into the emergency entrance at Presbyterian Hospital at 7:10 P.M., about the time Gailiunas and Larry drove up to Rozanne's house and precisely thirty-four minutes after the paramedics had first arrived on the scene.

Rozanne, whose pulse and respiration were still strong, was wheeled into the emergency room where doctors made a quick examination of her wounds. What they found was one bullet entrance hole squarely in the back of her head and another on her right temple. They could find no exit wound for either bullet. But when they examined the temple wound more closely, they saw that the bullet had not entered very deeply. In fact, it was resting just below the skin. A nurse grabbed a pair of forceps and probed the wound, easily removing a small, deformed slug. In one quick motion, she dropped the tiny piece of lead into a metal bowl, where it landed with a dull thunk.

RPD Officer Ken Roberts, who had joined May at the hospital, grabbed the bowl. Looking around for a container in which to store the evidence, Roberts spotted a small bottle of the type used to collect urine samples. Carefully, he lifted the pellet from the bowl and transferred it to the bottle, corking it with the rubber cap and dropping it into his pocket. Later, he sealed it and added his initials to a label verifying when and where it had been found.

The second bullet was somewhere inside Rozanne's brain. Realizing it would have to be removed, ER workers began feverishly preparing her for surgery. One nurse shaved her head, while another jabbed a needle into her arm and drew a vial of blood, which was sent to a commercial laboratory for analysis. It would be tested for drugs since doctors would need to know what, if anything, was already in her system before administering anything else.

By then, it was 7:25 P.M., give or take a couple of minutes, not even an hour after Duggan and Moore had first arrived at 804 Loganwood.

At 7:40, Rozanne was X-rayed and hooked up to a Portable Chest Unit, which would help her breathe. The idea was to do whatever was necessary to keep her alive and as strong as possible until a surgeon could open her skull, get into her brain, and determine the extent of the damage.

At 7:43 P.M., the on-call neurosurgeon, Dr. Morris Sanders, arrived and began readying himself for the operation.

At 7:55, Rozanne was given a CAT scan to try to pinpoint where the bullet had come to rest in her brain and to get a preliminary estimate of the extent of brain damage she had suffered.

When told by the uniformed officer that he would have to give a statement, Gailiunas announced that he would not say another word until he could get a lawyer. When the patrolman reported this to Mc-Gowan, the sergeant shrugged. Over the years, he had come to realize that was a fairly predictable reaction at the scene of a violent crime, especially if the person involved was a professional. The perceived need for an attorney, he had come to realize, was in direct proportion to a person's level of education.

Telling the officer he would be back shortly, Gailiunas walked across the street and knocked on the door of the house occupied by Page Billings, a seventeen-year-old student beautician, and her mother.

"I want to use your telephone," Gailiunas asked without preamble when Page opened the door.

As she was showing him where the instrument was, Gailiunas looked at her sternly and said sharply, "You didn't see me over here today, did you!" She did not reply.

When they got to the phone, Gailiunas asked Page and her mother to leave him alone so he could make his call in private. Even though they waited outside, they could hear him through the door. He called his lawyer and asked him to meet him at Rozanne's house. Before he left, he again glared at Page and her mother and told them: "Whatever you know, you need to keep to yourself."

Page regarded his words as a threat. Standing in the deepening twilight, the frightened teenager watched the doctor crossing the street in long strides.

Unlike Gailiunas, Larry told police that he was willing to cooperate.

"Good," the officer said, escorting Larry to a patrol car for the ride to police headquarters.

But once he got into the stationhouse and met Investigator Ken McKenzie, Larry changed his mind about being helpful.

Looking at the scratches Larry suffered in the bike accident earlier in the afternoon, McKenzie stared at Larry and asked him, "Why did you do it?"

"What?" Larry asked, not sure he had heard correctly.

"I asked, why did you shoot her?" McKenzie said belligerently.

Larry stared at him. "I'm not saying anything more until my lawyer gets here," he said, crossing his arms defiantly.

Asking for a telephone, he called Sandy Miller and asked for her help.

Digging through her files, she came up with the name of a criminal defense lawyer and recited it to Larry.

"You'd better call him," she said. "He's the only one I know of available at this time of night who would be able to help."

Larry thanked her and broke the connection. He then called the lawyer and briefly explained the circumstances.

"I'll be there in thirty minutes," the lawyer said.

While Gailiunas and Larry were waiting for their respective lawyers to arrive, Rozanne was wheeled into one of the hospital's operating rooms.

At 9:30, after she had been anesthetized, Dr. Sanders looked closely at the wound for the first time. What he saw was not encouraging. The bullet that had been fired into the back of her head, even though it was of a small caliber, much smaller in fact than the eraser on the end of a pencil, had evidently struck the perfect place to do the maximum amount of damage. It had entered the parietal area of her skull, below the crown and just to the right of center. The slug then apparently traveled downward and diagonally through the brain, coming to rest above and behind her left eye. From his long experience with gunshot wounds to the head, Sanders knew that as the bullet progressed it had literally cooked the tissue in its path, turning affected portions of the brain into mush.

The surgeon sensed immediately that the prognosis was extremely poor, that she was very close to death and probably would not survive for long. But he would do what he could. As he went to work, his immediate concern was to remove the bits of skin, bone, and hair the bullet had driven into the sensitive brain as it pierced her skull.

At 10:50, an hour and twenty minutes after surgery began, an operating room nurse sewed up the surprisingly small incision on the back of Rozanne's shaved head and wheeled her into the intensive care unit. She was classified as living because a machine was doing her breathing for her. But she was brain dead, which meant that her brain had ceased performing its vital functions. The condition was irreversible. Even if she lived, she likely would be nothing more than a vegetable.

7

While some officers began working door-to-door through the neighbor-hood, others began a methodical search of the house looking for clues. It was this group that ran into the first roadblocks; the inspection produced precious little. There were no fingerprints, no shoeprints, no cigarette butts, no empty glasses, no drops of semen or saliva—none of the usual things that might provide a lead to the identity of the murderer. The only blood found in the house was Rozanne's, and there was remarkably little of that considering the brutality of the crime. The only clues of significance in the house were the shell casing that Duggan had first spotted on Rozanne's pillow and the short lengths of rope that remained twisted around the bedposts.

The shell casing from the house, the other shell casing retrieved by Officer May, the two slugs, and the rope would be all the officers would have to work with for a long, long time. Overlooked as a possible clue—indeed considered part of the house's natural decor—was a small, inexpensive potted plant sitting on the floor against the wall by the front door. The significance of that pot would not become apparent for more than five years, and then its import would have to be spelled out to Detective McGowan.

As the investigators began straggling back, they also had little to add. No one had reported seeing an adult entering or leaving Rozanne's all day, although two neighborhood girls claimed they had seen Rozanne's son, Little Peter, playing peacefully in the front yard that afternoon. The remarkable thing about that bit of intelligence was the fact that the boy had been alone. According to the neighbors, Rozanne *never* allowed her son outside except under her direct supervision.

One of those who had reported seeing young Peter was the teenager from across the street, Page Billings, the same neighbor who had permitted Gailiunas to use her telephone earlier in the evening. The other was Dana Keller, a junior high school student who lived several doors away. Dana reported seeing young Peter outside at 3:45 and Page saw him at 5:20. Those reports puzzled McGowan.

Once Gailiunas's lawyer arrived, the doctor told Corley that he had been at home that evening waiting for Rozanne to bring their son to his house for dinner, but the boy called at six-fifteen and said Rozanne was "sick." Realizing that the situation was urgent, Gailiunas said, he asked his mother, to whom he had been talking when Little Peter's call clicked in, to telephone the paramedics and direct them to Rozanne's house. He denied being at the house earlier in the day.

"Ever since she moved out," Gailiunas added gloomily, "I was afraid something like this was going to happen."

"Who do you think did it?" Corley had asked.

Gailiunas did not pause. "I think it was either Larry Aylor or his wife, Joy," he said.

When Larry's lawyer arrived, he came barging into the small interrogation room in which Larry was sitting and slammed the door behind him.

Slapping his card down on the table, he leaned close to Larry and said, "All right, boy, I'm going to ask you a question and don't you fuck with me."

"What's that?" Larry stammered, surpised at the lawyer's belligerence.

"Did you shoot her?" he asked.

"No!" Larry replied.

"Okay," the lawyer said, adding he would need a $1,500 retainer before he could represent him.

Reaching into his back pocket for his wallet, Larry made out a check and handed it to the attorney.

"Now," the lawyer said brusquely, "are you willing to talk to these guys?"

"Sure," Larry replied, "as long as they don't accuse me of shooting Rozanne."

Nodding sagely, the lawyer opened the door and beckoned to Investigator Corley, who was waiting outside.

"He'll talk to you now," the lawyer said, walking out of the office.

It was the last Larry saw of the lawyer or his $1,500.

As calmly as he could, Larry explained to Corley about his plans to meet Rozanne that evening and about how he had been trying, without success, to telephone her. But the only time anyone answered the phone, he said, it was Little Peter. He had been talking to the boy when he heard a voice commanding him to hang up.

"About what time was that?" Corley asked.

"I think it was a little after six," Larry said.

"Do you have any idea who it was that yelled at him?" Corley asked.

"I think it was Dr. Gailiunas," Larry said without hesitation.

Several days later, when Gailiunas and Larry were alone, the doctor insisted that he had not killed his wife. "Did you tell them that I did?" he asked Larry.

Larry glowered at him. "Yes!" he said, and walked away.

In addition to the doctor and the contractor, there was someone else investigators needed to talk to that night, someone who could perhaps give them some very vital information about what had happened at 804 Loganwood. That was Little Peter.

When it was apparent that there was going to be no speedy resolution to the crime, investigators called Gailiunas's mother and asked her to bring the boy to headquarters so officers could talk to him. Grudgingly, she agreed.

After Peter arrived, Corley took the boy into his cluttered office and tried with only limited success to get him to open up. A hyperactive child with a short attention span, Little Peter wanted to talk about everything but the events leading up to the time he had found his mother. Although he was untrained in the techniques of interrogating a child, Corley nevertheless was able to establish that Rozanne had made him take a nap that afternoon as punishment for misbehaving in his ice-skating class. After he awoke late in the afternoon, he went into his mother's room and found her "sick." When Corley questioned him further about that, the boy replied that "she was tied up so she wouldn't fall in that stuff," obviously referring to the vomitus on the floor.

Corley, however, was unsuccessful in getting the boy to answer his questions about the presence of anyone else in the house that afternoon, and was about to give up when Gailiunas walked into his office. Without preamble, the doctor asked his son, in Corley's presence, "Who told you to hang up the phone?"

"You did," Peter replied.

But when Gailiunas repeated the question, his son gave a different answer: "Nobody."

Dissatisfied with the results he had obtained, Corley asked a female officer, Cynthia Coker, to give it a try. Coker, who also had no special training in handling children, and had no children of her own, thus no personal guidelines on how to respond to a four-and-a-half-year-old, had only marginally better luck.

Under the guise of a late-night play session, Coker questioned the boy about who had been in the house that day. Little Peter first told Coker that nobody had been in the house before his mother had gotten sick, but later told her that his father had been present both before and after Rozanne "got sick." The "after" visit apparently referred to when Gailiunas arrived with *his* mother, Peter's grandmother.

While she harbored inner doubts about the value of the statements she had taken from the boy, Coker placed enough credence in what he had said, backed by Larry's claim that he thought Gailiunas was the murderer, to form a basis for a request to have the boy temporarily placed under protective custody so he could not be influenced by his father or his grandmother until someone with training could question him more closely. That never happened. McGowan decided that the boy did not know anything of value and a youth expert was never summoned to interview him.

It was three A.M. Wednesday before McGowan, who was supposed to have finished his shift at eleven o'clock the previous night, got back to his office from 804 Loganwood Drive.

Gailiunas and Larry were still there, but rather than try to question them then, McGowan spoke to them only briefly and asked them to call later in the day to make an appointment to come back in a couple of days for a formal interview. He felt comfortable in letting them go because, although each had blamed the other, laboratory tests showed that neither had fired a weapon recently.

Also, McGowan's instincts told him that neither of the men had been the shooter. In most such cases, those close to a victim are generally regarded as prime suspects. Although neither Gailiunas nor Larry was out of the woods yet, the circumstances of the crime did not scream "crime of passion" to the veteran investigator. If Rozanne had been shot during a lover's spat, he reasoned, the house would have yielded some evidence of a struggle, which it did not. Also, he would have expected to find Rozanne crumpled on the floor rather than methodically tied spread-eagled across a bed. Despite the fact that Rozanne was found nude, there was no indication her shooting had been a sex crime either. Instead, given the details at the scene—really the *lack* of details— McGowan suspected that he would find that Rozanne had been shot by a stranger in a random act of violence. And that frightened him because it meant that somebody else might be in danger. He would not concede, not even to himself, for many, many months that it could have been a contract killing.

But before he could come to any hard conclusions about Larry and Gailiunas, McGowan would have to verify alibis, interview and re-interview other people, study the crime-scene findings, go over the evidence, even if it was pitifully little—in essence, sift and talk and examine and deduce: the basic ingredients of good detective work.

When McGowan finally left the yellow-brick police headquarters to drag himself home, he had a sinking feeling that the Gailiunas shooting was going to be a ballbreaker case, one that would strain his talents to the limit. He was right; before he could close his file on Rozanne, the investigation would consume almost a decade of his life.

8

Before either Larry or Gailiunas could come back for his meeting with McGowan, the investigation of the shooting of Rozanne Gailiunas took the first of several dramatic turns. It was not an unexpected change, but it was crucial nonetheless. On Thursday, October 6, the case became a homicide. Some forty-eight hours after Rozanne was wheeled into the operating room, after consecutive brain wave tests showed no resumption of normal activity, the breathing apparatus was shut off. At 8:56 P.M., two days and almost two and a half hours after she had been found, Rozanne Gailiunas was officially declared dead. She had never regained consciousness. At the time she died, Rozanne was thirty-three years and twelve days old.

Not long before she was shot, Larry and Rozanne had been discussing the status of patients being kept on life-support equipment and Rozanne had expressed her dislike for the procedure. Larry remembered this as he and Rozanne's sister, Paula, sat in Rozanne's hospital room, keeping watch over the unconscious victim. A few minutes earlier, doctors had told the two of them that Rozanne's case appeared hopeless. Larry and Paula had discussed the situation and decided to ask that the equipment be turned off.

Lightly holding Rozanne's arm since her hands were still covered with plastic bags in an attempt to preserve microscopic evidence that might help investigators identify her attacker, Larry whispered, "Rozanne, you told me if you were ever on one of these machines to take you off. Well, that's what we're here for."

When he said those words, Larry recalled later, Rozanne lifted her left hand and moved it toward the back of her head in one of her characteristic gestures. She then turned toward him and her eyes opened briefly. Tears ran down her cheeks as she died.

Not surprisingly, the mainstream Dallas news media did not immediately place a lot of emphasis on the attack on Rozanne. On October 5, the day after the incident, the *Dallas Morning News* and the *Times Herald* were understandably more interested in the state's effort to execute a killer named James David Autry. The attempt had been postponed after Autry already was strapped to a gurney and the intravenous tubes, designed to carry the lethal drugs into his system, had been plunged into his arm.

However, the Richardson newspaper, the *Daily News*, reported Rozanne's attack on the front page in a story headlined "Details Sketchy on City Shooting." The major source for the unsigned article was a neighbor of Rozanne's, who called the newspaper with the tip. The next day, Thursday, October 6, the *Daily News* fleshed out its account, identifying Rozanne and pinpointing the site of the attack. But there was little hard news to report because the city's police department had spread a curtain of secrecy over the incident.

On that day, Dallas's two daily newspapers were still unaware of the Richardson case. Instead, the *Morning News* and the *Times Herald* were much more concerned with a killing in the Casa Linda neighborhood in Northeast Dallas, a considerable distance from Rozanne's. Ironically, the two crimes had much in common. In Casa Linda, early on Wednesday, October 5, less than twenty-four hours after Rozanne was shot, a ten-year-old girl went to wake her mother and found her murdered. The woman, Margie Jo Wills, had been bound and strangled. It was the Richardson newspaper that first brought out the similarities of the attacks, noting that four comparable incidents had occurred in northeast Dallas since March.

The *Morning News* did not report the attack on Rozanne until after she had died, and then it was in a five-paragraph story buried deep inside the suburban edition.

On Friday, October 7, just a little more than twelve hours after she died, Rozanne's body was wheeled into the morgue at the Southwestern Institute of Forensic Sciences, near Parkland Hospital, for the required postmortem examination.

Conducting the autopsy was Dr. M. G. F. Gilliland, a petite, birdlike, humorless woman with a low tolerance for anyone who disagreed with her.

Methodically, Gilliland ticked off Rozanne's particulars: "brown hair . . . brown eyes . . . five-feet-five inches tall . . . 127 pounds . . . no significant scars . . . natural teeth in good repair . . ."

Moving systematically down Rozanne's body, Gilliland lifted her right hand and gazed at a ring encircling the pinky finger. The pathologist described it as a "yellow metal serpent ring with two red stones." It was the only thing in the report that hinted that the stiffening body with the shaved head and the half-open eyes—officially case number 2749-83-1299—had ever been a living, vibrant woman.

In stilted medical jargon, Gilliland recorded the physical facts of Rozanne's primary injury: "There is a history of a gunshot wound of the back of the head, slightly to the right of the midline at the torcula [sic] . . . . There is additional history the inshoot was surgically resected as was the underlying skull . . . . No powder or tattooing are mentioned in the description and none are visualized at autopsy."

Gilliland described the path the bullet had taken: "After perforating the skin and subcutaneous tissue, the bullet perforated the skull and brain, lacerated the dura over the left anterior fossa and ricocheted to lodge beneath the dura of the left frontal lobe." In layman's language: big trouble. This wound, Gilliland concluded, had been lethal.

The second gunshot wound was of lesser import. "Internal examination [of that wound] reveals diffuse right subscalpular [sic] hemorrhage," she dictated.

While contributing to her death, Gilliland concluded, that wound was not as serious as the one in the back of the victim's skull.

But there was something else that played a major role in the woman's murder: the strangulation attempt. In the pathologist's opinion, that also caused "an additional lethal injury." If Rozanne had not been so effectively shot in the back of the head, Gilliland noted, the strangulation could have killed her.

Gilliland's report, while it had the appearance of an unchallengeable scientific document that left little room for interpretation or dispute, would be highly contested years later and the pathologist's conclusions would be roundly criticized. Making the document and its conclusions particularly vulnerable was a single sentence Gilliland added, seemingly as an afterthought. In a section of the report labeled "toxicology" was a single sentence that read: "No antemortem blood available."

The report, and especially that sentence, would come back to haunt the pathologist. In spades.

At about the same time Gilliland was performing the autopsy, McGowan was gathering the facts as he knew them. They were pitifully few. The main clues were the bullets and shell casings, which told crime-lab experts that the weapon was a .25 caliber pistol and that the ammunition used in the shooting was of recent manufacture.

Even as the detective waited to interview Gailiunas, Larry, and Joy, his instincts told him that their alibis were going to check out perfectly. But just to make sure they were not playing games with him, he planned to ask each of the three to volunteer for a polygraph, commonly known as a lie-detector test.

At that stage of the investigation, McGowan had a distinct advantage: He knew more about the principals than they knew about him. Gailiunas and the Aylors were ignorant of the fact that McGowan had a reputation as a tenacious and determined investigator, a Texas version of a Canadian Mountie who never gave up until his quarry was in jail. To use a local analogy, the detective was like one of the snapping turtles that inhabit Texas creeks and rivers: Once he wrapped his jaws around a case, it would take considerably more than a clap of thunder to make him let go. He also had a special way with suspects, a sort of salesman's touch that made people instinctively like him and want to share their secrets with him. Whenever the situation called for a good-cop/bad-cop ploy, McGowan invariably filled the good-cop role.

Coming across as a friend in need, McGowan frequently was able to get suspects to open up and tell him things they would never confide to any other officer. And if his charm failed to work with a suspect, he could fall back on a sharp intellect that was hidden by his deceptively easygoing demeanor. Many a crook and overanxious defense attorney made the erroneous assumption that the detective's mind was as slow as his speech. Still, McGowan's experience was limited. Richardson had rarely experienced a crime involving a cold-blooded killer striking for no apparent motive.

But, being a methodical man, McGowan had a simple modus operandi. Whenever he investigated a violent crime, especially a homicide, he looked for three things: motive, method, and opportunity. Leaning back in his chair and plunking his boots on the desktop, McGowan considered what he had to work with.

He could put "motive" on the back burner, he felt, because all three of the principals involved in the case had a reason for shooting Rozanne; certainly Gailiunas and Joy had more motive than Larry. While no one knew what the investigation might turn up about the lovers' relationship, it was not a concern to the detective. Motive was definitely there, but he intuited that in this case "method" and "opportunity" were going to be more important to solving it.

"Opportunity" was going to be easy enough to check. Once Larry, Joy, and Gailiunas explained to them where they had been during the crucial hours, it would be easy enough to verify. The last person except the killer believed to have seen Rozanne before the shooting was the instructor at the ice-skating rink, who reported that Little Peter left with his mother at about two-thirty. The call to the fire department's emergency switchboard was logged in at 6:33, so that left a four-hour gap when nothing was known of her activities. Whatever she had been doing that afternoon, she apparently did it at home because Little Peter did not say they had gone anywhere once they returned to Loganwood Drive.

"Method," McGowan knew, was far and away going to be the most difficult issue to pin down, the one that was going to consume most of the investigator's efforts. The Richardson Police Department tended to take violent crime very seriously indeed and when an incident of the type that involved Rozanne occurred, it was department policy to throw every available person on the job until either the case was solved or every possible lead had been checked. In this situation, McGowan had seven investigators under his command and he felt he was going to need them all.

The first task, he told them at a hastily called conference, was to try to determine where the rope came from. The other was to try to trace the ammunition back to a specific pistol, which was not unlike trying to find a male Texan who did not own a pair of boots.

One by one, the three main characters in the drama filed into McGowan's office and gave him their alibis.

Gailiunas told the detective he had been at a clinic and then in his office on the afternoon of October 4, and he gave McGowan the name of another physician who could verify it.

Larry said he was in his apartment or with his sister Karen.

Joy, a quiet, seemingly shy blonde with an admirable ability to put others at ease, said she had been with her parents at a cottage they owned on a nearby lake.

McGowan was not surprised when their stories checked out. Nor was he astonished when each of the three agreed to take a polygraph and when the results revealed that they were not being deceptive in response to the questions asked of them.

In addition to answering the detective's questions, Larry repeated to McGowan his belief that Rozanne's murder was a contract job.

McGowan waved his hand in dismissal. "You've been watching too many movies," McGowan told him.

As a result of the lack of progress, the detective was left just about where he figured he would be: up a blind alley until, and if, solid detection could break the case open.

For three months, his investigators fanned out through Richardson and the surrounding communities, as well as into Dallas itself, talking to anyone they felt might have the slightest connection to the incident. Over the weeks, they questioned more than a thousand people. And when they were through, they had no more idea of who had killed Rozanne than they did on the night of the attack.

For McGowan, it was a depressing turn of events. He had never been faced with such a perplexing situation; despite the thousands of man hours and an incalculable amount of money spent investigating the murder of Rozanne Gailiunas, neither he nor the investigators under him had come up with a single solid lead.

After the turn of the year, when all possibilities had been exhausted and every potential lead run down, the investigative task force was dissolved. That left only McGowan, who was forced to rely on luck.

Since the night of the shooting, McGowan felt part of the answer to who had attacked Rozanne was to be found in her house, despite his own inability or that of his investigators to find it. Early on, he developed the habit of returning to the house to see if he could find the vital clue he was sure that he and everyone else had overlooked. Even after the task force was terminated and he went on to investigate other crimes, McGowan continued to visit Rozanne's house, pacing silently through the empty rooms, waiting, it sometimes seemed, for an almost-supernatural sign that might lead him to her murderer. Even after the house was rented to a new tenant, McGowan made arrangements with the latest occupants to visit the house when they were not home. The detective was not sure what he was looking for, but McGowan was certain he would find it, given enough time and sufficient determination.

9

Almost as soon as the autopsy on Rozanne was complete, Larry began making surreptitious plans to return her body to Massachusetts. Knowing that Peter Gailiunas would object and possibly try to get a court order to stop him, Larry made travel arrangements under an assumed name. Before he left Dallas, however, there was someone he had to talk to: Joy.

Driving to the house on Arbor Trail, Larry parked his truck in the driveway and knocked on the door.

"You know about Rozanne, don't you?" he asked when she answered.

"Oh, Larry," she replied sadly. "I'm so sorry. I know how much you loved her and how much it really hurt you."

Reminding her that their divorce was supposed to become final in just a few days, on October 10, Larry asked her to do nothing to try to prevent it from going through. "I'm just tired of the fighting," he said.

Tears brimmed in her eyes. "Do what you have to do with Rozanne," Joy told him. "Go and be with her family and when you get back, we can settle our business. I'm tired of the fighting, too."

But a week later when he called Joy from Boston and asked her if the divorce was final, she told him that she had postponed it.

"Why the hell did you do that?" Larry asked angrily. "I thought I told you I didn't want you to try to stop it."

"Because, Larry," Joy said, "it seemed like the right thing to do. The Richardson police are going to try to hang this murder on you and you need all the help you can get. My family is behind you and I want you home." Besides, she added, Chris, then just entering his teens, needed a father.

Larry was not happy with the situation, but he was too tired to argue. On the way out of Dallas he had stopped at his apartment and he had been all but overcome by the memories of Rozanne that still lingered: the remains of a pizza they had shared; some of her clothes that were hanging in the closet; strands of her hair on a pillow, the lingering scent of her favorite perfume, Chloe. "Okay," he told Joy reluctantly. "I'll come back."

But the readjustment was not easy. One evening soon after he returned, he and Joy were sitting in the den when the telephone rang. Joy answered it, listening in silence for several seconds.

"No," she said finally, "I can't. My husband and I are back together."

Again she listened, then replied, "Yep, that's the way I want it."

When she hung up, Larry asked her who that had been.

"You don't know him," Joy replied, adding, "it doesn't matter anyway. It was a friend of a friend who asked me out because he thought I was single."

"I'm not sure I like that," Larry said.

"Forget about it," Joy told him. "He won't call anymore."

Despite Larry's original diffidence to an attempt at reconciliation, it looked at first as though the effort might be successful.

Friends who ran into Joy and Larry at parties or in their old haunts said they acted like newlyweds, holding hands, hugging and smooching. Larry seemed to be giving Joy the attention and consideration that had been absent in their relationship a couple of years earlier, while Joy gave indications that she was ready to forgive and forget. Their business continued to prosper and the money rolled in. For Christmas, Larry bought Joy a $40,000 Porsche, a black 911 model, which several months later she traded in for a bright red 928, a more expensive and luxurious version.

But things were not as serene as they appeared on the surface. Although he had moved back in with his wife and son and had abandoned his divorce plans, Larry still carried a torch for Rozanne. He continued sending flowers to her grave and spoke of her often, even to Joy. This bothered Joy more than she let on. In public, she worked to create the image that they were again one happy family, but when she became pregnant soon after their reconciliation she decided to undergo an abortion rather than have the child.

On June 25, 1985, eighteen months after Larry moved back in with Joy, *she* filed for divorce.

Not long before, her younger sister, Elizabeth, twenty-five, announced her plans to marry a technical designer named Michael Goacher. According to a Dallas magazine, Larry's reaction to his sister-in-law's plans was bizarre. When he learned of the impending marriage, the magazine said, Larry threw a tantrum and threatened to beat Goacher. Even when he calmed down, he was unrelenting: He prohibited Joy and Chris from attending the wedding. Larry denies this. Although he admits that he did not attend the wedding, he said he did not tell Joy or Chris they could not go.

While the exact dynamics of Joy and Larry's marriage at that stage are not known, it seemed to continue on a roller coaster path. On January 8, 1986, six months after she filed for divorce, Joy withdrew the petition, telling friends and relatives that she and Larry were going to try yet again to make a go of their union. But something was strange. Even though they were ostensibly reconciled, the marriage slipped back into the same pattern that had predominated in 1982 and 1983, before Larry's affair with Rozanne. They were distant to each other and pursued separate lives.

Early in June 1986, Joy came to Larry with some very disturbing news. "We're broke," she said.

Larry was shocked. "What do you mean, 'broke'?" he asked. By his calculations there should have been almost $200,000 in their bank account.

There had been many unexpected recent expenses, Joy explained, and, what with the taxes they owed, their money had vanished. The situation was so bad, she said, they might have to borrow $30,000 from her father just to carry them through until Larry sold another house.

"Like hell we will," Larry said.

The next morning Larry went to see their accountant, who confirmed that there had been a lot of outgo but said he did not yet have all the records from Joy, who acted as the family bookkeeper, to give Larry any specifics.

Before he could get an answer to his questions about the money,

Larry and Joy's relationship took a decidedly downward turn. Within days, it had slipped to the point where they barely were speaking.

A few days after she told him about their financial problems, Joy told Larry that she wanted to meet him so they could have a lengthy discussion about their marital difficulties. She wanted a quiet place for the meeting, she said, someplace where they could both relax and get away from the distractions of everyday life. She suggested the ranch in Kaufman County. She asked Larry if he would saddle up a couple of horses so she and her mother could go for a ride. Then she and Larry would have time to talk.

Larry was puzzled. Neither Joy nor Frances Davis—*especially* Frances—had ever taken any interest in either the ranch or horseback riding. Joy, in fact, was not even sure where the ranch was. She was so uncertain of its location, she said, she wanted Larry to draw her a detailed map showing her how to get there.

Reaching for a piece of paper, Larry sketched the directions, conceding that it was relatively hard to find. The ranch was located near the center of Kaufman County, about an hour's drive from Dallas. The nearest town was Poetry, a flyspeck even on local maps.

Several days later, on the way to the ranch, Larry ran into an old friend, an ex-rodeo performer named Don Kennedy. Stopping to chat with him, Larry explained that he was on the way to Kaufman County to prepare a couple of saddle horses for Joy and her mother.

Kennedy, who knew both women, broke into a huge grin. "Joy?" he asked in disbelief. "And *Frances*? They're going to go *horseback* riding?"

"Yeah," Larry laughed. "Ain't that something?"

"I'd like to see that," Kennedy chuckled.

"Then why don't you come along?" Larry suggested. "Those horses we have aren't exactly the tamest in the world, but we can take them out for a run and get them tired before Joy and her mother show up."

Kennedy accepted the invitation, climbing into the passenger seat of Larry's red Suburban four-wheel-drive vehicle.

Hours later, after a long ride, Kennedy and Larry sat on the porch of Larry's ranch house, drinking bourbon and Coke and still waiting for Joy and Frances.

"I figured they weren't going to be here," Larry said in disgust. "It just sounded too impossible."

As he spoke, he looked up and pointed to a pickup truck driving down the road that ran in front of the ranch. "That's the third or fourth time that truck's been by here," Larry observed. "I wonder what the hell those two guys want?"

Kennedy shrugged. "Who knows?" Glancing at his watch, he asked Larry how much longer he planned to wait.

"To hell with it," Larry replied. "If they were going to be here, they would have shown by now. Let's go home."

Again, Kennedy slipped into the passenger seat and Larry got behind the wheel. Angry, because he had been stood up, Larry gunned the motor and pulled away in a cloud of dust. A few minutes later, however, after driving through the ranch's gate, he had to slow down to cross a narrow wooden bridge that spanned a small creek. Just on the other side of the bridge was a copse of trees, mainly the spindly pines that cover much of east and south-central Texas.

He had just crossed the bridge and was shifting into a higher gear when his driver's side window shattered and he heard a series of soft thuds followed by several popping noises. The first bullet had come through his window, narrowly missed, and buried itself in the seat behind him. A second bullet zipped through his hair. Seconds later, his friend Kennedy shouted, "I'm hit!" and grabbed his elbow. A third bullet had entered through a back window, passed between the seats, and hit Kennedy. The slug traveled down his arm and lodged near his wrist. "Where?" Larry screamed.

"In the arm," Kennedy moaned.

"Well, get down," Larry ordered. "They're still shooting."

Stunned, Larry floored the accelerator and sped away. Several hundred feet down the road, when there were no more shots, he braked to a stop. Turning to Kennedy he asked, "How bad is it?"

Kennedy grimaced in pain, still clutching his elbow, which was bleeding profusely.

"I don't think it's bad," he said, "but I'd better get to a doctor."

Larry and Kennedy were treated at a nearby hospital, Kennedy for the gunshot wound to the elbow, Larry for shards of glass embedded in his back.

While waiting for his friend to be released, Larry went to a pay phone on the wall nearby and called home. When he got no answer, he tried the Davises' home. Again he got no answer, so he made a third call: to the Davises' cottage on Cedar Creek Lake near the town of Gunbarrel. On that try he reached Joy.

"Where were you?" Larry asked testily.

"What business is that of yours?" Joy replied, also angry.

"You never showed up," Larry said. "Instead someone shot at me."

"Oh," Joy replied icily. "Whose wife are you screwing now?"

Later, when Kaufman County deputies examined Larry's truck, they found several small bullet holes in the front of the vehicle and deduced that the shots had come from a .22 caliber rifle, probably fired accidentally by sportsmen hunting illegally in the area.

But Larry was convinced that it had not been an accident. That evening, as soon as he got back to Richardson, he telephoned Investigator McGowan.

"Someone shot at me today," he said, his voice still shaky.

"Come by and see me tomorrow," McGowan replied disinterestedly, "and we'll talk about it."

Although McGowan dutifully took down the details and checked with the Kaufman County Sheriff's Office to see what they had found, he was highly doubtful that the attack had anything to do with Gailiunas or with Rozanne's murder. They were, he felt, too entirely different to be connected. In one case, a woman was tied spread-eagled on her bed and shot, execution-style, in the head. In the other, a pickup truck was hit by bullets in an area known to be frequented by hunters and poachers. Besides, the incidents occurred almost three years apart. He figured the Kaufman deputies had come to the right conclusion: that Larry and Kennedy had been victims of an unfortunate accident. In any event, he would not be investigating it since the incident had occurred outside his jurisdiction.

His advice to Larry was to forget about it.

But Larry had not received his last shock of the summer. Two days later the veteran philanderer discovered that Joy, then thirty-seven, was having an affair with a man named Jodie Timothy Packer, an athletic-looking, forty-year-old former husband of a Dallas civil court judge and owner of an interior-remodeling firm.

On the night of the sniping incident, Larry had returned to his house, but Joy was not there. When she did not show up several hours later, he again telephoned the Davises' cottage and asked for his wife.

"When are you coming home?" he asked her.

"I'm not," she said.

"Why not?" he asked.

"Because someone's trying to kill you and I don't want to be around."

Several days later, he returned home early one afternoon and, although the house was empty, he knew Joy had been there. He could smell her perfume, a brand called "Joy," which was sold at Dallas's most expensive department store, Neiman Marcus. Immediately, one thought flashed through Larry's mind: That woman has dolled up and gone out on me. Furious, he stomped into his office and picked up the telephone, punching the redial button. A voice at the other end answered with the name of a local plumbing company.

"I'd like to send you some material," Larry told the receptionist. "Where are you located?"

With the address in hand, Larry drove to the company. Joy's Porsche was in the lot. Nodding grimly, Larry settled down to wait.

Twenty minutes later, another car pulled up. Inside were Joy and a man whom Larry later identified as Jodie Packer, the man Larry believed to have been the jogger Joy had met at White Rock Lake some three years previously.

After confronting his wife and Packer, Larry climbed back into his truck and drove away. Outraged, he called his attorney and told him to draw up a new divorce petition. When it was filed in July, it was the third such request involving Larry and Joy Aylor. First, Larry had filed for divorce in June 1983, when he was having his affair with Rozanne. He withdrew it in the fall after she was murdered. Then Joy filed for divorce in June 1985, and withdrew the request six months later, in January 1986. However, the third filing ended the marriage.

On August 19, five days shy of what would have been Larry and Joy's eighteenth wedding anniversary, the divorce was granted. It was not an amicable settlement. After a bitter fight, Larry retained the contracting business, all furniture other than what was in their house on Arbor Trail, his own bank accounts, the bullet-riddled 1985 Suburban, the ranch in Kaufman County, his life insurance policies, $7,000 in cash, and a $20,000 promissory note covering a loan Larry and Joy had made to Larry's parents. Joy got the Arbor Trail house, the furniture, and the Porsche that had been a Christmas present from Larry after their seemingly happy 1983 reconciliation.

The two of them, in what would prove to be an extremely touchy arrangement, were named joint managing conservators for their son,

Chris, who was then sixteen. It would not be the last legal battle they would have involving Chris, nor would it be the most hostile.

Although each was now technically free of the other, they were not able to resume their lives as if nothing had happened. The terrible times they had endured in the early Eighties were only going to get worse. And, as time progressed, each would come to view their 1965 meeting at a high school football game as an encounter from hell. Despite the divorce, Larry's and Joy's lives would continue to be intertwined in a series of unusual and increasingly antagonistic encounters over their son. If they indeed once loved each other, that feeling came to be replaced by a pure and lasting hatred.

Joy, working at a series of minor jobs while trying to raise a teenage son, got the first indication that something was very wrong in 1987 when she received several mysterious and semithreatening telephone calls. Another more grotesque incident occurred one day when she went to her mailbox and discovered an unexpected package. Curious, she carried it into the house, opened it, and gagged. Inside was the rotting head of a fish.

On the surface, Larry seemed to drop back into everyday life with less trouble. He continued operating the custom home–building business and he found a new love, a woman named Jan Bell. On January 30, 1988, they were married. But Joy was not out of his life. Nor was he out of hers.

PART II

◄ 1988–91 ►

10

By the time 1988 rolled around, finding a solution to the murder of Rozanne Gailiunas was, along with winning the lottery, one of the last things that Mo McGowan expected to happen. Fifty-one months, more than enough time for someone to go through college or serve a term as president, had elapsed since the night he had first gone to 804 Loganwood Drive. In the interim, despite thousands of hours of work and prayer, not a single clue had popped up that might propel him on the path toward finding her killer. Although he still had nightmares about the case, the file had long since been relegated to the inactive drawer in a cabinet in a corner of his office.

But then the unexpected occurred. On a muggy evening in late April, as he was getting ready to go home, McGowan's telephone rang. The caller was Larry Aylor, from whom he had not heard since the summer of 1986. Larry was excited, as hyper as he had been when he had called the detective to tell him about the bullets slamming into his pickup truck.

"I have some information for you," Larry said eagerly.

"Go ahead," replied the laconic detective.

"I just had a conversation with a woman who said she had information about those people who shot at me," he said.

McGowan wanted to know what exactly the caller had said.

"She called while I was in the shower," Larry said, "and she told my wife, 'Tell him to get his butt in here right now if he wants to know who shot at him.' "

"Who were they?" McGowan asked.

"She wouldn't say," replied Larry.

"Then who was *she*?"

"She wouldn't say that either."

McGowan sighed. "Then what the hell am I supposed to do?" he asked in exasperation.

"She said she was going to call back," Larry said, his enthusiasm quickly waning.

"Well," McGowan told him, "if she does, let me know."

A few days later, to the investigator's surprise, he got another call from Larry.

"She called again," Larry reported.

McGowan asked what she had said that time.

"She said," Larry quoted: " 'Larry, I understand a friend of yours was murdered. The answer to the riddle is why.' "

McGowan considered what Larry told him. Did he have any way of substantiating his statements? McGowan asked.

"Yeah," Larry replied. "I got her last call on tape."

After listening to the recording, McGowan urged Larry to see if he could convince the woman to get in touch with him the next time she phoned. It was a shot in the dark; McGowan had little hope that he would ever hear from the mystery caller. However, a few days later he was shocked when he answered his phone and the woman was on the line.

She was, she explained, interested in the $25,000 reward for information leading to the arrest and conviction of Rozanne's killer, a bounty announced years previously by Peter Gailiunas. If she told the detective what she knew, she asked, would she be able to collect the money?

"Come see me," McGowan replied, "and we'll talk about it."

The woman who showed up at his office was slightly overweight and dowdy, with frizzy, dyed hair and eyes that bounced around like a basketball at an NBA game. Looking at her he thought, What have I gotten myself into?

Before he could say anything she stuck out her hand.

"Hi," she said, "I'm Carol Garland."

McGowan looked blank.

She smiled. "Carol *Davis* Garland," she said. "I'm Joy Aylor's sister."

McGowan's eyes widened in surprise.

Offering her a chair, he invited her to speak. "What do you have to tell me?" he asked.

McGowan, who was extremely good at listening, sat spellbound while Carol blurted out a confusing story of murder plots, blackmail, a secret marriage, not-so-secret affairs, and sisterly rivalry. He had been a police officer for nineteen years, but he had never heard a tale with as many soap opera elements as the one he was hearing from his guest. It was almost too much for him to digest.

McGowan listened intently as Carol continued on, sometimes almost hysterical, skipping about wildly in time and subject matter. Although she jumped ahead, flashed back, repeated herself, and left big holes in her narrative, essentially what she was saying was that her sister—Joy— had enlisted her—Carol—as a go-between in a plot to have Larry murdered. After she was involved in the scheme, she said, she learned that Joy had also been behind the murder of Rozanne Gailiunas. And *now*, she said, she believed that Joy was building a list of other people she wanted eliminated. So far, Carol claimed, there were five names on the hit list, including hers.

McGowan interrupted, firing questions at her, seeking names, dates, reports of conversations, anything he could get to help nail down the allegations that were spewing forth from this most unlikely source.

When she appeared about to collapse from exhaustion and tension, McGowan eased up. But inwardly he was ecstatic. At the very least, he thought, this is material I can use to renew the investigation. For the first time since October 1983 he felt confident he was on the way toward solving Rozanne's murder. Until Carol Garland walked into his office, he had not given much thought to the idea that Joy was connected to the killing, even though Gailiunas had suggested that very idea the night of his estranged wife's shooting. McGowan remembered what the doctor had answered when Investigator Corley asked him who he thought had shot Rozanne. "It was either Larry Aylor or Joy Aylor," Gailiunas had said. To suddenly discover that Joy might indeed be the one behind *two* unsolved crimes, especially one which he had not even considered a crime, was something the detective was going to have to adjust to.

Joy's alibi for the day of Rozanne's shooting had checked out, he reminded himself. Plus, she had passed the polygraph with flying colors. Suddenly, it came to him: Joy had been able to answer the examiner's questions about Rozanne's shooting without registering any deception on the machine because she, in fact, did not *know* any of the details. That meant that Carol might be right, that Joy had arranged for the shooting much as Larry once had handed out contracts to subcontractors.

According to Carol, Joy turned the job over to a man named Bill Garland. And this was where Carol's story really got confused. Bill Garland was Carol's estranged husband. She had met him while working as the contact between him and Joy. She had fallen in love with him, or thought she had, and married him on October 4, 1986, three years to the day after the attack on Rozanne and less than two months after Joy and Larry were divorced. Her new husband had ordered Carol not to tell anyone in her family, especially Joy, about the marriage. But now, it seemed, Carol and her husband were on the verge of a falling out. She had, in fact, filed assault charges against him, charges that were later dismissed. As a result, she was scared and angry, not only at her husband but at Joy, who she blamed for getting her into the position in which she now found herself. Also, several years before, her father, Henry Davis, had had a stroke, so he was largely incapacitated. Ever since he had become ill, his generous subsidy to her had evaporated. Now she was broke and the $25,000 reward was very appealing.

Carol had mentioned no one other than Garland as a participant in the plots, but McGowan considered that to be a lack of knowledge on her part. If the scenario was as complicated as Carol had given him reason to believe, the detective felt certain that others had to be involved. But he did not know how many or how. The long interview with Carol, the detective knew, had only cracked open a door.

Although McGowan, even today, is unable to go into details about his conversations with Carol for a number of legal reasons, Carol touched on the subject in an interview with Glenna Whitley, a writer for Dallas's *D* magazine, in 1991, three years after the initial meeting with McGowan.

Carol told Whitley that Joy began calling her in January 1986. She had been surprised to hear from her because she and Joy had not been on the best of terms for a long time. Plus, for reasons she would make clear later, she doubted that Joy would want to talk to her. The reason for Joy's call was to find out what Carol knew about Larry.

Carol told her, then asked her why she sounded so desperate to know.

Because, Joy allegedly said, she wanted to have Larry killed.

Despite her sister's shocking revelation, Carol's reaction was relatively mild. Rather than professing amazement, Carol, who had never liked Larry, asked only one question: Why?

Joy hesitated. It was, she said reluctantly, because she had just discovered that Larry was having an affair with their younger sister, Elizabeth, who was then twenty-six, a situation apparently going back several years. That, Joy said, helped explain Larry's strange reaction to the news in 1985 that Elizabeth was getting married.

"No kidding," Carol had replied sarcastically when Joy explained about Larry and Elizabeth. "I thought you knew that. Elizabeth and Larry were always together," Carol said. "They acted more like a married couple than you and Larry did."

After the murder attempt on Larry failed, Carol told Whitley, her husband involved her in an elaborate plan to blackmail Joy, a scheme that was successful to the tune of $12,500. It was in connection with that scheme, Carol said, that Joy began receiving threatening telephone calls and a packaged fish head.

As Carol came to the end of her story, McGowan's brain was ticking furiously. Slow down, he cautioned himself. Do this one step at a time. Start with Joy and see what develops. But first do some basic checking on what Carol has said so far. He was as skeptical of the source as he was of the information. How did he know that she was not just a vengeful, perhaps mentally disturbed woman seeking revenge against her husband and her sister? Seeking to buy time to do some quick investigating, he asked Carol to come back and see him again a few days later. Not happy with the idea, but knowing she had no other choice, Carol agreed. At the same time, he knew he was going to need a lot more facts before he could wrap things up.

When Carol returned for a second meeting, McGowan asked her just how serious she was in her determination to blow the whistle on her husband and her sister. Was she resolute enough, he wanted to know, to really help put a noose around Joy's neck? Would she help police trap Joy?

Carol blinked rapidly. Behind her thick glasses, her eyes seemed as large as silver dollars. Tears welled up and she took a long time to answer. "Yes," she said finally.

McGowan exhaled in relief. So much for Step One. "Would you be willing to wear a wire?" he asked. "Would you be willing to help us record your sister talking about her part in the murder and attempted murder?"

Again Carol hesitated, but again she said yes.

McGowan nodded solemnly. "Okay," he said, "let's work out a plan."

At Carol's request, Joy met her in a busy suburban restaurant, JoJo's, one of a number of outlets of the popular Dallas chain. Carol showed up carrying a briefcase, which, as casually as possible, she laid on the table. Inside the case, unknown to Joy, was a tape recorder.

She and Joy talked for almost an hour. Afterward, Carol was delighted with the way things had gone; she thought she had gotten Joy to make more than enough admissions to insure her arrest. What she was particularly pleased with, she told McGowan, beaming, was the look of complete shock on Joy's face when Carol told her she was married to Bill Garland.

But McGowan had bad news for her. The conversation between the two was all but obliterated by background noise; the tape was unusable. Carol was going to have to do it again.

Carol paled when she heard the news. Trying to entice Joy to make self-damaging statements on tape was dangerous enough the first time, she felt, but to repeat the performance was flirting with lunacy. She blew up, cursing and screaming. When McGowan finally got her calmed down enough to listen to him without flying off the handle, he explained that he knew he was asking a lot of her but he would not make the request unless it was absolutely necessary.

"You don't think I like having to ask you to go back and do it again, do you?" he asked. Without waiting for a reply, he pushed on. "But you are the *only* one who can help us with this. We desperately need your help. If you don't help us, the chances of getting Joy are pretty slim. We'll do everything we can to protect you, but we don't think you're in immediate danger."

Carol opened her mouth to protest, so McGowan spoke quickly.

"I mean, I don't think she's going to attack you right there. And if you can get her to incriminate herself, we'll arrest her and slap her in jail and there's not much she can do to you from there."

Carol considered what the detective had said. She really *was* pissed off at Joy and her husband. And she really could use the reward money. Besides, she figured, McGowan probably was right. If Joy was in jail, there was not much she could do to her, especially if her connections to Bill Garland were broken.

"Okay," she said reluctantly. "I'll do it."

McGowan gave her a lopsided grin. "I'll arrange it," he said.

Several days later the sisters met again, this time in a room in a seedy motel in a somewhat less than desirable section of the city, a locale that was so unlike a place Carol normally would have chosen that McGowan figured it would give credibility to her claim that she was hiding from her husband.

11

Although Joy had agreed to the meeting, she was suspicious from the beginning. The first thing she did when she walked into the room was scrutinize the surroundings.

"Would you like to look at the rest of the room?" Carol asked nervously, attempting to hide her concern with sarcasm. "I mean it's got a bathtub. Want to check under the bed?"

Joy grunted. "Okay," she said impatiently, plopping tensely on the edge of the bed, "what's the scoop?"

Carol gripped her hands together and tried to sound casual. "Well, Joy," she said nervously, "I'd say we're both in trouble."

Joy asked a simple question: "Why?"

Carol sighed. Garland was less than happy with her, she explained, because she had him arrested for assault. Additionally, he thought she had hidden his truck and was refusing to give it back. But most of all, Carol said, it was because she had a tape that allegedly implicated Garland in the plots against Rozanne and Larry.

"Before we go any further," Joy asked, "do you really have it?"

"Yes, I do," Carol said, sounding injured. "And it's going to stay in that safety-deposit box. It's not coming out ever."

It appeared to her, Joy said, that Carol could get Garland off her back simply by agreeing to drop the assault charges against him, giving him back his truck, and reassuring him about the tape. However, Carol disagreed, insisting that Garland was going to keep harassing her.

"With that tape, I don't really think so," Joy scoffed.

Joy's apparent lack of empathy infuriated Carol. "The man is sadistic," she said angrily. "He's crazy."

He may be as unbalanced as Carol claimed, Joy retorted, but he was not crazy enough to want to go to jail.

"He's schizophrenic," Carol replied. "He is not stable." He doesn't care about going to jail, she added.

Joy sighed. Okay, she conceded. Garland was not mentally well. So what did Carol suggest? What did *she* think could be done to alleviate the situation?

Carol slumped and stared at the floor, confessing that she was at her wit's end, that she was so frightened and confused that she could hardly think straight. What did she—Joy—think could be done? Carol asked.

Joy did not answer for several minutes, considering the possibilities. I'll call him, she said finally.

Carol was shocked at the suggestion. "To do what?" she asked incredulously. "What are you going to talk to him about?"

"Tell him to stop all this craziness," Joy said, explaining her logic. "It's the only way anybody's going to survive." She would persuade him to leave Carol alone, Joy said, because that was the only way they all could get on with their lives with a minimum of trouble.

Carol was not convinced. In fact, she was not even sure Joy fully comprehended the seriousness of the situation. "You're not with the program," Carol spat, her voice shrill. "The man calls three times last Sunday. Three times! None of which was he polite, kind, sweet, or anything else. He was aggressive, hostile, and very willing to tell me what he'd do to me. Now, I don't think getting him on the phone and saying, 'Oh, you really shouldn't do this,' is going to do a lot of good."

That was where the tape came in, Joy pointed out. If Garland knew that the tape would be turned over to police if he continued to pursue Carol, it would be a tremendous incentive for him to leave her alone.

Although the argument made sense to Joy, Carol was not convinced. Garland was going to keep after her, Carol maintained, whether she dropped the assault charge against him or not, whether there was a tape or not. "He's going to come after me," Carol asserted, "whether it's today, six months from now, or three years from now. He's got a lot of patience. And he holds a grudge a long time."

To Joy, no matter what her sister said, Carol's biggest insurance policy seemed to be the tape. "I don't suggest giving him the tape," she said dryly.

Joy didn't have to worry about that, Carol responded quickly; she didn't plan to give Garland *anything*. "There's not *one* concession I will make to him," she said with finality.

Sounding puzzled, Joy said she didn't remember what was on the tape.

"It's the same conversation you two carried on," Carol replied nonchalantly.

"Which was what?" Joy asked. "I don't remember."

It concerned Garland and Joy's discussions about money.

"I've forgotten a lot of this, Carol. It's been a long time."

It had been a long time for her as well, Carol responded: nineteen months of being married to an abusive man. As far as she was concerned, that was nineteen months of pure hell, a hell that she never would have had to endure if it had not been for Joy. "You created this problem," Carol told her sister accusingly, "and I suggest you find us a way out. In case you don't know it," Carol said, pointing a finger at her sister, "I am really angry with you."

"I can see your point," Joy said, attempting conciliation. "Yes, I started this, but you were willing at the time."

"*Willing?*" Carol said sarcastically. "You've lied to me. You deceived me. You didn't tell me the truth. You didn't come anywhere near telling me the truth. Now if I'd known you'd been stalking Larry for over two years, you think I would have had one thing to do with letting you have him call me at my house? Do you think one time I would have? No, I'd have punched your frigging lights out."

If that was the case, Joy responded coolly, why had she not said anything before?

"I did, Joy," Carol screamed. "And don't even jack with me anymore because I'm going to tell you something. I'll stand up and slap the peewaddling shit out of you in about three seconds if you tell me that again. Don't put that little innocent air on to me." Joy had put her in jeopardy, Carol contended, by placing her in proximity to Garland. He had, she said, pursued her intensely and single-mindedly, refusing to accept it when she wanted to put an end to the relationship. "And you put me in this situation," Carol screeched. "You did it. You didn't have enough guts to tell me at the beginning you'd been planning this for years.

Now you tell me that there's nothing going on, and about Larry and Elizabeth."

"That's true," Joy agreed. "That's true."

"Yeah," Carol said, still steaming. "But, Joy, you know the way you told it isn't exactly the way it was. Now is it?"

"The part about the sex is true, yes," said Joy.

"Oh, yeah," agreed Carol, "that part's real true, Joy. But you see, you didn't bother telling me you already had the man hired. You didn't bother to tell me you'd been doing this for years, just waiting for a chance to get him."

"To be very honest," Joy said, "I didn't really see any point in bothering you with that."

"Well, Joy," Carol said drolly, "you didn't mind involving me with a frigging killer."

Like fighters exhausted after a wild flurry of punches, the two sisters paused for breath, gathering strength for a battle that was still far from over.

"Joy," said Carol, recovering enough energy for round two, "any person who would involve somebody else in a murder and not tell them that they'd been planning this for years, no, you're not capable of telling the truth. I think you're flat insane." It was Joy's fault, Carol insisted. Her responsibility. "Your greed is the reason I'm in this," she said. And for what? she asked her sister. What was the reason? The necessity? "You could have walked away," Carol said. "All you had to do was file, put up three hundred dollars, and you're divorced. Instead, what did you do? You picked a way out that nobody who's rational would have picked. And then you involve me in it. You didn't tell me the truth. You simply said he was going to leave messages on the machine and to tell you so you could call him."

"Well," Joy managed to break in, "I didn't know y'all were going to get chummy."

"I didn't *intend* to get chummy, Joy," Carol said irately. "But unfortunately you sent me out there so somebody would know who I was. Why didn't you go? Because you knew better. Because you knew you'd been around him for a couple of years and you knew he's flat dangerous."

"I'd never seen him," Joy said defensively. "I've never seen the man."

That was immaterial, Carol contended. What was important was that Joy had put her in grave danger by throwing her together with a man involved in a murder plot, a man who had not only arranged one murder and one attempted murder but who may have been discussing *with her sister* as many as five other murders, including Carol's.

Joy waved her hand in the air, as if shooing away a fly. There weren't to be any other killings, she said. She only said that because Garland did not know who she was and she was trying to confuse him about her identity. "I was just talking," she promised Carol. Besides, she said, she was out of money and she was extremely weary of the whole cabal. "I wish I'd never done this," she said sadly. "I've paid for it. Really, I have paid for it, not only monetarily, but mentally." She paused and then repeated, "I've paid for this."

Carol, her anger expended, seemed to have run out of steam. She, too, had paid for it, she said. "Physically and emotionally and mentally."

"Okay," Joy said, "we all know that. Now how do we stop it? What do we do?"

"I don't know, Joy," Carol said dejectedly.

They were silent for several moments, each lost in her own thoughts. Finally, after what seemed a long time, Carol spoke up. "Why didn't you just divorce him?" she asked plaintively. "Joy, why did you ever start this? Couldn't you just have divorced the man? He was out of the house. He was out of your life. Because you didn't divorce him, I'm in the situation I'm in. Did you ever think of that?"

"Oh, he wasn't out of my life," Joy said testily. "Let's don't get on that. I said I made a mistake. I want to just work on the problems of today. I don't want to go back five years. That's not going to do anybody any good." Arguing over what had happened in the past was not going to solve the problem in the present, Joy maintained. What they had to do was figure out a plan to resolve the situation.

It wasn't going to be easy, Carol countered, not when they had to deal with a man as volatile as Bill Garland. "He's crazy," Carol repeated. "You don't understand. It's like watching two personalities at work. It's like Jekyll and Hyde. They're two distinct personalities and unfortunately Hyde is the one that's out lately. And he's out all the time now."

Garland was not a man who was going to give up, Carol persisted. "He will continue to come after me. And if he gets tired of playing with me, he'll just play with you."

Joy nodded. "I've already been played with, so I know what it's like."

Carol stared at her sister. "Oh yeah," she said, "well what if he decides to have you killed?"

Joy shrugged. "If he comes to kill me, he just comes to kill me," Joy said. "There won't be a dang thing I can do about it."

"What if he threatens Chris?"

Joy shivered, thinking of her teenage son. "Well, if he does, he just does. I can't stop him from doing anything. But," she added quickly, "I think that just sitting here and not doing anything is certainly not going to make it any better. It's not going to go away. And whether you realize it or not, we're all in big trouble. You're not invisible in all this."

Carol jumped on the defensive. "Hey, Joy," she said angrily, "*I* didn't plot to murder Larry. I certainly didn't plot to kill that woman. I didn't even know she was dead."

"No, but you participated," Joy said, referring to the plot against Larry.

"You'd planned his murder two years before that," Carol argued. "*I* didn't instigate a plan to kill him. *I* didn't have any reason to have him dead. I have no motivation—"

"Have you forgotten," Joy broke in, "how you said you'd do it yourself, how you said you were afraid for your daughter and all that?"

"Hey, wait a minute," Carol said hotly. "I said if he ever put his hands on Michelle I'd kill him out in front of God and everybody. I'm not going to go hire an assassin. I'd stand right out and kill Larry myself. Because if he put his hands on Michelle, he wouldn't have to worry about it. The sun would never set on him. But I don't go hiring an assassin, Joy, because I would have taken my chances with the courts." Her advice at the time had been simple, Carol reminded her sister: "Divorce the son of a bitch."

Joy glared at her sister. "You said, 'I want him dead,' " Joy pointed out. "Have you really forgotten that?"

That wasn't exactly what she had said, Carol contended. What she had said was, "If he puts his hands on my daughter, I'm going to kill him myself."

12

Again, the two lapsed into silence. And again it was Carol who was the first to speak.

"You know there's one thing that bothers me," Carol said.

"What?" Joy said.

"Why wasn't Larry first on the list?"

"I don't know," Joy said slowly. "Stupid, wasn't it? I thought about that, too."

"It would have been more logical," Carol pointed out.

"Yeah, it would," Joy agreed with a sigh. "I just want to get out of this shit," she added. "Finished. Done. I don't want to fool with this anymore. I know you don't either, and I'm sorry. I wish I could take it back. I wish I could go back, but I can't."

Carol shrugged. "Did you ever tell Larry you knew about Elizabeth?" she asked.

"Mm-hum," Joy mumbled.

"What did he say?"

"Oh, he denied it. He wouldn't say anything."

Inexplicably, Joy's apprehension resurfaced. "Let me ask you something," she slyly asked her sister. "When you called the other day on the phone, are you taping every conversation that we have?"

Carol did not answer directly. "I wasn't home," she said evasively.

"Were you taping it?" Joy persisted.

"Joy," Carol said, "do you see a tape recorder on the phone?"

"I asked you a question," Joy replied sternly, pointing out that she had been truthful with her and now it was Carol's turn to be honest.

"No, Joy," Carol said. "I did not tape it."

"Did you tape it the other night when we were at Denny's?"

"We weren't at Denny's the other night," Carol corrected her. "We were at Jojo's. I asked you if you wanted me to stand up and look for a tape recorder."

"You're not answering my question," Joy said sharply. "I said did you?"

"I've told you I didn't," Carol lied. "I offered you a chance to see if I was wearing one, didn't I? Did I offer you that chance or not?"

"I don't remember," Joy said. "I guess you did."

"I had on a thin silk dress," Carol said. "It would have been real obvious."

"Well, you had that big briefcase," Joy pointed out.

"Well, Joy, if I put it in the briefcase and I set it there, how are you going to hear anything? Tape recorders have a little microphone thing across the top and you've got to be able to hear. If I was going to tape it, I would have set the tape recorder out on the table, now, wouldn't I?"

"No, I don't think so," Joy said. "They put them under the tables and all that other kind of stuff now." Besides, she added, her sister seemed to have a proclivity for taping conversations; witness the tape she claimed to have incriminating her husband.

"I taped it off the answering machine," Carol replied quickly. And her husband knew it was running. "He wanted me to hear what you said to him. It was *his* idea to tape it."

"Oh," Joy said warily, "because you see you told me that it was a conversation that he had with you."

"No," Carol said hurriedly, "it was a conversation between you and him."

"Then you lied to me before," Joy said accusingly.

"No I didn't, Joy," Carol insisted.

"No," Joy said firmly. Carol had told her it had been a conversation Carol had had with her husband.

"I don't think so, Joy," Carol said, backpedaling.

"Yeah, it really is," Joy said with certainty. "That I do remember."

"That's not the conversation that's on the tape that's in the safe-deposit box," Carol insisted.

"Okay," Joy said, trying to pin down her sister. "You don't have that tape anymore? You said that he called you and you didn't have time to turn the tape off and you didn't know it, but it was running? Now whether *you* knew it or not, I don't know."

"Joy," Carol said as innocently as she could, "if I had that conversation with you, I don't remember it."

"Well, you did," Joy asserted.

"There were a lot of things that I don't remember at all," Carol said. "There were three or four days there that I don't remember anything that even went on. I had short-term memory losses. You could have stood right there and told me something, but I wouldn't remember what it was. The tape that is in the safe-deposit box is a conversation between you and him."

Several days later, on May 26, Mo McGowan, with evidence based in large part on Joy and Carol's recorded conversation, arrested Joy Aylor, then thirty-nine, and charged her with capital murder in connection with the death of Rozanne Gailiunas, an accusation that carried a possible death penalty. She also was charged with two counts of solicitation of capital murder and two counts of conspiring to commit capital murder. Almost simultaneously they arrested William Wesley "Bill" Garland, forty-six, and charged him with two counts each of solicitation of capital murder and conspiracy to commit capital murder.

To test whether Joy had been telling the truth when she told Carol that she had never seen Garland, detectives deliberately walked her through the room where Garland was being processed. Neither of them showed any sign of recognizing the other. Both were quickly released on bond.

Before they arrested Joy, McGowan summoned Larry to police headquarters to break the news to him first. As bitter as the fights between the couple had been, Larry was totally unprepared for the revelation that his wife had been the alleged mastermind behind Rozanne's murder and his own potential assassination.

"I don't believe it," he said in shock.

"Believe it," said McGowan, reaching into a desk drawer and pulling out an audio cassette. The detective then asked Larry if he remembered Carol calling Joy at home on the evening before Larry was ambushed.

"Yeah," Larry said slowly, struggling to recall the incident. "I remember now. I answered the phone and I was really surprised because Carol hardly ever called Joy. When I asked her what she wanted, Carol said she needed to talk to Joy about some concert tickets."

"What happened then?" McGowan asked.

"I think I went out in the garage to work on my car."

McGowan inserted the cassette into a recorder he had on his desk, explaining that it was a tape of the conversation between Joy and Carol that had been made by Carol. The detective then pushed the play button.

Larry's jaw dropped open when he heard Carol tell Joy that "everything was all set up" for the next day.

Joy sounded very nervous and Carol asked her what was the matter.

Larry was just in the garage, Joy whispered.

"Well, get rid of him," Carol suggested. "Send him to get some chicken or something."

Joy giggled uncertainly. "What will he think?" she asked Carol.

"What do you care what he thinks?" Carol said. "He won't be thinking at all tomorrow."

While McGowan should have been happy that he was making tremendous progress in a case that he had feared just a few weeks previously might never be solved, he was worried.

Joy, he was certain, had not been the one who actually pulled the trigger on Rozanne, much less ambushed Larry. From what Carol had said and from what his own instincts told him, the detective was also pretty sure that Garland had not been the one, either. That led him back to his earlier theory that others were involved, although how many and what parts they played still were unknown.

Operating on information received from Bill and Carol Garland, McGowan sent investigators to interrogate two more men: Brian Lee Kreafle, thirty-six, the owner of an auto repair shop in nearby Garland, and Joseph Walter Thomas, forty-seven, a contractor from McAlester, Oklahoma. Kreafle subsequently was charged with soliciting the murder of and conspiring to murder Rozanne, and Thomas with soliciting the murder of and conspiring to murder Larry.

At that point, McGowan knew he had a chain of middlemen, actually *two* chains, and he was trying to work his way to the end, to the point where he could find the actual triggermen. He did not yet know how many people he had to go through, but he had obtained two more names to keep him going: Buster and Gary Matthews, two ne'er-do-well brothers from Dallas. McGowan believed they were directly involved in the Kaufman County attack. Of all the people believed to be involved so far, McGowan discovered that only the Matthews brothers had previous criminal records.

What the investigation was showing at that stage was that Joy was believed to have set in motion dual plots that resulted in the creation of parallel pyramids of contacts, one leading to Rozanne, the other to Larry. McGowan grabbed a scratch pad and made some quick notes. Joy went first to a handyman named Carl Noska, asking if he knew someone who could scare Larry. Noska gave her Bill Garland's name. Beyond that, McGowan reckoned, Joy may have been ignorant of the other players. Apparently Garland, after being contacted by Joy, who was using the code name Mary, went to Brian Kreafle, who went to? That chain resulted in Rozanne's death. Then, when Joy allegedly decided to have Larry killed, she went back to Garland, using Carol as an intermediary. Allegedly, Garland went to Joe Thomas, who went to the Matthews brothers.

✓ Among the many blanks that McGowan still had to fill in was precisely how much money had changed hands. The detective was certain that each person along the chain pocketed *something* for his trouble, but he did not know how much. That, he knew, probably could not be determined until he found the last person in each chain. Since he had already questioned Joy, Carol, Bill Garland, Kreafle, and Thomas, the obvious next step was to pick up the Matthews brothers. The trouble was, they had disappeared.

Pulling the files his investigators had opened on the brothers, McGowan skimmed through them quickly, noting that the data traced a grim history of petty and not-so-petty crime. Opening Buster's folder, McGowan read the details more slowly.

Buster James Matthews, he read, born August 17, 1942, the oldest of seven children by William and Opal Matthews. He dropped out of school in the tenth grade to join the navy, but was given an honorable discharge when he was twenty because he was needed at home to help support his family. Apparently, the way he planned to do that was not exactly mainstream. In 1967, when he was twenty-four, he was sentenced to twenty years in prison from Dallas County for robbery by assault and armed robbery. While he was serving his time, he earned his high school equivalency certificate, then went on to get a mail-order associate degree in applied science, plus a certificate in radio and TV repair.

But his newfound educational capabilities failed to put him back on a lawful path. In 1978, at age thirty-five, he was sentenced to two-to-four years, again from Dallas County, for a series of drug violations and carrying a weapon illegally.

When he was approached about the Larry Aylor assassination plot, Buster was in his mid-forties, had been married to his third wife for five years, and had a two-year-old daughter. Almost all of his employment when he was not in prison was as a roofer. The meager money he made in his job did not go far toward supporting his family, so the idea of a supplemental income intrigued him greatly.

McGowan closed the folder and opened the other one. William Gary Matthews, called Gary. Born August 9, 1951, in Dallas, some nine years younger than Buster. Like his older brother, Gary dropped out of school when he was in his early teens, but got his high school certificate and three associate degrees while an inmate in the Texas prison system, to which he was introduced when he was nineteen. His first prison term was the result of a two-year sentence from Dallas County for theft of credit cards and possession of a forged instrument, plus three years for unlawful possession of marijuana. Two years later, presumably after being paroled, he was sentenced to three years from Newton County on a charge of assault with intent to murder without malice. And in 1976, when he was twenty-five, he was sentenced to eight years from Dallas County for burglary.

Unmarried, Gary was living in a Dallas suburb with his common-law wife and their three children when Thomas allegedly made the offer to him and Buster. When he wasn't in prison, Gary worked as a manual laborer; Thomas's money offer attracted him also. At the time of the Kaufman County incident, Gary would have been almost thirty-five.

Both men, McGowan noted, had convictions for violent crimes. Two of Buster's convictions involved weapons and Gary had done time for trying to kill somebody, presumably with a weapon as well. In any case, the detective figured, both men were seasoned veterans of the Texas Department of Corrections and looked like sure losers. It did not seem to bother McGowan considerably that his investigators had not been able to track down either of them for questioning, assuming that with their backgrounds they would show up sooner more likely than later, probably after committing another crime.

What caused him more concern were the blanks between Kreafle and Rozanne. How many people were in there? he wondered. Who were they? Even more important, who could tell him? He was almost certain that Joy had no idea how far the chain went beyond Garland. And Garland might not know who was involved beyond the next man down. What he had to do, the detective reminded himself, was work on Kreafle and come up with another ID.

He doubled his efforts and was gratified with the results. A few weeks later, he had something to go on. Kreafle had supplied him with a name: George Anderson Hopper, a car appraiser for a local Chevrolet dealer.

On July 20, investigators Rhonda Bonner and Ken McKenzie, the same officer who had accused Larry of being involved in Rozanne's shooting, drove to the dealership in suburban Dallas to talk to Hopper, who at that point in the investigation was simply suspected of fitting into the chain below Kreafle.

At first the two investigators were cordial with Hopper, a polite, clean-cut man of medium height with dark, slightly wavy hair. They were there to interview him, not interrogate him or arrest him, so the talk began on an almost friendly note. When the topic turned to Rozanne Gailiunas, however, Hopper became visibly nervous and politely refused to discuss her without first talking to an attorney.

McKenzie and Bonner had no choice; they had no evidence upon which to base an arrest, not even enough to haul him down to the Public Safety Department building for more determined questioning.

Okay, they reluctantly agreed. Talk to your attorney and we'll get back to you.

They never had the chance. A few weeks later he telephoned McKenzie and told him he did not plan to keep his promise for the next meeting. When McKenzie and Bonner went looking for him, they discovered that he, like the Matthews brothers, had disappeared. That left McGowan, who had been frustrated by the case for five years, in somewhat of a predicament; every time he neared what he hoped was the end of the chain, his suspects vanished.

13

His first name was George, but no one ever called him that. His middle name was Anderson, but no one called him that, either. To everyone who fell within his sphere, and that was a considerable number of people since he was by nature a gregarious fellow, he was known simply as "Andy."

"Andy Hopper," he'd say, proffering a friendly fist, "pleased to meet you." And he meant it; he meant it sincerely, honestly, and without reservation. In the eyes of his parents, his friends, his coworkers, and most especially the petite, shy blonde who became his wife, the person who probably knew him better than anyone else in the world, Andy Hopper was a paragon of amiability, a happy-go-lucky, friendly fellow who liked almost everyone and who, in turn, was universally liked and admired.

From the day he was born, October 6, 1955, the second of four children and the first son of hardworking, God-fearing parents who lived in a respectable, neat neighborhood in Houston, Texas, he was something special. He was a golden baby who grew into a young adult with a golden future, limited only by the extent of his own imagination. Andy Hopper was one of those people about whom others said—speaking in awe and envy and eventually in great sadness—"he could have been anything he wanted to be." And what he wanted to be, at least in his late teenage years, was a fundamentalist preacher.

He had grown up in a stern Christian home, a home where the parents lived by the austere tenets of the Assembly of God faith, a creed whose followers went to services on Sunday mornings and Wednesday nights and sometimes, for good measure, on Sunday nights as well.

True believers in the faith did not, among other things, drink alcohol, smoke tobacco, use drugs, indulge in premarital or extramarital sex, or willfully treat others badly. These were all principles that Andy would later, in one way or another, break repeatedly. But as a youth he followed them zealously, as he had been taught to do. As did his parents and his siblings and friends.

In the fall of 1974, just weeks before his nineteenth birthday, he enrolled in the Southwest Bible College, a small Assembly of God school in Waxahachie, in north-central Texas, not far from Dallas. His announced intention was to engage in a course of study that would lead to his ordination as a minister. There was nothing—absolutely nothing—in his background that would indicate he was not of ministerial caliber. He was bright, cheerful, and eager to learn; he got along well with everyone, and he was well rounded. At Sam Houston High School he had been a member of the thespian society, played on the golf team, and was popular with the other students, particularly the blushing, giggling girls. Not only was he personable, he was also strikingly good looking. In his senior year he was a runner-up for the class's Most Handsome title.

For social purposes, college was simply a continuation of high school. He was quickly accepted by his fellow students, especially the coeds, who regarded him as the top catch in the freshman class. He could have had his choice among the female students, but the one he picked was a slim young woman barely five feet tall, a fellow freshman from the Texas Panhandle named Rebecca "Becky" Thompson.

Like Andy, Becky had been brought up in an Assembly of God home, attending services two or three times a week, obeying the strict creed to the letter, and seldom socializing outside the circles of the local church. Her father owned a shop that specialized in repairing automobile radiators, while Andy's father was a department manager for a major Houston automobile dealership who later opened his own body shop. As teenagers, both Andy and Becky were ambitious, adventurous, hard-working, responsible, and anxious to experience what the outside world had to offer. Becky pushed herself through high school in Pampa on a demanding schedule, finishing a year early just so she could get out of West Texas and see what the rest of the world was like. The boundary of that world, however, extended no more than a few hundred miles; it ended in Waxahachie, where her path crossed with Andy's.

Soon after the two met, they became sweethearts. Eight months later, on April 19, 1975, they were married. She was eighteen; he was a year older. When they decided to wed, they also decided to drop out of college and to try to make a go of it on their own. Since both of them had been brought up in homes where prayer was preferred and pleasure was deferred, they were anxious to see what they had been missing.

After they were married, they moved to Dallas, which was the closest large city. Settling in a rented house, Andy went to work as manager at an upscale men's shoe store while Becky stayed home to tend to the house, as was expected of women in her faith. But selling shoes proved tedious for Andy, who also was homesick for his family and his old friends. Six months after moving to Dallas, they loaded their belongings into a U-Haul and pointed the vehicle south, toward Houston, where Andy had been promised a job as an appraiser in the body shop of an automobile dealership. He had an edge in getting the job because both his father and an uncle were well known and well respected in the business, but once he began working, he carved out his own reputation.

Quickly, he became recognized as a competent and reliable worker with a special flair for organization. He had not been working at the new job very long when he had a better offer, that of manager of a body shop for a Ford dealership in the heart of downtown. It was a tremendous compliment to his talent and potential ability. At the age of twenty-one, he was the youngest manager for a major automotive dealer in all of Houston, perhaps in all of Texas.

While almost everyone who knew Andy thought of him as a God-fearing, hardworking young up-and-comer, cracks were beginning to develop in his persona. Very unusual cracks.

In the spring of 1976, when Andy was twenty and not yet married for a year, a twenty-three-year-old woman named Frances Ferguson was cleaning a vacant unit in a small apartment complex she managed when a strange event occurred. She was in the bedroom of the unit, vacuuming the carpet, when she saw a movement out of the corner of her eye. Looking up, she saw a man, a youth actually, since she estimated he was even younger than she, standing silently in the doorway, watching her intently.

"May I help . . ." she started to say when she looked more closely. The youth's trousers were unzipped and his penis was exposed.

Ferguson's first thought was for the safety of her toddler, who she had left playing on the floor of the empty living room. Brushing past the youth—who made no attempt to stop her—she scooped up her son and ran out the door. Once she was safely in the courtyard, she stopped and turned to face the apartment. The young man, his pants by then zippered, was standing nonchalantly in the doorway, calmly leaning against the door jamb and staring back at her, smiling pleasantly as though nothing untoward had happened.

"If you're through, you can leave now," Ferguson said, feeling a growing anger. Swept up by a wave of outrage, she ran to her own apartment and pulled a pistol out of her dresser drawer. Depositing her child in his crib, she ran into the parking lot, where the young man was trying unsuccessfully to start his car. Calmly, she leaned across the trunk and leveled the pistol at his back. Sensing her presence, he turned and stared down the barrel.

"You want to come back and try that now?" she asked coldly.

Terror flashed in the youth's eyes. "Don't shoot me, lady!" he screamed and scrambled out of the car. As she watched with leveled pistol, he ran down the street and around the corner, abandoning his vehicle. Later, when police showed up in response to the manager's call, they traced the license number and discovered the car was registered to George Anderson Hopper.

At that time, the crime that had been alleged was not officially a serious matter, especially in Houston, which has one of the highest incidences of violent crime in the country. As far as police were concerned, it was a Class C misdemeanor, which meant that it was a finable offense and not even punishable by a jail term. To atone for a Class C misdemeanor, it was necessary only to mail in a designated monetary penalty, which in this case was $102.50, including court costs. The charge, according to court records, was criminal trespass. Why it was that rather than indecent exposure was never explained.

Some four months later, on August 1, 1976, Becky gave birth to a girl. She and Andy named the baby Ginny.

In that period, things were going well both socially and professionally for Becky and Andy. In the beginning, their life together, as it had for each of them when they were growing up, revolved primarily around the church. The people they mingled with, confided in, and called their friends were, for the most part, fellow members of the Assembly of God. Some of them, such as Buddy Wright and Randy Cain, were people Andy had grown up with. And others, such as Debbie Hosak, Randy Cain's girlfriend, were friends of friends. But there were others in their circle as well. Following his instincts as an irrepressible extrovert, Andy ventured outward socially and drew the shy and retiring Becky along with him. Typical among these new friends were Ken Swarts, who worked at the dealership with Andy, and his wife, Connie.

The Swartses and the Hoppers soon became close friends, and with that friendship came an introduction into a world radically different from the one in which Andy and Becky had been raised. Within a very short time, Andy and Becky began asserting their independence from the church. While their life, in one way, still centered around the faith, they also were discovering for the first time a certain freedom from the church and its strict canons.

It was 1978. Becky and Andy had been married for three years and their daughter, Ginny, was two. The incident at the apartment house was two years in the past, presumably forgotten. By 1978, however, the man who once wanted to be a minister and his devout young wife had come to realize that they didn't *have* to go to services twice a week anymore; not even once a week, in fact, if they didn't feel like it. They could drink; they could smoke tobacco; they could live, it seemed, as others lived. Together, along with some of their closest friends from the church, Buddy Wright, Randy Cain, and Debbie Hosak, they began to stray from the church's strict teachings.

Among other things Andy and Becky discovered in this period was drugs. Their favorite was a particularly potent form of homemade methamphetamine known on the street as "crystal" or "crank." At first, especially for Becky, crystal was a wonder drug, opening up entire new vistas both for her and her husband. One of its main benefits, Becky would say later, was that it gave her tremendous surges of raw energy. It made her, an ardent homemaker, want to dig out an old toothbrush and go through the house methodically cleaning the baseboards.

At this time, Andy was successful in keeping his social and business lives separate. During the day, he built a reputation as a popular and efficient manager in a business in which men his age simply were not given so much responsibility. Remarkably, he was not only handling the job, he was excelling at it. When he took over the shop, it had been in total disarray, but within months the young man, still barely in his twenties, had totally reorganized the operation and had it running as smoothly as a new LTD. The dealer was so impressed with Andy's performance that he rewarded him by putting him in charge of a new and larger operation in suburban Houston. But by then Andy was getting restless and, arguably, more dissolute.

Sometime earlier, Randy Cain had come to Andy seeking guidance in his romance. Randy, who was a couple of years younger than Andy, looked upon the older man almost as a brother. And, in a brotherly fashion, he asked for advice. His girlfriend, Debbie, a willowy brunette, was beginning to give him the cold shoulder. She had been the first girl he had ever slept with, he said, and he had experienced a feeling toward her that he thought was true love. But lately the attraction was ebbing on both sides. For one thing, he confessed, Debbie no longer wanted to have sexual relations with him.

"Why do you think that is?" Andy asked politely.

"She says she just doesn't like to have sex anymore," Randy replied. "She says she just can't stand the thought of being intimate with men."

"Bullshit," Andy said bluntly.

Randy was shocked. "What do you mean?" he asked.

"It isn't *men* she doesn't like," Andy replied. "It's you. She just doesn't want to sleep with *you* anymore."

Randy was disbelieving.

"It's true," Andy said as kindly as he could, anxious not to hurt his friend's feelings. "And I can prove it to you."

"How's that?" Randy asked skeptically.

"I'll bet you ten dollars I can get her to go to bed with me," Andy said.

Randy studied his friend. He knew in his heart that his relationship with Debbie was on the verge of collapse and it appeared there was no way it could be rescued. At the same time, he didn't want to believe that he was personally unattractive. Yet Andy's arrogance made him uncomfortable. He thought about it for a few seconds. "You've got a bet," he said.

A few weeks later, Andy telephoned his friend. "Tonight's the night," he said. "Becky's out of town and Debbie's coming over. Drive by any time you want and you'll see her car parked outside."

Three times that night and early the next morning, Randy cruised by

Andy's house. Each time, even at 3 A.M., Debbie's car was parked outside.

Years later, when Randy related this story from the witness stand, tears welled up in his eyes.

"And you know what," he said, choking back a sob, "I never paid him that ten dollars, either."

14

One of Andy's least visible character traits, perhaps recognized at that time only by Becky and a few very close friends, was his burning ambition to be rich. What he wanted, he confided to his wife, was not just to make a good living, which is what he was doing, but to make more money than he could ever make working for someone else. And he wanted to make it quickly. Feeding this desire was Ken Swarts, who was fueled by a similar aspiration. For hours, they huddled together over cold beer, dreaming up highly improbable plans to make a million.

Finally, they felt they had worked out a scheme: They would open their own business, one that dealt in movable outdoor signs. Swarts's mother would finance the venture. They figured they would soon pay her back and then begin reaping really big bucks. This suited Andy perfectly. At age twenty-four, with a proven talent for management and a valuable occupational skill to fall back on, he seemed driven to find out how far he could reach.

In late 1979, only a few months after the birth of Becky and Andy's second daughter, named, ironically, Crystal, Andy was ready to make his move. He and Swarts, together with their families, would go to Florida and launch their enterprise there. Almost immediately, though, Becky voiced her objections. With two children under four, Becky was not at all convinced that a move to a state where neither had ever been to undertake a risky new business was the right thing to do. By leaving Houston they would be abandoning a world in which they were secure, one in which they had become entrenched, both socially and occupationally. In the end, though, she followed her training more than her instincts; in the Assembly of God, wives followed their husbands and never complained.

In retrospect, Becky's doubts proved to have been valid. The Hoppers had been in Florida only six weeks before the new business went belly-up; in that period they failed to sell a single sign and Swarts's mother announced that she was withdrawing her financial backing. The Hoppers and the Swartses had no choice but to return to Houston.

By then, too, the friendship between the two couples had cooled considerably. Perhaps it was because of their shared experience as unsuccessful entrepreneurs. When they returned to Houston, Becky resumed her role as homemaker and Andy went back to the Ford dealership.

It was only temporary, though. By then, Andy's father had opened his own body shop business. It was not long before Andy quit his regular job at the dealership and began doing independent car appraisals for his father, working on his own as a self-employed businessman. Again, it was something Andy proved he could do well. But after a few months he became disillusioned with Houston and decided to move Becky and the family back to Dallas, where he planned to operate his own business doing appraisals for an insurance company he had come in contact with through his father.

For the Hoppers, in many respects, things were still good. Becky and Andy led an active social life, characterized in large part by enthusiastic parties at their home on Friday nights. Among many of their friends, they were regarded as a perfect family. Ginny and Crystal were beautiful young girls who got along marvelously with their playmates. Andy was a hardworking and apparently successful young entrepreneur. And Becky was an ardent homemaker who doubled as her husband's secretary and bookkeeper. They settled into a neat three-bedroom brick house on a corner lot in the peaceful suburb of Garland.

On the surface, the Hoppers appeared to be classic yuppies. The facade they presented to the world was that of a young, white, fairly prosperous, all-American family. But there were shadows in their relationship that no one but they could see. Andy's business, though improving, was not taking off as spectacularly as he had hoped; they were still having trouble making ends meet.

But that may have been the least of their problems. At this stage in their lives both Andy and his wife were using crystal and marijuana on a regular basis. To help pay for their drugs, they had worked out an agreement with a notorious Dallas marijuana dealer named James Lee Carver, Jr.

In the days before he became a major drug-world figure, Carver worked as a repairman for Andy's father at a Houston automotive dealership, which was how Andy had first met him. By the time Andy and Carver connected again in Dallas, Carver was well on his way toward becoming, by his own admission, the country's second largest marijuana dealer. When he was arrested and convicted in 1986, he estimated his net worth at $20 million and claimed to rule an empire that included houses, boats, airplanes, and bank accounts around the world.

Andy and Becky were never big players in Carver's schemes, but where they fell short in volume, they made up with in enthusiasm. Almost as soon as they returned to Dallas, Andy and Becky worked out an arrangement with Carver whereby he would let them have marijuana at a cut-rate price and they would resell it to their friends, generating enough profit to pay for their own drug use. According to Becky, it was never a major operation, although Carver later claimed the couple was dealing as much as ten to fifteen pounds of good-grade marijuana a week.

During this period, the years of drug use seemed to catch up with the Hoppers, especially Andy. There were days when he worked furiously, from dawn until well after dark. And there were days when he did not work at all, electing to spend most of the day in bed or moping around the house in a state of semi-depression. His wildly fluctuating moods caused an increase in tension inside the family and began to undermine what was quickly becoming a fragile relationship. By the summer of 1983, it was apparent to both of them that their fast living was wrecking the marriage. Arguments were becoming more frequent and the potential for serious violence was growing.

Frightened by a vision of what that could lead to, Becky convinced her husband that the two of them should give up using crystal, although the marijuana smoking and dealing continued. Andy may have continued using speed on the sly, as well as cocaine. If he was, it might help explain some of the things that happened later.

Unnoticed by others for the most part, Andy and Becky, for all their public compatibility, were discovering that they had a basic personality difference. Andy, outwardly convivial and easygoing, actually had a hair-trigger temper and a perfectionist streak that sent Becky up the wall. For her part, Becky had uncovered within herself a feistiness that had never surfaced before, along with an uncontrollable impulse to needle her husband in areas where he was particularly sensitive. At home, she would provoke, he would respond, and the result would be a terrible battle in which Andy sometimes went beyond words.

Once, during such an argument, Andy shoved her. Although it didn't seem that he had pushed her especially hard, she was wearing socks and standing on a newly waxed floor. As a result, her feet flew out from under her and she fell on her back, striking her head sharply on the floor. Andy was immediately contrite. Apologizing profusely, he lifted her body, weighing less than one hundred pounds, off the floor, set her on the couch, and ran to the kitchen to get ice to put on the growing bump. During another dispute Andy threw a plastic toy in the general direction of his wife, who was in another room. The toy hit a cushion, bounced up and hit Becky on the side of the face, giving her a black eye.

But these encounters were not all one-sided. One night in October 1983 Andy and Becky had made plans to attend a toga party, but at the last minute Andy said he was not sure he wanted to go. At first, Becky was surprised and puzzled by his reluctance since he was usually the one ready to party at any excuse. But the more she thought about his diffidence, the angrier she got. Although she nagged him into going, he was clearly reluctant. As a result, by the time they were ready to leave, the stage was set for a full-scale fight.

En route, Andy's resolve not to attend returned. By the time they got to the house where the party was being held, Andy refused to go inside. Instead, he sat in the car brooding until he got bored and went to fetch Becky to go home. At Andy's insistence, and over her objections, they left a few minutes later. Almost immediately they began to argue. She threw her glass of beer into Andy's face. In response, Andy hit her in the chest with the back of his hand. Angry, she crawled into the backseat. They went to bed that night without speaking and four days later she initiated a separation and decided to take their two daughters, then seven and four, for an extended visit to her family in Pampa. In her mind, the separation might help bring both of them to their senses. Becky and the girls left Dallas on October 12, 1983, for the long drive across the barren West Texas plains.

Unknown to Becky until five years later, Andy was already in serious trouble. What Becky did not know was that some time earlier her husband had accepted a plain white envelope, allegedly from a body shop owner he knew named Brian Kreafle. By taking the envelope, he set into motion a series of events that forever changed his and Becky's lives as well as those of many others.

15

By the summer of 1983, Andy had changed considerably from the bright-eyed youth who had gone off to a religious college nine years earlier with the intention of becoming a preacher. His zeal for religion, once absolute, had all but disappeared, as had his desire to excel in his vocation and his dedication to his family's welfare. The deeper he got into financial trouble, the more drugs he took, and the more drugs he took, the worse his financial difficulties became. It was, nevertheless, a vicious circle that he was desperate to break. There must be a way, he told himself; there *had* to be a way. According to Andy, Brian Kreafle approached him outside his body shop one afternoon in mid-September 1983. Andy thought at first it might be an answer to his prayers.

"Do you know anyone who would like to make a little extra money?" Kreafle allegedly asked him. "Tax-free money," he added quietly.

"How's that?" Andy asked, suspecting that Kreafle was going to propose something illegal.

He knew some people who wanted a job done that involved a certain woman, Kreafle allegedly said.

"What kind of job?" Andy asked suspiciously.

"They want her taken care of," Andy quoted Kreafle as saying.

Andy gulped. He knew what Kreafle meant: Somebody wanted the woman killed. His stomach turned over, but he was desperate enough for money to want to know more.

"I might know somebody like that," Andy answered carefully.

Kreafle gave him a slow grin. "Think about it," he said, handing

Andy an unmarked envelope. "The people who want it done want it to look like a burglary or something."

Andy nodded and accepted the envelope, tossing it through the window onto the seat of his car. A few minutes later he drove away. A few blocks away, he reached slowly for the envelope and ripped it open. Inside was $750 in cash, a promise to pay $750 more on completion of the job, a picture of a dark-haired woman who looked a few years older than he, and a typewritten data sheet. Skimming the information, Andy learned that the woman in the picture was named Rozanne Gailiunas; she was thirty-two years old; she lived with her young son at 804 Loganwood Drive in Richardson; she worked part-time for a pediatrician; and she drove a brown Cadillac Seville. He needed money, he told himself, but he didn't need it that badly. At least that is what he thought at the time.

For the next few days, the envelope never left Andy's mind; it remained in his possession, sitting unobtrusively in his car like a radioactive rock. I can get someone else to do the job, he told himself, quietly making contact with a guy he knew from high school, a guy Andy thought might be willing. But when he outlined the idea to his old high school chum, the guy laughed.

"That's not enough money for that," he chuckled. "If you're thinking about doing it, you're stupid."

The idea ate at Andy; he couldn't forget it and he couldn't ignore it.

A few days later, he was driving by the intersection of Central Expressway and Belt Line Road when he saw his friend and drug supplier James Lee Carver.

"I want to talk to you," Andy yelled out his car window.

"Okay," Carver replied, pointing to a nearby restaurant. "Meet me in there."

Over a cup of coffee, Andy told Carver that he had been approached about "making a hit" on a woman.

Carver stared at him. "That's ridiculous," he said. "Why would you want to do that?"

"I need the money," Andy replied simply.

Thinking that he was trying to work up to asking him for a loan, Carver told him to forget about the hit. "If you need money, sell more pot," he said.

Andy appeared to consider the suggestion. Thanking Carver for his advice, Andy left the table and returned to his car, leaving Carver with the impression that he had taken the drug dealer's advice.

But Andy could not get the idea out of his mind. One afternoon he drove to Richardson to see if he could locate 804 Loganwood Drive. He found it with no difficulty and stopped in front, carefully studying the house. There was no car in the driveway, but Andy wondered if it was inside the closed garage. For several minutes, he sat silently watching the house for any indication that anyone was inside. Sitting there staring at the building, he began to get nervous. Get out of here, Andy, he told himself. Go away and forget about it.

He drove off, but he did not forget. A few days later he was back again, staring at the exterior and debating what to do. In the time since he had accepted the envelope, Andy had dipped into the cash, taking the money down to Dallas's trendy Oak Lawn district where he bought crystal.

I'm using the money, he reminded himself. I'm going to have to replace it or the people who put up the cash are going to come looking for *me*, never mind the woman they want eliminated. The problem was, he did not have the money to replace what he had used. That left him no alternative. I'm going to have to kill the woman, he told himself.

One night in late September, he drove by the house yet again. It was the first time he had been there in the evening and the darkness gave him added confidence. Parking his car several doors down, he slowly walked by the residence. There were no lights on inside. In his pocket, Andy had a suction cup and a glass cutter. If no one was home, he planned to force his way in and wait for her to arrive. In the movies he had seen how a burglar could put a suction cup against a windowpane, then use it to keep the glass from falling and breaking when it was cut. That was the movies. In practice it did not work out that way, at least not for him.

Quietly he slipped into Rozanne's backyard and stealthily approached the rear door. He was not surprised when he found it locked. Nervously, he produced the suction cup, wet the surface with his tongue, and clamped it onto a window near the door. When he started to etch the surface with the cutter, however, he ran into trouble. Instead of cutting neatly, as he expected it to do, the pane shattered. To him, it sounded like a whole wall of glass coming down. Frightened, he pocketed the suction cup and left at a near run.

For several days after that, Andy deliberately stayed away from that part of town. Then, in the early afternoon of Tuesday, October 4, 1983, he had to go appraise a damaged car at a location not far from 804 Loganwood Drive. Unable to resist the temptation, he detoured down the street and cruised slowly past the house. This time, the woman's brown Cadillac was in the driveway. She's home! he thought. This is the time!

He drove hurriedly to the in-town condominium of a friend, Terry Harmon. He had met Harmon through his work and the two had gotten to know each other well. Generously, Harmon had given Andy a key to his condo, saying Andy could use his desk to prepare written appraisals so he would not have to drive all the way back to Garland simply to take care of paperwork. Andy knew his friend had a pistol and he knew where he kept it.

Letting himself into the empty dwelling, Andy moved quickly to Harmon's desk, removed the a tiny .25 caliber automatic that Harmon kept there, along with some extra bullets, and slipped them into his pocket. As quietly and as quickly as he entered, he left.

From Harmon's condo, Andy drove to a nearby supermarket where he bought a pair of yellow latex gloves and a small coil of rope. Then he went next door to a florist shop where he bought a potted plant. Finally, before leaving the strip center, he stopped and hurriedly re-moved a set of license plates from a parked car, which he put on his own car. Then he headed back to Richardson.

Shaking with anxiety, he drove past Rozanne's house, noting with an uneasy satisfaction that her car was still there. Parking well away from Rozanne's house, Andy got out of his car, palmed the pistol in his left hand, hiding it with the flowerpot. The rope and gloves were in his pocket. He walked quickly to the door and rang the bell. Within a few seconds Rozanne answered. Her dark hair hung loosely around her shoulders and she was clad in a dark robe.

She saw the plant in his hand, smiled, and opened the door wider. Moving quickly, Andy swung open the screen door, transferred the plant to the other hand, and gripped the pistol by the butt. Pointing it at her, he ordered her to step aside as he moved in rapidly behind her. Rozanne's expression, at first puzzled, dissolved into terror when she realized what was happening.

Once inside, Andy glanced quickly around the living room and was tremendously relieved to see no one else was there. "Where's the bedroom?" he asked nervously.

Tears were building in Rozanne's eyes. "Why are you doing this?" she stammered.

"Shut up," he replied brusquely, setting the flowerpot on the floor. "Where's the bedroom?"

She pointed down a hall, which opened off the living room.

"Let's go," he said, pointing with the pistol.

A few feet down the hall, he looked through an open door and saw a young boy asleep on a bed. Quietly, he closed the door. Moving more discreetly, he shoved Rozanne into the master bedroom and softly closed that door as well. Looking around, he noted that the room had a cluttered, disorderly look. An ironing board was set up in front of the closet and several dresses were strewn about. On the wall, hanging slightly askew, were two prints, one of a nude man, and one of a nude woman.

Swiveling his gaze back to Rozanne, he barked a sharp command: "Take off your robe."

Rozanne sobbed heavily; tears rolled down her cheeks. "Please," she stammered.

"I told you to shut up," he growled.

Still crying, she took off the robe. She wore nothing underneath.

"Get on the bed," Andy demanded, pointing with the gun at the four-poster that sat in a corner of the room, carefully made with pale yellow sheets decorated with a cheerful flower pattern in green and red. "On your stomach."

Nearly hysterical, Rozanne did as she was told. Roughly, Andy grabbed her right wrist and tied it to the right bedpost with the rope he had brought along. Then he tied her left hand to the left post and her two ankles to the foot posts. When he finished, she was nude and spread-eagled.

Succumbing to a sudden urge, he kneeled on the bed and tried to pull his penis from his pants, intending to enter her from the rear. He ejaculated prematurely, however, spurting semen over his hand. Cursing softly, he climbed off the bed and went into the bathroom that opened off the master bedroom. He wiped his hand with toilet tissue, flushed it, and went back into the bedroom, where Rozanne was crying and trying to free herself.

Grabbing a stocking from a nearby chair, Andy again knelt on the bed and twisted the nylon around her throat. Making a makeshift noose, he began to tighten it, but the stocking had too much stretch. Quickly, he reached over and grabbed the sash from the robe. Roughly, he looped it around her neck. He was strangling her with that when Rozanne managed to free her left hand and began trying to swing at him.

Panicking, Andy pulled the pistol from his pocket, where he had put it once he had her tied up, and clamped a pillow over her head. Without thinking, he fired twice through the pillow. Rozanne jerked and lay still.

(Prosecutors would imply later that Andy, in an attempt to make sure she died, then stuffed tissue paper down her throat to restrict her breathing. Although paramedics did indeed find tissue lodged in her throat, Andy denied putting it there.)

His heart beating wildly, Andy leaped off the bed and ran out the door. On the way down the hall, he looked quickly in the boy's room and saw that he was still sleeping soundly. Being careful not to make any more noise than he had already, Andy slipped out the door, walked briskly to his car, and drove away.

A few minutes later, he stopped at a do-it-yourself car wash where he carefully vacuumed the interior of his car. He removed the stolen plates and replaced his own, dumping the stolen ones in a convenient trash can. Then he shredded the information about Rozanne that had been given to him and threw that into the can on top of the stolen plates. Still shaking, he drove unsteadily away.

Andy then returned to Garland and tried to resume a normal life. When he went back to collect the other half of the money, the body shop owner told him that the woman had not been killed outright but had died two days later, on October 6—Andy's twenty-eighth birthday.

No one would mention Rozanne's name or the incident to him for almost three years.

16

After the attack, Andy retreated into himself, becoming something of a hermit. It was an existence that was totally uncharacteristic for the normally ebullient car appraiser, and it puzzled Becky greatly. Naturally, Andy was unable to explain to his wife *why* he was in such a mood. Since he could not tell his wife what was troubling him, Andy had to let her assume the worst. And she did. She had already made up her mind to take the children to Pampa, but the length of her stay was open-ended, depending on how Andy reacted to her absence. Her determination to go was only strengthened by Andy's melancholia.

She left Dallas on October 12, less than a week after Rozanne died, unaware of the entire situation. By the time she left, her attitude had hardened and she had resolved that she was not coming back. But she had not counted on Andy's persistence, either. He telephoned her daily, begging her to return. She finally relented after he promised to see a marriage counselor.

After she came back on Christmas Day 1983, Andy gave up his own business and went to work as an office manager for a car appraisal firm while Becky took a job with a floral-design company. It was a move of necessity more than desire; with two growing girls and the debt Andy had built trying to get his own company started, they needed the money.

While the financial situation caused some tension, this was basically a time of healing for Andy and Becky. He kept his promise about seeing the counselor, and for awhile their marriage seemed to have a new life. He became attentive to her and the girls and plunged into his new job with enthusiasm. No matter what his other faults, Andy was a devoted father.

But not even the girls were enough to make Andy change. As the weeks wore on, he slipped back into his wild ways, taking drugs and having brief liaisons. He had at least one short liaison with a young married mother who worked at an insurance company, although she later admitted that she was the one who initiated the affair. Apparently, there were others as well. Andy's drug-dealing friend, James Lee Carver, swore that Andy was a womanizer of considerable magnitude who used to brag about his conquests and flaunt his women until Carver told him to quit bringing them around his shop because his wife and Becky were friends. According to Carver, Andy once telephoned him and boasted that he was calling from another woman's bed.

Then, barely five months after Becky had returned, Andy had his first brush with the law since the indecent-exposure incident in Houston in 1976. That peculiar second episode began when an insurance company employee named Glenn Johnston entered Andy's life.

In May 1984, Johnston went to police officers in Richardson to complain that a man who apparently had stolen his wallet while he was shopping for a birthday card for a relative had traced him through identification in the billfold and was trying to extort more money from him. Later, the story would prove more complicated, but what Johnston initially told investigators was that the pickpocket, after a week-long series of telephone calls demanding money, said he was going to leave the $200 to $300 worth of traveler's checks that had been in the wallet hidden in a stack of bricks at a construction site. Johnston was to go to the site, remove the checks, make them out to "G. Hopper," sign them, and return them to the hiding place, where the extortionist could pick them up at his convenience. If Johnston did not do as he was told, the man allegedly told him, harm would come to his wife and children.

Richardson Detective Ken Roberts planned a trap for Andy. After getting Johnston's agreement to cooperate, Roberts told the insurance man to do as the caller had suggested in every respect except for signing the traveler's checks. Instead, in case the man was watching him, Johnston was only to *pretend* to be signing them. There would be officers at each end of the road leading to the construction site and when the man came to pick up the checks, they would close the net. Roberts and a female detective named Melody Accord would be in one unmarked vehicle, and another officer, Ken McKenzie, would be in another.

When the time for the transaction rolled around, Johnston did as he had been told. And when a man came to pick up the checks, the police moved in. Roberts blocked one end of the street with his car while he and Accord crouched behind the vehicle with drawn pistols. McKenzie, in his unmarked truck, drove the extortionist toward Roberts and Accord—like a hammer to an anvil.

To a certain extent the plan worked. A man came to pick up the checks and McKenzie moved in. The man jumped in his car and drove away from the approaching policeman, toward Roberts and Accord. But when he got to their vehicle, rather than stopping at the roadblock, he swerved around the police car, drove down the sidewalk, and sped down the street. McKenzie allegedly gave chase.

McKenzie later testified that he chased the extortionist for quite a distance, sometimes at speeds approaching eighty mph. The man, he said, was driving recklessly and was endangering innocent bystanders. At one point, according to McKenzie, he pulled up alongside the extortionist, but before he could make a move, the man swerved his car into the detective's path, forcing the policeman to drop back. A few minutes later, McKenzie lost the other vehicle. During the chase, however, he said he had gotten close enough to get the license number of the other car, and he traced it to Andy. At Andy's trial, the defense would challenge some of the details of McKenzie's description of the chase.

That evening, McKenzie and several other officers went to Andy's house and arrested him in front of his wife and children, dragging him away in handcuffs. The next morning, Becky borrowed $77 from drug dealer James Carver to post Andy's bond.

Curiously, no charges were ever filed against Andy in connection with the incident, either by Johnston, the extortion target, or by the police.

Andy never denied trying to extort money from Johnston. The reason charges were not filed in connection with the extortion was allegedly because Johnston was not able to positively identify Andy as the thief who took his wallet. But it was never satisfactorily explained why police did not file charges themselves in connection with the alleged high-speed chase, which, inexplicably, was never joined by Roberts and Accord. Later, McKenzie would say that *he* did not file the charges against Andy because it was not his case.

The incident resulted in one significant development: Investigator

Ken McKenzie appeared in Andy's life. Not only was he the one who chased Andy through the streets of North Dallas, but he was the one who arrested him at his home that evening. For the next several years McKenzie would weave in and out of Andy's life at crucial moments. Over time, he became Andy's archenemy, one of the few people whom Andy admitted disliking intensely. Years later, Andy's loathing of the detective made it easier for Richardson police to use the good-cop/bad-cop routine when he was being questioned about Rozanne's murder. McGowan was the good cop; McKenzie, Andy knew immediately, was the bad cop.

While Andy's sexual affairs were usually short-lived, there was one that was not. In 1986, to help bring in extra money, Andy joined three friends in the operation of a nightclub called Beethoven's. This put Andy into contact with a crowd that included a barmaid named Shelley Zachary, who seemed to strike up an immediate friendship with Andy's wife, Becky.

Over the weeks, Shelley became a faithful guest at the Hopper's Friday-night bashes. The evenings had become something of a tradition in their own right, frequented not only by Andy and Becky's new friends in Dallas, but by some of their old friends from Houston as well. The way Texans measure distances, 250 miles was only a hop and a skip away, certainly not too far to go for a good party. One of the regular commuters from Houston was Andy's boyhood friend Buddy Wright, who quickly became enamored of the Hoppers' new friend, Shelley. Unknown to Wright and to Becky, though, Shelley's eyes were on Andy.

Shelley, like Investigator McKenzie, would play an important role in Andy's future.

One of those from this period of Andy's life who would later claim a special insight into Andy's dark side was James Carver, the drug dealer. "I think I know him as well as anybody," Carver contended, "and there's definitely a 'tiger' in him. He appears to be subtle, but he's not; he's more fearless than you would imagine."

Several weeks after the attack on Rozanne, Carver said he again accidentally bumped into Andy and again they sat down for a friendly chat.

"I killed that woman," Andy bragged to Carver almost as soon as their coffee arrived.

Carter, a major law breaker in his own right, didn't want to be saddled with unwelcome revelations from others. Still, Andy seemed bent on filling him in on the details.

"She kept squirming the whole time," Andy added, pausing for emphasis.

"Hold it right there," Carver told him. "If you killed somebody, I don't want to know about it."

"It wasn't a big deal," Andy continued. "It wasn't the first time. I've done things like that before."

Carver said he again tried to shut him up, but Andy seemed compelled to boast about his experiences, real or imagined.

"You wouldn't believe the power you have when someone's life is in your hands," Andy said.

At that point, the drug dealer got up and left.

The next time Carter heard from Andy, he testified later, was in 1986 when Andy telephoned asking for a job in Baltimore, where Carver had moved his drug-dealing headquarters.

"Forget about it," Carver told him.

Needless to say, the drug dealer never reported these conversations to the police until years later, after he had been convicted in connection with his drug activity and was serving time in a federal prison in East Texas. Ironically, when Carver did tell the story, it was to Detective Ken McKenzie. But by the summer of 1988, except for the Johnston incident four years earlier, Richardson detectives were not interested in Andy and certainly didn't suspect him of shooting Rozanne Gailiunas. Only after McGowan began delving into the seemingly unrelated events surrounding Larry and Joy Aylor did his name emerge.

17

Considering his experience with Investigator McKenzie in the Johnston incident, Andy was not exactly delighted to see the detective when he showed up with Rhonda Bonner at the Chevrolet dealer's body shop where he worked in July 1988. It had been roughly twenty-four months since the two of them clashed, but as soon as he saw the officer coming, the Johnston incident flashed through Andy's mind. As the two investigators approached, Andy considered what to do. Although he had no idea what they wanted, he knew that it was not going to be to his benefit. He thought about running, but decided against it. I'll tough it out, he told himself. See what they have in mind and make my move from there.

But when they asked him about Rozanne, he thought he was going to give himself away. Nevertheless, he managed to get through it all right and was happy that he had at least been able to stall them; at first he thought McKenzie was going to haul him off in handcuffs as he had before.

As soon as they were gone, Andy went to his boss, Carl Joplin, and asked if he could take off early. "I have some personal things to take care of," he told Joplin. "I may be gone for a few days."

"Is there anything I can do?" Joplin asked solicitously.

"No," Andy said, "but thanks anyway. The police are trying to put something on me and I need a few days off to take care of it."

At the mention of the word *police*, Joplin's pulse quickened. He didn't like the sound of that, but he had too much respect for his employee to question him about it. Ever since Andy had come to work for him more than a year earlier, he had proven to be an exceptional employee. He kept his records in perfect order, he regularly showed up on time, he hardly ever called in sick, and he was never, *ever*, rude to the customers. Andy, Joplin knew, was roundly liked and admired both by the people he worked for and those he worked with. "Don't worry about it," Joplin told him. "Take as much time as you need."

When he left the dealership, Andy went home and sat down with his checkbook. He was making roughly $40,000 a year, but he had next to nothing in the bank, no cushion that Becky and their two daughters could fall back on. As he went over the bills to be paid and thought more about the visit by McKenzie and Bonner, he got increasingly depressed. It brought back too many memories. Putting aside the financial records, he called a lawyer he knew and set up an appointment. Then he got more discouraging news. Before he would even talk to him, the lawyer wanted a hefty retainer. Andy simply did not have the money, but he knew he would have to find it somewhere.

Desperate for cash, he dialed his old boyhood friend in Houston, Buddy Wright. "Buddy," he said when he got him on the line, "I'm in a bit of trouble and I need some money."

Like Joplin, Wright respected Andy too much to ask him what kind of trouble. Instead, he asked: "How much do you need?"

"Five thousand," Andy replied.

"Okay," Wright replied. "I'll see what I can do."

Over the years Wright had been buying stock in the company he worked for, Continental Airlines. He had access to the $5,000 that Andy needed and he didn't hesitate. The next day, cash in hand, he flew to Dallas to deliver the money personally to Andy's lawyer.

Andy, in the meantime, had told Becky little more than he had told Joplin, that the police were trying to "put something on him" and he was going to have to hire a lawyer to help get it settled.

Unlike Joplin, Becky knew about Andy's experience with the Richardson police. Like Andy, she vividly remembered the encounter with McKenzie, the time the detective had come to their house, searched the dwelling, taken some of Andy's clothes, and then dragged her husband away while their two daughters stood by in shock and embarrassment. McKenzie had been rude to her then, she recalled bitterly, yelling sarcastically at her to "get a job" as he led away her husband. She also remembered that nothing had ever come of that incident. No charges had ever been filed against Andy. If her husband was telling the truth then, she reasoned, why might he not be telling the truth now? Maybe McKenzie *was* just out to get him.

Becky's support did little to help Andy's spirits. Despite her attempts to be cheerful, Andy's mood continued to sink. One night he called her and said he was at a motel. In an alcohol-slurred voice he said he had gotten so worried about his situation that he had had too much to drink. Since he didn't want the girls to see him drunk, he had checked into a motel.

A day or so later, Becky got really frightened when Andy told her he had borrowed a pistol from a friend. Afraid that he might try to shoot himself, Becky called Buddy Wright and poured out her problems. Wright took the first available flight to Dallas and sat down for a long talk with Andy. When he left, Andy's spirits seemed to improve. As far as Becky could tell, her husband was over the hump and was working at becoming more like his old self.

Unknown to Becky, however, Andy had asked Wright for another $2,000, explaining that the lawyer was hitting him up for still more cash up-front. What he really wanted the money for—although he did not tell Becky—was to help finance his escape. Wright said his slush fund was empty, but suggested that Andy call another mutual friend. Andy did and the friend sent the money.

On Sunday, July 31, Andy went to the dealership to work on his books. Ever since McKenzie and Bonner had come to see him earlier, he had spent very little time on the job. Joplin had been very supportive of Andy and did not pressure him to return. That Sunday afternoon, with the place to himself, Andy closed out the month and placed his records in a neat stack on Joplin's desk. Then he went home. That evening, his daughter Ginny invited several of her friends over for a small party to celebrate her twelfth birthday, which was the next day. There was no hint that anything was wrong.

The next morning, Monday, August 1, Becky asked Andy to drop Ginny off at cheerleading practice on his way to work. Andy said he had not yet shaved and he would not be ready to leave for several minutes yet. He was going to his office, he said, and that afternoon he had another appointment with his lawyer.

"Okay," Becky said with resignation, "in that case you'd better shave. I'll take Ginny." Grabbing her car keys, she headed for the garage. "Come on, girls," she yelled. As Ginny and Crystal, then nine, ran to join their mother, Andy grabbed his younger daughter and hugged her tightly. "No matter what happens," he told her cryptically, "always remember that I love you."

Becky would also remember it. Years later, both she and Andy would break out in tears as she recounted the incident to a jury that held Andy's life in its hands.

As soon as Becky and his two daughters were out the driveway, Andy quickly packed a small suitcase, filling it with a number of improbable items: black dress socks, a heavy coat although it was the middle of summer, a pair of boots, jeans, and a single shirt. Throwing it in the back of the car, he drove to the house of Shelley Zachary, the former barmaid from Beethoven's who had befriended Becky. In actuality, Shelley had exaggerated the friendship as a cover to be close to Andy, with whom she was involved in a torrid affair. Telling Shelley only that he was being sought by police who were trying to frame him, Andy begged her to drive him out of the city in an attempt to escape.

A few hours out of Dallas, after they had crossed the border into Oklahoma, Shelley left Andy on the side of the road and headed back to Dallas in his car. When she got back to the city, she parked the vehicle on a quiet side street and left it. For awhile, Shelley went to stay with Becky and continued to pretend to be her friend. Days later, she led Becky to Andy's car. It was a double shock for Becky. Shelley's action made it clear that the barmaid and her husband had been having an affair and that Andy was not coming back. Hurt and rejected, she packed up and again took the children to Pampa. There was nothing else she could do; Andy had left her with very little money in the bank and a stack of unpaid bills.

Over the next few months, against her instincts, she kept in touch with Richardson police, hoping they would give her some news about Andy. Her contact was McKenzie, whom she still did not like. Later, she recalled, it was McKenzie who told her about Andy's affair with Shelley. And it was McKenzie who continued to harass her with requests for information that might lead him to her missing husband. By that time, too, McKenzie had learned about the Hoppers' dope-selling escapades and Becky feared that the officer would use it against her, possibly even jailing her and charging her with selling narcotics.

* * *

In the meantime, McKenzie's boss, good-cop Mo McGowan, was pursuing other avenues in an attempt to track Andy. A few weeks after Andy disappeared, a man identifying himself as a friend of Andy's from Houston contacted the detective and volunteered to help police find him.

McGowan also had been in touch with Shelley, who, when she learned of the seriousness of the suspicions regarding Andy, had volunteered to help police track him down. Since Andy continued to telephone Shelley periodically from wherever he happened to be, the investigator felt it would be only a matter of time before Andy would suggest a rendezvous with his lover. When that happened, McGowan wanted to be prepared. Explaining his plan to Shelley, the investigator asked for her help in baiting a trap. To his delight, she agreed to cooperate.

Andy had been gone less than a month when McGowan's prediction proved accurate. Shelley called the detective and told him that Andy had telephoned from Idaho and that he wanted her to fly up to visit him.

McGowan went to his boss and got him to okay expenses for the detective and Shelley to fly to Boise in the hope that Shelley would be able to get Andy to talk. At that point, all McGowan had was a strong suspicion that Andy was somehow involved with Rozanne's murder. When he had followed the chain of allegations from Bill Garland to Brian Kreafle, the next name down the line was Andy's. Later, McGowan would swear that he did not believe then that Andy had been the triggerman. When asking for permission to pursue Andy in distant Idaho, McGowan explained to his captain that he did not have enough evidence to arrest him and charge him, nor was he sure that Andy was the final person in the Rozanne chain. However, the investigator hoped that with coaxing from Shelley, Andy would open up and talk about his involvement, that he could provide information that would lead police to the killer.

When McGowan and Shelley flew into Boise on a bright, late-summer day, two plainclothesmen were waiting at the airport to offer their assistance. Andy was there as well.

McGowan let Shelley deplane separately to meet Andy alone. The detective feared that Andy might connect him to Shelley if they were seen together and he didn't want to blow the opportunity. While Shelley went off with her lover on the back of a motorcycle Andy had obtained since skipping town, McGowan climbed into an unmarked car with the two Idaho detectives. At that point, the investigation began to resemble an episode out of the *Keystone Kops*.

Although McGowan had arranged in advance for Shelley to lead Andy to a specific motel where a bugged room was awaiting them, Andy had ideas of his own. He took Shelley to a motel of *his* choice, frustrating investigators who had gone to considerable lengths to prepare the trap. Since McGowan could not approach Shelley in Andy's presence without exposing the would-be trap, there was nothing McGowan could do except wait and hope that Shelley would contact him. Fortunately, he had given her a telephone number where he could be reached just in case something like this occurred.

That night, she took advantage of Andy's temporary absence and called the detective. "Get him to our motel!" McGowan ordered.

The following day, Shelley convinced Andy to change inns and they checked into the one where a room had been prepared for their arrival. McGowan and detectives from Boise were in the room next door, anxiously listening to Shelley and Andy's conversations, hoping Andy would tell her something that would further the Texas investigation.

The bugs worked as planned. McGowan picked up a lot of heavy breathing and the dialogue from "Donohue," which was playing in the background. But Andy adamantly refused to talk about Rozanne or any connection he might have had with her.

The next morning, Andy climbed on his motorcycle and disappeared into the mountains. The last view McGowan had of him, he was heading north, toward the Canadian border.

Later, when he testified at Andy's trial, McGowan looked embarrassed as the defense pounded away about the Idaho fiasco. Clearly, he did not regard it as one of the finer moments in his investigative career.

18

If he had come up empty-handed in his effort to get Andy, McGowan could take some consolation in the fact that the Matthews brothers had finally surfaced and, as he had expected, come to the attention of law officers by committing another crime.

Before they were picked up, McGowan had learned some of the circumstances under which they had been hired. When Joy allegedly finally decided to make her move against her husband and asked Garland to make the necessary arrangements, the pest exterminator turned accused fixer went through the same chain he had used for Rozanne. More than two years before Andy fled from Dallas, he was approached with an offer to kill Larry. But Andy was not even slightly tempted. Instead, he made up a story so he could gracefully back out of the offer.

After he had accepted the money to kill Rozanne in the fall of 1983, Andy, anxious not to let on that he was doing the job himself, claimed that the actual hitman was someone from Houston. When Andy was approached about the planned murder of Larry in the spring of 1986, he replied he'd check with the man to whom he had given the money to kill Rozanne. A couple of days later, Andy reported that the man from Houston had gotten married, settled down, and was no longer interested in that kind of work.

It was then, supposedly, that Garland went to Joseph Walter Thomas, who, in turn, allegedly went to Buster Matthews, a burly roofer. Apparently feeling the job would be more attractive if he painted the potential victim as a true blackguard, Thomas allegedly told Buster that he knew someone seeking a rough-and-ready type to "hurt" a man named Larry

Aylor, who Thomas claimed was a child molester and wife abuser. The job paid $5,000, Buster learned: $2,500 up front and the balance upon completion. It didn't take him long to reply that he and his brother, Gary, might be willing to perform the task.

Once Buster and Gary agreed to do the job, they were told that a plan had already been worked out and they only had to follow orders. The scheme was simple: Their target would be lured to a rural area where they would ambush him. In preparation for the attack, which had changed from a proposal to "hurt" Larry to one to kill him, they were driven to Kaufman County and shown possible locations for the trap. They picked a copse of trees near the entrance to the target's ranch.

On June 16, the brothers hid in the trees and waited for Larry to drive into range. In the way of armament, Gary was waiting with a .22 caliber rifle, not exactly a high-powered ambush weapon. To make the task they had set for themselves even more difficult, the rifle was only a semiautomatic, which meant the shooter had to pull the trigger each time he wanted to fire a round.

Except for the weapon and the choice of assassins, the plan worked perfectly. Larry walked right into the trap. But there were two crucial things not included in the scheme: the friend Don Kennedy, whom Larry had brought along, and Gary being an incredibly bad marksman.

It was later estimated that Gary fired close to a dozen shots at Larry's pickup from a distance of eighty to one hundred feet. Fewer than one fourth of the rounds even struck the truck and none of them found their mark. The only wound suffered by either man was a nick on Kennedy's elbow.

The only phase of the ambush that succeeded was that Buster and Gary, despite their bumbling, easily escaped in the confusion. And they successfully disappeared again in the early summer of 1988 when McGowan tried to track them down. But in August of that year, they ran out of luck.

As would so many others involved in the tangled series of events swirling around Joy and Larry, when Buster and Gary Matthews discovered that authorities were looking for them, they decided to get out of town. They headed west into New Mexico, setting up camp in the Lincoln National Forest in the south-central part of the state. Obviously, they had picked the area for its remoteness. To the south of their camp site was the thinly populated Mescalero Apache Indian Reservation. Immediately to the west was a barren area known as The Malpais, an incredibly desolate expanse of sharp, black rocks, a river of jagged stones left behind by some ancient lava flow. Just a little farther in that direction was the even more desolate parched tableland known as the Jornado del Muerto, or Plain of Death. It got its name from the fact that it had been a deathtrap for the Spanish conquistadors who tried to cross it without adequate water. In the northeast corner of the Jornado, snuggled up against an arm of the moonscapelike San Andres Mountains, was Trinity Site, the place where the world's first atomic bomb was detonated on July 16, 1945. Furthermore, in an ironic thrust, Buster and Gary had chosen as their place of refuge New Mexico's notorious Lincoln County, one of the bloodiest counties in the history of the Old West and the former stomping ground of the infamous William H. Bonney, a.k.a. Billy the Kid.

Buster and Gary certainly had found isolation; they probably were as removed as they could be from investigators in Richardson and Kaufman County and still be in the United States. But they had not counted on the locals.

They bolted to New Mexico in August, a time when Lincoln County's pleasant, sunny afternoons are often shattered by thunderstorms that gather like the ghosts of ancient Indian warriors over the mile-and-a-half-tall peaks. When the thunderstorms dissipate after drenching the Ponderosa pine- and fir-covered slopes, it is almost as if God has turned on His air conditioner. Temperatures drop rapidly and a warm sweater becomes a necessity. It is even more comfortable if a camper has a toasty fire to huddle over. When fellow-Texan Robert Lindquist found the hapless Matthews brothers at 7:15 on the evening of Saturday, August 27, 1988, they had neither.

A sixty-three-year-old retiree from Fort Worth, Lindquist had come to Lincoln County for much the same reason as Buster and Gary: its remoteness. The difference was, there was no one on his trail; he was there simply to enjoy the clean air and perhaps snag a trout for dinner. On that evening he had been fishing at nearby Eagle Lake and had, himself, been caught unprepared in the usual afternoon downpour. When the fish quit biting, Lindquist, interested only in a hot shower and warm clothes, was driving down Highway 532 en route to the vacation cabin where he was staying when he spotted the Matthews brothers standing underneath the crumbling canopy of an abandoned gas station. In a neighborly fashion common to the rural West, he stopped and asked if they needed help.

"Yeah," mumbled a wet and bedraggled Buster, "we'd like to get to town."

"Hop in," said Lindquist, opening the door of his pickup. "I'll drive you there. I don't have anything else to do anyway."

Exactly why he picked them up remains something of a mystery; they were a rough-looking duo. At six feet tall and 190 pounds, Gary sported a thick, dark beard, a tattoo reading "Sherry" on his right bicep and a knife scar along the right side of his neck. And he was the more presentable of the two. Buster, with wild bushy hair and a bulging beer belly (he packed 230 pounds on his 5-foot-10½-inch frame), had eyes as cold and dark as a December night and the personality of a chain gang boss.

Lindquist, however, seemed not to be put off by the two men and happily drove them up and down a sizable section of Lincoln County in search of a particular motel they said they had heard about. After a lengthy and unsuccessful search, Gary asked Lindquist if he would stop at a convenience store while he and his brother got a cup of coffee. When they climbed back in the truck, Buster made Lindquist an unusual offer: He told the Texan he could have all their camping gear if he would just drive them to their camp site to pick it up. "We're through camping," he said, claiming the two of them were disgusted with the cold mountain nights and the daily soakings, and were anxious to get back to civilization.

When they got there, Buster curtly ordered Gary to load the gear into the bed of Lindquist's truck, standing back, as Lindquist later related to sheriff's deputies, like a man who disdained soiling his hands with manual labor. When it looked as if everything had been loaded, Lindquist and Gary were ready to climb into the truck's cab when Buster stopped them.

"Did you get the shovel?" Buster asked his brother.

"No," Gary said, shaking his head and stalking somewhat unhappily back into the trees.

Lindquist watched him walk away, then turned to Buster, shocked to see the man holding a large black pistol. Lindquist's eyes popped when he noted that the gun was pointed directly at his heart.

"Don't fool around now," Buster told him with a mean edge in his voice. "Lay down on your stomach with your hands folded out or I'll kill you right now. I have no reason not to."

"Okay," stuttered Lindquist. "Okay. I'm getting down."

"I don't like to do this," Buster added, "but if I don't get to California by tomorrow they're going to put me in prison."

Lindquist, who figured he was in no position to argue, stretched out on the ground and gritted his teeth as Gary systematically went through his pockets, removing his money, his wallet, a pocket knife, a fingernail clipper, even his drugstore reading glasses. The only thing they left him was a soiled handkerchief.

After he had been stripped of everything of value, Lindquist was ordered to climb into one of the sleeping bags, which Gary then zipped up to his chin. Then Gary grabbed a roll of twine and began wrapping it around the outside of the sleeping bag, sealing Lindquist inside. When he saw what they were doing, Lindquist moved his arms and legs slightly away from his body so, once they left, there would be some slack in the binding.

Trussed up like a calf at a rodeo, Lindquist watched as Buster and Gary climbed into his 1984 Ford pickup and Buster turned the key in the ignition. When it refused to start, Lindquist grimaced apprehensively.

"God," he mumbled to himself. "I hope that son of a bitch runs and gets 'em out of here." Lindquist breathed an audible sigh of relief seconds later when the engine caught.

Propping himself up on his elbows, he watched the brothers and his truck disappear up the road that led to the top of the mountain. As soon as they were out of sight, Lindquist wiggled out of the sleeping bag and hurried down the same road. He went no more than a few hundred yards when he spotted a turnoff to a cabin nestled protectively in the trees. Shaking with anger and fright, Lindquist pounded on the door and asked the startled inhabitants to call the police.

A few minutes later, Lindquist was standing in front of the cabin, excitedly telling a sheriff's deputy what had happened.

"And what," the deputy asked, "does your truck look like?"

When Buster and Gary drove away from the campsite in the Texan's truck, they headed up the mountain, evidently intending to drive over the crest and continue westward toward California. However, they were unfamiliar with the area and did not know that the road they were on deadended at the peak. When they got to a barricade, they had no choice but to turn around and come back down the mountain.

The deputy had no sooner asked Lindquist to describe his vehicle when the Texan glanced toward the road. He did a double take and broke into a huge grin. "As a matter of fact," he drawled, pointing toward a pair of taillights, "there it goes right there."

When the deputy pulled the vehicle over a few minutes later, Gary and Buster both ran into the woods. The corpulent and out-of-shape Buster soon collapsed. Panting in the thin mountain air, he gave in to the inevitable, surrendering meekly to the deputy. But the lithe Gary bolted into the trees and disappeared. He was arrested early the next afternoon, several miles away on the other side of the mountain, trying to thumb a ride. The two brothers were thrown into the tiny jail at nearby Carrizozo and charged with stealing Lindquist's truck, armed robbery, and false imprisonment.

Once they were behind bars, the Matthews brothers worked quickly to make sure they secured a place at the top of the inmate pecking order, bragging to the meeker inhabitants that they were the meanest *hombres* in the lockup, and that their dominance of the situation would not be challenged without dire consequences for the challenger. One of the perks that went with being at the top of the prisoner heap was possession of the remote control device that determined what all the inmates would watch on the jailhouse TV. With the clicker firmly in hand, Buster made sure he and his brother got to watch their favorite program: reruns of "The Flintstones."

19

After he sped up the road into the northern Idaho mountains, Andy dropped out of sight again and did not resurface until just before Christmas. In mid-December, he called Shelley and told her he was on his way back to Dallas. She reported the conversation to McGowan, who told her to go home and wait. Anxious not to let him slip through his grasp yet again, McGowan called the telephone company and arranged for a device called a trap to be installed on Shelley's phone. It was different from a tap in that it would not pick up a conversation but was designed only to record the numbers from which incoming calls were made. That way, McGowan could backtrack and find the phone Andy was calling from and, hopefully, speed there in time to grab him.

On December 18, before the trap could be activated, Andy called Shelley again and said he was in the city. Fatefully, this information did not go first to McGowan, but to Ken McKenzie, Andy's nemesis. According to Shelley, Andy was going to come to her house that night, a Sunday.

McKenzie, who had by then notified McGowan, left immediately for Garland, where Shelley lived with her mother, to stake out her house until McGowan and other reinforcements could arrive.

While McKenzie was waiting on the darkened street in an unmarked pickup truck, he glanced in the rearview mirror and watched nervously as a figure emerged from the bushes several houses behind him. As he watched with growing anxiety, the figure walked steadily down the sidewalk toward McKenzie's vehicle. As the man got closer, McKenzie hunched further down in his seat, hoping he would not be seen. But when the man got abreast of the truck, he spotted the policeman out of the corner of his eye.

Figuring he had no alternative but to show himself, McKenzie sprang from the truck and drew his pistol. The man started running away, heading for the shadows alongside a nearby house.

"Halt!" McKenzie yelled. "Police!"

The man kept running.

"Andy!" McKenzie hollered. "Police! Freeze!"

As soon as he yelled "Andy," the man screamed loudly, lifted his knees, and spurted away faster.

Testifying about this encounter later, McKenzie said that it was the first time in his fourteen years as a police officer that he felt his life was in danger.

The man disappeared, outmaneuvering the detective for the second time.

Later that same night, meter reader Merle Ward was watching "Designing Women" on TV and thinking about going to bed when there was a knock on the door of her home in northeast Dallas. Ward, who lived with her roommate, Rebecca Trammell, was an old dope-smoking friend of Andy's. Still, she failed to recognize him as he stood at her door, dressed in scruffy, dirty clothes, his lower face covered in a scraggly, unkempt beard. But as soon as he identified himself, she let him inside without a second thought.

"Are you in trouble?" she asked him as soon as he was seated on her couch.

"Yeah," he admitted, a sheepish look showing through his exhaustion. "I passed some money to have someone killed and they're looking for me."

With a pleading look, he asked Ward if he could stay at her house for a couple of days until he figured out what he was going to do.

Ward considered his request. "It's okay with me," she said, shrugging, "if it's okay with Rebecca."

Andy sighed in obvious relief. Stretching out and relaxing for the first time since he had crossed the threshold, Andy grinned and asked Ward if she had any marijuana.

Ward laughingly replied that she did. Switching the channel to ABC, Andy and Ward watched the Monday night football game and quietly got high.

After Trammell came home, the three of them sat around the kitchen table while Andy repeated his story for Trammell's edification. He had made a mistake, he told her, by agreeing to pass along some money to a fellow he knew named Chip. The money was payment to kill a woman. He himself had not been the killer, he stressed, but he was still afraid that his role could result in a death sentence if he were caught. In the meantime, he needed to find Chip so he could clear his name.

Trammell was dubious. "I didn't know you could get the death sentence unless you were the actual triggerman," she said.

Andy waved off her statement, assuring her that he was in big trouble and he needed their help.

"How do you feel about being a fugitive?" Trammell asked, curious to see how he would respond.

"I enjoy it," he admitted. "Being one step ahead of the law gives me a kind of high."

"Don't you think they're going to find you eventually?" she asked.

"If they do," he said, "it will be because I'm trying to see Shelley."

"Aren't you worried that they're going to catch you in some simple way, like asking you for an ID?"

"I've got that taken care of," Andy said, digging out a slip of paper which he handed over for Trammell and Ward's examination.

It was a document purporting to be a birth certificate showing that the bearer was born in Georgia. On one corner was an official-looking seal. Trammell studied the seal and her mouth fell open.

"The birth certificate says Georgia," she exclaimed, "but the seal says South Dakota. How are you ever going to explain that?"

Andy shrugged. "No one will ever notice," he said confidently.

Seemingly excited in her own right by the idea of harboring a dangerous fugitive, Trammell fixed Andy a sandwich and, while he was eating, she dug out clean sheets and made a bed for him in a spare room. The next day she volunteered to drive to a park where Andy said he had hidden his belongings in some bushes and retrieve them for him. Then she went to work.

That afternoon, when Ward returned from her job, Andy was talking on the telephone. Covering the bottom half of the phone, he mouthed to Ward that he was talking to Shelley. When he got off the phone, Ward told him that she had discussed the situation with Trammell and they had decided that Andy was going to have to leave.

He nodded silently. "I understand," he said quietly, promising to depart as soon as he could get his things together. He would vacate by the next day at the latest, he said. As it turned out, it was sooner than that; the telephone trap had caught up with him.

Thirty minutes after Andy hung up with Shelley, someone knocked on Ward's front door. When she went to answer it, she was confronted by a uniformed policeman who asked her to step outside. Once away from the door, the officer told her to stay where she was and not to move. Looking around, she could see that police had the house surrounded.

Brushing past her, McGowan entered the house and found Andy alone in a back room. He offered no resistance.

Once the cuffs had been placed around Andy's wrists, he was hustled into a squad car and taken straight to the Richardson Public Safety Department for processing. The whole thing took place so quickly that McGowan did not even stop to read Andy his Miranda rights until they got to the police station.

Without giving him a chance to settle into his cell, McGowan hustled Andy into a small interrogation room and pointed to a chair. Then, making himself as comfortable as possible, McGowan opened the conversation in his customary folksy style, an approach designed to impart to Andy that the two were simply brother Texans having a friendly chat over a Coca-Cola.

The investigator began by explaining that seven people had been arrested so far in connection with the attacks on Rozanne and Larry, but the moving force behind both incidents appeared to be an interior decorator named Joy Aylor, who had been indicted on five felonies, including murder. Intuiting that the name meant nothing to Andy, McGowan added, "She's a lady that's got a lot of money and that kind of thing."

Attempting to ingratiate himself with the new prisoner from the very first, McGowan quickly apologized for his lack of foresight in sending investigators McKenzie and Bonner to interview him at the dealership the previous July instead of going himself. Also, he said, there was one other thing he regretted regarding Andy's situation: "I wish you hadn't of run," he said wistfully.

For the next few minutes, McGowan detailed for Andy how he had been hot on his trail for the last five months and how investigators had almost caught him in Minot, North Dakota, missing him by just a few minutes at a truck stop where he had stopped to try to collect some money that had been wired to him from Texas. "But the time for running and all that crap is over with," the detective added, not unkindly.

McGowan related how investigators had talked to others allegedly involved in the dual plots, including Brian Kreafle. "You already know Brian's given us everything he's done," McGowan explained. "He's been indicted and there will be some others."

Andy, feeling a response was required, said simply, "Yeah." Otherwise, he seemed to show little interest in the proceedings except to ask disingenuously if there was any chance he might be released on bond pending further developments.

McGowan shook his head. "I mean, it's not hard to figure out why," he said. "That's why I say I wish you hadn't have run. I mean, we don't have any guarantee it wouldn't happen again. You have to be honest with yourself: Would you run?"

"I don't think so," Andy replied. "I'm tired of running."

"Well, I imagine you're tired of the whole fucking deal," McGowan clucked sympathetically, "just like a lot of people are. Well, where we go from here, that's up to Andy. There's nobody else now."

Andy looked puzzled. "What do you mean?" he asked.

"Well," McGowan replied, "you can get on our team and help us or not. That's your business."

"Shouldn't I be talking to an attorney?" Andy asked suspiciously.

"That's up to you," McGowan said. "What I'm telling you is it's over. We know the whole story but Andy's."

When Andy showed no inclination to respond, McGowan added: "Two things are going to happen. If you ask me a question I can answer, I will. And I ain't never going to lie to you or bullshit you about nothing. *Nothing!*" he repeated emphatically. "Those are my rules and I go by them with everybody."

Andy showed no signs of softening, so McGowan spread it on a little thicker. "All I can do," he said to the unresponsive prisoner, "is tell you where I'm coming from and where I've been. I've been involved in this son of a bitch for five years, and it ain't been easy. That's where I got all this fucking gray hair. But at the same time, I got a good idea it hasn't been easy on Andy, either."

When Andy did not respond, the detective slowly shook his head again. "I just wish the fuck you'd never run," he said.

Andy's spirits improved a few minutes later, after McGowan told him he could make a telephone call. With the detective sitting silently at his elbow, Andy dialed Shelley's number. He spoke for a few minutes, hung up, and turned slowly to McGowan. "Is she the one who turned me in?" he asked with bitterness.

McGowan shook his head. "Not really," he said, explaining how he had been tracked through a device on her telephone. She was only one in a string of people, he explained, who had helped investigators.

"I want to tell you up front," McGowan said, "that you got to understand something. People in their lives, everybody around you when you were here, wanted this deal over with. Nobody likes cops coming in asking them stuff: 'What about this?' 'What about that?' It was tearing a lot of people up. They wanted you caught so they could sleep at night." But what had happened in the past was over with, he continued, and what was going to happen in the future depended on Andy.

For his part, Andy remained skeptical, alluding again to his wish for an attorney.

Ignoring what Andy's trial lawyers later would heatedly argue was only one of a number of requests from Andy for counsel, McGowan went on. "Andy's the one," he said. "His fucking lawyer ain't the one. Andy's the one that can make or break himself. And either you get on our side or you don't. That's your choice. *I* can't make it for you. Can't *nobody* make it for you."

"I know," Andy relied, "but I'm going to have to have my attorney present before I do it."

McGowan seemed to give in. "Mighty fine," he replied. "But are you going to do it?"

"I'm going to have to talk to my attorney," Andy replied.

McGowan ignored him, claiming that if Andy refused to cooperate, the district attorney's office would look with disfavor upon his resistance and treat him more harshly than if he went along. Seemingly as much to organize his thoughts as for Andy's benefit, McGowan outlined his theory about Joy being at one end of the chain that led to Rozanne while the other end was still a question mark. However, he added, from where he was right then, Andy was the last person in line. "If it needs to stop at you, that's fine," McGowan said, toughening his stance, "because I'm going to tell you that we're going to get Joy Aylor. And if we have to, we're going to get you. Now that's just the way it has to be."

Although sobered by the remarks, Andy refused to open up. "I need to hear from my dad saying he's going to get me an attorney or he's going to have one court-appointed."

"I understand that," McGowan replied, shaking his head slowly. "But I want you to know where I'm coming from, too."

To help break the ice, McGowan suggested they discuss less sensitive issues, ones that did not require Andy to face the issue of Rozanne's attack directly. "Let's talk about some bullshit stuff," McGowan said lightly. "Stuff that don't have nothing to do with nothing."

"Not on the record?" Andy asked skeptically.

"Nothing on the record," McGowan confirmed. "Just bullshit stuff."

20

For twenty minutes or more, McGowan and Andy chatted about how investigators had traced him, lost his trail, picked it up, then lost him again before finally catching up with him after he returned to Dallas.

Andy, relaxing more by the minute, related how he had used three different aliases on his travels through Nevada, New Mexico, Idaho, Oregon, and the Dakotas. "I probably could have stayed gone forever," he added.

"Why didn't you?" McGowan asked.

Andy shrugged. "I don't know."

"I thought there would be a point where you would turn around, come back here, and do the right thing," McGowan said. "I thought you would sit down with me and we could get it right."

Again, the conversation drifted away, this time to talk about Andy's daughters, the two young girls he had not seen in five months and missed terribly. Life on the run had its downside, Andy agreed, and one of the most prominent disadvantages was not being able to see family and friends.

"Well, hell, I know that," McGowan commiserated. "A guy that's used to having a home, a family, a job, goes to work, comes back home, even got a girlfriend on the side, he isn't ready for that kind of shit. For the kind of guy that's killed fifteen people, that's an easy life, probably the best one. But for a guy that's an everyday guy, that shit ain't going to work."

Just when it appeared that McGowan and Andy were approaching a rapport, Investigator Ken McKenzie entered the room, feigning a casualness that immediately raised Andy's hackles. "I'm sorry," he told McGowan, nodding at McKenzie, "but I won't say another word with him in here."

McGowan nodded, inwardly pleased with the opening moves in the good-cop/bad-cop scenario that was beginning to be played out. Claiming a sudden craving for a cup of coffee, McGowan excused himself and briskly left the room, anxious to see what would happen when McKenzie and Andy were left alone together.

As soon as the door closed, Andy turned to McKenzie and stared sullenly at him.

"I know I'm not your favorite person in the world," McKenzie began unctuously, claiming he knew that Andy felt a great deal of hostility toward him. "But I do know some things that you probably want to know." The main thing, McKenzie said, was that Andy's daughters were doing well, that they had no knowledge about what had been happening in the last few months while their father was being sought as a fugitive.

Andy glared at McKenzie, scorning what he considered his bogus attempts to sound friendly. He responded only when necessary, and then only in monosyllables.

"You know this isn't the end of the world," the detective pointed out. "You read the newspaper. You know that people have gone up against a lot bigger walls than what you're going up against. And they climb those walls to go on to lead productive lives.

"What I'm saying," McKenzie blurted, rushing on when Andy failed to respond, "is you can read the paper every day and there's articles in there about people that have committed a lot worse crimes than you've committed and within a short period of time they're back out on the street."

Andy looked at him coldly. "I say I want to speak to my attorney before I talk to y'all and you say, 'Well, that makes us think you did it; we think you pulled the trigger.' " Didn't that mean, Andy asked, that he might be a prime target for execution?

"Well," McKenzie added hurriedly, "let me tell you there are a thousand people killed here in this state every year. You hear maybe about one or two that get death and that's usually after about ten or fifteen years. What you hear about a lot of times are people who have committed several murders and they're back out on the street."

When Andy again sat silently, McKenzie decided to take the direct approach. "Why did you kill Rozanne Gailiunas?" he asked abruptly, the same thing he had asked Larry Aylor on the night Rozanne was shot.

Andy went rigid. "I want to talk to my attorney," he blurted.

Again, McKenzie ignored him, pointing out instead how he knew that Andy had been dealing drugs, how he had gone through some tough times, but how he had come through the situation as a better and stronger person. "Answering my questions, Andy, all it's going to do is just let me know more about you," McKenzie added.

"I'll wait until I have my attorney present," Andy repeated.

McKenzie leaned forward. "This case *is* going to go to trial," he said unequivocally, adding that it would be better for Andy to tell them what he knew so the courts would look more favorably upon his situation.

Andy stared at the table without answering.

"What are you thinking of?" McKenzie asked. "What are you thinking right now?"

"I want my attorney," Andy responded.

McKenzie leaned back in his chair. "Want a Coke?" he asked.

McGowan returned to the room in time to hear the last few exchanges between McKenzie and Andy. Figuring it was time to raise the good-cop flag, he sent McKenzie for coffee. As soon as the abrasive investigator was out the door, McGowan turned to Andy and said softly, "After he brings the coffee back, I'm going to ask him not to stay in here if that's all right with you."

"Yeah," Andy said angrily. "He doesn't care what he does. He was downright rude and hateful to Shelley, to me, to my wife . . ."

"I'm listening," McGowan broke in, explaining that not all investigators handled things the same way.

"The fact remains," Andy said, "I've been told by two different attorneys not to say anything without my attorney."

McGowan tried to temporize, explaining how most people he met on the street would tell him to never trust a cop. But those people, he added, were not in serious trouble.

"I have some good friends that are cops," Andy interjected.

"Well," McGowan philosophized, "it's like riding a motorcycle. You can't tell somebody what it's like to have a wreck on a motorcycle until you've had one."

Effortlessly, McGowan switched from motorcycles to wives and families. "A guy says 'I'm going to get married.' You try to tell him, man, you ought to think about that, maybe live with 'em for awhile, that kind of thing, because that marriage, that's a heavy responsibility. How many of 'em listen to you?"

Without waiting for an answer, he continued: "That's right. You got it! I didn't. You didn't. And it's a lot of fucking responsibility. Marriage sounds like fun, you know. You got your wife and she's there all the time, but there's a lot of extra shit that goes with it. The arguments, the hassles, even children are the same way. We love 'em to death, but at times they're a pain in the ass. They get sick, have doctor bills . . ."

"I'm prejudiced," Andy broke in, "but mine were never a pain in the ass. I've been real fortunate with my little girls. I was fortunate to have healthy, damn good girls."

"But you know what I mean," McGowan insisted. "And it's kind of the same thing [with lawyers]." Lowering his voice, playing the part of confider, the detective cautioned Andy to be careful about picking an attorney.

"Don't fall in a trap and get you some bloodsucker," he warned, pointing out that attorneys were expensive. "You have any idea what it's going to cost?" he asked, explaining that in a capital murder case a lawyer would probably go home with $250,000.

Before McGowan could say anything else, McKenzie returned to the room. McGowan gave him a pointed glance. "Ken," he said firmly, "leave us alone for a bit. Would you please?"

McKenzie nodded and left.

"Okay," McGowan said, turning back to Andy, "we're going to get first things out of the way first. I don't want you saying no shit about 'I want to see my attorney' because I ain't going to use nothing right now against you. This is all fucking off the record from this point forward."

"But Mo—" Andy began.

McGowan raised his hand. "Listen to me first," he said. "If we get one issue out of the way, the odds are split. Some people say yeah, some say no. We get one issue out of the way, Andy! Then you got everything to gain by getting on this team over here. That's the truth and that's what some others have done. It's a hell of a lot easier; it's less of an obstacle. You see what I'm getting at?"

Andy looked puzzled. "No," he admitted. "I'm waiting for you to explain it."

"All right," McGowan sighed. "McKenzie said it a different way. He says you did it. Now I'm asking you straight out if you did and I want you to tell me yes or no, and that's it. Nothing else. That's what I want to know and then we'll go from there."

Andy stared at him. "If I shot the girl?" he asked cautiously.

"Yeah," said McGowan.

"No!" Andy replied quickly.

"Then, Andy," McGowan said easily, "you got every fucking reason in the world to get on this fucking team, son. Every fucking reason you can think of for you to be over here." If he did not cooperate, McGowan said, the district attorney's office would come after him with everything it had. Dismissing McKenzie's references to Andy's involvement with drugs, McGowan declared that was the least of the things they were interested in. No matter what else investigators might have against him, McGowan said, it was of little consequence compared to the murder of Rozanne Gailiunas.

"We're interested in one thing," he said, "and if you're telling me the truth, son, you've got everything to gain and probably plenty to lose. Now we've beat around the bush," he said soberly, "and we've talked some because I was personally interested. But business is business and you ain't been doing shit right lately. And being scared and all that shit, that's fine. A lot of people are that way and I'm not sure I wouldn't be the same way. But I ain't in your shoes and if I was, I know what decision I'd make, because you got a lot to fucking gain if that's true."

If he were telling the truth about not being involved in the attack on Rozanne, McGowan promised, he would stand behind Andy all the way. "But I got to have the truth," he said. "I got to know so that I can get the right one. The ones that don't get on the team, we're going to fucking handle." One or two of the people they had questioned had proved uncooperative, McGowan pointed out, and they were paying the price. "I'm throwing you a pass," he told Andy, "and it's up to you to catch it. Conspiracy is a hell of a lot better than the big motherfucker."

Andy appealed again to McGowan. "Don't you think I should also have the right to at least talk with an attorney—"

"Sure—" McGowan interjected.

"—and make that decision after talking with him?"

"Sure," McGowan repeated, adding, without making a move to rise, "if that's what you want to do."

"There's no doubt in my mind," Andy said, "that sitting here right now, Mo, knowing that if I'm going to trust anyone, you're the person.

But I'm still drilled with the idea that it should be with an attorney to talk to."

"A lot of people are drilled with that same thought," McGowan said sympathetically.

"I would like to talk to an attorney," Andy asserted.

"Okay," McGowan said, "I ain't got no problem with that. But what I'm telling you up front—"

It was Andy's turn to interrupt. "Are you saying that after I talk with an attorney that I don't have any chance to come on your side?"

"You're not going to be dealing with me then," McGowan said firmly. "I'll tell you that now." Instead, McGowan added, the case would be taken over by the district attorney's office.

Andy tried to ask if he could request that McGowan remain on the case when McGowan's boss, Captain David Golden, knocked on the door and motioned McGowan into the hallway.

"He's done asked for an attorney six times so we ain't getting anywhere with this deal," Golden whispered in disgust. "He could drop to his knees and confess all day long, but we ain't going nowhere now."

"I'm going after information," McGowan explained.

"Why don't we let him call an attorney in here?" Golden asked.

"Because all a lawyer is going to do is tell him to shut up and that's it," McGowan said impatiently. "Right now I want the information."

"So you want to go for inadmissible information?" Golden asked incredulously.

"Basically, yeah," McGowan said. "I'm kind of laying groundwork for the future."

Golden suggested that any information obtained would be usable against other defendants.

McGowan agreed. "Yeah, against the other person."

Golden sighed. "All right," he said. "Let's go and get it over with."

Picking up where he left off in the conversation, McGowan told Andy that if he weren't the triggerman he ought to just tell McGowan what happened.

When Andy did not respond, McGowan added: "Let's face it, you've asked for your attorney enough times now. I'm not going to be able to use a fucking thing you say. Even if you wrote me a confession, I couldn't use it. That's the law. But let's get down to brass tacks now because I have to know your part because that's going to take me in someplace else."

McGowan repeated how others involved in the case had agreed to cooperate and it would be to Andy's advantage for him to do the same. He hinted that with some cooperation, he might even be released pending trial. But that, he added, depended on Andy's willingness to talk. "How can we know you're going to get straight, even offer you a bond, until we know for sure what's going on?" the detective asked in mock sincerity.

When Andy still refused to respond, McGowan decided to end the session. But he did not want to go without the last word. "Everybody can give you advice," he said, "but I want to tell you the truth. I'm going to lay my cards on the table. I ain't asking you to put a fucking thing in writing. Nothing. But I'm going to shoot straight with you from the word go. And I'll be there."

21

While preparations were under way in New Mexico to dispose of the cases involving the Matthews brothers stemming from the Lindquist incident, thus clearing the decks for their trials in Texas for attempting to kill Larry, McGowan was also moving ahead in an attempt to seal up the other side of the dual murder schemes and write an end, finally, to the investigation of Rozanne's killing.

On Wednesday, February 22, 1989, McGowan appeared at the Dallas County Jail to take Andy's formal statement. During an unrecorded interview conducted in a small room at the jail, Andy gave his first formal version of events of his alleged involvement in the death of Rozanne Gailiunas. It later became known as the "Chip statement."

Andy admitted to the detective that he accepted an envelope containing money and some biographical data from Brian Kreafle. In late September, he said, he went to Rozanne's house with the intention of killing her. Using a glass cutter to remove a pane in a back window, he reached through the hole and unlocked the door, letting himself inside. Once in the house, he told McGowan, he appropriated a steak knife to use as a weapon and hid in the darkened house waiting for Rozanne to return. While waiting, however, he became worried that Rozanne might not be alone, that she would return with a man. Not anxious to face a confrontation of that sort, Andy said he left.

A day or so later, he said, he decided to extricate himself from the plot. He kept $500 of the money and turned over the rest to a man from whom he claimed he had bought drugs, a man whom he knew only as "Chip," with the expectation that Chip would fulfill the contract.

A few days after that, Andy said, he ran into Chip, who told him that "everything had been taken care of." Andy said Chip also warned him that if he ever told anyone about what had happened between them, he would take revenge on Andy's family.

In the period between visits with McGowan, Andy's demands for an attorney finally had been met. Jan Hemphill, a respected criminal defense lawyer with a reputation for being tough and unyielding, was appointed to represent him.

Hours after the February 22 session, as soon as McGowan and lawyers from the Dallas County District Attorney's Office had a chance to go over the Chip statement, one of the prosecutors called Hemphill and asked for her permission to check Andy out of the county jail. They wanted to take him to Richardson, the prosecutor said, to give him a polygraph examination in an attempt to verify that he was telling the truth about Chip. Although polygraphs are not admissible in Texas courts, the tests are used routinely by both prosecutors and defense lawyers in an attempt to establish basic veracity. If Hemphill had acted correctly, she would have told the district attorney's office that she would not allow them to polygraph Andy until she had a chance to have her own expert test him first, or at least to be present when the exam was given. But she ignored her instincts. Much to her later regret and embarrassment, Hemphill agreed to let Andy be taken alone to Richardson to be strapped to a lie detector.

On Monday, February 27, RPD Investigator Brent Tourangeau picked up Andy and took him to the police department, a twenty-minute drive away, where the polygraph would be administered.

Unfortunately, Andy did poorly on the test. According to the examiner, Andy indicated deception in his responses to three crucial questions: 1. Were you in the house when Rozanne was attacked? 2. Do you know who murdered her? 3. Did *you* murder her?

As soon as the examiner told McGowan that he thought Andy was hiding something, the detective escorted Andy to a tiny interrogation room on the ground floor of the Richardson Public Safety Department building, motioned Tourangeau inside, and closed the door. The room was barely large enough to accommodate the three men and a tiny table. McGowan said later that his intention had been to question Andy further about the inconsistencies uncovered during the test. But before he began there was one detail that he felt needed to be attended to: McGowan ordered Tourangeau to read Andy the list of rights he was entitled to under the Supreme Court's Miranda decision. Andy stared at the table-top while Tourangeau went through the procedure in a dull monotone.

If McGowan had followed the correct procedure, Andy's lawyers would argue vigorously at his trial, the detective should not even have been in the room with Andy. The detective should have returned him to the Dallas jail as soon as the test was over, regardless of the results. Then, if investigators wanted to talk to him further, they should have called Hemphill and made new arrangements. Hemphill, they asserted, had agreed to release him *only* to be tested, not to be interrogated about his responses during the test. Instead, they argued, what McGowan did was a further violation of Andy's rights: He was questioned without his attorney being present even though he was represented by counsel, which just added to the clear-cut desecration of his rights that had occurred when McGowan and McKenzie ignored Andy's repeated requests for an attorney on the night he was arrested.

The back-to-back decisions—Hemphill's concurrence with the request for Andy to be taken alone to Richardson to be given a polygraph, and McGowan's impulsive interrogation *after* the test—would be irreversible acts that would later have a tremendous detrimental influence on Andy's future.

In the five days that had passed since Andy had first told McGowan about Chip, McGowan had sent investigators on an emergency search to try to uncover the mystery man's identity. Their success was phenomenal. They had not only learned Chip's full name, but had tracked him to southern California, where he now was under surveillance at the request of the Dallas authorities. When McGowan went into the interrogation room with Andy, he had in his pocket a picture of Chip.

Hunched over the table in the small room, McGowan leaned close to Andy and asked him to tell his story yet again. "Tell me *exactly* what happened," he urged, "from beginning to end."

Andy repeated the tale he had told the detective on February 22: that he had kept some of the money he had received in the envelope from Kreafle to use for drugs, that he gave the rest of it to Chip, and that he believed Chip was Rozanne's assailant.

McGowan responded skeptically. "If I go find Chip, what is he going to tell me?" he asked, putting pressure on Andy. "Who is that going to bring me back to?"

Andy obviously did not like the idea that McGowan might try to contact Chip; the suggestion made him visibly nervous. "That would bring it back to me," he answered uneasily.

Realizing that Andy was vulnerable on two counts—rattled because of the unsatisfactory polygraph and by being without his lawyer—McGowan played his trump card, certain he would never have a better shot at extracting more details from Andy. Reaching into his shirt pocket, McGowan slowly removed the picture of Chip he had brought with him and slapped it down on the table with a flourish.

"Who is this?" he asked coldly.

Andy was stunned; apparently he had never considered the possibility that Dallas police would be able to track down the elusive Chip on the slim leads he had provided to his identity.

"That's Chip!" he exclaimed in horror.

"That's right," McGowan replied with satisfaction. "That's Chip."

The investigator was on a roll and he knew it. Andy was reeling, so McGowan pushed harder. "I haven't contacted him yet," he confided to the confused prisoner, "but if I do and I ask him his involvement, where would that leave us? If I put Chip on the polygraph and he passes it, where would that leave us?" "

"It would come back to me," Andy said softly, slumping in his chair.

"That's right," McGowan agreed, realizing in that instant that he had won, that Andy was going to tell him everything he wanted to know.

Tourangeau, who had been watching the procedure as a fascinated participant, gazed in awe as Andy deflated like a collapsing hot-air balloon. He swiveled toward McGowan, wondering what the veteran detective was going to do next.

McGowan had forgotten that Tourangeau was there; he was focused on Andy with deadly concentration. Extending his right hand, palm flat and perpendicular to the floor, McGowan drew an imaginary line on the wall behind him. "On this side of the line is Joy Aylor," McGowan said, "and on the other side is us. Andy," he said earnestly, "I want Joy Aylor, and I want you with us. I want you to testify against Joy Aylor."

Still in shock over the Chip revelation, Andy showed his bewilderment. "Can I go back to the jail and think about it?" he asked softly.

At that point, McGowan was not about to let go; it would be like cutting the line when the record-setting fish is almost in the net.

"I need the whole truth," McGowan pressed, letting a note of urgency creep into his voice. "Regardless of what it is, I want the truth. If you were there, tell me."

Andy gave it one more try, acting more out of instinct than conviction. "Can I go back and think about it?" he repeated halfheartedly.

McGowan leaned closer and tried to lock eyes. "Andy, I need it *now!*" he said firmly.

Andy's head sank to his chest and he stared listlessly at his hands for what seemed a long time but actually was no more than half a minute. Then he whispered, "I did it."

His response was so soft that McGowan was not sure he had heard him correctly. "What did you say?" he asked, leaning forward.

"Mo," Andy said, using the detective's nickname, "I did it! I killed her!"

McGowan shook his head sadly. Motioning to Tourangeau, he quietly told the investigator to fetch a tape recorder.

One of the things that came out during Andy's confession was how he gained entry to Rozanne's house. When he explained that he had bought a plant at a nearby supermarket and then posed as a floral delivery man when Rozanne answered the door, McGowan's eyes bulged in surprise.

Later, when Andy had been returned to the Dallas County Jail, the detective dug through his files and extracted the photos taken in Rozanne's house the night of the shooting. To his amazement, the pictures corroborated Andy's claim. Sitting not two feet from the front door was the plant Andy had in his hands when he confronted Rozanne. It was the clue McGowan had been looking for, and had never been able to find, on his repeated trips to 804 Loganwood Drive.

For the first time in almost five and a half years, McGowan felt himself truly relaxing; his long search for Rozanne's killer was, in his mind, successful. When Andy was taken back to the Dallas County Jail late that afternoon, McGowan was confident that he had finally solved Rozanne's murder. And he had a detailed confession to back him up.

There were, however, three points stemming from the *way* the confession was obtained that would be debated heatedly during Andy's trial. One was whether McGowan had violated Andy's constitutional rights by conducting the interrogation without the explicit permission of Andy's lawyer, Jan Hemphill. Another was whether McGowan had further violated Andy's rights by continuing with the interrogation despite Andy's two requests to "go back and think about it." According to the defense, a prisoner was entitled under Miranda to terminate an interview at any time. The question was whether the words "go back and think about it" constituted a request to stop the discussion. The third and touchiest of the points was whether Andy's lawyer had acted ineffectively by allowing him to be polygraphed without her being present. It was primarily because of Jan Hemphill's absence, Andy's trial lawyers would argue, that McGowan was able to conduct the improper interrogation that led to the confession.

22

In March 1989, some two weeks after Andy's confession, Buster and Gary were brought into court in Carrizozo, New Mexico. In addition to the charges already pending against them in connection with the Lindquist incident, Lincoln County prosecutor Scot D. Key asked that both be considered habitual offenders because of their previous records, a move that could result in stiffer prison sentences if District Judge Richard A. Parsons agreed, which he did.

On March 9, Parsons sentenced Gary to eight years in the state penitentiary at Santa Fe. And six days later, he sentenced Buster to six years. Both men had pleaded "no contest" to the charges, which meant trials were unnecessary.

McGowan, more than six hundred miles away in Richardson, found the news interesting, but his role in those proceedings was relegated to that of a long-range spectator. He would not be directly involved in any action against the brothers until they were returned to Texas to be tried for the attempted assassination of Larry, and then McGowan's role would be that of a spectator because the attempt did not occur within his jurisdiction and he was not an investigator in the case.

At that point, with Andy's confession in hand and the Matthews brothers safely locked away—secure in the belief that the "Larry chain" ended with the hapless Matthews brothers—McGowan figured his job was done except for the necessity of testifying at the other trials. Joy, Garland, Kreafle, and Thomas all were under indictment and it appeared that the situation was well in hand. The only thing that remained for him to do, the detective reckoned, was to turn over his material to the district attorney's office. For virtually the first time in years, he felt, he could draw a breath without worrying about what was going on in the seemingly endless drama swirling around Joy Aylor and the murder of Rozanne Gailiunas.

The only thing wrong with McGowan's reasoning was that it was premature. When the department gave him a badge and a gun, they had neglected to furnish him with a crystal ball.

After the trauma of February and the shock of Andy's confession, the rest of 1989 slipped by relatively quietly for McGowan, at least as far as developments went in the cases involving Rozanne and Larry.

In November, a Dallas County grand jury indicted Carol for soliciting her former brother-in-law's murder and conspiring to kill him, the same charges faced by her husband, Kreafle, and Thomas. The fact that she was indicted when she thought she was going to be rewarded infuriated Carol, as did McGowan's alleged refusal to help her get into the witness protection program. She vented some of her anger in her interview with D magazine, telling Glenna Whitley that she was having her lawyer look into the possibility of filing suit against the Richardson Police Department.

Sometime that year, Joy's younger sister, Elizabeth, divorced her husband and moved into her parents' house. Her actions had absolutely no connection to the criminal cases other than the fact that her alleged affair with Larry may have been the event that pushed Joy over the edge and supposedly made her decide to try to kill her husband.

There were developments on the civil front, but they, too, had nothing to do with McGowan or with the criminal cases. Larry filed suit against Joy, seeking millions of dollars in damages and recompense for money he claimed she stole from their joint bank account to pay blackmailers in connection with Rozanne's murder. Since it was Joy's father who had the real money, Larry tried to get the court to make him a party to the suit, contending that Henry Davis was involved in the conspiracy. The court refused to go along and Davis's name was later dropped from the document.

But in December a tragic event, while not directly connected to the criminal cases, would nevertheless play a major role in events that followed, events that *did* have repercussions on the criminal cases.

After his parents were divorced in August 1986, Chris Aylor ostensibly went to live with Joy, although he spent as much time with his grandparents Henry and Frances as he did with his mother. From Chris's point of view, it did not seem like such a bad deal: His parents and his grandparents could afford to lavish expensive gifts upon him, and what Chris wanted Chris got. His grandparents saw that he was expensively clothed and his parents kept him supplied with pocket money. For his high school graduation, Larry gave him a $2,500 Rolex. And just before Christmas in 1989, when Chris was nineteen, his grandparents gave him an almost-new Corvette.

On Christmas Day, Chris went out with friends to celebrate and show off his new wheels. For reasons that were never explained, he let a longtime friend, Raymond Slupecki, Jr., drive the car. At 1:30 A.M., technically the day *after* Christmas, Chris and Slupecki were speeding eastward on the eight-lane LBJ Freeway, a sort of inner loop around the city, racing with another car. Near the Marsh Lane exit, Slupecki lost control of the vehicle and ran onto the shoulder. Bouncing off the guard rail, the Vette smashed into a disabled vehicle that had been abandoned along the highway. Both cars burst into flames. Slupecki burned to death behind the wheel. Although Chris was still alive when he was pulled from the wreckage, he was rushed to Parkland Hospital in critical condition, where he died shortly afterward.

When police called Joy about the accident, she sought support from a new friend, a lawyer named John Michael "Mike" Wilson, whom she had met several months previously when she went to an attorney's office with a cousin who was seeking a divorce. Wilson and the divorce lawyer shared office space, and while Joy's cousin was closeted with her attorney, Wilson and Joy struck up an acquaintance. An admitted addict who was later convicted of conspiracy to distribute cocaine, Wilson eventually became romantically involved with Joy.

Exactly why Joy decided to call Wilson that night is not known since at the time she hardly knew him. In any case, the lawyer responded immediately to Joy's plea. He picked her up and together they kept an all-night vigil in Chris's room. The youth died at 11 A.M., some nine and a half hours after the crash. He would have been twenty years old in four more months.

Although it seemed on the surface to be nothing more than a pathetic accident, doubt continues to linger about the incident and the events leading up to it. For one thing, in the months preceding the crash, Chris underwent a remarkable physical change. From a buoyant, slightly beefy teen, he slimmed down considerably and took on the look of a much older youth. Part of that may have been normal adolescent development, but his father worried that some other forces may have been at work. Larry had seen one of Chris's friends go through the same transformation and when he asked Chris about it, Chris had said that his friend had a "nose problem." Although Chris had always exhibited an extremely low tolerance for alcohol or drugs or anyone using them, the thought did indeed cross Larry's mind that his son may have changed.

The previous autumn Chris and Larry had gotten into an argument when Larry refused to defend Joy in regard to the criminal charges filed against her. Chris sped away from Larry's house in a huff and the two did not speak for almost two months. By the time the holiday season rolled around, however, they had reconciled and Chris had told his father that he planned to come to Virginia to live. He was supposed to make the trip after spending Christmas with Joy and his grandparents.

There were several other things that made Larry suspicious as well. One was a sizable collection of weapons that were found in Chris's room after his death. The youth had been reared as a hunter and Larry was not surprised to learn that his son still had his old hunting rifles and two shotguns, along with a .22 caliber rifle that the two had used to hunt prairie dogs. But it was the other weapons that made Larry wonder what Chris may have been involved in before his death. Also found in Chris's room was a long-barreled .357 Magnum pistol complete with telescopic sight, a nine-millimeter automatic pistol, an AK-47 assault rifle, and an Uzi machine pistol, weapons generally regarded as "street guns" and commonly outside the interest of casual collectors.

Also curious was a report given him by the police officers who investigated the crash, which said Joy and Mike Wilson arrived at the site soon after the accident occurred, apparently before going to the hospital. Some of Chris's friends who were at the crash site said Joy and a man none of them recognized arrived soon after the fire was extinguished. While Joy searched the interior of the burnt-out shell of the car, the man began picking up pieces of the wreckage, which they took with them when they left. The same youths who then went to the hospital said Joy and the man, whom they later learned was Wilson, had decorated Chris's room with bits of the car: the Corvette symbol, part of the grill, and pieces of the fiberglass body, creating a macabre homemade shrine.

Another strange development was the death of another youth, a close friend of Chris's and Slupecki's. Within a couple of hours of the accident, even before Chris died, twenty-one-year-old Kirk Mauthe drove to a quiet park near his home and shot himself in the head with a .357 caliber pistol. His death was ruled a suicide.

Joy took Chris's death extremely hard. After that, she seemed to collapse mentally, becoming increasingly more agitated. The fact that she and Larry became locked in an incredibly hostile legal battle over Chris certainly did not help.

Larry, who had rushed to Dallas from his home in Virginia as soon as he heard about the accident, arrived in time to stop Joy from claiming Chris's body.

Joy wanted her son to be buried on the Davis family farm in Alma, in East Texas, but Larry argued that he would never be permitted to visit the gravesite because it would be on private property. Chris's body lay in the county morgue for nearly three weeks while Larry and Joy fought over where the youth would be interred. Eventually, the judge ruled in Larry's favor and Chris was buried in a Dallas cemetery.

The bitterness between Larry and Joy engendered by the fight over Chris's body would be total and lasting. From then on any possibility of an amicable relationship between the two, if the probability had ever existed after the attempt on Larry's life, was irrevocably crushed.

The trauma Joy underwent as a result of that fight was increased by the pressure of her legal difficulties. As spring 1991 approached, Joy's trial date seemed to be drawing closer and she became increasingly worried about what was going to happen to her despite the fact that her lawyer, Doug Mulder, had a reputation as one of the best defense attorneys in the city, if not in the entire state. His reputation, however, was not entirely unblemished. A cloud still hung over his head due to an incident that had taken place while he was one of the county's most high-profile prosecutors.

23

In a single sentence the English novelist Charles Dickens once commented on the presence of evil in the world and the need for dealing with the situation in an organized, civilized manner: "If there were no bad people there would be no good lawyers." Certainly there has been no dearth of bad people traveling through the Dallas judicial system. And just as certainly, there has been no dearth of good lawyers to either prosecute them or defend them. Doug Mulder, a husky, dark-haired man with a Texas-sized ego and, reputedly, a bank account to match, qualified on both counts.

As a prospective graduate of the Southern Methodist University Law School in 1964, the young Mulder—a youth of some privilege from Des Moines, Iowa, who chose SMU because he was impressed with the city of Dallas—applied for a job with then–District Attorney Henry Wade, reasoning that a career in criminal law might be more exciting than following in the footsteps of his father, a banker of local renown who had died when Mulder was still in high school.

At the time, Wade had been in office for more than a dozen years and had become nationally recognized because of two events: the recent conviction of Jack Ruby for the murder of Lee Harvey Oswald, and as the titular defendant in *Roe* v. *Wade*, the country's landmark abortion case.

As a result of his prominence, Wade could pick and chose among the cream of the prosecutorial wannabe crop. But he felt an immediate affinity for Mulder despite the fact that the applicant's grades were only slightly better than average and he had shown his professors nothing that would have predicted his future success. At his first meeting with the ambitious student, Wade listened to his inner voice and offered Mulder a position without even a second interview. It was, Wade recalled later, the first time he had ever acted that impulsively.

Wade may have felt a temporary twinge of regret for his impetuousness not long afterward when Mulder, who had been assigned as a third-team prosecutor in the misdemeanor court division, tried and lost his first case, that of a man accused of drunk driving. But Mulder, who hates to lose as much as he hates being without the trappings of wealth and power, bounced back and won his next trial. And the one after that and the one after that. By the time he left the prosecutor's office some sixteen years later, he had compiled the best conviction record in the history of Dallas County.

As he kept winning, he also kept moving closer to Wade's inner circle. As a result, before Mulder was thirty, he had been named the chief assistant to the irascible district attorney, a colorful figure who literally defined law and order in Dallas for thirty-six years.

Before long, Mulder had carved out his own reputation not only as a relentless and persuasive prosecutor but as a ruthless administrator. He became Wade's top trial lawyer as well as the office hatchet-man. In some circles he was snidely referred to as "Mad Dog" Mulder.

The beginning of the tarnishing of Mulder's extraordinary reputation as a prosecutor had begun shortly after midnight on November 28, 1976. At that time, a Dallas patrolman named Robert Wood, a full-blooded Choctaw Indian and a veteran of two tours in Vietnam, stopped a car on a quiet street in West Dallas to warn the driver that his parking lights were on.

Wood, whose friend and fellow policeman Alvin Moore had been shot to death when he answered a domestic-violence call in a nearby neighborhood earlier in the month, cautiously approached the car from the front. As Wood walked up to the vehicle, the offending driver rolled down his window. Before Wood could deliver his warning, the driver opened fire with a .22 caliber revolver. One hollow-point bullet hit Wood's finger, causing only a minor wound, but another struck him squarely in the chest. As he began to fall to the pavement, two more bullets slammed into his back and a fifth bullet hit him in the back of the head. Wood's female partner, shocked by the sudden violence, pulled her pistol and fired several shots, but by then the driver was speeding away. Minutes later, Wood was pronounced dead at nearby

Parkland Hospital. Almost a month later, a twenty-eight-year-old itinerant laborer named Randall Dale Adams was arrested and charged with the policeman's murder.

Adams told officers that on the afternoon before the morning Wood was shot, his car had run out of gas as he was returning to his motel apartment. He was trying to get more fuel when he was picked up by a youth whose name he later learned was David Harris. Harris took Adams back to his stranded vehicle, Adams said, and he put some gas in the tank while Harris waited. Then Harris followed Adams back to the motel where Adams left his car and the two of them drove away in Harris's vehicle. After a stop at a pawnshop to get some ready cash, Adams and Harris had a few beers, picked up a bucket of fried chicken, and went to a drive-in movie. After the movie, Adams said Harris dropped him at his motel and drove off. He was back in his room in time to watch the ten o'clock news, Adams contended. Wood was murdered more than two hours later.

Officers traced Adams through Harris, who had been arrested on another charge in a city in southeast Texas several hundred miles away. Harris, seemingly anxious to curry favor with the local authorities in order to clear the charges against him there, volunteered that he knew who had killed the policeman in Dallas. The cop killer, he said, was Randall Dale Adams.

A Dallas County grand jury, acting on Harris's words, indicted Adams. Mulder was the prosecutor. The trial began on March 28, 1977, almost exactly four months after Wood was killed. After listening to the testimony and deliberating for more than nine hours, the jury convicted Adams of capital murder and sentenced him to death in the electric chair.

For Mulder, it appeared to be simply another capital murder conviction. During his career in the DA's office he sought the death penalty twenty-four times. And, incredibly, he notched up twenty-four victories. However, the Adams case, far from being routine, would turn into a nightmare for the gung-ho prosecutor.

In June 1980, more than three years later, the U.S. Supreme Court overturned Adams's death sentence because of irregularities in the jury selection process. After the reversal, DA Wade asked Governor Bill Clements to reduce Adams's sentence to life in prison so another trial would not be necessary. Although Mulder was not involved in the jury

Above: Chris Aylor, left, a
best friends who died
each other, Chris in a fa
Kirk in a suicide whe
news. (Ken Hardesty)

Right: Carol Davis G
woman with a histor
stability who claims to
blackmail her sister,
Englade)

Prosecutors believe that Rozanne Gailiunas's
affair with Dallas builder Larry Aylor ultimately
proved fatal. (Courtesy of Judge Pat McDowell,
Dallas Criminal District Court #5)

Left: Andy Hopper, a devout fundamentalist Christian whose plans to become a minister derailed when he discovered drugs, a deadly temptation that ultimately led him to commit murder. (*Dallas Morning News*/John F. Rhodes)

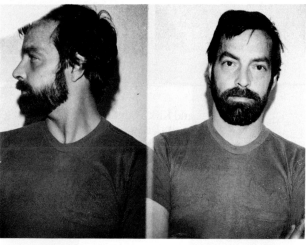

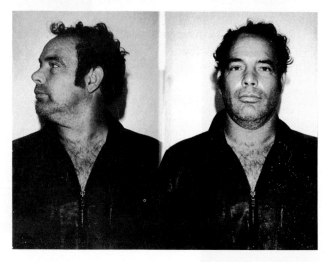

Jodie Packer, anothe[r]
lovers, is currently
sought by authori[ties]
allegedly helping Jo[y]
and concocting an e[laborate]
passport fraud s[cheme]
(Courtesy of the U.[S. Mar-]
shal's Office)

Buster, top, and Gary Matthews, ne'er-do-well brothers with long criminal histories whose desperation almost resulted in the murder of Larry Aylor. (Courtesy of the Otero County District Attorney's Office)

Above: Investigators Ken McKenzie, left, and Morris McGowan, whose dogged persistence led to the conviction of Rozanne's murderer but whose blatant disregard for the suspect's rights may lead to a new trial. (Richardson Police Department)

Right: Peter Lesser, left, and Larry Mitchell, well-known Dallas attorneys whose defense of Andy Hopper came close to upsetting the prosecution's case. (Ken Englade)

Right: A publicity-shy Joy trying to hide behind her famous attorney, Doug Mulder, after a court appearance that precipitated her flight. (*Dallas Morning News*/Richard Michael Pruitt)

Below: The villa in St. Paul de Vence, a sleepy village in the south of France where Joy was living quietly under the name of a woman taken from a headstone on a Dallas grave. (Ken Englade)

selection snafu that led to the appeals court reversal, the Adams case would soon come back to haunt him in a much more significant way.

Almost five years later, in 1985, the Adams saga took another strange turn. In March of that year Adams was approached by a film producer named Earl Morris, who was working on a documentary on a Dallas psychiatrist, Dr. James P. Grigson, commonly called Dr. Death or Dr. Doom because of his frequent testimony in favor of execution in capital murder trials. One of the many defendants Grigson had testified against had been Adams.

As he progressed with his research, Morris angled away from Grigson as his main subject and began focusing on a handful of cases in which Grigson had testified. He later refined his search still further, zeroing in exclusively on Adam's case.

Released in 1988 under the title *The Thin Blue Line*, Morris's film hinted strongly that Adams was innocent of Officer Wood's murder. Of equal importance, the film also revealed discrepancies in the prosecution. On March 1, 1989, twelve years after Adams was convicted, the Texas Court of Criminal Appeals overturned the verdict and cited Mulder for suppressing evidence and allowing perjurious testimony during Adams's trial. The DA's office, by then under a new chief, John Vance, decided not to retry Adams, who was released from prison three weeks later.

Harris, who had exonerated Adams of shooting Wood by admitting that Adams had not been in the car when the policeman was shot, had in the meantime been convicted of another murder.

But what ended well for Adams ended badly for Mulder.

In the aftermath of the appeals court decision, two Houston lawyers, proclaiming that they had to do it because no attorney in Dallas would dare to attempt such a move, asked the Texas Bar Association to investigate Mulder for his role in the Adams trial. It was not the first complaint dealing with Mulder's conduct at the trial. Shortly after Adams was convicted, his then-attorney Dennis White went to the bar association with an almost identical grievance.

In both cases, after studying the charges, the TBA dismissed the complaints. Still, Mulder's reputation was heavily damaged. Adams's defender, White, who had known Mulder in law school and had worked with him as a prosecutor before becoming a defense attorney, was so unnerved by Mulder's actions that he quit practicing law altogether.

Tracked down by a reporter for the *Dallas Morning News* thirteen years after the Adams trial, White said that in his mind Mulder was no better than Stalin or Hitler, and labeled him a "disgusting" attorney who deserved to be disbarred.

But by the time Adams was freed, Mulder was long gone from the district attorney's office. In December 1980 he had been offered $100,000 to defend a man accused of murder. Since he was earning only $65,000 a year as a prosecutor, the possibility of earning half again as much for handling a single case was a powerful temptation. By then his mentor, Henry Wade, had retired, leaving Mulder faced with having to start over again with a new boss as he reached the peak years of his career. Mulder had no desire to begin again at the bottom. He resigned as a prosecutor and took his first job as a defense lawyer. The man he was hired to champion never went to trial, but Mulder collected his fee anyway.

His next case involved the son of a wealthy surgeon who had been charged with killing a college student during the commission of a burglary. Not only had the victim been brutally killed (he was stabbed a dozen times), but the accused had signed an eight-page confession.

While many skilled lawyers would have been hesitant to take on such a case, Mulder leaped at the chance. Claiming that his client acted in self-defense, Mulder put on such a convincing defense that the jury returned a verdict of guilty to a much lesser charge of voluntary manslaughter. For Mulder, it was a remarkable victory.

Mulder walked the tightrope again in the late 1980s when he agreed to represent an ambitious Methodist minister named Walker Railey, who was suspected of trying to murder his wife so he could continue an extramarital affair with the daughter of his former bishop. Railey's wife survived a horrible physical attack, but has never regained consciousness and remains in a vegetative state.

When a grand jury was asked to investigate the case and Railey was called before the group, Mulder gave him a single piece of advice: Take the Fifth. Railey apparently did just that; he reportedly answered practically every question with a refusal to answer claiming the right of protection from self-incrimination under the Fifth Amendment.

Although Mulder was severely criticized for allegedly trying to stymie an investigation into an attempted murder, he shrugged off the verbal attacks by arguing that his primary responsibility was to his client. As a result, the grand jury failed to indict the minister. At least at that time.

Several years later, late in 1992, a different grand jury, after a new review of the case, *did* indict Railey, who again hired Mulder as his lawyer. The former minister's trial began in March 1993 in San Antonio, to where it was moved because of the excessive publicity the case had received in Dallas. On April 16, 1993, Railey was acquitted of all charges.

According to those who have watched him in action, there are several elements to Mulder's success in the courtroom. One is the amount of time and energy he is willing to spend on preparing a case for trial. Reportedly, he interviews virtually all the witnesses in a case himself rather than delegating that chore to an associate. Mulder routinely works seventy-hour weeks, longer ones when he is involved in a major trial.

For another thing, Mulder has a reputation as a genius for spotting holes in the prosecution's case. Because of his experience as an assistant district attorney, he also knows how to take advantage of even the slightest crack. He is especially devastating when cross-examining opposition witnesses, skilled at opening up wedges in their testimony. He delights in cross-examining expert witnesses and ripping apart the occasional witness who tries to spar with him.

Plus, when it comes to picking a jury, Mulder is said to have a sixth sense about which veniremen will ultimately be sympathetic to the defense and maneuvers the process so he can get as many of them on the final panel as possible.

To jurors, Mulder appears as suave, charming, and extremely confident—a debonair, well-dressed straight shooter, the latter characteristic being one which is *always* appreciated by Texas juries. Among fellow lawyers, though, Mulder has a reputation as a snob. Even when he seems to want to be sociable with his colleagues, he comes across as aloof and superior. An often-repeated story about Mulder deals with the time a group of lawyers decided to attend a baseball game and Mulder was invited along. As they gathered in the parking lot to enter the stadium, Mulder arrived, fashionably late, in his chauffeur-driven limousine.

Mulder's main recreational outlet is golf, and to hear those who have played with him tell it, he is a tough competitor. He should be, some of them say, since he brags that he has been playing the game since he was ten. In golf, as in law, Mulder is good and he knows it. There is little room in his life for amateur duffers, just as there is little room in his life for those who might criticize or belittle his lawyering skills. When the Adams case was at the height of its controversy, a reporter asked Mulder if he would concede a prosecutorial error.

Mulder shook his head. "I think we got the right man," he said. "And I think he should have been executed."

Weeks later, after Adams had been freed, Mulder was asked to speculate what the results would have been if he had been Adams's attorney instead of the prosecutor. Mulder didn't hesitate. "I'd have gotten him off," he bragged. "There's no doubt in my mind."

24

Like Mulder, Mike Wilson had once been a rising star in the Dallas District Attorney's Office. But his reputation had never shone as brightly and he burned out a lot quicker.

In the early days of his broken six-year career as a prosecutor, Wilson had been assigned more than his share of high-profile cases. Among those he prosecuted was a well-known madam named Sherry Blanchard, who kept a diary listing the names of prominent Dallasites who had been her clients. Her trial had created a media orgy, and Wilson reveled in the publicity. He also handled the case involving the infamous movie entitled *Debbie Does Dallas*, which was something of a classic in the hard-core porn era of popular entertainment.

A sandy-haired, cherubic-looking extrovert with a sharp sense of humor and a born-comedian's instinct for the absurd, Wilson grew up in Winnsboro, a tiny oil town in East Texas, a town, Wilson liked to quip, that was so small its residents had to take turns being the village idiot. He was the quarterback on the high school football team and a recognized leader among his peers. Early on, it was apparent that he was going to leave Winnsboro behind and move on to bigger and better things. If he lived long enough, that is. Along with his budding talents, the young Wilson also proved to be something of a magnet for tragedy, a trait he carried with him at least into middle age.

When he was in high school, he and several friends were out Christmas caroling when he was run over by a hay wagon. The accident almost killed him. He eventually recovered, but for eight months he had to wear a colostomy bag as a result of the internal injuries. Then, when he was a sophomore at the University of Texas in Austin, he was out waterskiing with his first wife-to-be, a Fort Worth socialite named Lucy Brants, when he was bitten by a water moccasin. If a friend with whom they were double dating had not been along to rush him to a hospital, Wilson might have died then, too.

In 1965, while still a student at UT, Wilson married Brants and they eventually had three sons. But in 1969, after graduating from UT, he became worried that he was going to be drafted and sent to Vietnam. One way he might postpone his induction, he figured, was to stay in school. A friend of his had enrolled in law school at SMU and Wilson reckoned that sounded like a good idea.

In the spring of his last year of law school, 1971, he was impressed by an assistant district attorney who had come to speak to his class, so impressed, in fact, that he applied for a job with the DA's office as soon as he graduated. Already working in the office at the time was another SMU graduate named Doug Mulder.

As excited as he had been to adopt the title of prosecutor, Wilson soon became disillusioned by what he considered the slow progress of his career as an ADA. An ambitious, competitive attorney, Wilson was anxious to try the murder cases that got a lot of press, the kinds of cases that seemed to crop up with amazing frequency in Dallas. However, those cases just as invariably went to the office superstar, Mulder, who had preceded Wilson as an ADA by seven years.

In 1974, Wilson decided to escape from Mulder's shadow to try to make it as a defense attorney. But, in his typical bad-luck fashion, he moved too soon; he quickly discovered that he did not have the experience he needed to make his way successfully as a defender. His bank account made no appreciable leaps. The more he thought about his problems, the more he turned to alcohol as a means of escape. By 1976, he had developed what even he recognized as a real problem with booze. After drying out at a special treatment center, Wilson reapplied for a job in the DA's office. His application was accepted.

For the next few years, Wilson fought a continuing battle with the bottle. Before the Seventies were over, he had been in and out of one facility after another at least a half dozen times. Booze was Wilson's black cloud. He left the DA's office for the final time in 1981, taking a good job as a civil lawyer with a railroad. Not long after he joined the company, however, he was fired for getting drunk, making a scene, and embarrassing his employers.

His career was not the only thing that suffered. His marriage also was on the rocks. Frightened by his alcohol dependency, Wilson once more entered an alcohol treatment center and stayed for thirty days. Upon emerging, he joined AA and made a determined, apparently successful fight to stay away from the bottle. But a new gremlin soon arose to take the place of alcohol.

After being fired from the railroad job, Wilson went back into private practice as a defense lawyer. This time, he was eminently more successful; it was not long before he began pulling down $300,000 a year, which was about six times what he had been making as a prosecutor. But the job had its downside: The bulk of his clients were drug dealers. Wilson began using drugs himself in 1987 and, although he had apparently won his fight against alcohol, he became addicted to cocaine.

On February 24, 1988, a year before he met Joy and some two months before Carol went to McGowan, Wilson and a client who was on probation for possession of cocaine were arrested at a routine traffic stop. In the car was a pistol and a small amount of coke. Since police could not prove which of the men the dope belonged to, they did not prosecute. But at that point, Wilson became a target for the Drug Enforcement Administration, which suspected that he was involved in drugs in a big way.

By this time, too, Wilson's first marriage had ended in a bitter divorce. But he was an engaging, charming fellow and within a few months he was seeing another woman seriously. In February 1989, about the time Andy confessed to killing Rozanne, Wilson married Mona Brunson. Three months later, he met Joy Aylor.

The more he saw of Joy, the closer they got, much to the frustration of his second wife. Joy and Wilson's relationship was cemented when Joy called him after Chris's accident and he went running to her side. For months after the tragedy, Wilson and Joy were virtually inseparable.

But whatever Joy brought to the relationship with Wilson, it was not a change of fortune; the hapless attorney's bad luck soon got even worse.

After Chris's accident and Wilson's infatuation with Joy, Wilson's bride of only thirteen months filed for divorce. Then, on March 20, 1990, he and a male friend went to a local motel to confirm that a suitcase containing almost fifty pounds of cocaine was secreted in one of the rooms waiting for them to pick it up.

The next day, a Wednesday, Wilson returned to the motel, transferred nearly half of the coke to a canvas overnight bag he had brought along, and was exiting through the parking lot when DEA agents, who had been watching the attorney since soon after his first arrest, swooped down. Despite Wilson's contention that the more than twenty pounds of coke in the bag was strictly for "personal use," he was charged with conspiracy and possession with intent to distribute cocaine, a serious offense that could net him a long term in a federal penitentiary. Authorities further asserted that Wilson was given the drug in lieu of legal fees to represent an alleged dope dealer, which put him in even hotter water with the state bar association. Because of his standing as an attorney, he was released on his own recognizance pending trial.

The car he had driven to the motel—the visit that resulted in his arrest—was Joy Aylor's Porsche. There was one further irony as well: The motel at which Wilson was arrested was the same one in which Larry Aylor was staying while he was in Dallas to attend a hearing in one of his court cases.

After his arrest, Wilson went into a state of deep depression. Not only was he in serious legal trouble—possibly losing his license to practice law was the least of his problems—but his personal difficulties were mounting as well. His second wife was about to get her divorce. He also found out that his father was fatally ill with cancer, and the youngest of his three sons, the last one still at home, had abandoned him and gone to Houston to live with his mother, Wilson's first wife. There was no doubt that at that time Wilson and Joy were feeding off each other's troubles.

Joy had hired the highly regarded Doug Mulder to defend her and was moving steadily closer to trial. Her case had been assigned to Judge Patrick McDowell, a distinguished-looking, graying Irishman with a reputation as a no-nonsense jurist. Worse yet, from Joy's point of view, was McDowell's apparent determination to bring the issue to a speedy conclusion. It had been almost six and a half years since Rozanne's murder and three and a half years since Larry had been ambushed. McDowell was deceptively easygoing, an impression hiding the fact that he could be stern and uncompromising when he felt certain limits had been reached. He had decided that it was time to air the charges against Joy in the courtroom.

On February 23, 1990, a little less than a month before Wilson's arrest at the motel, McDowell had ruled that Joy and Andy would be tried separately on charges stemming from Rozanne's murder. Indications were that Joy would be tried first. At the time, Andy was in jail without any hope of getting out, at least until he was tried. Joy, on the other hand, was free on a $140,000 bond.

But as Joy's trial date grew closer, she became increasingly more agitated, not only because of her legal difficulties but because of the grief she still suffered as a result of Chris's death just a few months before and her painful court battle with her former husband over their son's body. That her new lover, Wilson, also was under extreme stress did not help. Both Joy and Wilson dreaded the prospects of going to trial.

Quietly, they decided to do something about it. In anticipation of needing some ready cash in the near future, Joy began building an emergency fund, using money withdrawn clandestinely from her accounts in deliberately small amounts so the banks would not have to report the transactions to federal authorities. A U.S. grand jury would later contend that she had help in this project from Dallas businessman Jodie Packer, her ostensibly rejected lover. Packer would deny helping Joy in any way.

Joy's legal situation came to a crisis on Friday, May 4, when she, with Mulder at her side, appeared in McDowell's court for what she thought was going to be another uncomplicated bond hearing. In fact, the session proved to be hardly routine. Once she got in the courtroom, she discovered that the judge had a more significant plan in mind: He told her he was ordering jury selection to begin in her case on May 14, a scant ten days away. Turning to Mulder and the prosecutors, ADAs Kevin Chapman and Daniel Hagood, McDowell ordered them to meet with him three days hence, on May 7, for a final pretrial hearing.

Shocked by the unexpectedly rapid movement toward trial, Joy panicked.

25

Joy left McDowell's courtroom as quickly as she could. Running to Wilson, she proposed a radical suggestion: Let's split. Wilson felt there was nothing in Dallas worth waiting around for as far as he was concerned. He readily agreed.

The next day, Saturday, May 5, Joy and Wilson fled with the help, according to investigators, of Joy's cousin, Hugh Bradford "Brad" Davis. Authorities contend they left Dallas in Davis's vehicle, headed for the same part of the country in which Andy Hopper had lost himself almost two years earlier: the Rocky Mountain West.

Wilson had a small suitcase and Joy brought along her purse, which contained an American Express card and a voter registration card belonging to Jodie Packer. She also had a bag. In it was the emergency fund she had been building, some $300,000 in cash.

Investigators believe that Joy's escape was far from impulsive. According to an indictment handed up by a federal grand jury in December 1992, Jodie Packer methodically made the rounds of several Dallas banks beginning in April 1990, withdrawing money to help Joy flee. The withdrawals made by Packer allegedly ranged from $7,000 to $25,000 and totaled $64,000.

Additional funds also may have been withdrawn on Joy's behalf by others. A few weeks before she fled, Larry's father was in his bank when he saw one of Joy's relatives making a large withdrawal. Slipping away unseen, Clyde Aylor called Larry, who called the assistant district attorney assigned to Joy's case, Kevin Chapman.

"I think Joy's getting ready to run," Larry reported breathlessly.

"I hope she does," Chapman replied. "That will just make my case better."

Brad Davis allegedly drove the couple to Cheyenne, Wyoming, where he dropped them at a Jeep dealer. Using $7,800 from Joy's stash, she and Wilson paid cash for a 1984 Wagoneer. After that, Davis returned to Dallas while Joy and Wilson headed west.

As soon as he discovered that Joy was missing, McGowan sent investigators to Joy's home to see if she had left any clues. A few minutes after they left empty-handed, another set of law enforcement officers showed up: uniformed patrolmen from Dallas. They had arrived in response to a shrill burglar alarm set off by the Richardson detectives.

From Cheyenne, Joy and Wilson drove their new vehicle to Cut Bank in northwestern Montana, on the edge of the Blackfoot Indian Reservation. But they stayed there only long enough to register the Jeep, pick up Montana license plates, and buy new clothes from a western-wear store. They hit the road again for Vancouver, Canada, where they stayed for three weeks in an apartment rented under the aliases Mr. and Mrs. John Storms.

By the first week of June, about a month after they left Dallas, Wilson was getting increasingly despondent and Joy was becoming extremely nervous.

After she learned through a telephone conversation with a friend or relative in Dallas that Brad had been arrested and charged with perjury for telling Richardson authorities that he had left the couple in Denver, Joy was ready to go again.

Unknown to her, Wilson had been in touch with an old law school friend with whom he had gone into practice the first time he left the DA's office, Bob Fain. Fain had left Texas years before and had opened a practice in Montana. He and Wilson had kept in contact.

When Wilson told Fain how depressed he was, Fain feared that he might be contemplating suicide. As a result, Fain began trying to convince him to surrender. Go back to Dallas to face the consequences, he told him. It was no worse than living on the run.

About the time Joy learned of her cousin's arrest, Wilson had also decided that Fain was right. He and his old friend had worked out a plan whereby Wilson would recross the border into the United States and surrender to federal authorities in Billings.

While Wilson was working out his own agenda, Joy had decided to go to Mexico.

Wilson, unwilling to let Joy know he was giving up the fight, led her to believe that he planned to follow her once she had gotten to Mexico and determined that it was safe. He told her to call him once she arrived, signaling him to take the next plane.

On June 7, traveling under the handy unisex name of Jodie Packer, Joy took a Japan Air Lines flight from Vancouver to Mexico City. Wilson, in the meantime, had moved to a rural resort in backcountry British Columbia, three hundred miles from Vancouver, still using the name John Storms.

A federal warrant charging him with unlawful flight to avoid prosecution had been issued in Dallas on May 10, three days after Judge McDowell issued a similar warrant for Joy when she failed to show up for her pretrial hearing.

Wilson, getting jumpy himself, changed hotels before Joy could reach him. But when he left the first hotel, he told the clerk that he would call with a number where he could be reached in case someone—Joy—was looking for him.

Unknown to Wilson, soon after he checked out, the hotel manager, Judy Culos, received a call from a Canadian immigration official, who said his department was looking for "John Storms." Frustrated when told that he had left only hours before, the official asked Culos to notify him if Wilson/Storms came back.

A few hours later Wilson called Culos and wanted to know if he had received any telephone messages. Thinking quickly, Culos said a woman had called and asked for him but she did not identify herself.

"Oh, good," Wilson said. "If she calls back, tell her I'm staying at the Safari Beach Resort in Osoyoos, British Columbia." He gave her the number, but added that he would be moving to another motel later that day.

Culos called immigration officials, who notified the RCMP. Within an hour, eight armed officers had surrounded the small hotel where Wilson was staying, a pleasant, peaceful inn on the bank of Lake Osoyoos. One of the officers then dialed Wilson's room and, once the lawyer was on the line, suggested he "come out with his hands up." Wilson quickly complied. Seemingly relieved that his ordeal was ended, he offered no resistance.

* * *

Joy, however, proved much more elusive. McGowan and the Dallas County DA's Office continued to keep a watch for her in Dallas just in case she tried to slip back into the city. However, they figured that she was safely out of their reach in a foreign country, probably Mexico, and would not be back to Texas. The soundness of their reasoning was proved early in August 1990, some two months after she fled from Vancouver, when a Dallas woman, Stephenie Grimes, called authorities and said she had been friends with Joy—whom she knew as "Jodie Packer"—a few weeks earlier when they both were attending Spanish language classes in Cuernavaca, Mexico. The two had even shared a room in the home of a Mexican family. In late July, "Jodie" told Grimes that she and her husband were having marital problems and she had to drop out of school in order to meet him in Mexico City. She said good-bye to Grimes and left. After "Jodie" was gone, Grimes discovered that her Mexican travel visa had been stolen, apparently by Joy, ever resourceful in her search for new identification.

Grimes added that she did not know who "Jodie" really was until she saw Joy's picture in a Dallas newspaper. But, when Grimes had last seen her, Joy/Jodie told her that she planned to come back to the language school for the fall term, which was to begin in mid-September. Authorities then set a trap for her, hoping she would show up as she had indicated she would. Not surprisingly, she did not.

In Dallas, other things were happening as well.

On July 12, 1990, Civil Court Judge Dee Miller dismissed Larry's claims that Joy's father, Henry Davis, had been part of a plot to steal his money. But on August 6, another civil court judge, Bob O'Donnell, issued a default judgment against Joy, awarding Larry $31.2 million in damages from his ex-wife: $200,000 for fraud, $300,000 for embezzlement; $10 million for pain, suffering, and mental anguish; $20.6 million in exemplary damages, and $100,000 in court fees. Since Joy was not there to testify in her own behalf, the judge accepted Larry's testimony on its face.

McGowan and the DA's office, however, could not have cared less about the civil cases. They were interested only in the criminal proceedings. As far as they were concerned, default judgments were valueless; they wanted Joy back so she could be tried for capital murder and sentenced to die in the state's lethal injection chamber. They would have a long wait.

On September 14, 1990, Joy got national publicity when her case was aired on Fox Television's "America's Most Wanted," the popular television show. Dallas actress Suzanne Savoy played the part of Joy. Although the program drew a lot of responses, there was nothing that would lead authorities to Joy.

In actuality, she was getting even farther away, slipping ever deeper into the strange netherworld of the serious fugitive. By the time of the TV show, Joy had been missing for five months and her trail was getting colder. In retrospect, it is clear that a large part of her success in eluding authorities was because she had help, and that aid apparently came, according to federal officials, from Jodie Packer.

After Joy left Canada for Mexico and it was discovered that she had used identification under the name of her ex-lover, authorities contacted him and asked how she had obtained his voter registration card and credit card. That was easy to answer, he said: She stole them. That claim began to seem dubious when, some months later, authorities began to suspect that Packer may have been helping Joy all along.

In July 1990, Packer allegedly went to a post office in the northern Dallas suburb of Plano and, using fraudulent documents, applied for a passport in the name of an uncle, Donald Averille Airhart. The real Airhart had been killed in a hunting accident a quarter century earlier. From what authorities pieced together later, in September someone went to Oklahoma City and applied for a passport in the name of Elizabeth May Sharp, a Dallas woman who was about Joy's age and who had died several months previously. Soon, Joy would bring Sharp back to life, if only temporarily. But all of that was discovered after the fact. In reality, by the fall of 1990, some six months after Joy fled with Mike Wilson, Dallas authorities had no idea where she was, how she was surviving, what names she was using, or where she was going to turn up next.

From what was later made public, it appeared that Joy, after leaving Cuernavaca in July, traveled randomly, perhaps through Central or South America, before flying to Frankfurt, Germany. From there, it is believed she took a train to Zurich, and then went either by train or car to Nice, situated along the French Côte d'Azur.

In December, she rented a villa in the town of St. Paul de Vence, a village considerably off the beaten path, tucked away in the hills above Nice and Cannes. Traveling up the winding, plunging roads, she found a furnished flat of the type the French call a *mueble*. Essentially, it consisted of the upper half of a two-story house at 1370 Rue de St. Jeannet. It was within walking distance of a former residence of the well-known artist Pablo Picasso. The apartment was composed of one bedroom, one bath, and an L-shaped living room/dining room. The main part of the flat, including the large, attractive bath, overlooked the *collines de Vence* (the Vence hills) and a garden maintained by the landlady, who lived below. For this, Joy paid an off-season rate of 3,500 French francs per month, about $700 U.S. During the high season, the same place would cost almost twice as much.

Joy told the landlady that her name was Elizabeth May Sharp, that she and her "husband," a man named "Don," had driven from Switzerland and had fallen in love with the area. She said they had two sons in college in Texas but she wanted to stay for a few months in France while "Don" traveled through Europe and the Middle East. She wanted a place that would make her feel as if she were at home, a place with a garden and flowers.

26

In the meantime, Jodie Packer, apparently traveling under the name of his late uncle, Donald Airhart, was building a cover story in Dallas to explain his frequent absences. Since he allegedly was flying regularly to France to see Joy, he needed some kind of excuse to protect himself at home. He told friends and employees he was trying to line up business in the Middle East, thus he would be gone quite a lot. After the Gulf War, he refined the tale by claiming that he was vying for contracts involving the rebuilding of Kuwait.

In France, Joy worked to build a new identity. Soon after she arrived in Vence, she had a hairdresser cut her wavy, dark hair short and add blond highlights. And, unlike in Texas where she dressed very casually, Joy began affecting well-made French and Italian clothes, preferring pants to skirts and blouses. On her wrists and fingers, she began sporting tasteful, expensive jewelry.

The Gulf War, for unknown reasons, was apparently a particularly traumatic event for Joy, who seemed to be suffering from rampant paranoia.

Telling her landlady that she feared imminent doom as the result of the conflict, and that she was particularly afraid of biological warfare, she sealed the windows, doors, and vents of her flat with thick layers of newspaper and masking tape. And, although she was known as a compulsive house cleaner when she lived in Dallas, she went to the opposite extreme in France, letting the trash pile up in cupboards and corners. A half-inch-thick coating of grease was allowed to accumulate on the stove, and she neglected to dust the furniture or sweep the floors.

From the day she arrived, she was regarded as somewhat eccentric by her neighbors, reclusive but not altogether unfriendly. Virtually the only times she ventured out of the apartment were to work in the garden or to go to lunch with the landlady. On those occasions, Joy always picked up the check and always paid in cash.

But, after the war began, her eccentricity tipped over into fixation. After the United States started bombing Iraq, she seldom went out of the flat except at night, and when she did she wore a pair of large, dark glasses and was always snugly muffled so as little of her face as possible was visible. Her connection to the outside world dwindled until it consisted mainly of infrequent, hurried shopping trips and irregular French lessons from a female tutor who came to her flat.

In early March 1991, when her short-term lease was scheduled to expire, Joy arranged to rent another apartment not far away. But two weeks before she was scheduled to move, an event drastically changed her plans.

When Joy rented the villa she also rented a small car, an Opel Corsa. Early in March, on one of her infrequent excursions away from her flat, she was involved in a minor road accident. At that point, she panicked, abandoning the vehicle on the side of the road and scurrying back to her hideaway.

For some reason, French police, in the process of investigating the accident, became suspicious and began checking the background of "Elizabeth May Sharp." In the process, they discovered that Sharp was really Joy Jeannine Davis Aylor, who was wanted in Texas for murder.

They formed a task force and went to her house to arrest her, slipping down the steep driveway that led to her flat in the cold, predawn darkness. Just in case she tried to run, they surrounded the dwelling.

Once the officers were in place, a French police inspector named Roland Seja knocked on her door. It was a few minutes before seven on the morning of Saturday, March 16. When Joy answered, Seja told her he needed for her to come with him to police headquarters so he could clear up the matter of the wrecked rental car.

"Of course," Joy replied, but since he had caught her before she could perform her morning toilette, would she be permitted to shower first?

"*Mais oui, madam,*" Seja replied politely, pulling up a chair.

Joy disappeared into the bathroom and Seja heard the water running. A few minutes later, she reappeared, wearing a shapeless sweat suit. A few minutes later, they left together for the short ride to Nice.

Once they were at police headquarters, Seja confronted her with the evidence that proved she was actually Joy Aylor. When she saw that she had been found out, Joy's composure collapsed. Obviously distraught, she asked to be allowed to visit the ladies room. Shown where it was, she went inside and closed the door. When she did not come out a few minutes later, a matron forced the door open and went inside. Joy was sprawled on the floor, bleeding from slashes on her wrists.

Before she went with Seja, officers determined, she had palmed a razor blade and hidden it in the waistband of her jogging suit. Then she had used it to cut her wrists once she was alone in the restroom. The injuries were not life-threatening; she had been discovered in time.

Joy was rushed to a local hospital, where her wounds were treated and she was placed under guard until she could recover sufficiently to be sent to jail.

As soon as her family was notified of her arrest, her younger sister, Elizabeth, along with Michelle Mulder, daughter of Joy's Dallas attorney, flew to Nice to see what they could do to help. The first sight Elizabeth had of Joy was in the hospital, where she found a thin, wan woman propped up in bed with casts on her wrists up to her elbows. After they greeted each other, Joy gave her sister a scrawled list, almost illegible because of the casts. It was, she said, an accounting of her possessions at the flat. Would Elizabeth please go and collect them?

Elizabeth was amazed by Joy's incredible command of detail. The list not only catalogued her possessions but detailed exactly where each could be found, right down to a needle Joy had dropped while sewing a new button on a blouse.

Soon after her arrest, Mulder himself flew to France to interview his client, converting some details of that meeting into an anecdote he seemed to revel in relating. When he showed up for that first meeting, he had tucked under his arm a huge box of chocolates, which he gave to Joy's matron as an expression of appreciation for helping Joy through a difficult period. The gift, he said, was well received.

Although the interview with Joy was beneficial, it grew tedious when Joy kept asking him, with different variations, three basic questions: When can I get out? What are they going to do to me? Am I going to have to go back?

As helpful as he wanted to be, Mulder said that by the end of the day he was weary of hearing those three questions. It was with some relief that he knew he would not be able to visit Joy again the next day, a Saturday, because that was a day reserved for families. Finally, when he was ready to leave, he told Joy he regretted that he could not come back because of the family-only rule. His excuse, however, was shattered when the matron to whom he had given the candy interrupted. "Because your lawyer has been so nice," the guard told Joy, "I'm going to make an exception and let him come back on Saturday."

At that point, Mulder said with a sigh, he had no choice but to return and try to figure out new ways to calm Joy's fears.

In a more serious vein, French police were glad they had taken precautions when they went to the villa to arrest Joy. When they searched the flat, they found a half dozen credit cards, each bearing a different name, and a bag filled with currency from a number of countries, including several in Central and South America. Given the slightest warning, Joy would undoubtedly have fled again. During her ten months on the run, Joy is believed to have used a number of identities, calling herself at various times Mrs. John Storms, Jodie Packer, Jodi Packer, Leigh Curry, Stephenie Grimes, J. Taylor, and Elizabeth May Sharp. If she had other aliases, they have not been revealed by French or U.S. authorities.

At the time of her arrest, it had been almost eight years since Joy, then forty-one, had allegedly begun planning the murder of Rozanne Gailiunas.

The French media delighted in telling Joy's story, often referring to her as *la femme diabolique de Dallas*—"the devilish woman from Dallas." She got particularly good coverage in *Paris Match*, a slick magazine best described as a cross between *People* and *Newsweek*. Her story was given two full pages in the April 1991 edition. French journalists, however, made few references to her alleged accomplice, Jodie Packer, a.k.a. Donald Airhart.

Authorities are circumspect in talking about Packer's activities, but apparently he was somewhere in the vicinity when Joy's deception was uncovered, perhaps en route to the villa for another visit. On March 18, two days after Joy's arrest, he is believed to have left Nice for Zurich, where he purchased $49,000 in traveler's checks. On March 19, he left Zurich and flew to Mexico City, returning to Dallas on March 21.

Almost two weeks later, on April 2, Packer was arrested at Joy's family's home at Cedar Creek, near Austin, and charged with passport fraud. In his possession were traveler's checks totaling $9,500, and two airline tickets, one open-ended to Costa Rica, and the other an April 22 return ticket to Nice via Mexico City.

Three days later, Packer was released by a federal magistrate without bail and ordered to reappear on July 23. Soon afterward, he denied to reporters that he had been to France to see Joy or that he had helped her in any way.

When he failed to show up for his scheduled court date, he was declared a fugitive. On December 18, 1992, he was indicted by a federal grand jury in Dallas and accused of violating federal financial reporting laws by attempting to cover up transactions, allegedly in an effort to help Joy. If Packer is ever found, tried, and convicted of the crimes with which he is charged, he could be sentenced to as many as fifteen years in prison and fined a half million dollars.

In Dallas, District Attorney John Vance, a mere five days after Joy's arrest, announced that he would be willing to forgo his plans to seek the death penalty against Joy if only the French, who have abolished capital punishment, would agree to return her to Texas, where prosecutors were attempting to tie up the loose ends and bring as many of the peripheral cases to trial as they could in anticipation of her extradition.

On January 7, 1991, two months before Joy's arrest, Mike Wilson went on trial in federal district court in Dallas on the drug distribution charges. Testifying in his own defense, the forty-five-year-old Wilson claimed that alcohol and drugs had been problems for most of his adult life and that they were responsible for the breakup of his first marriage and the loss of a good job. After his addiction to cocaine, he confessed, he went rapidly downhill. When he was caught at the Dallas motel in 1988, he asserted, he had been on a cocaine high for five days and was not even aware of what he was doing.

The jury, but not the judge, believed him. Deliberations began on January 18 and, a few hours later, the panel came back with a verdict of simple drug possession, a conviction that carried a maximum sentence of one year in prison. However, Judge A. Joe Fish was less than pleased with the verdict. Utilizing his judicial prerogative, he set the decision aside and ordered jurors to return to the deliberation room and reconsider their action. Four days later, after pondering the situation over the weekend, the jury came back with a second verdict that was more to Fish's liking. The second time, the group found Wilson guilty of conspiracy to distribute cocaine, a much more serious charge. The maximum possible sentence was life.

On April 30, 1991, Judge Fish sentenced Wilson to twelve years in prison and fined him $20,000. Fish said he ordered a relatively mild sentence, considering what he could have assessed, because Wilson had provided authorities with "substantial information" about a "person" in another case and had agreed to testify against that "person" at a future trial. Although the "person" was not identified (Wilson could have been handing over information about one of the drug dealers he had come into contact with during his period of drug abuse), it most likely was his former lover, Joy Aylor, who had hardly been mentioned at all during Wilson's trial.

There is no parole in the federal system; Wilson will not be eligible to be released until he has served his full sentence.

While waiting for the trials of the major participants—i.e., Andy Hopper and Joy Aylor—to begin, ADA Kevin Chapman, who had been assigned full-time to the series of cases, decided to help clear the decks by disposing of the cases against Buster and Gary Matthews. They would be tried separately on charges of conspiring to murder Larry.

Buster, meanwhile, had helped the process along by requesting a speedy trial, mindful in his jail-smart way that it would be to his advantage to get the proceeding over with so he could serve the New Mexico and Texas sentences concurrently. Chapman undoubtedly figured it was not up to him to deny Buster's request. In December 1991, Buster went before Judge McDowell, who also would be handling the Hopper and Aylor trials.

The prosecution's contention was simple: According to Chapman, Buster accepted money from Joseph Walter Thomas to kill Larry. He allegedly waited for him outside the entrance to the Kaufman County ranch and ambushed Larry when he came along in his four-wheel drive. The fact that the attempt was conspicuously unsuccessful did not mean that the intent was not serious.

In his defense, Buster claimed that Larry had been described to him as a wife beater and child abuser who deserved whatever punishment was administered, that he considered he was performing a form of public service. Additionally, he said, it was his brother who did the actual shooting, not him. He had been little more than a bystander. Buster's attorneys, Michael Byck and King Solomon, argued that to their client's credit he later volunteered to help police clear up the case, going so far as to try to get Gary on tape admitting to the shooting.

Apparently, however, the jury was not impressed. After hearing four days of testimony and deliberating only briefly, jurors convicted Buster of conspiracy to commit capital murder and recommended a life sentence.

Gary was tried seven months later before Judge Gary Stephens, sitting in for a busy Judge McDowell. After two days of testimony and arguments, the jury, on Wednesday, July 15, 1992, took only a few hours to convict him. He also was sentenced to life in prison, which in Texas means a minimum of fifteen years.

On the civil side, as a result of default judgment, Judge Dee Miller, on October 15, 1991, ordered Joy to pay Donald J. Kennedy, who was slightly wounded during the attack on Larry Aylor, a total of $2,000,149.35, which included $500,000 for pain and suffering, $1,500,000 in exemplary damages, and $149.35 for medical expenses.

The trials of Carol and Bill Garland, Brian Kreafle, and Joseph Walter Thomas were put on indefinite hold because prosecutors feared that trying them would reveal too many details of Joy's alleged part in the complicated murder schemes and would seriously damage chances of convicting her. The others would not be tried, DA John Vance decreed, until Joy could be extradited from France.

As a result, going into 1992, there was only one other trial that could be held before Joy was returned: that of Andy Hopper. In the end, despite the prosecution's weapon, Andy's confession, defense attorneys would drop a bombshell that almost wrecked the state's case. As it turned out, testimony during the trial opened the door to a number of thought-provoking issues and prevented the proceeding from being the slam-dunk conviction that prosecutors expected.

PART III

◂ 1992 ▸

27

Andy's first lawyer, appointed by Judge McDowell on December 29, 1988, was Jan Hemphill. However, when the charge is capital murder, as it was in this case, it is customary in Dallas County for a second lawyer to be named as well. The way it usually works is that the original lawyer, in this case Hemphill, is allowed to choose an aide.

Since courtroom tactics were her specialty, she planned to examine and cross-examine witnesses herself. For an assistant, therefore, she needed someone adept at taking care of the other details that always need attending to during a complicated trial. To perform this function, she chose Lawrence Mitchell, a balding, soft-spoken attorney, a former president of the local bar association, with a reputation as a top-notch appeals man, a talent that Hemphill figured would be very convenient if Andy were convicted. And, considering the gruesome blow-by-blow confession her client had made to McGowan, that seemed a good possibility.

When Hemphill picked Mitchell, she was aware that up until then he had never been involved in a trial in which a man's life was at stake. But this was immaterial to her since his job would be primarily that of an observer. His responsibility would be to sit like a fly on the wall during the trial, making detailed notes on Judge McDowell's perceived mistakes.

But then events took an unexpected turn. Before Andy could come to trial, Hemphill was appointed by Texas's new governor, Ann Richards, to fill a seat on the district court bench. That left Mitchell as Andy's lead counsel, a position in which he was decidedly uncomfortable since his experience was in the library rather than the courtroom.

Mitchell had come to Dallas from Wichita, Kansas, in the Seventies to attend law school at SMU. After he graduated, he and a classmate, an expatriate New Yorker named Peter Lesser, went into practice together, specializing in criminal defense law. The partnership eventually dissolved, with Lesser branching out and building a reputation as a controversial trial lawyer and unsuccessful politician, while the quieter, less flamboyant Mitchell concentrated on more scholarly pursuits, serving as an associate justice on the court of appeals in Texas's Fifth District while honing his talents for searching out and highlighting potential legal errors. But even as the two went their different ways, they remained good friends. By the late Eighties, they even shared an office on the seventh floor of a modern building not far from Dallas's downtown airport, Love Field.

In light of the unanticipated developments, Mitchell knew that his first duty to his client was to find someone to fill the role that Hemphill had assigned to herself in Andy's case: someone experienced in courtroom roughhousing. What he needed, Mitchell felt, was a blunt, aggressive, knowledgeable attorney who could work under pressure, who could be merciless on cross-examination and was unafraid to mix it up with witnesses and prosecutors alike, and who would not be intimidated by the well-oiled machine known as the Dallas County District Attorney's Office. The only person he could think of who best met those requirements, even if he too had never tried a capital murder case, was his old friend Peter Lesser.

A slender, long-limbed, aesthetic with fiery, dark eyes, midnight black hair that tumbled below his shoulders, and a bushy, wiry beard turning rapidly gray, Lesser was a man with a well-deserved reputation for making waves. In two attempts to win election as district attorney and one unsuccessful race for mayor, Lesser had won the attention, if not the ballot-box support, of Dallas residents. Not only had he retained enough of the aggressiveness he had developed while growing up in New York City's Washington Heights to be painted as a Yankee-hippie-troublemaker among ultra-conservative Dallasites, but he was also a high-profile Jew in one of the country's most aggressively fundamentalist Christian cities.

Before he and Mitchell opened their practice, Lesser worked as a courthouse reporter for Channel 13, a local PBS station, winning the grudging respect of the city's other journalists, most of whom had little inclination or training to actually try to comprehend the workings of the local legal system. Virtually alone among the local newspeople, Lesser became known for his ability to fathom the issues involved and then explain them in terms comprehensible to the majority of television viewers. During this period he also developed a reputation as a committed iconoclast, a description that follows him to this day and one illustrated superbly by his handling of a 1991 case that drew more than its share of public attention.

That summer, about the time Joy was beginning her fight against extradition, Lesser signed on to defend Glen Anthony, a twenty-six-year-old handyman with a previous felony conviction for theft. It was one of the more sexually and racially explosive cases in the city in many years, one in which a black man, Anthony, was charged with kidnapping a thirty-seven-year-old white woman named Nancy Jane Taylor, the socially prominent wife of a member of the board of DART, the city's high-profile public transportation system.

Anthony was accused not only of kidnapping Taylor and holding her hostage for eleven hours, but of assaulting her and forcing her to cash a $1,200 check.

At the trial, a standing-room-only event for the entire two weeks it lasted, Taylor testified that she had never seen Anthony before the afternoon of the attack when he came to her house posing as a deliveryman. Once he talked his way inside, she said, he pulled a .357 caliber pistol from his belt and forced her to leave with him in her black Jaguar, subsequently performing the other actions leading to the charges against him.

Anthony, on the other hand, told a completely different story. When he took the stand in his own defense, Anthony denied *kidnapping* Taylor, swearing that the white, well-to-do socialite willingly went with him. In fact, he said, to the shock and revulsion of Dallas's upper crust, the two had been involved in a secret but nonetheless highly charged sexual liaison for several months. Anthony asserted that the affair began weeks before the alleged kidnapping incident when Taylor, out for a jog through her exclusive Highland Park environs, stopped to compliment him on the work he was doing on a neighbor's garden. A little later that day, he said, they met at his modest apartment and had sex for the first time. That encounter, he claimed, led to three other trysts preceding the incident in which Taylor said she was kidnapped.

On that day, Anthony insisted, Taylor came to him and told him that she was very upset with her husband, was thinking about leaving him, and asked him to meet with her at her home so she could discuss the situation. After that meeting, she filed charges against him.

The story was as improbable as it was salacious. While it made for excellent news copy and spirited gossip, there were not many in white Dallas, including the six-man, six-woman jury hearing the case, who were prepared to believe Anthony's version. The jury deliberated for less than two hours before finding Anthony guilty of aggravated robbery and recommending a ninety-nine-year sentence. As of April 1993, he still faced kidnapping and assault charges.

The point, however, was that Lesser, a rabble-rouser in a city and a profession not known for its tolerance of anti-establishment thought, may have been the only attorney in Dallas who would have dared mount such a defense. The fact that it was unsuccessful did not diminish the boldness of the move or the fervency with which he argued his client's case. His performance did little to diminish his reputation as an out-of-the-mainstream liberal, while at the same time it also enhanced his fame as an unpredictable, quick-thinking defense attorney, a lawyer who could be infuriatingly exacting and combative to the point of being overbearing, but one who also was aggressive and imaginative. It was a mix that would be confirmed in coming months.

District Attorney John Vance has made it his policy, as did his predecessor, the eminent Henry Wade, to let his first assistant assign lead counsel, choosing among the one hundred and fifty or so assistant district attorneys the one who would take a particular case into court or negotiate a plea bargain. Under Wade, that duty had fallen to Doug Mulder. Under Vance, the task is performed by Norm Kinne, a crew-cut graduate of Texas A&M who sets the example for the militaristic attitude that prevails in the suite of offices atop the new Frank Crowley Criminal Courts Building. Kinne picked a rising thirty-six-year-old ADA named Kevin Chapman, a slight, trim man with a soft, raspy voice and a rapidly disappearing hairline, to steer the prosecution team in the Aylor/Hopper cases.

A native of Midland in West Texas, Chapman got both his undergraduate and law degrees at the University of Texas in Austin, compiling an extraordinary 3.8 average in undergraduate school and finishing law school in the top 10 percent of his class. He joined the district attorney's staff immediately upon graduation in 1981. Over the next ten years, Chapman prosecuted and convicted hundreds of criminals. He sent three of them to death row.

By the time of Andy's trial, because of his courtroom record, his dedication, and his proven ability to produce, Chapman was supervisor of activities in three criminal district courts and head of the DA's special projects section.

As is customary among attorneys appointed to defend someone accused of capital murder, the lead prosecutor also selects another ADA as an assistant. As Mitchell had picked Lesser, Chapman chose Dan Hagood.

A tall, athletic man with a permanent scowl on his face and a boot-camp haircut, Hagood was known around the courthouse as "the colonel," not only because he actually *was* a lieutenant colonel in the Marine Corps reserve but also because his bearing and attitude seemed rather Prussian.

Despite his no-nonsense demeanor and the absence of a verifiable sense of humor, Hagood also was known as one hell of a lawyer. The son of one career military man and the brother of another, Hagood earned his undergraduate degree at the University of South Carolina and went straight into the Marine Corps upon graduation. Four years later, he accepted a scholarship at the SMU law school. As a student, Hagood consistently made the dean's list and served in the prestigious and much-sought-after position of moot court judge. He went to work in Vance's office after he graduated in 1982.

By the time Andy's trial came along, Hagood, then just two months shy of forty, was in charge of the office's organized crime division, a unit specializing in the most serious prostitution, gambling, and drug cases the county prosecutors had to handle. Like Chapman, Hagood had hundreds of trials under his belt and two more capital murder trials than his teammate, for a total of five. As Chapman's had, all Hagood's capital murder trials had resulted in convictions and death sentences.

Unlike defense lawyers, who came and went depending on who was on trial, Chapman and Hagood were in for the duration, coordinating not only Andy's trial, but the trials of Joy and the others in the dual "chains." Andy had Lesser and Mitchell to defend him; Joy had Doug

Mulder; and the others would hire still other attorneys. But Chapman and Hagood were constants.

However, because of the complexities of the cases, a third lawyer was appointed to the prosecution team for Andy's trial: a relative neophyte named Jim Oatman. Much as Lesser and Mitchell had divided the responsibilities of the defense, the three ADAs divided the prosecutorial duties. Hagood and Oatman worked virtually alone in the jury selection process with Chapman making only an occasional appearance. Once the case was set for trial, however, Chapman assumed responsibility for presenting the prosecution's case, while Hagood, who could be ferocious and sharp-tongued, was delegated to handle most of the cross-examination. Oatman took over much of the behind-the-scenes work.

The other major figure in the courtroom for Andy's trial was Judge Patrick McDowell. Like members of the prosecution team, McDowell was a permanent fixture in proceedings related to Joy; by the time jury selection began for Andy's trial in the summer of 1991, McDowell had been involved in the case or its spin-offs for almost three years.

A slim, middle-aged man with a patrician nose and a head of judicially gray hair, McDowell was an experienced lawyer who had seen both sides of the criminal bar before taking the bench. He began his legal career as a prosecutor, then, in a move common in the city's legal community, he switched sides.

As a defense attorney, he participated directly in two cases involving men accused of capital murder, and assisted colleagues in three others. Additionally, as a judge, McDowell had presided at three other capital murder trials, all of which ended in convictions and death sentences. While McDowell appeared easy-going, he could be very exacting and he had a quick temper.

In the months it took to pick a jury and try Andy Hopper, McDowell's patience and judicial acumen would be tested a number of times, not only by the esoteric legal issues that would arise with amazing frequency throughout the proceedings, but by his need to be a combination of scholar, moderator, father confessor, and referee, especially the latter since, from the beginning, the opposing lawyers clashed bitterly and frequently over the tiniest of details.

28

The first step in Andy's trial was the selection of a jury, a process commonly referred to by its Latin name, *voir dire*, literally, "to say the truth." And, since it was going to be a special sort of a trial, a capital murder case, special procedures had to be followed in picking the panel of citizens to determine Andy's fate.

In Texas, a capital murder trial is actually *two* trials. In the first one, the jury determine's the defendant's guilt or innocence. If the verdict is guilty, the second trial begins, one in which the end result is either a sentence of life in prison or death by lethal injection. As a result of this dual or bifurcated trial system, a jury has to be selected with care. Each potential juror has to be meticulously grilled to make sure that he or she is not philosophically opposed to the death sentence, and is capable of making an unbiased judgment.

Because the jury selection process in a case like Andy's can be so long and tedious, not every accused murderer is actually *tried* for capital murder. In fact, the percentage of such trials is remarkably small considering the number of murderers. There are more than six hundred killings each year in Dallas County, but John Vance and Norm Kinne typically pick only three or four of the accused killers to prosecute for capital murder.

One criterion in deciding who gets tried for capital murder and who doesn't is the heinousness of the crime. Rozanne's murder definitely met that requirement. Another requisite is "winability." Vance and Kinne constantly ask themselves if there is a strong likelihood that a conviction is going to be forthcoming.

Over the years, stretching back to Henry Wade's days, the district attorney and his first assistant have gotten quite good at this. By the time Andy went to trial, the DA's office, beginning when the death penalty was reinstituted in Texas in 1974, had a 56-0 record on capital murder convictions. That is, not once in fifty-six consecutive capital murder trials had prosecutors failed to convince a jury to convict. And of those fifty-six convictions only twice had the jury failed to follow through with a death sentence.

A third, and probably the most important, factor in determining if a defendant should be tried for capital murder was deciding if the crime fit within the state's death penalty statute.

In Texas, the death penalty is of restricted applicability. It can be sought only if the crime meets certain particulars, called "special circumstances." These include someone accused of multiple murders, or of the single murder of a policeman, a fireman, or a prison official. Another special circumstance—and this was the crucial one as far as Andy was concerned—was a murder perpetrated during the commission of another felony. Burglary is a felony. If a burglar kills a homeowner in the process of breaking into his or her residence, that person can be tried for capital murder. Since Andy entered Rozanne's house illegally, it could be presumed from a technical point of view that he was there as a burglar. Whether he actually stole anything, or even intended to, was immaterial.

While there was at least one other special circumstance that could have applied in Andy's case—murder for hire—prosecutors decided not to raise that issue. The reasoning was sound: If Chapman and Hagood had sought to try Andy as a hired killer, they would have had to reveal whatever evidence they had against Joy, his alleged employer. That they did not want to do for fear of ruining their chances of convicting her later. It was much more convenient from the prosecution's point of view simply to legally label Andy a murderous burglar.

Since Judge McDowell had issues to deal with beside the Hopper case, he announced that potential jurors would be questioned no more than three days a week, depending on his own schedule. In practice, some weeks were skipped altogether, either because of McDowell's workload or to accommodate the lawyers's schedules.

As a result of the jerky work schedule and the care exercised by both teams in questioning the veniremen, it took from June 3 to November 18—with fifty-six working days—to pick the panel of thirteen: twelve regular jurors and one alternate. Courtroom observers pronounced it as the second longest voir dire in county history in terms of actual days spent at work, and *the* longest in the number of days consumed by the process.

The panel eventually selected was composed of five women and seven men. The woman alternate would be used only if one of the regular jurors was forced to drop out before the trial was finished. They ranged in age from their mid-twenties to their sixties, and most of them were blue-collar workers. Two of them were black, one woman and one man.

Although the jury was picked before Thanksgiving, Judge McDowell was reluctant to start the trial immediately because he feared that it would drag into the holiday season and wind up being a major inconvenience for everyone.

As a rule, capital murder trials in Dallas County took a week, two at the very most. But this looked from the beginning as if it was going to be an exception. Defense attorneys already had warned McDowell and the prosecutors that they expected it to take a minimum of four weeks. As it turned out, it would take almost twice that long. In any case, though, the last thing the judge wanted was to have to sequester a jury during Christmas. So he set a target date of January 21. In the end it didn't matter; it was late getting started anyway.

First there was a difficulty over a conflict in lawyer's schedules, which pushed the beginning date back to January 27. Then, on the day the proceeding was scheduled to commence, it was postponed again because of a jury problem, the first of several that would plague Andy's trial from beginning to end and set courtwatchers to mumbling about the "snakebit"—unlucky—panel. With all the court personnel in place except for the jury, McDowell sadly announced that one of the jurors had a medical emergency in her family and had not shown up that morning.

The next day, Tuesday, January 28, with a full panel sitting nervously in the jury box, the trial formally got under way. It was a hot start; spectators got a hint of just how far apart the defense and prosecution would be as soon as Chapman and Lesser presented their opening statements.

Designed to be freewheeling speeches with the purpose of giving jurors a preview of what they could expect from each side during the trial, Chapman and Lesser's presentations outlined the gulf that separated the two sides, a remarkable gap considering the general belief that the prosecution had an airtight case against Andy Hopper.

Chapman's oration lasted for sixteen minutes and was fairly predictable. Essentially, he recounted details about the crime that had already been made public through media reports. Andy, Chapman contended in a steady, soft Texas drawl, accepted $1,500 for killing Rozanne, an act he performed by strangling and shooting her after he had forced his way into her house (the burglary). After he was arrested, Chapman continued, Andy first tried to lay the blame on a man named Chip. However, Chapman continued, Andy changed his story after a polygraph examination failed to confirm his version of events. Admitting that he had lied earlier, Andy then gave two separate statements in which he admitted that he, not Chip, had been the killer.

Chapman promised that the prosecution also would introduce tangible physical evidence proving that Andy had told Morris McGowan, now a lieutenant, the truth when he admitted to the attack. That evidence would consist primarily of the pistol Andy said he had used, a weapon that ballistics experts would testify had been the one that fired the bullets into Rozanne's head.

The ADA left it to the jurors to make the connections: Andy admitted taking money for the crime . . . he admitted the attack . . . he led police to the pistol he said he used . . . scientific tests would show that the pistol was the one that fired the shots . . . ergo, Andy was the killer.

The impression the prosecutor left with the members of the jury was that it was a pat case, one that was all wrapped up and needed only their verdict to make it official.

But when the defense got its turn, Lesser threw an unexpected curveball at the prosecution. The scenario he presented had tremendous potential for derailing the district attorney's expected express.

As Chapman settled back into his chair, Lesser strolled casually to the front of the room and stopped in front of the judge's platform. It was Lesser's normal strategy not to make an opening statement. Why, he reasoned, should he tip off the prosecution to the case he was about to make. In this instance, however, he made an exception. Exactly what made him take that tack was a puzzle, since he did not know until he stood up that he was going to do it. In retrospect, he felt that the opening statement he made was his first mistake of the trial.

Nonchalantly sticking his hands in the pockets of his dark suit, Lesser affected a relaxed pose. In the next few days, he began in a controversial tone, he and Mitchell would share with jurors what radio newscaster Paul Harvey called "the rest of the story."

While not contradicting Chapman's contention that Andy was in Rozanne's house, Lesser said he would show jurors that the tale was much more convoluted than the prosecution had led them to believe. For one thing, he said, he would attempt to tie Rozanne's estranged husband, Dr. Peter Gailiunas, Jr., to her death. Furthermore, the defense attorney added, the incident did not begin on October 4, 1983, the day Rozanne was attacked, but had its roots in a series of events set in motion weeks previously by Joy Aylor, whose estranged husband was having an affair with Rozanne. This affair, he said, was the reason for Rozanne's murder.

Aware that he was treading on dangerous ground—that the prosecutor and Judge McDowell would strenuously resist his efforts to drag Joy into Andy's trial to any substantial degree—he deftly switched gears and swung the focus back to Peter Gailiunas.

"Testimony will show," he said almost matter of factly, "that Rozanne's four-year-old son claimed that 'Daddy' was there before *and* after 'Mommy' got sick." Additional testimony would show, he continued, that Joy's former husband, Larry, called for Rozanne that afternoon, but the phone was answered by the boy. "Larry will say that he heard in the background someone yell, 'Put the phone down, goddamnit.' Larry Aylor will say the voice was that of Dr. Gailiunas."

But Lesser was saving his big news for last. In addition, he said, he planned to introduce medical records from Presbyterian Hospital showing that the drug Thorazine was present in Rozanne's system when she was admitted. What the defense was going to try to show, Lesser was saying, was that even if Andy had tied, strangled, and shot Rozanne, he may not have killed her: The weapon that pushed her over the edge may have been a mystery drug that the pathologist who performed the autopsy had not found because she never obtained blood to test. "The presence of this drug was totally missed by the medical examiner's office," he said heatedly, abandoning his over-the-back-fence tone. Even more ominously, he added, was the fact that the discovery continued to be ignored. Thorazine was not a commonly used drug, he continued, although it would be readily available to Gailiunas, a kidney specialist, because it was frequently used in the treatment of people required to undergo dialysis.

Delving into the subject just enough to pique the jurors' curiosity, Lesser said he planned to elicit testimony showing that Gailiunas was at one time a suspect in his estranged wife's murder, that he did not have a verifiable alibi for two crucial hours on the afternoon that Rozanne was attacked, and that he had at one time allegedly threatened her with a shotgun.

What Lesser was telling the jury was that the prosecution might think it had a tight case within certain narrow boundaries, but he intended to open up the possibilities and show more than one side.

It was vintage Lesser, a brazen attempt that could, at the very least, create among jurors a reasonable doubt about the involvement of someone other than, or in addition to, his client. He was deliberately vague on some points, such as the thread, if any, between Joy and Dr. Gailiunas, or between Larry and the physician. Just how Andy fit into the defense scenario also was unclear. Lesser was particularly obscure on that point, saying only that he intended to challenge the statements his client made to investigators, hinting that he would try to show that Andy was trapped into making the admissions through a clever scheme by prosecutors and investigators to keep Andy's lawyer—at that time Jan Hemphill—from knowing exactly what was going down at the Richardson Police Department.

With a verbal wink and the tantalizing lure of startling revelations to come, Lesser sauntered back to his chair. It took him twenty minutes to present the bare outline of the defense's case; he implied it would take several weeks to round out the argument.

Later, when he had time to reconsider his words, Lesser regretted mentioning the Thorazine to the jury in the opening statement. Although the prosecution was aware of the report attesting to the drug's presence, Chapman and Hagood apparently had attached no special significance to it, although Lesser did not know that at the time. By mentioning it before testimony started, he had done what he most wanted to avoid: He had tipped off the prosecution in plenty of time for Hagood and Chapman to try to devise a plausible explanation to counter his and Mitchell's argument of why the drug was in Rozanne's body. Even worse, Lesser felt he had overestimated the prosecution's capacity for preparing for all eventualities. It was a mistake, he felt, that the defense would pay for dearly.

29

In line with what could be expected from the district attorney's office, the case built by Chapman over the next few days was workmanlike, incriminating but hardly flashy. That was no reflection on Chapman; it was simply the way the office worked, and it had worked that way long before Chapman signed on.

Over the years in the last third of this century, the reigning district attorneys, first Henry Wade and then John Vance, built a reputation for thoroughness and persistence, not flamboyance. The office philosophy was a model of conservatism: ADAs wore dark suits, white shirts, conservative ties, highly polished shoes or, in a nod to the local culture, western boots, as long as they were not the ostentatious type favored by dancehall cowboys. The head hair was to be short, preferably army style. Beards were verboten. When it came time to present the case in court, ADAs followed the same orthodox plan: Tender the facts as they saw them as unsensationally and as narrowly as possible, then keep pounding away at those premises relentlessly, inflexibly, and unswervingly. Be hard-nosed . . . be merciless . . . and be unyielding. Leave the showboating to defense attorneys like Lesser and Mitchell. Borrowing the Boy Scouts' motto, the DA's creed demanded that prosecutors, above all, be prepared.

Chapman fit this mold perfectly. A low-key litigator who rarely raised his voice, Chapman was known as a perfectionist and an obsessive preparer, a tireless worker who firmly believed that the key to courtroom success was groundwork rather than histrionics, that organization was more crucial than dramatics. This philosophy was readily apparent to even the most casual courtroom observer. At the beginning of proceedings each day the prosecution team wheeled in a bright red dolly sturdy enough to support a refrigerator. Stacked one atop the other on the dolly's platform were some two dozen black looseleaf binders, each at least three inches thick. Those were Chapman's trial notes.

Running as smoothly as a finely tuned engine, Chapman began building his case, calling a series of witnesses to set the scene for Rozanne's murder: the dead woman's father, a couple of glass-company employees who replaced the broken windowpane on her house, a locksmith who changed her locks, young Peter's day-care teacher, his skating instructor, a neighbor, and the paramedic Winfred Duggan.

Ironically, given the publicity the case had received over the months and years before Andy's trial, the drama was playing to a virtually empty house. Except for a few courthouse employees and a journalism class from Southern Methodist University that visited sporadically, the only regular spectators were members of Rozanne's family, Dr. Peter Gailiunas's mother, and, invariably, Andy's parents. Rozanne's family members remained stoic throughout the vivid testimony in which Rozanne's last hours were detailed, staring straight at the wall behind Judge McDowell or at their feet. Andy's parents, his father clad in work clothes and his mother in a neat, carefully pressed dress, sat immediately behind their son on the hard wooden bench. When the testimony got too graphic, Andy's mother buried her head in an inspirational book or a religious tract, while his father seemed not to hear.

Gradually, as the trial dragged on, the prosecution's game plan swung into focus. Chapman had begun at the bottom of the list, and as he moved upward through the preliminary witnesses, the pertinency of the testimony grew. His aim was to build a seamless box around Andy. But, contrary to his plan, as the trial drew on, the box became increasingly less airtight.

One of the weaknesses of the prosecution case developed on the fourth day when Chapman called Dr. M. G. F. Gilliland, the pathologist who had performed the autopsy on Rozanne.

Gilliland mesmerized the jury with projected color slides of portions of Rozanne's body magnified to many times life-size. The marks on her neck, projected on the screen, were as large as a weightlifter's arms. Her face was the size of a beachball, magnified so jurors could clearly discern the tiny blemishes caused by popped blood vessels. And the two ugly bullet wounds in her head grew as large as baseballs. Definitely, Gilliland said in a tone that bordered on the supercilious, it was those wounds, combined with strangulation, that had caused Rozanne's death.

Seeking to defuse the defense's tip about Thorazine, Chapman asked Gilliland if, given the severity of Rozanne's wounds, the drug would have made any difference in her potential for survival. The pathologist puckered her thin lips and pondered the question for several seconds before responding with a crisp, unequivocal "No!"

Archly, she added: "Thorazine was not the cause of death or even a contributing cause," ignoring the fact that from a legal point of view the point was immaterial. If the drug was administered with the *intention* of killing Rozanne or hastening her death, that person would be just as culpable as the person who shot and strangled her even if the drug had not killed her.

When Mitchell got his shot at Gilliland during cross-examination, he pointed to the footnote in her report that read "No antemortem blood available." The defense attorney challenged her thoroughness, claiming that blood was indeed available because a sample had been drawn from Rozanne when she was admitted to the hospital. He accused Gilliland of negligence in not tracking down that information when it could have been vital in determining the cause of death.

To the defense, the Thorazine was an important, if not crucial, issue. A powerful drug used primarily in mental hospitals to control violent psychotics (it induces a zombielike state referred to among medical people as "the Thorazine shuffle"), its presence in Rozanne's body was sinister, a mystery that threw into doubt the prosecution claim that her death resulted solely from Andy's brutal attack. It was a point that the defense team would come back to repeatedly throughout the trial, but what Mitchell wanted to do with Gilliland was force her to admit that the drug may have been a contributing factor. She refused to cooperate.

Calling on her personal experience as a psychiatrist, a specialty she practiced briefly before switching to pathology, Gilliland speculated that Rozanne, a registered nurse, could have had access to Thorazine and may have medicated herself to help relieve depression or anxiety over her stormy marital situation.

Mitchell scoffed at that idea. Thorazine, he pointed out, was not a "happy" drug. It was not a medication people took voluntarily in an attempt to raise their spirits. It was, he said, a system depressant with decidedly unpleasant side effects.

Gilliland, seeing where Mitchell was going, waved off his allegations. The amount of the drug that Rozanne may have had in her body originally, perhaps 150 milligrams, was, according to the pathologist, within the therapeutic range.

Mitchell disputed that point of view, citing medical reference texts indicating that that dosage might be normal, but only for persons who had been taking the drug long enough to build up a resistance to it. The amount that Gilliland had mentioned—150 milligrams—was only 50 milligrams shy of the amount used to treat hyperactive psychotics, he pointed out. For a normal person without any tolerance to the drug, Mitchell contended, 150 milligrams was enough to make that person comatose.

Despite his efforts, Mitchell could make no headway against Gilliland, who refused to concede that Thorazine was a factor worth considering in determining Rozanne's cause of death.

The defense team, however, had better luck in their cross-examination of some of the state's peripheral witnesses.

Lesser, for example, scored points when he got Merle Ward, the longtime friend of Andy's who sheltered the defendant in the hours immediately preceding his arrest, to admit that the two of them had been smoking marijuana from the time Andy showed up at her house and that her recollection of events may have been influenced by drug intoxication. He also successfully painted Ward's former roommate, Rebecca Trammell, as a fanciful, adventurous young woman who may have surrendered to hyperbolic style when she composed a written statement about Andy's visit for investigators.

Trammell was not called as a witness, but Lesser made his point by having the defense trial associate, Jean Bauer, read a sixteen-page statement drafted by Trammell for investigators. It was replete with imaginative descriptions of Andy's visit, including an aside about how the author of the document was sufficiently worried about Andy's presence that she took a .38 caliber pistol to bed with her.

"Needless to say, in a fugitive's reach, sleep was had by none that night," she wrote. There were other references to how the house felt "eerie" with Andy in it, and unfounded speculation that he may have had ties to organized crime.

To counter the twenty-one-year-old Trammell's report, Lesser elicited testimony from Ward in which she said she considered Andy anything but threatening. Ward also told how Trammell had volunteered to retrieve Andy's belongings from a park where he had hidden them just before he knocked on Ward's door.

Did Ward, Lesser wanted to know, feel that Trammell was being overly dramatic in her allegations to police?

The witness shrugged. "She was just a kid," said Ward, who was a dozen or more years older.

The first real clash between prosecutors and the defense came on the fifth day of the trial after Judge McDowell ordered a special hearing— a *Jackson* v. *Denno* proceeding, so-called because of a Supreme Court decision setting the law for dealing with the admissability of a confession—to determine if the jury would be allowed to see and hear Andy's confession, which was on both videotape and audiotape.

This was a critical issue for the defense, probably the most crucial of the trial. Without that confession, the state's case would be considerably weakened if not demolished. Although Chapman and Hagood had a pistol they claimed they could link to Andy, *and* prove it was the weapon that fired the shots into Rozanne's head, the prosecutors had no fingerprints from the weapon or from inside the house tying Andy to the scene. They had no eyewitness testimony placing him there, and they could discover no motive for him being there except from what other highly questionable sources had told investigators. If Andy had not confessed and had stuck to the allegations he outlined in the "Chip statement," it would have boiled down to his word against Chip's. But that possibility evaporated when Jan Hemphill gave her permission for Andy to be polygraphed.

The defense's best hope of keeping the confession from the jury was to prove that it was illegally obtained. To do that, they would first try to get Lieutenant Morris McGowan to admit that he acted improperly in pressuring Andy to confess. The hearing began with McGowan taking the stand as a prosecution witness.

McGowan projected the image of a cop's cop: shrewd, intelligent, experienced, well-spoken, dedicated, and incredibly persistent. He had, after all, doggedly continued the investigation into Rozanne's murder for more than five years, long after many other homicide investigators in a similar situation would have shoveled the papers into the "unsolved" file and gone on to something else.

Under minimal guidance from Chapman, McGowan related how he worked to build a relationship with Andy and parlayed that into getting Andy—with Hemphill's permission—to come to Richardson to take a polygraph to determine the veracity of his "Chip statement."

At that time, McGowan said, he honestly did not believe that Andy had been the triggerman; he only became suspicious when Andy did so poorly on the polygraph. Even after the test showed he was trying to be deceptive, Andy repeated the Chip story. But McGowan got him to change his tune. "I told him I didn't think he was telling us the entire story," McGowan drawled.

It was only after the investigator proved to Andy that he knew who Chip was that Andy's resistance crumbled.

" 'Andy,' " McGowan testified he told him, " 'we can't go any further until I hear it from your lips. I don't know if you were in the house, but whatever I need to know the truth.' "

At that point, McGowan said, Andy confessed. Afterward, McGowan added, Andy asked him what was going to happen to him and he told him that he didn't know.

"It was an emotional time for both of us," the investigator said softly.

Then Andy asked to call his wife, Becky, saying he wanted to explain to her what he had done.

When the man who had been in the room with McGowan and Andy, Investigator Brent Tourangeau, at the time little more than a rookie, finished testifying (covering basically the same ground as McGowan), Jim Oatman wheeled in a rack with a TV and a VCR. It was time to see the tape itself.

In a courtroom empty except for the judge and the lawyers, Andy's parents, Rozanne's father, sister, and her husband, plus a few diehard spectators, mostly courthouse workers dropping in to chart the progress of the trial, Oatman kicked off the tape.

The picture flashed on the screen in full color. It showed Andy sitting calmly at a table dressed in a white prison jumpsuit, smoking a cigarette, and occasionally taking a sip from a can of Coke. As the camera zeroed in, Andy began speaking in a matter-of-fact voice. But as the minutes passed, as he described in gruesome detail how he had attacked Rozanne, his voice got more emotional.

The recording lasted a little more than ten minutes. When it was finished, the courtroom was hushed. Andy stared at his hands and showed no emotion. His mother sobbed on his father's shoulder. It was a powerful piece of evidence, one which undoubtedly would have a tremendous impact on the jury.

On cross-examination, Lesser was unable to shake the unflappable McGowan. In order to show that the investigator had simply used the polygraph exam as an excuse to get Andy into his web where he could put pressure on him to confess, Lesser would have to get McGowan to admit that he thought that Andy was the killer even before he brought him to Richardson.

McGowan would not do that. Despite persistent questioning, he insisted that his only motive had been to clear Andy as the triggerman.

"I thought Andy had been in the house, but I didn't think he was the killer," McGowan said.

"How about after the polygraph?" Lesser asked.

McGowan nodded slightly. "After the test," he said dryly, "I thought his involvement was greater than he had led me to believe."

The day ended inconclusively as far as the admissibility of the confession was concerned. The next day, in a last-ditch attempt to keep the statement away from the jury, the defense planned to call Jan Hemphill. It was not a task that Lesser and Mitchell relished.

30

On February 3, day six of the trial, defense lawyer-turned-judge Jan Hemphill made the first of what would be several appearances in Judge McDowell's courtroom, all of them outside the jury's presence.

A blocky, middle-aged woman with a puckish sense of humor and a Gary Cooper complex that seemingly prohibited her from answering any question in more than two words, Hemphill calmly took her seat in the witness chair, a strange position for her since she was more accustomed to looking down on that spot from her perch behind the bench.

It was a delicate situation for Lesser. If he was going to help Andy, he was going to have to attack not only a former colleague for whom he had tremendous respect but also a sitting judge before whom he might one day have to appear. Not only did he have to attack her but he had to try to demonstrate that she had acted incompetently when she represented Andy. Still, he and Mitchell knew that if anything would sink Andy, it would be the confession, a confession he made on Hemphill's watch.

In a strong voice, Hemphill forthrightly admitted that she blundered. "I didn't expect the man to make a confession," she answered, adding in a steady voice that she blamed herself for abandoning him. "It was a big mistake," she conceded. "I should have been there."

Why had she let him go alone? Lesser asked.

"I was convinced he would pass the test," Hemphill replied. "It was a big mistake," she repeated. "Even if he had passed, it was still a big mistake."

However, she said she did not blame Hagood and Chapman for misleading her about McGowan's plans for Andy. Perhaps, she conceded, they should have called her after the polygraph and before initiating an interrogation, but she had not given them specific instruction beforehand on what to do in such an eventuality. "I did not say, 'Now don't take a confession from him,' " she admitted. On the other hand, she added, neither had she given permission for an interrogation.

When Hemphill finished, the defense said it had two requests of Judge McDowell: 1. To not let the jury see or hear Andy's confession. 2. Barring that, to allow Hemphill to testify before the jury about how that confession had been obtained.

McDowell pondered the pleas. Even at such an early stage of the trial, he already was exhibiting a pronounced tendency to rule in favor of the prosecution on the close calls. He had made it clear from the beginning that he was not going to allow the defense to introduce details about Joy Aylor, that he regarded Andy's and Joy's cases as distinctly separate and to waver in that respect would be to open a Pandora's box that would totally confuse the jury and possibly result in a mistrial. He took the same position in connection with the defense requests surrounding the confession. He apparently felt that he had to hold the line on what the jury could or could not consider because to do otherwise would obfuscate the issues and pave the way to disaster. In that frame of mind, McDowell rejected both entreaties.

It was a double blow for the defense. While Mitchell and Lesser would have celebrated a McDowell decision prohibiting the introduction of the confession as a major victory, they felt it would have been a good consolation prize for the judge to allow the jury to listen to Hemphill's story. When McDowell announced that he was denying both, Mitchell's and Lesser's spirits plummeted. The trial had more or less just started and they had not even begun their case, but already the defense attorneys felt they were fighting an uphill battle.

Shaking off their disappointment, they told each other that they still had some cards to play. Jurors had not yet heard from McGowan because they were excluded from the *Jackson* v. *Denno* hearing. Mitchell hoped they could regain some ground by ruthlessly cross-examining the detective in front of the panel. However, that opportunity did not come until February 5, day eight of the trial, and it again proved a frustrating experience for the defense.

If Lesser and Mitchell had their way, the trial would be as much about police procedures, botched evidence, and leads that were not followed up as it would be about Andy Hopper. They would never try to claim that Andy did not shoot Rozanne, but they *would* try to create a major doubt about whether it was the bullet wounds that actually killed her. The trial, as much as the defense could make it, would be about Morris McGowan, Dr. Peter Gailiunas, Thorazine, and, hovering in the background like an unutterable entity, Joy Aylor.

The defense's first major effort to broaden the scope of the proceedings came when McGowan was seated before the jury. By then, the prosecution strategy seemed clear: Zero in on a theme, keep the focus as narrow as possible, stick to it with aggressive singlemindedness, and divulge as little as possible to the defense. And nowhere was this approach articulated better than through the star witness of the district attorney's office's, Detective McGowan.

On direct examination, in response to softball questions lobbed to him by Chapman, the detective repeated essentially the same story he had told at the *Jackson* v. *Denno* hearing about following the trail to Andy, his arrest and subsequent collapse. But the real test for the witness came on cross-examination.

Remaining polite, the investigator nevertheless was contrary to the defense. He was never openly antagonistic, but his attitude was clear in the way he answered Lesser's questions. After awhile it seemed to become something of a game. If Lesser asked a question in exactly the right way, using the precise wording that the detective had determined was necessary to prompt a response, McGowan would answer positively. If the defense attorney did not hit upon the correct code, the response was negative.

For example, at one point Lesser was trying to learn from McGowan how the detective had gotten information about Andy's presence at Merle Ward's house. Lesser had a good idea that Andy had been betrayed by his, Andy's, telephone call to his girlfriend, Shelley Zachary, but he wanted to make sure.

The defense attorney began by asking McGowan how many wiretaps he had used. McGowan said he had not used any, which prompted a series of questions from Lesser designed to see if some agency other than Richardson PD had used wiretaps. When that drew a string of negative answers, Lesser wanted to know how many wiretaps had been sought, even if they had not been used. That led to a deadend as well. Some fifteen minutes later, however, Lesser was able to wring from McGowan that the information had not come from a telephone *tap* but from a *trap*. The difference in the two, as explained by McGowan, was that a wiretap permitted someone to listen to a conversation while a trap merely recorded the numbers of the calling parties.

The jury eventually learned what Lesser was trying to elicit, but McGowan's apparent obstinacy gave the impression that the detective was deliberately trying to be evasive. This impression was bolstered by Lesser's fruitless attempts to get McGowan to reveal to the jury the details regarding the investigation culminating in Andy's arrest. The usual way of learning about the progression would be to induce Mc-Gowan to read from notes he had made at different stages of the inquiry. But that avenue was closed off very early when McGowan confessed that he had made virtually no notes, and those that he had taken had long ago been incorporated into a formal statement and the originals destroyed.

Lesser also was frustrated in getting details on the investigation by McGowan's refusal—backed vigorously by repeated objections from Chapman and Hagood—to reveal what any investigators working under him had uncovered. Even though McGowan had been in charge of the investigation, he refused to reveal any information he did not develop on his own, seeking refuge in the contention that anything told to him by anyone else was hearsay, and thus safe from disclosure. If the purpose of this stance was to prevent the defense from learning any more than absolutely necessary, it proved amazingly effective.

The basis of the prosecution's objections was that the defense was trying to obtain information to which it was not legally entitled, that is, investigatory reports. Judge McDowell repeatedly sustained Chapman's and Hagood's protests, effectively slamming that door on the defense. Although the prosecutors were successful in keeping the information from being disclosed, they were risking a backlash from the jury, some of whose members might look upon the prosecution's complaints as an attempt to hide or cover up information that would tend to point a finger at anyone but Andy. Chapman and Hagood did not stand to gain by coming across as if they were interested in convicting Andy at any cost and had no tolerance for conflicting details.

Lesser had begun his cross-examination of McGowan on Wednesday morning, February 5. He did not finish until Friday morning. The questions about the search for Andy took up only part of the time because Lesser and Mitchell were interested in a much broader view of the investigation. What they wanted to do was make the jurors question the entire process by trying to show that Richardson police, acting in concert with Chapman and Hagood, had taken a wrong step early on and that had led them down a false path. While the prosecution's trail to the end of the chain that led to Rozanne ended with Andy, Lesser and Mitchell contended that the true path should have been in another direction, that there were enough warning flags along the way to have alerted investigators to the fact that the conclusion was not as simple as they wanted the jury to believe.

One thing the defense hoped to accomplish by grilling McGowan so thoroughly was to get the jury thinking about the possibility that the investigator had been too quick to reject Rozanne's estranged husband as a suspect, or ignored him altogether when the trail to the attacker diverged toward Andy. They also wanted to plant in the jurors' minds the possibility that Andy might not have been involved in the attack on Rozanne at all despite the confession, but even if he had, he may not have acted alone, as the prosecution wanted them to believe. Finally, they wanted the jury to begin thinking that McGowan acted improperly in pumping Andy to confess.

Needless to say, these were not ideas that the prosecution was interested in seeing promulgated. If Lesser and Mitchell thought the going was tough in extracting details about how investigators tracked Andy, it was easy compared to attempts to drag other details out of McGowan. As soon as Lesser mentioned Gailiunas, for example, the prosecution tried to shut down the questioning completely.

After attacking from several angles in an attempt to find a way around prosecution objections, Lesser eventually was able to pry from McGowan an admission that the detective had, for a long time, considered the possibility that the doctor had been the perpetrator, although the detective had eventually eliminated him as a suspect.

As soon as he saw which way Lesser was moving, Chapman tried to deflect the defense questions, arguing that McGowan had no personal knowledge of Gailiunas's involvement and that interviews with the doctor had been conducted largely by McGowan's subordinates, therefore were safe from disclosure under the hearsay rule.

Probing as diligently as a dentist performing a root canal, Lesser found a small hole in this argument by resorting to lawyerly tricks. Rather than asking McGowan what his investigators had told him about Gailiunas, Lesser asked the detective what conclusions he himself had drawn from what they had told him.

"What was your *state of mind* about him being a suspect?" Lesser wanted to know.

Judge McDowell let the question pass.

"He was," McGowan replied taciturnly.

"Why?" Lesser asked, touching off a hearsay objection from Chapman.

McDowell sustained it, forcing Lesser to take another tack.

"Was Peter Gailiunas living with Rozanne?" he tried, searching for a way to get the detective to testify about his personal contact with Gailiunas.

"He was not," McGowan replied.

"Did you have a conversation with Peter Gailiunas that night?"

"Yes."

"How did he appear?"

"He was acting upset."

"What did he say?"

"He said he was her husband."

"Did *you* feel that the attacker had been her husband?"

"I never completely ruled him out."

"Why?"

"I felt he had the most motive," McGowan said. "They were estranged and his wife was seeing another man." For McGowan, it was a remarkably loquacious reply.

Step by step, Lesser also was able to get McGowan to admit that Gailiunas did not have an alibi for part of the time period during which Rozanne must have been attacked, that Larry Aylor evidenced his own suspicions about Gailiunas when, soon after he was notified of the incident, he blurted to McGowan, "The doctor did it," and that he had never completely rejected Gailiunas as a suspect until Andy came along.

Lesser also scored points supporting his contentions about Gailiunas as a neglected suspect when he got the detective to admit that he had paid little attention to the fact that Thorazine had been found in Rozanne's system. McGowan said he did not learn this until 1985, two years after Rozanne's death, when he got the news from a Massachusetts investigator looking into details of the killing on behalf of Rozanne's family.

"Did the fact that Thorazine was found in her system surprise you?" Lesser asked.

"No sir," McGowan answered.

"Do you have any explanation for how it got in her body?" Lesser asked.

"No sir," McGowan replied, effectively ending *that* attempt.

31

Searching for a weak spot, Lesser bore down on Detective McGowan about his actions leading to Andy's confession. Lesser insisted that the detective relate how he had tried to present himself to Andy as a sympathetic soul, the helpful half of the legendary good-cop/bad-cop team that historically has proven so effective in breaking down a criminal's defenses.

McGowan admitted that he had, under the guise of trying to find out if a lawyer had yet been appointed to defend him, telephoned Andy during the Christmas holidays in an attempt to get Andy thinking about him as the good cop.

"You were trying," Lesser said, "to ingratiate yourself with the prisoner so you could get his confidence?"

"Yes sir," McGowan acknowledged.

From then until the time Andy admitted attacking Rozanne, Lesser contended, McGowan did everything he could to break down the prisoner's resistance, including skillfully manipulating the situation so that Andy was deprived of his lawyer when he needed her the most.

McGowan answered noncommittally.

Once he had him in the interrogation room, Lesser continued, it was simply a matter of applying enough pressure. "You were trying awfully hard to get him to make an admission," Lesser said accusingly.

"Of his involvement, yes sir," McGowan replied politely, adding that he did not feel obligated at that stage to suggest to Andy that he call his attorney. He had already read Andy his rights, which included telling him that he could call an attorney. In addition, he added, he had not regarded Andy's statement that he would like time to think about the situation as a request to stop the questioning, as is required under the Miranda rulings. As far as Jan Hemphill went, McGowan candidly admitted that he had not expected her to let him get as far as he had with her client.

"Is it fair to say that if the man had an attorney present, these things may have turned out differently? That you may not have gotten the statement that you did?" Lesser asked.

"That's correct," McGowan replied.

Before winding up his cross-examination, Lesser—despite Judge McDowell's edict against bringing Joy Aylor into the Hopper trial— managed to open the door a crack by asking the Richardson detective how he had first learned about Brian Kreafle, who allegedly had given Andy the envelope that contained the money to kill Rozanne.

As soon as he moved into that area, Hagood was on his feet objecting to the jury being allowed to hear testimony that was irrelevant to whether Andy had killed Rozanne.

Judge McDowell gritted his teeth, angry at the backdoor attempt to slip Joy into the proceedings. He knew that he eventually would be presiding at Joy's trial and he did not want anything in Andy's trial to taint that process in advance. Reluctantly, he ordered the jury out of the room while he and the lawyers hashed out which, if any, questions Lesser would be allowed to repeat in front of the jury.

With the courtroom empty of everyone except trial participants and a handful of spectators, McGowan testified that he got Kreafle's name from Carol Garland, who, in turn, led him to Bill Garland.

What, exactly, did Carol say about Bill Garland's possible involvement in the attack on Rozanne? Lesser asked.

"She kept saying that '*they*' killed Rozanne," McGowan replied. "She assumed '*they*' included Bill Garland."

Judge McDowell interrupted. "I don't think Bill Garland has anything to do with this trial unless he was the killer," he commented.

This time it was Mitchell who was on his feet.

"Your honor," he said, "we believe that Carol will testify that Bill told her that *he* killed Rozanne and that Andy Hopper was a sacrificial lamb."

"But he didn't tell *Detective McGowan* that," the judge pointed out.

"Bill Garland's involvement in this trial is irrelevant unless he said he did it." Turning to McGowan, he asked: "Did Garland say he did it?"

"No sir," the detective answered.

Frustrated by what he considered the judge's decision to go along with the prosecution's attempt to keep the jury from hearing any evidence that Rozanne may have been killed by Bill Garland, or by Garland and someone else, rather than by Andy, Mitchell argued angrily. "What I'm hearing," he said loudly, "is that the court doesn't care how the crime was committed."

Judge McDowell struggled to keep his temper. "The jury is trying to focus, as I am," he said coldly, "on Andy's guilt or innocence. I'll sustain any objection about whatever Bill Garland told Lieutenant McGowan."

To soothe the defense somewhat, the judge gave Mitchell the opportunity to make what is called in legal terms an Offer of Proof, which basically was a statement outlining what testimony the defense would *expect* to elicit from a witness if it had the chance.

Conceding that he was operating strictly from supposition, Mitchell hesitated only slightly before launching into the defense theory. He had never talked to Bill Garland, he explained, and he had never seen any statement Garland had made to investigators. But from what he had been able to piece together from scraps of what he knew of Carol's statements, Mitchell said he "believed" that Garland would say, if forced to testify under oath, that he was present at the time of the attack on Rozanne, that he had been the one who shot her, and that he later disposed of the weapon by tossing it into a lake. He also believed that Garland would testify that Andy was not there when the attack occurred.

"Our position," Mitchell continued, "is that Bill Garland admitted it, that Brian Kreafle was involved, and that all have made deals with the government" to keep from coming to trial. "They're all out on low bonds and they haven't had a court date set for two years," he added.

Judge McDowell shook his head. "All I have right now is a theory."

Mitchell persisted. "The court is prohibiting the defendant from getting a fair trial. It's an issue that they lied about the involvement of Andy, that the evidence that led to Andy is a product of lying by others. The evidence we have is that Bill Garland and Brian Kreafle are parties to the crime."

The jury never got to hear this argument, although several days later both Bill and Carol Garland made cameo appearances in a juryless courtroom. They were called during the first week that McDowell had given the jurors off. When the formerly married couple showed up, each was accompanied by an attorney.

A ponderous, six-foot-five, barrel-chested man with his hair in a Fifties-style crewcut and the type of unlined, boyish face that, had he lost seventy-five pounds, would have made him look twenty years younger, Garland shuffled nonchalantly to the stand when he was called by Mitchell. In a surprisingly small voice coming from such a large man, Garland declined to answer each of Mitchell's questions on the grounds that to do so would violate his Fifth Amendment right to protection against self-incrimination.

After a half dozen repetitious responses, the judge interrupted Mitchell to ask Garland if he would continue to answer in the same vein if the questions continued. When he replied that he would, Judge McDowell nodded, announcing that he was going to honor Garland's right not to answer, thereby ending any chance that Garland would divulge any pertinent information—or any information at all, for that matter—during Andy's trial. When he was excused a few minutes later, it was with the understanding that he would not be seen again in McDowell's courtroom until Joy's trial or his own.

When Carol appeared, it actually was the second time in a week she had been before Judge McDowell. The previous Wednesday she had been dragged in against her will because she had refused to accept the defense's subpoena to appear. When she fled from the process server, the man called the police, who tracked her down and slapped her in handcuffs.

A pudgy, frumpy-looking woman with long blond hair and outsized purple-framed glasses, Carol was still seething over the incident by the time she got to Judge McDowell's courtroom, complaining loudly that the arrest and handcuffing constituted police brutality.

The judge, undoubtedly remembering the way her sister, Joy, had skipped on the eve of her own court appearance, sternly asked Carol if she anticipated a problem in obeying the subpoena.

"No," she replied haughtily. She would appear, she added contemptuously, but she would not answer any questions.

Judge McDowell's eyebrows went up. That would be up to her and her attorneys, he told her. But his tone said, We'll see about that.

True to her word, when she was called by Mitchell, she appeared only minutes after her ex-husband had left the room. And, as she had promised, she remained essentially mute, also claiming protection under the Fifth Amendment.

McDowell said he needed time to consider her position because she apparently did not fall into the same category as her former spouse. The charges against her had nothing to do with Andy Hopper, while Bill Garland was in the Rozanne "chain."

On Friday, February 7, day ten of the trial, Chapman told Judge McDowell that he was almost through with his case-in-chief and the prosecution intended to rest on Monday. Since the judge had promised to give the defense a week to fine-tune its presentation, the judge indicated he would recess the proceeding at the end of the day and bring the jury back on February 17.

Mitchell and Lesser accepted the judge's announcement with sighs. They figured they were going to need all the time they could get. Lesser was almost through with his cross-examination of McGowan and they had been looking forward to the week off to prepare their witnesses, especially their medical expert who would expand on the Thorazine issue and try to discredit Dr. Gilliland's autopsy report. But first, there were a few more questions Lesser wanted to put to the detective dealing with his preparations in anticipation of the trial.

What material, Lesser asked the detective, had he read to get ready for his testimony?

To the defense attorney's surprise, the detective admitted to virtually no preparation, confessing he was relying instead entirely on memory.

In response to another question, McGowan admitted that he had taken no notes during the entire investigation with the exception of a few scribblings he had made in the days immediately after the attack. But, he added hastily, he had destroyed those when he incorporated them into a formal report. "I operate from memory," he said.

When Lesser then asked him if he had reviewed any reports that might help him remember what had transpired, McGowan answered that, on orders from Chapman, he had read very few reports.

"What do you mean?" Lesser asked incredulously.

"Mr. Chapman told me to read some reports and not to read others," McGowan said.

"Which ones were you told not to read?" Lesser pressed.

He said he had been told not to read anything dealing with events that transpired between 1984, after Rozanne's death, and the time Andy was arrested late in 1988.

"Is it your habit *not* to review all the reports before you come to testify?" Lesser asked.

"Yes sir," McGowan replied. "That's so I can testify only about what I did myself."

The note issue surfaced prominently again later in the day when Lesser asked the detective to list in detail the sequence of events that occurred after Andy was taken into the interrogation room following the polygraph.

"My memory is I went up to see him," McGowan said.

"I don't guess you took any notes?" Lesser asked sarcastically.

"No," McGowan replied.

"Do you have *any* notes on what you did on that day?"

"No," McGowan replied.

Throughout the remainder of the trial, Lesser would return to the theme again and again, quizzing every police officer who testified about his or her note-taking practices. The defense attorney wanted to establish that it was department policy rather than just personal idiosyncracies that stopped investigators from taking notes. If they did not take any notes, Lesser pointed out, no notes could come back to haunt them years later. While this practice could save a lot of embarrassment and headaches for the investigators, it made it difficult to put together a clear picture of events that had transpired nine years previously.

Veteran Dallas defense lawyers smile knowingly when asked about the no-note policy, accepting it as an unhappy but unchangeable fact of life. "Don't forget," one of them commented cynically, "that Dallas County investigators questioned Lee Harvey Oswald for twelve hours before he was killed and none of them took notes."

A few minutes later, Lesser announced that he was through with McGowan, thinking as he did so that the detective would not be back on the stand again during Andy's trial. He was wrong.

At that point, however, both sides had come away with something as a result of the detective's extended testimony. The prosecution got to present to the jury a sanitized and incomplete version of events that led to Andy's confession, as well as to demonstrate the tenacious police work that went into Andy's capture. Once jurors had these facts, Chapman hoped, they could not help but come to the same conclusion as the

DA's office: that Andy, acting alone, had cold-bloodedly shot and fatally wounded Rozanne Gailiunas.

The defense, on the other hand, longed to expose a side of the investigatory process that the prosecution would have preferred to keep hidden, that is, that McGowan may have acted precipitously in targeting Andy exclusively, and may indeed have violated Andy's rights in his eagerness to bring the long investigation to what he considered a fulfilling conclusion. Furthermore, Lesser and Mitchell believed they had planted in juror's minds a suspicion that McGowan—whose dedication to his job could not be doubted—nevertheless harbored an instinctive distrust for the defense, an attitude that was clearly shared by Chapman and Hagood. The defense lawyers hoped that they could persuade the jurors that the district attorney's office was more interested in convictions than in truth.

Later, as the lawyers packed their files and prepared to leave the building for the week-long recess, Chapman handed Mitchell two audiocassettes, explaining that they were recordings of the interview with Andy on the night he was arrested. The move caught the defense lawyers by surprise; they did not know such tapes existed.

Originally, Chapman did not plan to give the tapes to the defense, but Judge McDowell had a copy of the transcript and Chapman knew the judge felt it was information the defense should have. If he had not voluntarily surrendered the tapes, Chapman feared that Judge McDowell would have ordered him to do so.

The tapes, although Mitchell and Lesser did not know it at the time, would necessitate a major shift in defense strategy, pave the way for two more appearances by Jan Hemphill, require another long stint in the witness chair for McGowan, and lead to some of the most revealing testimony of the trial.

32

On February 17 Carol made her third appearance in Judge McDowell's courtroom, again outside the jury's presence. The judge had bad news for her: He said his research convinced him that she was not entitled to take the Fifth Amendment in the current trial because the charges against her stemmed from the attack on Larry Aylor, not the one on Rozanne. That meant that as far as he was concerned, she could not incriminate herself in a proceeding in which she was not involved. However, before allowing the lawyers to question her, the judge cautioned Carol not to bring her sister Joy into her testimony.

Joy, who was in jail in France, was not an issue in the case currently being tried, the judge warned Carol, and he did not intend to let her become one. The prosecution, worried that even the slightest mention of Joy during Andy's trial might derail chances to prosecute her later for her alleged connection to Rozanne's murder, had pleaded with Judge McDowell to keep out any testimony relating to her.

Despite the judge's admonition, when Lesser tried to question her, he got no further than the second question, which was what Bill Garland had told her about the attack on Rozanne. In response to his question, Carol began, "He said my sister had hired him—"

Hagood leaped to his feet. "Objection," he roared, professing concern that testimony along those lines might hinder her future prosecution. It was an odd basis for complaint, considering that the district attorney's office had made no attempt to bring Carol to trial in the two years since her indictment.

Startled by the prosecutor's reaction, her emotions fed by her own dominant unease, Carol suddenly became very wary.

In his statements to her, she said apprehensively, her former husband had implied that he was "more or less a broker" in arranging for Rozanne's murder.

"Was he a shooter?" Lesser asked.

"No," she responded.

"Did he say he threw away the gun?" he persisted, trying to get her to repeat statements he believed she had made earlier to investigators.

"No," she said, adding that Garland had never told her directly that he had been present when the attack occurred, but that was the impression she had gotten from his graphic description of the scene. Of course, Garland could have learned the details from various other sources.

Lesser's suggestion that Carol be allowed to read a statement she had made to Richardson police in order to refresh her memory touched off another series of objections from Hagood.

"I'm real worried about the future prosecution of this witness," the ADA repeated.

"I think she ought to be allowed to refresh her memory," Judge McDowell interjected, setting off a complaint from Chapman, who suggested that the judge take the three-inch-thick stack of transcripts, which included Carol's various statements, into his chambers and review them privately before allowing the defense to continue its examination.

McDowell glanced at the digital clock on the wall above the jury box. It was 11:15. The judge had promised the jury he was going to dismiss them at noon, which would leave him no time to comply with Chapman's proposal. Plus, the issue could not be put off until the next day because Carol had a dawn flight to Hong Kong and she was not coming back for two weeks.

"It's a very simple one-two question," McDowell explained, mindful of the advancing clock. "Mr. Lesser just wants to know if your husband said he killed Mrs. Gailiunas and threw the gun away."

"No," Carol replied, looking flustered.

"Why is it mushrooming like this?" Lesser asked, frustrated by the lack of progress. "There's just one statement—"

Chapman interrupted him, claiming that Carol had made several statements.

Lesser, who was not privy to the statements because the prosecution guarded them zealously as "work product" information and therefore material that was not required to be supplied to the defense, repeated his demand that Carol be allowed to see the document in which, Lesser believed, she claimed that Garland acknowledged his presence in Rozanne's house. If Lesser was successful in getting that information before the jury, it could help his client tremendously. And Carol was his last hope in that regard because Judge McDowell had already ruled that Garland, in light of the charges against *him*, could not be forced to testify about the situation because such testimony would be self-incriminating.

Lesser's demand struck a sore spot with Chapman, who until then had never raised his voice or given any indication that he was under stress. In a rare display of temper, Chapman yelled across the courtroom at Lesser.

Judge McDowell, in an attempt to reestablish order, instructed Chapman to show Carol the transcript of the statement the defense had been alluding to.

Some fifteen minutes later, Carol resumed her testimony, but it was vaguer than ever.

Getting impatient, Judge McDowell took over the questioning. Did your ex-husband ever tell you "directly" that he killed Rozanne Gailiunas? the judge asked.

"No," Carol responded firmly, "it was always 'we' or 'they.' "

McDowell nodded sagely. As far as he was concerned, that negated the value of her testimony.

"He never said distinctly that he killed her?" the judge repeated, seeking to make sure that door was closed.

"No," she replied.

Turning toward the lawyers, McDowell explained that he had two reservations about allowing Carol to testify. "One," he said, "Garland never said he did it. Two, I have a problem with trying to corroborate anything she has to say."

That was good enough for Hagood and Chapman. Taking his cue from the judge, Chapman objected to any further questioning of Carol on grounds that anything else she had to say was hearsay and, additionally, was irrelevant to the charges against Andy.

To Mitchell, however, Carol's use of the word "we" in quoting her ex-husband was significant. "The fact that Bill Garland said 'we' makes him a participant and we think that is an exception to the hearsay rule," he argued. "Plus, what she has to say is definitely relevant."

McDowell was unmoved and was ready to dismiss her when Lesser slipped in one more question. Did her husband ever mention the name Andy Hopper, he asked.

Carol looked blank for a moment. "I think that's a name they gave me," she said, obviously referring to investigators.

Judge McDowell rolled his eyes. With the clock moving rapidly toward noon, the judge abruptly cut off debate. He would not allow the jury to hear from Carol at that time, he decided, adding that she could always be recalled after she returned from Asia.

It was another costly defeat for the defense, which had been relying heavily on Carol's testimony to create doubt among the jurors and make them question the validity of the state's clear-cut contention that Andy alone was involved in Rozanne's death.

In a near parody of the Fifth Amendment claims raised by Garland and Carol, Carl Noska was the next to raise the specter of self-incrimination.

A cabinetmaker who allegedly was the initial go-between linking Garland with Joy, Noska showed up in response to a defense subpoena with his own newly hired lawyer, who promptly announced that Noska also would be seeking protection under the Fifth Amendment.

"How can he get up and say he's taking the Fifth just because he's a witness?" asked an outraged Mitchell. "He hasn't even been indicted."

"I'm inclined to let him take the Fifth if there's any hint that what he's going to say is self-incriminating," said Judge McDowell, dealing the defense another blow.

"We believe that he knows Joy Aylor," Mitchell said hurriedly, as if afraid either the prosecution or the judge was going to cut him off. The defense also believed, he added, that Noska would testify that Joy had asked him to help her find a "scary-looking" man to "take care of something" for her. The person Noska allegedly turned to, Mitchell claimed, was Bill Garland, who had a shop next to his. The arrangement between Garland and Joy allegedly led to Brian Kreafle, who in turn led to Andy Hopper. It was Noska, Mitchell was arguing, who was at the beginning of the chain, even above Bill Garland, and because of his position, what he had to say was important to Andy's fate.

"We believe this could be testified to without endangering his Fifth Amendment privilege," Mitchell said. "We don't believe he is the subject of an investigation or that he is likely to be indicted."

McDowell, obviously unimpressed by Mitchell's argument, decided to honor Noska's claim to Fifth Amendment rights. However, he kept defense hopes barely alive by promising to do additional research on the subject, adding that if he changed his mind, he would let Mitchell and Lesser question him.

It had not been a good day for the defense. Mitchell and Lesser had been thwarted at every turn with no one upon whom they could take out their frustration. For the two lawyers, especially the pugnacious Lesser, it was a sobering experience.

In some respects, policemen and lawyers are similar, especially when it comes to digging information out of reluctant witnesses. Defense lawyers, particularly, have to be adept at this procedure. When there are two defense lawyers involved in a case they frequently adopt the good-cop/bad-cop ploy, thus becoming a good-lawyer/bad-lawyer team. However, this did not hold for Lesser and Mitchell. Instead, they adopted a stance under which each was aggressive. Rather than "good" and "bad," they became "mean" and "meaner." Sometimes, too, it was hard to tell who was who. Although Lesser did most of the cross-examination and had to wear the "mean" mantle when it came to asking incisive and embarrassing questions, Mitchell donned the "meaner" cap when it came time to throw barbs at the prosecutors or to try to push the judge into making a reversible legal error. They tread a fine line, which is what a good defense team was supposed to do.

Most people familiar with the Hopper case felt that it would be an easy victory for the district attorney's office. But once testimony got under way, the defense skillfully extracted statements that chipped away at the prosecution. Lesser and Mitchell had shown particular aggressiveness in attempting to introduce an element of doubt about Andy's culpability, an issue the defense hoped the jurors would remember when it came time to debate his guilt or innocence.

Being realists, they knew that after the confession was played for the jury, they had virtually no hope of getting their client acquitted. But if they could get jurors to believe that he had not acted alone in causing Rozanne Gailiunas's death—*and* if they could get Judge McDowell to give jurors an option when it came time for them to begin their deliberations—they might be able to save Andy from execution. As far as Mitchell and Lesser were concerned, a life sentence for Andy would be a victory.

At this stage of the trial, this did not yet seem an impossible goal. They felt they had done fairly well in discrediting several prosecution witnesses, particularly Detective McGowan, and they had not yet even started to lay their own case before the jury. The judge's decisions involving the testimony of Bill and Carol Garland and Carl Noska had hurt—but not nearly as much, admittedly, as McDowell's decision to let the jury hear Andy's confession and his refusal to let Jan Hemphill testify. To recoup, they were going to have to make a lot of points with their own medical expert and with two hostile witnesses they figured would be important to their case: Dr. Peter Gailiunas and Larry Aylor.

But there were other factors at work in the courtroom that had nothing to do with the testimony of witnesses. And in the long run, these factors might be just as important.

33

By this time, with the trial at the halfway point in the guilt/innocence phase, the proceeding was beginning to take on its own unique character. And, in this instance, there were some disturbing undertones. Whenever the jury was present, the opposing lawyers gave little hint of the animosity that existed among them. But when the jury was absent, the lawyers seemed strained to maintain an appearance of cordiality and respect. As the days went by, the prosecution and defense teams grew increasingly curt with each other. At times it seemed as though they would have been happy, literally, to strip to the waist and fight it out with bare knuckles.

In addition to the matchup of arch liberals against arch conservatives, there were several reasons that made this trial and the relationships among the participants atypical. For one, the long voir dire had left a lot of open wounds. It had been a tedious process during which attorneys from both sides had rubbed on each other's nerves.

Yet it was more than that. In some trials, once the proceedings are finished, opposing lawyers can bury their differences, go out and have a drink or a meal together, and commiserate about the state of the judicial system. In the case of Mitchell/Lesser and Chapman/Hagood, there was virtually no chance of that happening.

On the surface, the tension seemed to be most evident between Lesser and Hagood, but that was simplistic. The *real* animosity existed between Lesser and Chapman because it was Chapman who was calling the shots for the prosecution team.

Lesser felt it had been Chapman's idea to try Andy for capital murder rather than simple murder; that it was Chapman who wanted to see Andy executed, not just tucked away in prison for much of the rest of his life, but strapped down on a gurney and pumped full of lethal drugs. During the voir dire, Hagood had approached the defense lawyers and asked them if they would be willing to let Andy plead guilty to murder as an alternative to trial and a possible death sentence. However, Hagood stressed that the final decision would be up to Chapman. "I'll go to bat for you, but don't tell Kevin," Hagood proposed.

After considerable debate, Mitchell and Lesser decided to take Hagood up on the offer. But the whole idea went down the tube shortly afterward when Hagood told the defense that Chapman had flatly refused to bargain, that he wanted the death sentence against Andy.

Maybe, Lesser decided later, Chapman had made that decision out of frustration with the inability of the government to come to an agreement with France to get Joy back. Deeply disappointed because the district attorney's office had been precluded from seeking a death sentence for Joy, Chapman may have been looking for a scapegoat, and that happened to be Andy Hopper. At any rate, it was Lesser's perception that Chapman was the true enemy, a feeling that prompted him to privately refer to his opponent as "the angel of death."

Judge McDowell was well aware of the situation and he struggled stalwartly to keep it under control. At all costs, he wanted the rancor hidden from the jurors. The last thing he wanted was a mistrial.

To a large extent the judge had been successful up to a point. So far, most of the dueling had occurred off-stage, while the jurors were not there to witness it. However, the judge was slightly less successful when the jury was absent, as was the case very early on, when Chapman had made a blatant attempt to cripple the defense position even before the jury had been sworn and the lawyers had made their opening statements.

One of Chapman's first actions after he walked into the courtroom on Monday, January 27, was to file a thirty-nine-point document, called a *motion in limine*, which, if it had been approved by McDowell, would have restricted the defense both in what it could do to defend Andy *and* in presenting its own case.

If the prosecution had had its way, the defense would have been prohibited from making "any comment regarding the whereabouts of any person who has not testified," or from making "any comment regarding Joy Aylor fleeing Dallas." It would, in fact, have effectively prohibited the defense from even mentioning Joy's name. But what really made Mitchell and Lesser angry was a clause in the proposed motion that would have put tight restrictions on virtually anything the defense attorneys might say if they strayed at all from the path predetermined by the prosecution.

The effect this motion could have on the trial became evident quite quickly. While Mitchell was urging Judge McDowell not to go along with the prosecution proposal, he expressed puzzlement about one of the points, claiming he was not sure what the prosecution had in mind. Hagood, unwilling to pass up the opportunity to zing his opponent, blurted sotto voce, "What do you mean you don't know? You're a big-time, board-certified lawyer."

Before Mitchell could respond, Lesser leaped to his feet and pointed a threatening finger at Hagood. "See, judge!" he yelled angrily. "That's what we mean. We don't need that kind of comment."

Judge McDowell slowly shook his head, looking like a tired father unhappy at having to referee disputes among his squabbling children. "Okay," he said calmly, "let's get back on track."

But the defense was not ready to give up. Early the next morning, Mitchell and Lesser presented their own motion in limine, which was designed to restrict the prosecution in *its* presentation. Where the prosecution motion had contained thirty-nine points, the defense motion strained to list forty, including a clause requiring the prosecution to preview the testimony of each of its witnesses outside the presence of the jury before the witness could testify. If that proposal had been approved by Judge McDowell, it could have extended the trial well into the spring and maybe even the summer. Another point would have prohibited the prosecution from presenting *any* evidence until its relevance could be determined in a hearing without the jury being in the room.

Clearly, the document that Lesser privately referred to as the defense's "chicken-shit motion" would have been impossible to enforce. It was introduced solely in an attempt to harass Chapman and Hagood, to show that the defense did not intend to surrender without a fight.

Again, Judge McDowell shook his head. "I'm denying both motions in their entirety," he said, firmly explaining that the trial was going to run under *his* rules and that he was not going to surrender his authority to the opposing lawyers. Furthermore, he added sternly, the two sides were going to conduct themselves as professionals or there was going to be hell to pay.

That was for the record. When the lawyers retreated to Judge McDowell's chambers, things *really* got raucous. At more than one such meeting the "fuck you's" flew as thickly as mosquitoes swarming along the Trinity River. At times, McDowell feared the opponents would actually come to blows.

This enmity, initially expressed subtly but gaining in perceptibility as the trial progressed, apparently was not going to simply disappear. Before the trial was over, one particularly bitter clash between Hagood and the defense would lead Judge McDowell to angrily threaten to throw them both in jail. The unusual display of open antagonism between the opposing pairs of lawyers—far exceeding the belligerence expected in a normally competitive environment and at times seeming to border on actual hatred—would haunt the trial, severely test the judge's patience, and force one of the city's most even-tempered jurists into a tantrum of his own.

One particular incident when the trial was well under way seemed to effectively demonstrate the lengths to which the lawyers would go to try to wound the other side. It involved Andy's parents, who had been in the courtroom faithfully every day since the proceedings started, including the lengthy jury selection process. They had become fixtures: two inoffensive, middle-aged people who were immediately recognized by the jurors and the regular spectators.

On February 5, day eight of the trial, Chapman asked Judge McDowell to invoke the rule banning potential witnesses from the courtroom. That meant expelling Andy's parents, who the defense tentatively planned to call to testify about Andy's childhood.

At the start of the trial, the defense and prosecution teams had agreed to exempt Rozanne's and Andy's families from the rule holding that potential witnesses would not be permitted in the courtroom, at least until after they had given their testimony. The reasoning behind the agreement to ignore the rule regarding family members was that none of them would be able to give substantive testimony relating to the facts of the case. To exclude them from the proceedings, when the issue affected them so deeply, would be cruel and unnecessary.

Early in the trial, Chapman had called Rozanne's father, Henry Agnostinelli, as an historical witness to testify about Rozanne's early life in Massachusetts. And, although the Hoppers were standing by, Lesser said he did not plan to call either of them until the punishment phase of the trial. Even then they would be, as Rozanne's father had been, historical witnesses only.

For the first seven days of the trial, Andy's father and mother sat quietly in their seats in the first row on the far-left-hand side of the room, immediately behind their son. Hopper's mother, especially during the more sanguinary testimony, usually immersed herself in a religious tract. Rozanne's family huddled on the opposite side of the chamber, behind the prosecution table. Allowing them all to remain seemed like a humane arrangement. For that reason as much as anything else, it came as a shock when Chapman asked Judge McDowell—with the jurors absent—to order the Hoppers to leave the room and be prohibited from returning.

What made the act especially astonishing was its timing. Chapman made his request only hours after the jury viewed Andy's confession and almost immediately after Rozanne's family returned to Boston. The prosecutor never explained his reasoning, leaving the impression that it was a petty impulse, that he had gotten what he wanted out of the agreement to let the families stay and, once that was accomplished, he wanted to wound the Hoppers and the defense. The last time the jury had been in the courtroom, the Hoppers had been sitting in their customary seats. When jurors came back, they could not help but notice that the Hoppers were missing.

Lesser, remaining uncharacteristically calm under the circumstances, opposed Chapman's proposal to eject the Hoppers, arguing that the results of the banishment could have an adverse effect on the way the jury viewed Andy. For the Hoppers to suddenly and inexplicably disappear could raise serious questions in the jurors' minds about Andy's guilt. The most logical conclusion the jurors could draw, Lesser argued, would be that the Hoppers were so revolted by their son's confession that they abandoned him. If the jurors thought the Hoppers felt that way about their own son, they would be more inclined to look upon him without mercy themselves.

"I'm more concerned about the appearance their absence will create than about the rule being invoked," Lesser argued to no avail since Judge McDowell said he was powerless to deny the prosecution request.

"It's not going to be for the rest of the trial," Chapman said in an attempt to soften the blow, "but only for the testimony that is coming up." He did not elaborate.

However, for the next several days, the Hoppers remained in limbo. To prove that they had not forsaken their son, they camped on a hard bench in the hallway just outside the courtroom, where jurors had to pass them as they came and went.

Then, as unexpectedly as he had demanded their expulsion, Chapman reversed himself and told the judge that he would have no objections if the Hoppers wanted to return. His reason for asking for their removal—or for changing his mind—was never made clear. As far as Lesser was concerned, though, it was simply additional evidence of the prosecutor's pettiness; it did not help to relieve the tension between the two.

One of the results of this animosity among the lawyers affected the pace of the trial. It slowed.

The amount of time the jury spent out of the courtroom, particularly during the presentation of the state's case, was far more than usual. One of the reasons for this was because the trial was breaking new ground, particularly as far as admissibility of a confession was concerned. There also were frequent long and bitter arguments about what was hearsay and what was not, an issue that, to the best that Judge McDowell could determine, was not adequately spelled out under existing Texas law. These were arguments, understandably, that demanded the jury's absence.

As a result of these issues and others, in the first ten days of the trial, the jury probably spent more time out of the courtroom than inside it. One day, for example, when the lawyers were engaged in particularly acrimonious debate, the jurors were in the room for less than two hours.

Hagood and Chapman also proved exceptionally quick to object. Every time momentum built in the trial, testimony got sidetracked under a deluge of protests from the prosecution. This was part of the strategy of the district attorney's office in order to keep the focus as narrow as possible and to attempt to censor any testimony that did not fit with its contention that Andy acted independently in the attack on Rozanne.

In most trials, the objection tactic is preempted by the defense, which is anxious to keep out testimony harmful to a client. In this case, it seemed, the prosecution was being extremely cautious because it feared that revelation of any material that did not deal specifically with Andy Hopper might hinder the future prosecution of Joy Aylor, or give information to her lawyer. Still, by taking this stance, Chapman risked alienating the jury. By the time the defense got to its case-in-chief, jurors were audibly groaning about the yo-yo treatment they were receiving, constantly being asked to retire to their cramped quarters behind the courtroom while the lawyers fought out whatever issue was being raised. Most of the time the objections were raised by the prosecution.

Two other factors also contributed to the trial's slow progress. One was McDowell's attempt to keep up with his usual workload in addition to trying Andy Hopper. And then there was the string of unfortunate circumstances that seemed to plague the proceeding, particularly members of the jury, a stream of misfortune that veteran courthouse employees could not recall ever before occurring during a single trial.

The most serious of the incidents was when one of the jurors, who later came in red-eyed and shaken, had stopped for gas on the way home and was fueling his car. A twenty-year-old soldier on furlough walked into the station seeking help for his broken-down vehicle. While he was talking with an attendant, a car with five teenagers drove up and the youths began yelling obscenities at the soldier's half-sister. The soldier yelled something back and one of the group produced a shotgun, which he leveled at the soldier. He missed with his first shot, but the second blast caught the soldier squarely in the chest, killing him instantly. The juror witnessed the entire incident. As a result, he spent most of the rest of the night at the police station giving statements and being questioned about what he had seen.

And then there was the incident that occurred on day ten of the trial. The prosecution was examining Larry Fletcher, the state's firearms expert, in an attempt to connect the gun allegedly used by Andy to shoot Rozanne and the bullets that were recovered. The problem erupted when Fletcher opened a small vial purportedly containing the slug taken from the wound near Rozanne's right ear. To his and everyone else's surprise, the container was empty. The missing bullet subsequently was found in the property room at Richardson PD and, although it was admitted into evidence over defense objections, its value was unquestionably greatly diminished.

These ups and downs, ironies, inconsistencies, bouts of pugnacity, and childish digs at each other were hardly more than one might expect, one courtroom wag pointed out, in a trial that featured a fundamentalist Christian being defended by two liberal Jews before a Roman Catholic judge.

34

Larry Mitchell and Peter Lesser, who had been impatiently waiting for the eleven days it took the prosecution to wind up its case-in-chief, summoned as their first major witness the medical examiner from San Antonio, Dr. Robert Bux.

An affable and articulate witness, Bux had been called by the defense to give jurors another version of what might have caused Rozanne Gailiunas's death—a common practice in many murder trials—and fill them in on the properties of Thorazine, the powerful drug discovered to be in Rozanne's system the night she was attacked.

Before delving into the Thorazine issue, however, Mitchell led Bux through a painstaking reexamination of Gilliland's autopsy report, beginning with the least serious of all the wounds inflicted upon Rozanne: the second gunshot wound to the head. In that case, the bullet never penetrated the skull, but struck a glancing blow and lodged just below the skin on her right temple. The pathologist, who had performed more than 2,600 autopsies, scoffed at Gilliland's conclusion that this wound contributed to Rozanne's death.

"There was no evidence of severe bleeding from this wound. There was no evidence it hit anything vital. There was no evidence that the wound was septic. In my opinion," he said, brushing aside Gilliland's contentions, "you can eliminate this."

Significantly, he added that he did not believe that the tissue found stuffed down Rozanne's throat had been a contributing cause in her death. It may have made it difficult for her to breathe, he said, but it had no effect on her fate. Since it was removed by paramedics at the scene and since it left no telltale signs that it ever had been inserted, it was not even mentioned in the autopsy report.

Lesser and Mitchell had wanted to make sure that Bux's statements about the tissue were in the record for a very specific reason: Andy denied ever cramming the material in her mouth. But getting Bux to testify about it was part of the strategy. The defense lawyers wanted to lay the groundwork for this claim in case they ever got the opportunity to try to prove that someone other than Andy was involved in Rozanne's death. To Lesser and Mitchell, the presence of the tissue was another indication that someone knowledgeable about physiology had been involved because the idea of trying to suppress a person's breathing in such a way would never have occurred to the ordinary person.

In the end, the defense team was not able to get the issue before the jury. But the tissue's presence, like that of the Thorazine, was never satisfactorily explained.

Different from the tissue, however, but still questionable as a cause of death in Bux's point of view, was the attempt at strangulation. In her testimony, Gilliland had detailed the wounds at great length, concluding that the attempt was a contributing cause of death.

Bux also questioned her opinion on that issue. In the first place, he pointed out, he did not believe the sash from her robe and the stocking, both of which were found on Rozanne's bed, had been the ligatures used in the attempted strangulation. From his examination of the wounds, Bux concluded that in his opinion the instrument that had done the most damage was a piece of rope, which the assailant apparently carried away with him. In any case, though, no one could argue with the fact that Rozanne was alive and breathing on her own when paramedics arrived. "If you're going to say that strangulation was a cause of death, she should have been dead at the scene," Bux contended.

But, he added, he could not *prove* Gilliland wrong about the strangulation because the necessary evidence did not exist, again thanks to an apparent mistake on Gilliland's part.

Pathologists commonly take tissue slides from the brain to determine if a victim has been strangled. Scientists have been able to determine that sudden oxygen loss, as would occur if a person were throttled, creates a distinguishable change in the tissue in a particular area, a change that can be as readily observed as a black eye. Apparently, Bux said, Gilliland tried to do this, but she took the slides from the wrong section. If she had only taken the slides from the correct area, Bux said, it would have shown conclusively whether strangulation played a role in Rozanne's death.

The jury, far from being bored with the medical terminology that was flying around the courtroom like jetliners circling DFW, hung on Bux's every word, much to the consternation of Chapman and Hagood.

What particularly disturbed him about Gilliland's autopsy, Bux said, was her failure to examine blood that had been drawn by hospital personnel when Rozanne was admitted and she was still alive. In his view that was an inexcusable error that could not be dismissed with the notation on Gilliland's report that no antemortem blood was available.

"It's the primary responsibility of the medical examiner to obtain that blood. It was available, but they just didn't get it," he said. As a former hospital blood bank administrator, Bux said emphatically, he *knew* that such blood had been available from two separate sources because a hospital's failure to keep such material would be a flagrant violation of blood bank rules. If a hospital was found in violation of that rule, he pointed out, it could loose its accreditation.

"Gilliland's failure to get that blood doesn't allow a judgment about the effects any drugs may have had at the time," Bux said, leading up to the hospital report, made independently, that Thorazine had been found in Rozanne's system.

"Hospital records show she had .22 milligrams per liter of Thorazine in her blood when she was brought into the emergency room," Bux said, adding that it should have triggered a warning when it was discovered that Rozanne had been a nurse and her estranged husband was a physician.

"When you first saw that report on Thorazine, what effect did that have on your thinking?" Mitchell asked.

Bux paused, carefully composing his answer. "That is not a drug you typically see abused," he replied, explaining that he had found it in cadavers only a half-dozen times in his career, and in every case the deceased had been a patient in a mental institution, where Thorazine is used fairly frequently because of its ability to control psychotics.

"The first thing I asked myself was had this drug been administered on a one-shot basis or had Rozanne been a chronic user," Bux said.

Mitchell asked if the mere presence of Thorazine in someone being admitted to a hospital was unusual.

Yes, Bux replied, especially in someone who was not institutionalized. "Thorazine is used frequently on psychotics because it brings them closer to reality." It also is used, he added, to control vomiting and nausea, but normally it is not administered in such situations outside of a doctor's office or an institution.

Working backward from the amount of Thorazine found in her blood when she was admitted, Bux estimated that the initial dose, which probably had been administered intramuscularly with a hypodermic needle since no remains of pills were found in her vomitus, had been between 125 milligrams and 175 milligrams. That, he added, was a strong dose for someone who had not been a chronic user, that is, someone who did not use the drug regularly enough to build up a tolerance.

Under Mitchell's guidance, Bux said if a dose of the size that apparently was administered to Rozanne had been given during the morning, she would not have been able to perform the functions that other witnesses had described: picking up her son at the day care center and then taking him to lunch and an ice-skating lesson. She would have suffered from blurred vision, her heart rate would have increased considerably, and she probably would have felt faint. "She would have been incapacitated," he said.

With the morning eliminated as a likely time for the drug to be administered, Mitchell said, that left only the afternoon, sometime between 2:30 P.M., when Rozanne picked up her son at the ice-skating rink, and 6:36 P.M., when the paramedics arrived at her house.

Using those parameters, Mitchell asked, was it possible to tell if the drug was administered before or after she was shot?

Bux shook his head. "No," he replied, "I can't tell that. But I can say that if it was administered before the killer arrived, she would have been sedated and would not have been walking around."

According to Andy's confession, Rozanne answered his knock on the door, carried on at least a limited conversation with him, walked on her own to the bedroom, and struggled against the restraints.

"Was there any indication the drug was administered at the hospital?" Mitchell asked.

"No," Bux replied.

"Was there any indication it was taken voluntarily?"

Bux looked mildly surprised. "No!" he said emphatically. "That drug is not going to make you feel good."

Treading delicately since the answer to the next question was pivotal to the defense theory that Dr. Gailiunas had administered the drug in an attempt to push his mortally wounded but still breathing wife over the edge, Mitchell asked Bux what effect the drug would have had on Rozanne if it had been administered *after* she was shot.

"It would have sedated her and compounded the injury to the brain caused by the gunshot," Bux replied without hesitation. "It would have had an effect on her breathing pattern and caused additional swelling of the brain. It would have made her chance of survival virtually nonexistent."

Zeroing in for what he hoped would be an injurious blow to the prosecution's case, Mitchell also carefully phrased his next question. "If you eliminate the Thorazine, is it possible that this was a survivable wound?" he asked.

Bux swiveled slightly to face the jury. "Yes sir!" he answered crisply.

Mitchell sighed in relief. Winding down his examination, he summarized Bux's testimony.

"You agree that death was caused by the gunshot?" he asked.

"Absolutely," Bux replied.

"Hypothetically, if she had received immediate medical treatment and if she had not been given Thorazine, is it possible she could have survived?"

"Yes sir," said Bux.

"Did the Thorazine sabotage her treatment?"

Bux answered unequivocally: "Yes!"

Chapman began his cross-examination with an apparent effort to rile Bux, hoping perhaps to get him to lose his temper and thereby weaken the effect of his testimony on the jury. During Mitchell's questioning, Chapman had complained several times that Bux was giving narrative answers when he should have been responding to questions monosyllabically.

"Just answer my questions yes or no," Chapman directed. "In other words, if I ask you what time it is, don't tell me how to build a clock."

The remark drew smiles from several jurors and a scowl from Judge McDowell.

"Thorazine alone would not have killed her, would it?" Chapman asked.

"No," Bux replied. "There's no doubt about that. It would not." But, he added, if her brain was already swollen from the gunshot wound, the Thorazine would have made the injury worse.

"Do you think Peter Gailiunas came in and injected her?" Chapman asked.

Bux said he did not know the answer to that question.

Then, the ADA asked, was it possible that whoever shot her could have injected her?

Bux said it was, but he added that that person would have had to have access to medical supplies because Thorazine was not a "street" drug.

In an effort to undermine Bux's contention that Rozanne might have survived the gunshot wound to her brain, Chapman tried to get the medical examiner to admit that if she had lived, she probably would have been in a vegetative state.

Bux conceded that may have been the case, but otherwise gave little ground.

Bux was a powerful witness, a bright light in a defense case characterized up to then mainly by disappointment and frustration. The best benefit that Mitchell and Lesser could hope to reap from Bux's testimony was that it had created grounds for doubt among the jurors, that it might make them question if the prosecution's case against Andy was as airtight as Chapman and Hagood wanted them to believe. However, the defense attorneys were astute enough to realize that the pathologist's testimony alone was not going to save their client; they were going to have to expand upon the small opening that Bux had provided for them. One of the ways they hoped to do that was through the testimony of their next witness: Dr. Peter Gailiunas.

35

From everything they had heard about the kidney specialist, Mitchell and Lesser had him pegged as a volatile man, someone with a quick temper, a sharp tongue, and an overbearing, condescending attitude. However, when he took the stand on February 18 he exhibited none of those traits, much to the disappointment of the two defense attorneys.

Rather than being abrasive, Gailiunas spoke softly and rationally in a deep and not unpleasant voice devoid of a regional accent despite the fact that he was educated primarily in Boston. The only hint that he might have been nervous was the fact that he chewed gum throughout the time he was on the stand and admitted, after prodding from Lesser, that he had taken a tranquilizer before he was called to testify.

Under questioning from an unexpectedly restrained Lesser, Gailiunas detailed his training and explained how he had met Rozanne when their jobs threw them together in the late fall of 1977. They married and at his urging they moved to Dallas, where their son, Peter III, was born on April 19, 1979. In the autumn of 1982, he said, they decided to build a new house and contracted with a homebuilder whose name Gailiunas had seen on a sign. That man was Larry Aylor.

At the time, Gailiunas said, speaking slowly and deliberately, he had every reason to believe that his marriage was stable and that his wife, Rozanne, was content with him and their relationship, although she had been less than excited about being uprooted from her home in Massachusetts and being moved to the middle of the North Texas prairie.

"When did you first become suspicious that things were not going as well?" Lesser asked.

That would have been in late April or early May 1983, Gailiunas answered, but he did not begin to get really worried until June, when Rozanne announced that she was leaving him and moving into a house of her own. It was then, Gailiunas added, that he hired a team of private detectives to watch his wife in an attempt to reveal the identity of the man with whom she was involved.

He said the discovery that it was Larry Aylor shocked him to the core. After that, he said, he began taping all telephone calls coming into or going out of his house, including one in which Larry and Rozanne described their respective spouses in less-than-glowing terms. He then played the tape for Joy Aylor, he said, to prove to her that her husband was seeing another woman.

He was angry and hurt because of Rozanne's decision to leave him for Larry. It left him dispirited to the point that he sought temporary relief in alcohol, he said. But even after he knew that Larry was Rozanne's lover, he did not entirely give up hope of getting her back. One night, at the height of his despair, he asked his mother to accompany him when he went to confront Larry.

"Did you and Mr. Aylor have a friendly conversation?" Lesser asked disingenuously.

"I'm not sure it was friendly," Gailiunas replied. "I told him I wanted him to stop seeing my wife and he denied he was seeing her."

Up until then, Gailiunas, who had not appeared voluntarily as a witness but had to be subpoenaed by the defense, had indicated that he was willing to cooperate. But his mood subtly shifted when Lesser began questioning him about Thorazine and whether it was a drug commonly used by people in his medical specialty, nephrology.

Testifying that he was only "vaguely familiar" with the drug, Gailiunas said he did not use it in his practice and did not know what the normal doses were or what its effects would be.

"Isn't it used by nephrologists?" asked Lesser, whose wife is a physician and was the one who had first alerted him to the significance of the Thorazine that had been found in Rozanne's system. "Don't they use it to help combat nausea and give it to patients who are undergoing kidney dialysis?"

"Not that I'm aware of," Gailiunas answered calmly. "There are other drugs that are available for that."

Although he admitted that Chapman had told him several weeks previously that Thorazine might be an issue in the Hopper trial, he said he had not done any independent research on the drug in an attempt to find out more about it.

"And you were never aware that Thorazine was found in your wife's blood before 1992?" Lesser asked, his voice rising in disbelief since Detective McGowan had testified that he discovered that fact as far back as 1985.

"No," he replied. "The first I heard of it was from Mr. Chapman several weeks ago."

"When you were told about the Thorazine in your wife's blood, what was your reaction?" Lesser asked.

Gailiunas looked puzzled. "I was perplexed," he said in a tone that made it sound more like a question than an answer.

"Do you have any idea why it was there?" Lesser persisted.

Gailiunas looked as though he were smothering a grin, as though that were a question he had been waiting for. "I was told there wasn't a struggle and I've always wondered why," he said. "When I found out about the drug, I figured your client used it to subdue Rozanne so he could murder her."

Lesser looked as though he wanted to bite off his own tongue for asking such a question. "How about if you administered it?" he asked, trying to recoup.

"That's ridiculous," Gailiunas responded.

"Do you know how Thorazine would be acquired?" Lesser asked.

Gailiunas jumped on the opportunity to show a little disingenuousness of his own. "In a pharmacy, I suppose," he replied sarcastically.

"Would it be fair to say that Thorazine would not be a drug your wife would have taken on her own?" Lesser ventured, hoping to damage the prosecution's contention, which Gailiunas was not aware of, that Rozanne may have medicated herself with the drug because she was upset over her marital situation.

"I would think that's correct," Gailiunas answered noncommittally.

"Why would anyone need Thorazine if he had a gun?" Lesser asked.

"If she were sedated, that would solve everything," Gailiunas said, meaning it would make her entirely pliable. He did not mention the fact (although Lesser would later bring it up) that the killer would first have to inject the drug, then wait thirty minutes or longer for it to take effect.

Despite his persistent probing for soft spots, Lesser was unable to punch any major holes in Gailiunas's claim to be nothing more than an aggrieved husband who reacted in a not abnormal way to the dissolution of his marriage and the fact that his wife was having an affair with someone with whom Gailiunas continued doing business.

When Chapman took over the questioning the next morning on cross-examination—anxious to get Gailiunas's position unequivocally before the jury—he jumped right to the point.

"Did you go into the house that day?" he asked.

"No," Gailiunas said.

"Did you inject her with a drug?"

"No."

"Would it be reasonable for you to do that?"

"No, it would be unthinkable."

"Does it make sense that you would be accused?"

"No."

"How do you feel about your son?"

"I love him more than anything in the world."

"How does it feel to be accused of these things?"

"I'm stunned that anyone would even suggest it."

Without breaking stride, Chapman then popped the question most of the jurors would have liked to ask if that had been possible. "Who did you think had murdered her?"

Gailiunas, obviously ready for it, responded quickly and firmly: "Joy Aylor or Larry Aylor."

While Chapman had the momentum going, he machine-gunned questions at Gailiunas in an attempt to destroy any possible headway Lesser may have been able to make the previous day.

Although Gailiunas had characterized his drinking as "occasional" when being questioned by Lesser, the physician admitted to Chapman that there was a period in the fall of 1982 and the summer of 1983, about the time Rozanne moved out, that he had "perhaps" imbibed too freely. And he had repeatedly claimed that his memory of events on the day Rozanne was attacked was either hazy or nonexistent. Although in response to questions from Chapman, he reeled off remarkable details of a conversation he had with his son late that afternoon, the conversation during which he first found out that there was a problem at Rozanne's house. It was that call, he said, that sent him rushing to 804

Loganwood after instructing his son to lock the doors and not allow anyone inside.

A few minutes later, when he got the witness back on redirect, Lesser was openly skeptical of the reported telephone conversation between father and son.

"You told him to close and lock the door," Lesser said. "How did you know it was open and unlocked?"

"I just wanted to make sure," Gailiunas said.

"Were you aware that when the paramedics arrived the door was unlocked?"

"No," Gailiunas replied.

"You had been taping conversations in and out of the house," Lesser reminded him. "Was that conversation taped?"

"No," Gailiunas said, explaining that the taping had been done earlier, before Rozanne moved out.

While he had been almost gentle in his handling of Gailiunas the previous day, Lesser was rougher on redirect, asking more pointed questions and firing them at him rapidly in an attempt to trip him up.

"Did your wife think you were a violent person?" Lesser asked.

"I don't think so," Gailiunas answered calmly.

The answer was hardly completed before Lesser bombarded him with a series of similar queries: "Did your wife think you had an ungovernable temper? Did she think you were unpredictable? Did she think you abused her?"

To each question, Gailiunas had an identical answer: "I don't think so."

"Did she think you harassed her?"

"I think she was under the impression that I did," Gailiunas answered. "She was under the impression I was having her followed. I told her if someone was following her, it wasn't me."

Lesser raised his eyebrows, pointing out that Gailiunas had admitted hiring two sets of detectives to tail his wife.

"That was earlier," Gailiunas said. "That was in June or July. I'm talking now about August or September."

"Was your wife in fear of you?" Lesser asked sharply, only to be cut off by a prosecution objection that was sustained by Judge McDowell. Although Lesser tried to go at it from a different angle, pointing out that Rozanne was able to get a restraining order against him, Chapman and

Judge McDowell repeatedly blocked his attempts to go into detail on what the order said or why it was requested. The best he could do was question Gailiunas about his anger.

"I'm not saying I wasn't angry," Gailiunas said, "but that wasn't my overriding emotion."

If Dr. Bux had been a plus for the defense, the best Lesser and Mitchell could rate Gailiunas as was a draw. He had not fallen apart or exploded as they had hoped he would do, but his testimony about his unfamiliarity with Thorazine may have made him come across as less than credible.

However, since jurors typically have their own mysterious criteria about judging witnesses and their trustworthiness, the defense had to be content with the knowledge that they had done the best they could under the circumstances. The closer Lesser and Mitchell got to opening up testimony about possible participation of anyone other than Andy, the more frantic the prosecution got with its objections and, seemingly, the more Judge McDowell became inclined to agree with Chapman and Hagood.

Although it was obvious the prosecutors were trying to protect their case against Joy and others not tied directly to Andy—Bill and Carol Garland, for example—the attempts to keep Andy's trial so narrowly focused was, at the least, frustrating for Mitchell and Lesser.

More seriously, it also could prove damaging to the prosecution—possibly undermining Hagood and Chapman's own strategy—because the jury, which was not privy to much of the discussion about collateral issues, could end up totally confused.

Although the trial was almost two weeks old by the time Gailiunas finished his primary testimony (Lesser indicated he wanted to call him back later to ask him some more questions about Thorazine), the jury had been in the courtroom only about half that time.

A good example of just how tightly the prosecution wanted to restrict testimony was evident when the defense called its next unwilling witness, Larry Aylor.

36

Dapperly attired in a dark blue suit, a white shirt, and a red, white, and blue rep tie, Larry Aylor grudgingly took his seat on the witness stand, looking like he would rather be in a proctologist's office than by Judge McDowell's left hand.

By the time he was called, it was late Wednesday and he had been in town for five days. His weekend was spent meeting with members of the defense and prosecution teams. Since then, he had been kept on hold, nervously twiddling his thumbs, waiting to be called.

He had not wanted to be a witness in the first place; Lesser and Mitchell had to get a court order to drag him back from his new home in Virginia so he could point an accusatory finger at Dr. Gailiunas as a possible principal in the murder of Rozanne.

In Larry's view at that point, *everybody* was the enemy, including the prosecutors. For their part, Hagood and Chapman feared that he inadvertently was going to say something on the stand about his former wife, thus giving the defense a priceless wedge into opening up the testimony.

Once he was seated in the witness chair, Larry stared straight ahead and clenched his teeth. All four attorneys stared back at him. The defense team wanted to bleed him for every little fact, but if Larry and the prosecution team could have their way, his testimony would consist of two words: No comment.

The former Dallas homebuilder had hardly settled into the witness box when Hagood asked Judge McDowell to send the jury out while attorneys held an impromptu hearing on the admissibility of what he might say. These hearings, or procedures within a procedure, were becoming commonplace in the trial. There had been so many in just the first fifteen days that everyone had lost count.

With the jurors confined to their quarters behind the main courtroom, Hagood launched into an argument against allowing Larry to testify about a long list of items, especially about details of his affair with Rozanne and his suspicions about Gailiunas's involvement in Rozanne's death. To allow Larry to testify about these subjects, Hagood said, either would be a violation of the hearsay principle, which prohibits a witness from commenting about anything beyond his own personal range of experience, or irrelevant as far as Andy's guilt or innocence was concerned. "Hearsay" and "irrelevance" had become prosecution mantras.

For example, the prosecution claimed it would be hearsay if Larry were to be allowed to tell the jury anything that Rozanne had told him about Gailiunas if Larry himself had not been present. This would include several alleged incidents that the defense desperately wanted the jury to hear, such as Larry's claim that Rozanne told him how she and Gailiunas once engaged in a literal tug of war over young Peter, each of them pulling on one of his arms. The incident allegedly ended with Gailiunas brandishing a shotgun and threatening his estranged wife. There was another time, Larry related, when Rozanne told him how Gailiunas had threatened to inject himself with an unknown lethal substance. And there was a third, more innocent tale in which Larry related how his and Rozanne's affair had begun.

After listening to this preview of what the defense wanted the jury to hear, Hagood urged McDowell to purge it *all*, particularly the testimony about the alleged threats with the hypodermic needle.

Judge McDowell rejected the prosecution request to censor the testimony about how the affair began, but he quickly agreed to disallow any testimony about the shotgun incident. He seemed puzzled about the needle episode. Why did the defense think that was important, he asked, since it did not involve a threat against Rozanne?

Lesser jumped at the chance to answer. "We think it shows Dr. Gailiunas's predisposition to use a needle as a means of death," Lesser replied.

The judge shook his head. "That's too farfetched for me," he said, ruling that the jury would not be allowed to hear the tale.

The first thing Larry told the jury when they returned to the room was about his lunch with Rozanne that marked the beginning of their affair.

The second major incident he recounted was about the telephone call to Rozanne's house on the evening of the attack. Since he had personally participated in that event, the prosecution could not score with a hearsay objection. It was one of the few even mildly controversial issues about which Larry was allowed to testify without a torrent of protests from Hagood.

"On October 4, 1983, did you call Rozanne at home?" Lesser asked.

"Yes," Larry said, "and young Peter answered the phone."

Larry said when he asked to speak to Rozanne he heard a man in the background yell, "Hang up the goddamn phone." After that, the connection was severed.

Lesser asked if Larry thought he knew whose voice that had been.

"In my opinion," Larry answered emphatically, "it was Dr. Gailiunas."

After his unsuccessful attempt to reach Rozanne by telephone, Larry said he drove to the house and found that police were already there. He identified himself as "Rozanne Gailiunas's boyfriend" to an officer at the door.

"And then what?" Lesser prompted.

"I asked him what had happened," Larry said. "I asked, 'Did the doctor beat her up or shoot her?' "

A few minutes later, he said, he was asked to go to the police station for questioning and for chemical tests designed to determine if he had recently fired a weapon. After he was accused by one of the detectives of committing the crime, Larry said, he called an attorney and asked him to come to the police station to represent him.

"After October 4 did you ever tell Dr. Gailiunas that you thought he had killed his own wife?" Lesser asked.

Before Larry could respond, Hagood leaped to his feet. "I object, your honor," he bellowed at parade-ground volume. "That's irrelevant to what we're discussing here."

"Sustained," Judge McDowell said tiredly.

Lesser tried from a different direction. "Do you believe," he asked Larry, "that Peter Gailiunas had anything to do with Rozanne Gailiunas's death?"

"Yes, I do," Larry answered smoothly. "I've had that belief since 1983."

During cross-examination, Chapman tried valiantly to discredit Larry's version of the telephone incident. Chapman succeeded in getting Larry to admit that he was only 50 percent sure it was Dr. Gailiunas's voice he heard on the phone, and that in his initial statement to police he had said only that it was "a man's voice." Homing in on the telephone call, Chapman said, "Tell me *exactly* what happened."

Chapman listened carefully to Larry's recitation, then asked him if he remembered that he had first told officers that he had made the call at 6:40 P.M., which would have put it five to ten minutes after police arrived at the scene. The implication was that it was one of the police officers who had ordered young Peter to hang up, not Gailiunas, as Larry believed.

Chapman did *not* say that none of the officers who had testified up until then could remember the phone ringing while he was in the house.

Eventually, after considerable prodding by Lesser on redirect, Larry explained that it was an extremely stressful day and that he might have erred in the time he estimated making the call by as much as forty minutes, which would have set the time of the occurrence before the paramedics and police arrived.

Before letting Larry leave the witness stand, Lesser had one more item he wanted to question him about, one that might cause additional doubt in jurors' minds about the prosecution contention that Andy operated in a vacuum when he attacked Rozanne.

In response to the defense attorney's questions, Larry prosaically related how, on the afternoon of the attack on Rozanne, he had been riding his bicycle down a little-used road in the suburb where he lived when a car mysteriously appeared behind him and struck the rear of his bicycle, sending him and the bike sprawling into a ditch. He suffered only minor scratches and bruises.

"Did you see who was driving the car?" Lesser asked.

"Not clearly," Larry replied, "but it looked like a little old lady."

"Are you sure?" Lesser asked.

"Well," Larry responded, "it could have been a man with long hair or someone wearing a wig."

What Lesser was trying to do was raise the possibility that someone was trying to kill both Larry *and* Rozanne, that there were simultaneous hits planned for that day and that forces greater than Andy were at work. But it was too far beyond the jurors' grasp of the case; Lesser's attempt slipped by without impact. While there was later an obvious attempt on Larry's life, it did not come for almost three years, and Judge McDowell definitely was not going to let him testify about *that*.

In any case, Chapman quickly demolished this testimony when he got Larry back on recross.

"Do you think the driver of that car was Dr. Gailiunas trying to take you out?" the prosecutor asked bluntly.

Larry, who had little reason to protect Gailiunas but every reason to try to punish him, replied firmly: "No."

When Mitchell and Lesser first tried to call two Richardson police officers who had questioned young Peter about his father's presence at the house on the day of the attack on his mother, Judge McDowell refused, honoring a prosecution objection that the officer's testimony would be hearsay. The defense argued that the statements from the boy were what is known in the law as "excited utterances" and were, therefore, an exception to the hearsay rule.

At first, the judge agreed with the prosecution, saying that remarks made hours after the event could hardly be considered "excited utterances," which were generally recognized as statements blurted during the heat of the moment. He changed his mind, however, after listening to testimony from a health care professional named Jan Marie Delipsey, who specialized in working with children and adult victims of post-traumatic stress disorder.

Delipsey, called by the defense, explained out of the jury's presence that children, particularly a child as young as Peter Gailiunas was at the time, did not react to stress the same way as adults. It took them much longer to focus on traumatic events. Often, she said, they went through a period of denial, especially when a loved one was involved.

Under the circumstances, she said, Little Peter's reaction—first claiming and then denying his father's presence—was more typical than unusual. His comments, she said, even though they came hours after the event, could, under the principles of applied child psychology, be considered "excited utterances."

Obviously impressed with Delipsey's testimony, Judge McDowell changed his mind and told Mitchell and Lesser they could call the officers.

Lieutenant Mike Corley, who had been a detective at the time of the attack on Rozanne, working on the case under McGowan, and Officer Cynthia Percival, who had been Cynthia Coker at the time, testified that young Peter had implied in separate interviews that his father had been at the house at 804 Loganwood Drive on the afternoon of the attack.

Although the prosecution tried to discredit the boy's observations, Lesser was successful in getting Percival to admit that she placed enough credence in what the boy had said to use the statements, together with Larry's claim that Dr. Gailiunas had shot Rozanne, as a basis for a request to have the boy placed under protective custody so he could not be influenced by his father or his grandmother. Little Peter told officers it was his father who ordered him to hang up the phone, and Larry had testified that he thought the voice had been Gailiunas's.

To discredit this, Chapman called Wayne Dobbs, a husky, balding policeman with a radio announcer's deep voice. He said he had been the first patrolman to go inside Rozanne's house on the day of the attack. When he walked inside, he said, he was attacked both verbally and physically by Little Peter, who obviously was upset by events. Dobbs testified that he had gone into the back bedroom to see if he could help the paramedics and was returning to the front of the house when the telephone rang. Little Peter answered the call, he said, and was talking into the instrument when Dobbs ordered him to hang up.

"There is a very strong possibility that I cursed at him," Dobbs said primly, explaining his lapse of professionalism by claiming that he was "scared and faced with the worst crime scene I'd ever been faced with before or since."

On cross-examination, Lesser pounded at Dobbs, pointing out that the officer, who at the time was a veteran of more than five years with the department, should have had more presence of mind than he admitted to. Besides, Lesser said, Dobbs had previously said he did not remember being the one who gave the command to young Peter. Was he lying then, Lesser implied, or was he lying now?

In response to Lesser's questions, Dobbs admitted that his recollection of the telephone incident was recent.

"How do you account for that?" Lesser asked sharply.

"Delayed recall," Dobbs replied smoothly. "It's quite common in cases like that."

Lesser gaped at him in amazement. *"Delayed recall,"* he repeated sarcastically. Boring in, he asked, "Do you remember participating in a test in which your voice and Dr. Gailiunas's voice was played for Larry Aylor so he could try to determine exactly whose voice he had heard instructing Little Peter to hang up the goddamn phone?" Lesser asked.

Uncertainty flickered in Dobb's eyes. "No," he said slowly, "I don't remember that."

"That's good," Lesser shot back, "because it never happened."

Dobbs had stepped over the landmine.

37

By February 26, Lesser and Mitchell were nearing the end of their list of witnesses. While they felt Bux, Gailiunas, and Aylor had made an impact on the jury, they knew they had still not come close to overcoming the damage done by Andy's confession. If anything was going to clinch a verdict against their client, it would be that damning admission. Their lifeboat was the set of tapes of the December 20 interrogation, the recordings that the defense lawyers did not know existed until they were handed over nonchalantly by Chapman a few days previously.

Lesser and Mitchell's first line of defense, made clear early in the trial, had been to try to keep the confessions, especially the videotaped one, from going before the jury. When they failed in that attempt, all the defense attorneys could do was try to modify the impact.

Although there were several ways they could have done that, each attempt had, up until then, been blocked by rulings from Judge McDowell. They had sought, for instance, to introduce testimony from Bill and Carol Garland, which they hoped would at least cast doubt on the theory that Andy had acted alone. But the judge had closed off that avenue.

Then, they hoped to be able to soften the blow by demonstrating through a rigorous cross-examination of McGowan that Andy had been coerced into making the admissions by a devious detective, who they claimed ran roughshod over Andy's constitutional rights in the process. But they got little satisfaction from their questioning of the investigator.

As a backup, the defense attorneys had Jan Hemphill, who would testify about the prosecution's maneuverings to get the confession. But again, they had been thwarted by Judge McDowell, who rejected their request to let Hemphill appear in front of the jury.

The tapes represented a new, and almost certainly last, opportunity for the defense team to do any serious repair to the damage caused by the confessions. But they also knew that getting this information before the jury was not going to be easy. By then, Judge McDowell was showing the strain of being required on a daily basis to referee the increasingly bitter squabbles between the prosecution and defense attorneys and still keep the trial on track. As a result, he seemed to be exhibiting a growing tendency toward the prosecution, repeatedly shooting down defense attempts to stray from the corridor defined by Chapman.

Lesser and Mitchell were going to have to present their case carefully. They *knew* they were going to get strong opposition from the prosecutors. They were *almost certain* that, under ordinary circumstances, the judge was going to come down in the state's favor. So they had to set up the request in such a way as to get McDowell thinking about how his action—if he denied them the chance to pursue this new field of inquiry—was going to look to an appeals court. Given his druthers, no one in the courtroom wanted to try the case again.

Gingerly, Mitchell broached the subject of the tapes. And, predictably, the prosecution responded with a cascade of objections. Judge McDowell sent the jury out of the room. "Okay," he said abruptly, setting his jaw, "let's hear the arguments."

Mitchell hurriedly began making his case. On December 20, Andy had asked for a lawyer no less than a dozen times, he said, and each time he had been ignored. Those repeated refusals to summon a lawyer were the same as McGowan's refusal to let Andy "think about it" before he broke down on February 27, Mitchell contended, and both were clear violations of Andy's constitutional rights. For that reason, the defense lawyer continued, Judge McDowell should tell the jury to disregard the confessions.

Chapman disagreed, arguing, disingenuously it seemed, that McGowan had never *refused* to stop the interrogation in February. "He just told Andy, 'I want it now,' " which the ADA asserted was not the same thing, that if Andy had wanted to stop the interview he should have been more explicit.

Judge McDowell weighed the arguments. Finally, he said, in his opinion, the words "I want to think about it" did not, of themselves, raise the issue of voluntariness. That is, just because Andy said he wanted to think about it did not mean that because he was *not* given time to think about it, that it meant that his subsequent confession was coerced or was given involuntarily. The fact that McGowan had not specifically told Andy "no" when he said "I want to think about it" was significant. Since the detective had not said "no," he had not violated Andy's rights by going ahead.

Mitchell shook his head. "Your honor," he pleaded, "we believe those words—that he wanted time to think about it—was an attempt by Andy Hopper to invoke his right to remain silent and end the interview."

Staring at Judge McDowell challengingly, he added, "We believe this is a question of fact, not of law," meaning that in the defense's view it was a question that was not open to judicial discretion, that Judge McDowell's opinion was not important because it was not an issue that was within his purview to decide.

Chapman, anticipating a defense request to re-call McGowan to the stand, jumped to his feet.

"It doesn't raise a factual issue upon which the confession turns," the prosecutor argued, explaining that there was too big a time gap between the December 20 interrogation and the February 27 confession for there to be a connection between the two events, therefore there was a question of relevancy.

Judge McDowell agreed with Chapman. "I still don't see a 'fact' issue," he said. "I sustain the state's objection."

Mitchell persisted. "I didn't address the issue of relevancy," he said. "I just wanted to see if you would instruct the jury to disregard the confession."

"I've determined that the confession is admissible and I don't think the jury is the proper forum to review my decision," Judge McDowell replied sternly. "I *do* have legal basis for my rulings."

Mitchell had reckoned that was coming. If the judge would not tell the jury to disregard the confession, he said, the defense would like to re-call McGowan, Investigator McKenzie, and Jan Hemphill to query them *in front of the jury* about the process under which Andy gave his confession, using the December 20 interrogation as an example of how investigators had systematically worked on Andy, setting the stage for his eventual breakdown. The tapes, he added, amply demonstrated how investigators had violated Andy's constitutional rights, and the defense wanted the jury to be aware of that.

"I don't think anything would be served by getting Lieutenant Mc-

Gowan or Judge Hemphill before the jury," the judge said. "I'm not going to permit new testimony from Lieutenant McGowan to go before the jury if the state objects."

On cue, Chapman objected.

"Sustained!" Judge McDowell responded quickly.

Mitchell did not want to give up.

"I'd like to call Lieutenant McGowan [before the jury] and start asking him questions," he suggested. "Then, if the prosecution has objections they can make them then."

Judge McDowell was faced with another close call. What the lawyers were arguing about was a fine point that was not clearly defined in any of the case histories he had been able to find. Also, he was weary of the constant bickering.

"I'd like to get *something* before the jurors," he sighed. "They haven't heard any substantial testimony for five days."

Sensing an opportunity, Mitchell continued. The defense's earlier cross-examination of the detective had been done before he and Lesser knew about the tapes of the December 20 interrogation, he said, and therefore they did not have all the facts available upon which to base their questions. If the judge would let them re-call McGowan, they could question him more thoroughly.

Besides, Lesser said, entering the debate, the long time between the December session and the one in February was immaterial because what had happened at both sessions demonstrated the attitude of investigators. "It relates to police conduct," he contended.

Chapman resorted to form: "What the defense wants to go into is irrelevant," he said, lighting Lesser's fuse.

"How can proof of lying ever be 'irrelevant' in a trial?" he screeched. "The jury has the right to know what kind of truth teller this witness is. It goes to his credibility. It proves he lied to the jury under oath."

McGowan was a "liar," the defense attorney proclaimed loudly, reminding Judge McDowell that when he had cross-examined McGowan earlier—*before* he knew about the December 20 tapes—he had specifically asked the investigator what he would do if someone he was interrogating asked for a lawyer. In response, McGowan had replied that he would stop the questioning immediately and accede to the request. Lesser said the tapes undeniably showed that McGowan did not practice what he preached, that he had willfully and repeatedly ignored Andy's requests for a lawyer, which violated Andy's constitutional rights.

"It's clear that Mr. Hopper asked for a lawyer a dozen times," Lesser continued. "In response, Lieutenant McGowan disparaged lawyers, called them 'bloodsuckers,' and said he didn't need one, that all one was going to do was tell him to shut up. *This*," Lesser contended, "is the heart and soul of the defense case. This confession was involuntary."

What the defense wanted, he summarized, was a chance to impeach McGowan.

Judge McDowell considered what Lesser had said. Viewed from that perspective, he said thoughtfully, the defense had the right to impeach a major prosecution witness. And the tapes *had* given the defense evidence on which to base a renewed attack. Possibly worried as well about how an appeals court was going to look at the record, he promised Lesser and Mitchell that he would let them re-call the investigator if the defense lawyers would strictly limit their questions to the issue of whether Andy had, under the legal definition, been requesting an attorney.

Willing to take whatever opportunity presented itself to grill McGowan again, Lesser and Mitchell readily agreed.

It had become more and more evident, however, as the trial progressed that things would not move smoothly. Virtually nothing up until then had been accomplished without acrimonious debate and snide comments by lawyers from both sides. The tape issue was not going to be an exception. Despite McDowell's announced intention to allow a new cross-examination of McGowan, the prosecution raised new objections the first thing the next morning, even bringing in one of the district attorney's appeals experts to bolster their arguments.

"They're just trying to use this issue to bootstrap into more questioning of Lieutenant McGowan," Hagood argued, adding that whatever answers the investigator made were irrelevant to the case before the jury. "Their theory is that just because Lieutenant McGowan may have been bad on December 20 he was bad on February 27. They can't do that," he contended.

Indeed they could, Judge McDowell announced. "I just feel I *have* to let the defense do it."

"Impeachment for bad acts are not allowed unless those acts result in a conviction," Chapman persisted. "What McGowan would have done if the defendant had asked for a lawyer doesn't matter because he never asked for a lawyer on February 27."

Judge McDowell, running out of patience, tried to put an end to the debate. "Men," he said sharply, "I'm going to stay with my ruling. I've got to do this. I think it's the right thing to do." Turning to Lesser, he reminded him that he was going to strictly limit his questioning to make sure it did not stray outside his announced boundaries.

Unwilling to give any unnecessary ground, Chapman demanded that the defense reveal its specific questions before McGowan was called. "I'm very concerned about getting inadmissible evidence before the jury," he contended.

Judge McDowell shook his head. "I can't tell the defense what questions to ask," he said.

McGowan and the jury were summoned at 10:49. Within thirteen minutes the jury was sent out for the first time. In that brief time span, Hagood and Chapman objected six times to Lesser's questions. Before the examination was over one hour and forty-five minutes later, the prosecution filed an additional thirty-nine objections—an average of about one every two and a half minutes—and the jury was removed three more times.

Despite the frequent objections that slowed the pace of the questioning and prohibited the defense from building momentum, the defense was able to underline its point that it believed McGowan had violated Andy's constitutional rights to have a lawyer present during an interrogation.

For his part, McGowan denied that, claiming the discussion he and Andy were having had nothing to do with the crime itself and, therefore, Andy had no need for a lawyer. The detective said he knew that whatever details he extracted from Andy could not be used against him; that he was seeking "information" rather than material that could be used at a trial.

His voice rising, Lesser argued that whatever McGowan had thought about the purpose of the interrogation did not matter because Andy had the *right* to have an attorney there. The detective countered that Andy had never specifically asked for an attorney.

Lesser was flabbergasted. He pointed out that Andy had said that he "thought" he should have an attorney with him, that he "should be" talking to an attorney, that he did not "want to say anything else without an attorney," and that he was going to "wait" until his lawyer was there before saying anything else. Flipping through the transcript of the

December 20 tapes, Lesser found a passage he thought was particularly pertinent.

"Here," he said, pointing to the transcript, "Mr. Hopper says, 'I want my attorney,' and McKenzie responds: 'Want a Coke?' and you say, 'Well, I want some coffee,' and the interrogation continues. What would he have had to say to put an end to the interrogation?"

"He would have to say, 'Put me in my jail cell; I have nothing more to say to you,' " McGowan shot back.

Didn't the investigator think that Andy was entitled to an attorney? Lesser wanted to know.

"It depends on the circumstances," McGowan replied. "I was after *information*," he said, trying to emphasize the distinction, at least in his view, between *information* and *admissible evidence*.

"So then it's all right to violate his constitutional rights?" Lesser asked, setting off an objection from Hagood that was sustained by Judge McDowell.

"Every time Mr. Hopper is asking for an attorney, isn't that an attempt to invoke his constitutional rights?" Lesser asked, approaching from a different angle.

"Objection!" Hagood yelled. "Mr. McGowan can't answer because that is a legal conclusion."

"He doesn't have to be a lawyer to understand the Miranda rights," Lesser countered.

The judge sustained Hagood's objection.

"He *has* to know that when a man says he wants a lawyer, he has to stop talking," Mitchell interjected.

"If he tells me he did it, the interview would end right there," McGowan replied, adding that in his view Andy's references to a lawyer were simply his way of saying that he did not want to talk about the crime itself. "I didn't see it as any indication that he wanted to stop talking to *me*. He just didn't want to talk about the offense."

Lesser's frustration was evident. "He kept saying he wanted an attorney—" he began.

"He said he wanted *an* attorney," McGowan interrupted, his voice rising as well. "That's not the same as him asking me to get him one."

Lesser took another tack. "Did you read him his rights when he was arrested?"

"I don't think so," McGowan replied. "I wasn't asking him anything then." He read Hopper his rights when they got to the jail.

But what about when he asked for an attorney during the interrogation at the jail? Lesser asked.

"I wanted information that may have been inadmissible," McGowan said.

"So that gave you the right to ignore Miranda?" Lesser yelled.

"No sir," McGowan said before Hagood jumped to his feet and yelled at Lesser, who yelled back.

Judge McDowell, visibly displeased, sent the jury out of the room. Standing with his hands on his hips, the judge took both Lesser and Hagood to task.

"I'm not going to have any more interchanges between the lawyers in the presence of the jury," the judge said angrily. "The next time there is a sidebar remark addressed by any lawyer to the other lawyer, I'm going to send the jury out and I'm going to sanction that lawyer for contempt of court. If you have to come down here every day and try the case out of the jail, that's going to be the way it's done."

Both Lesser and Hagood sank into their seats, appropriately chastised.

The exchange between Hagood and Lesser effectively ended McGowan's cross-examination on the December 20 interrogation, but the investigator was called back one more time before the day was over as a rebuttal witness for the prosecution.

By calling McGowan, Chapman hoped to counter the defense's contention, raised earlier, that there was a sizable time gap on the afternoon of the attack on Rozanne during which Dr. Peter Gailiunas had no alibi. According to defense witnesses, Gailiunas had been unable to account for the time between roughly 3:45 P.M., when he was seen at Parkland Hospital, and about 5 P.M., when an associate said he chatted with him outside his office door.

Under Chapman's questioning, McGowan told how he had driven from Parkland Hospital to Rozanne's house by three different routes and was convinced that Gailiunas could not have made it to 804 Loganwood Drive and back to his office within the prescribed time limitations.

"How long did it take you to make those trips?" Lesser asked on cross-examination.

"I don't know," McGowan replied, adding that he had taken no notes on the experiment.

Throughout the trial the defense had pounded away at the investigators' failure to take notes to substantiate their testimony. In every instance, investigators said they were relying strictly on memory. This practice was thrown in the detective's face a few minutes later when Lesser asked him to describe what he had found to be the quickest route between Parkland Hospital and Rozanne's house. After the investigator recited the list of streets he had taken, Lesser pointed out that he could not have taken the route he claimed he had because two of the streets did not intersect.

"Oh," McGowan said in surprise. "I forgot Central Expressway."

Lesser pounced. "That goes to show just how faulty memory can be, doesn't it, lieutenant? Doesn't that prove the adage that a short pencil is better than a long memory?"

"Yes sir," McGowan answered sheepishly.

38

Before resting its case and handing the baton back to the prosecution for rebuttal, Mitchell and Lesser wanted to make one more attempt to let the jury hear Jan Hemphill.

Unlike McGowan, whom Judge McDowell reluctantly had allowed to be questioned before the jury, Hemphill was to be heard first outside the jury's presence. If the judge then determined that what she had to say should be shared with the panel, jurors would be summoned and the process would be repeated. But, since it was midafternoon and the judge anticipated that Hemphill's questioning might take some time, he sent the jurors home for the day.

In an almost-empty courtroom, Lesser began for the second time the unpleasant task of making a colleague publicly confess her mistakes. He started at the beginning.

Hemphill, poker faced and as terse as usual, answered his questions directly and concisely.

She had been appointed to defend Andy on December 29, 1988, she said, and in her first interview with him she told him the same story he had told investigators: that he had passed $1,000 of the money and the data on Rozanne along to Chip. As far as she knew at the time, there was no physical evidence linking Andy to the attack. At that point, she did not know that a pistol had been recovered.

"On the basis of what the prosecutors had told you, what was the evidence at that time against Mr. Hopper?" Lesser asked.

"It wasn't great," Hemphill replied succinctly.

Did you have a copy of the December 20 tapes? Lesser wanted to know.

"I don't think I *ever* got those," Hemphill said, adding that she certainly did *not* have them by the time in February when Hagood asked for permission to polygraph Andy.

According to Hemphill's memory of the sequence of events, Chapman had told her that Andy had fingered Chip as the "shooter," but the prosecutor wanted to talk to Andy to help investigators track down Chip.

"Chapman wanted the first and the last people in the chain," Hemphill said, "while those in the middle were out on bond." Because she thought Hopper fell in the middle, she was not particularly worried about his fate. She was so unworried, in fact, that she agreed to let Hopper go to Richardson to be polygraphed.

"Why would you let him take a state polygraph without first giving him one of your own?" Lesser asked.

"No good reason," said Hemphill.

"Did you request to be present?"

"No."

"Would a competent lawyer let his client be questioned in a capital murder case without that lawyer being there?" Lesser asked uncomfortably.

Hemphill did not hesitate. "Obviously not," she replied dryly.

Lesser quickly followed with two more questions relating to competency: Would a competent lawyer let her client be polygraphed, or go to police headquarters without specific instructions on how to respond?

Hemphill answered both questions negatively.

"Would a competent lawyer keep on representing her client under those circumstances?" Lesser asked.

"I should have withdrawn," Hemphill replied candidly.

Finally, Lesser got to the most important question of all. In a sad voice he asked Hemphill if she thought her actions amounted to ineffective assistance of counsel, one of the most damning accusations that can be leveled against a defense lawyer.

Hemphill looked directly at the prosecution team and answered unwaveringly, "Yes. I fell below the standards."

If she had been there after the polygraph was administered, Lesser asked, did she think the results would have been different?

"The questioning would have been cut off," she replied.

Chapman, apparently surprised by Hemphill's responses, asked permission to pursue that issue. Judge McDowell agreed.

"You would have stopped the questioning?" the ADA asked.

Hemphill shot him a withering look. "I sure would have," she replied.

Chapman asked her how she could say that since the ultimate decision on whether to continue rested not with the lawyer but with the defendant. "That would have been his decision, would it not?"

Hemphill shot him a contemptuous look. "Of course," she said.

His rhythm broken, Lesser tried to reestablish the pattern of his questions. In a brusque series that the defense attorney and Hemphill had obviously worked out beforehand, Lesser confirmed that Hemphill felt retrospectively that it had been her duty to be with Andy when he was taken to Richardson and that by the time he had confessed it was too late for her to try to make a plea-bargain arrangement with the district attorney's office.

After he confessed, why did she continue to let investigators have access to her client? Lesser asked.

"I didn't see how he could be any worse off," Hemphill replied.

Hagood rose, objecting that Lesser was intentionally trying to embarrass Hemphill.

"Do you think I'm trying to do that?" Lesser asked Hemphill softly.

"I think you're trying to protect your client," she responded.

Once the questions were over, Chapman asked that the jury not be allowed to hear Hemphill's testimony. How she felt about her representation of Andy was irrelevant, he argued.

Judge McDowell agreed; the jury never got to hear Jan Hemphill.

The defense had run out of witnesses. Feeling they had been consistently and unfairly rebuffed in attempts to present testimony pertinent to Andy's defense, Mitchell and Lesser reluctantly surrendered the initiative to Chapman and Hagood for rebuttal. It was 2:30 P.M., Wednesday, February 26, day sixteen of the first phase of the trial.

During the remainder of that afternoon, and all of the next two days, the prosecutors brought forth still more testimony designed to seal Andy's fate. During that period, Chapman and Hagood scored with two powerful witnesses.

The first was a clean-cut twenty-nine-year-old convict named Michael Matthews, who was serving a twenty-year sentence for burglary and robbery.

In October 1990, Matthews said, when he was sharing a cell with

Andy, Andy told him that he had been hired by a woman named "Joy" or "Joyce" to kill another woman. Andy also claimed, Matthews said, that he gained entrance to the victim's house by posing as a floral deliveryman, that he had tied the woman's hands, stuffed cotton in her mouth, and shot her.

"What was your reaction?" Chapman asked.

"I didn't want to hear any more," Matthews said, obviously nervous about being called to testify, mindful of what could happen to snitches in prison.

"What was Mr. Hopper's demeanor when he told you this?" the prosecutor pressed.

"Looking into his eyes was like looking into the eyes of a fish," Matthews replied. "He had no emotion; no remorse."

Mitchell objected to Matthews's testimony on the grounds that it was too vague; that he could not identify the victim, and that the facts of the crime, as related by Matthews, were only partially correct.

"Overruled!" Judge McDowell said.

The second witness was Andy's boyhood friend Buddy Wright. His testimony was more emotional and potentially much more damaging than Matthews's.

Wright said he had kept up with Andy in the years since they were childhood members of the same church and was not surprised when he received a telephone call from him in midsummer 1988. The purpose of the call, however, did surprise him.

Andy told him, Wright said, that he had been accused of killing someone and, although he was innocent, he needed money to help pay for a lawyer. Wright said he scraped together $5,000 by selling some stock he had been holding on to and flew to Dallas to personally deliver the money. Soon afterward, Andy fled and Wright did not hear from him again until March 1989. Wright did not know it, but by then Andy had confessed to McGowan that he had attacked Rozanne. The contact he had with Andy at that time, Wright said, was via a letter.

Mitchell and Lesser froze. They were aware that a letter existed, but they had never seen it and Hopper's memory of what he had written was vague. When Wright testified that Andy had admitted in the letter that he had killed Rozanne, Lesser's jaw dropped.

With a theatrical flourish, Chapman temporarily broke off his questioning. Assuming a position immediately in front of the jury box, Chapman, in a soft uninflected voice, dramatically read the letter.

"I am the one who killed this person," Andy wrote. "I know that by telling this that I am taking a chance of receiving the death penalty, but Buddy even if this is my destiny I have been given such a peace with God that what ever shall be is His will."

Chapman paused and looked up at Wright. Both he and Andy were crying. He continued: "Buddy, I have been so bound by this for five and a half years that every time I got on my knees to pray and ask for forgiveness, I couldn't even ask without feeling so guilty for what I've done. Now, Buddy, I know God has forgiven me of all my sins and is preparing a home for me someday."

Chapman again looked up at Wright. "How do you feel about this letter?" he asked.

Wright fought to control his voice. "I wish I'd put 'return to sender' on it and sent it back," he groaned.

One of the prosecution's last witnesses was Peter Gailiunas III, Rozanne's son. The bespectacled youth, who had been only four and a half when his mother was murdered, was a twelve-a-half-year-old seventh-grader when Chapman called him to the stand, ostensibly to try to set the record straight on whether his father had been in the house that afternoon.

Dressed in a Sunday suit and tie, with comb marks clearly discernible in his short brown hair, young Peter peeked over the edge of the witness stand and, in a squeaky little boy's voice, related how he remembered going ice-skating that fateful afternoon in 1983 and being picked up by Rozanne, whom he now referred to as his "first mother."

They went home, he said, and he went into his room to take a nap. When he awakened and was unable to rouse his mother, he called his father.

Did he remember speaking on the telephone at any other time that afternoon after talking to his father? Chapman asked.

"No," young Peter said without hesitation, pushing his horn-rimmed glasses up on his nose.

"Did you go outside?" Chapman asked.

"I don't recall," the boy replied.

The prosecutor asked Peter if he had seen *anyone* at his house from the time he and his mother got home until the paramedics arrived.

"No," he said firmly.

Figuring they had nothing to gain and everything to lose in the eyes of the jury, who might regard any questions as an attempt at badgering, Mitchell and Lesser waived cross-examination.

Factwise, the boy contributed nothing to the prosecution's case, but his appearance was important nonetheless: Chapman carefully planned the scene to win sympathy from the jury.

Since the first day of the trial when the defense had first made Thorazine an issue, prosecutors had been haunted by the apparently inexplicable presence of the drug in Rozanne's body. At first they tried to make it sound plausible that Rozanne had taken the drug on her own to help relieve depression she was suffering as a result of her marital problems. But that explanation fell apart under the weight of medical testimony that indicated it would be very unusual for *anyone* to take Thorazine voluntarily since it had such unpleasant effects, much less a registered nurse who would know better.

In another attempt to try to resolve the Thorazine mystery, prosecutors called Robert Nalepka, a bearded chemist at the laboratory that performed the test on the sample of Rozanne's blood for Parkland Hospital on October 4, 1983.

Chapman asked Nalepka if he believed in 1983 that Thorazine had been correctly identified in the blood sample.

"I certainly did," the chemist replied.

"Do you still believe that today?" Chapman asked.

"I would say it would be hard to say whether it was or was not," Nalepka equivocated.

"Why do you doubt it?" Chapman wanted to know.

Because, Nalepka explained, he had later learned that there was a contaminant that gave an identical reading as Thorazine. He estimated the odds that it had indeed been Thorazine in the 1983 blood sample at about 50–50.

On cross-examination, however, Lesser ripped apart Nalepka's testimony.

Had the chemist seen any articles in professional journals relating to similar problems with a contaminant, Lesser asked?

No, said Nalepka.

Could he recall recording any other such false positives at the lab in the same general time frame?

Nalepka said he could not.

Did you see any similar results after that? Lesser wanted to know.

He had not, Nalepka admitted.

In light of your answers, Lesser asked, what do you now think were the odds that Thorazine had been correctly identified in 1983?

Nalepka refigured. "About sixty-six percent," he now replied.

With his testimony in doubt as a result of Lesser's aggressive questioning, the chemist's claims were all but demolished the next day when the defense called Dr. James Garriott, the former chief toxicologist for the Dallas County Medical Examiner's Office. Garriott also had been one of the founders of the lab at which Nalepka worked and had devised the testing process the facility had used to identify Thorazine.

Garriott testified that under the double-check system he had instituted at the lab, it would have been difficult to misidentify Thorazine since a contaminant would have to create a false reading in two separate sections of the automated test report.

"In my opinion, it appears that Thorazine was properly identified," he said.

Asked to review the laboratory records for the month before and two months after the time that Rozanne's sample was tested—some four hundred and thirty tests—Garriott testified he could find only three other reports of Thorazine, two of which also showed another drug commonly administered along with Thorazine. In the single case where Thorazine alone was found, it proved to be in a sample from a patient at a psychiatric hospital.

"Would you expect to see more false positives if it had been caused by a contaminant?" Mitchell asked, intent on destroying the state's new claim that Thorazine had been misdiagnosed.

Garriott nodded. "The fact that there have not been lends more credence to the belief that it was a positive identification," Garriott replied.

Looking satisfied, Mitchell asked: "Do you have an opinion about that report?"

"There is nothing," Garriott answered, picking his words carefully, "that leads me to believe it was not a valid reading."

*   *   *

Chapman was unable to shake Garriott's testimony, and an attempt to refute it by calling still another prosecution expert ended abruptly with an attack from Lesser.

The third expert, who worked under Garriott for a long period, wilted when Lesser compared his credentials and experience to Garriott's, and pointed out that the witness was working on equipment designed by Garriott when he claimed to have found the possible error.

"Do you think you know more than the creator?" Lesser barked, seeking to make quick work of the witness.

Startled by the harshness of the question and the accusatory tone in which it was asked, the witness stammered that he did not.

Both sides agreed to end testimony at 3:20 P.M. on February 28, eighteen working days after the parade of witnesses began. Already it had become the longest guilt/innocence trial in the county in recent memory as well as one of the most bitter. But, true to the spirit of the proceeding, it would not end without a final dispute.

After sending the jurors home for the weekend with a caution to bring a suitcase on Monday in anticipation of the beginning of deliberation, Judge McDowell announced that there would be one more witness: a public defender in Judge McDowell's court improbably named King Solomon.

The judge said he was calling Solomon as his own witness, outside the jury's presence, to give still another side to the defense-raised issue of whether Jan Hemphill should be allowed to testify.

When he took the stand, Solomon said he remembered a comment Hemphill made about the prosecutors in a case she was handling: "I can't believe what the bastards did to me." It was his interpretation, Solomon said, that Hemphill was referring to the Hopper case and how she had been treated by Chapman and Hagood.

When Solomon finished his brief testimony, Judge McDowell swiveled to Mitchell and Lesser.

"I understand you would like to put that before the jury," he said, not unkindly, "but right now I think the jury's heard all it's going to hear."

39

For three hours late in the afternoon and evening of Sunday, March 1, the opposing lawyers, taking advantage of the weekend day by showing up in jeans, cutoffs, Bermuda shorts, and baseball caps, met in an empty courtroom in an empty building to discuss the items that Judge McDowell proposed to include in the list of instructions, commonly called a "charge," that he would deliver to the jurors the next morning.

The fact that it appeared to be a democratic session was somewhat misleading; although the judge had asked for their input, in the final analysis what went into the charge was strictly up to him. And what he decided was not propitious for the defense.

The indictment against Andy read capital murder. If the judge's charge was to follow the indictment literally, he would tell the jury that there were only two possible verdicts: 1. Not guilty. 2. Guilty of capital murder.

In the highly unlikely event that the jury would find Andy not guilty, he would walk out of the courtroom a free man. Not even Lesser or Mitchell dared hope for that.

If the jury found him guilty of capital murder, the proceeding would then move immediately into what is called the penalty phase, in effect a second trial at the end of which the same jurors would decide what the punishment would be.

However, it was within Judge McDowell's purview to give the jurors a choice of a third verdict, and that was what Lesser and Mitchell urged. Realizing there was virtually no chance the jurors were going to acquit their client in light of the confessions, the defense lawyers beseeched the judge to give jurors the option of finding Andy guilty of a reduced charge of *attempted* capital murder.

If that option were to be given and accepted by the jury, Andy would then be sentenced to prison for a term to be decided by McDowell. The jury would be dismissed and no second trial would be required.

After considering the defense request, Judge McDowell refused. He did not say why he had made that decision, nor did he have to.

At that point, Andy's fate was all but sealed.

The next morning the lawyers filed silently into the courtroom. The mood was tense. The trial had reached the stage where all the testimony had been heard and there remained only two things to do before the case went to the jury for a verdict: Judge McDowell had to deliver his charge and the lawyers had to present their closing statements.

With little preamble, the judge solemnly began laying down guidelines for the jurors to follow when they locked themselves into their deliberation room and started debating Andy's fate. The first thing they should do, he said, was agree not to rely strictly on a confession as a determinant of guilt since that alone was insufficient under the law.

"There must be evidence independent of the confession that the crime alleged was committed," he cautioned, adding, "and if you have a reasonable doubt that the crime alleged was committed, then you will acquit the defendant."

Possibly as a result of the defense's aggressive attempts to prove that one or more others might have participated in the attack on Rozanne and were responsible for an action that at least contributed to her death, Judge McDowell also explained the legal interpretation of reasonable doubt, instructing the jurors in what to look for and how to come to grips with it. Above all, they had to be careful in distinguishing "reasonable doubt" from "all possible doubt."

"A 'reasonable doubt,'" he explained, "is a doubt based on reason and common sense after a careful and impartial consideration of all the evidence in the case. It is the kind of doubt that would make a reasonable person hesitate to act in the most important of his own affairs."

But, he explained, "all possible doubt" was not the same thing, and it was not the prosecution's job to prove guilt to that degree. Still, if the jury felt there was a reasonable doubt about Andy's guilt, it was their duty to acquit him.

From a practical point of view, the mini-lectures on the differences between "reasonable" and "all possible" doubt may have been splitting hairs. What it boiled down to, really, was that the jury had only two choices, each of which McDowell laid out in stilted legalese, which nevertheless was perfectly intelligible.

"Now, therefore," he read from a prepared statement, "if you find and believe from the evidence beyond a reasonable doubt that on or about the fourth day of October 1983, in Dallas County, Texas, the defendant, George Anderson Hopper, intentionally caused the death of Rozanne Gailiunas . . . by shooting . . . or by strangling . . . while the said defendant was in the course of committing or attempting to commit the offense of burglary . . . then you will find the defendant guilty of the offense of capital murder."

Then he gave them the lone alternative: "Unless you so find and believe from the evidence beyond a reasonable doubt, then you will acquit the defendant and say by your verdict 'not guilty.' "

It was barely 9:30 when Judge McDowell finished delivering his charge, a remarkably early hour considering the erratic hours to which most of the participants had become accustomed during the previous five weeks. But it promised to be a busy and nerve-wracking day and the judge was anxious to get started.

Without further comment, he signaled the lawyers to begin their closing statements. Under the ground rules hashed out the evening before, each side would have ninety minutes to sum up its case. The prosecution would begin and the defense would follow. Then the prosecution would have one more opportunity to speak before the jury began deliberating.

First up was ADA Jim Oatman, who had sat virtually silent at Hagood's left elbow throughout the trial. While he was an unknown quantity to the spectators, he was not unknown to the jury since he had been Hagood's partner during the tedious five-month-long voir dire. He planned to take one third of the prosecution's allotted time.

A sober, soft-spoken man in his early thirties, Oatman walked confidently across the open space between the judge's bench and the jury box and carefully thumbtacked two blowups of Rozanne to the wall behind the witness stand. One was a color portrait of Rozanne alone, the other was a blowup of a snapshot of Rozanne and Little Peter. The pictures were a signal that Oatman's narration would be an emotional one, one designed to gain the jurors' sympathy rather than an outline of the hard facts of the case.

True to those expectations, Oatman returned to center stage and calmly, in a slow, low-pitched drawl, began by expanding upon Judge McDowell's directions.

"Don't return a verdict of guilty unless you're dead-gut, one hundred percent sure of the defendant's guilt. If you think Thorazine killed that woman," he said, pointing to the pictures, "and not strangulation and gunshot wounds, then you need to acquit that man sitting right over there."

It was not Oatman's intention to speak more than necessary about acquittal, however, so he quickly left the subject, addressing instead the viciousness of the crime and the effect it had upon a number of lives.

He began by reminding the jury about how, at the end of September, just days before Rozanne was killed, workers had to come to her home to install new locks and to replace glass broken in an apparent burglary attempt. The experience had left her shaken.

"She was feeling fear and uncertainty in the days before she was murdered," he said, while at the same time, on the opposite end of the emotional spectrum, she was eagerly anticipating a visit to her family in Massachusetts on October 10, a trip she never got to make. Her son, Little Peter, never got to make the trip either, Oatman pointed out, because of the murder of his mother.

"Here was a little four-year-old boy who tries to wake up his mother, but he can't. So he goes to get a glass of milk and his teddy bear and he takes them to his mommy. Then he realizes that Mommy's not going to get any better." She was not going to get any better, he added, because she was "tied up like an animal, lying in her own blood and vomit, making a sound that Chief Duggan hopes he will one day be able to get out of his mind."

Moving systematically through the evidence as it was presented to the jury, Oatman paused to heap scorn upon the defense contention that Thorazine may have been at least partially responsible for Rozanne's death. The prosecution's main medical witness, neurosurgeon Dr. Morris Sanders, Oatman reminded the jurors, had testified that Rozanne was so badly wounded by the bullet in her brain that Thorazine would not have made "a damn bit" of difference. "It's like a man who takes a sleeping pill and then someone comes along and beats him to death with a baseball bat. It ain't the sleeping pill that killed him."

Pointing at Andy, who had remained virtually motionless throughout the trial, Oatman labeled him a skilled liar and manipulator, a man who had tricked or misled a whole string of people ranging from longtime friends Merle Ward and Buddy Wright to the members of a family that befriended him in North Dakota. But then, Oatman said, Andy had the bad luck to run into Morris McGowan at the Richardson Police Department.

"Once again he tried to lie and manipulate, but that time he wasn't talking to someone from North Dakota," Oatman said. "His lies and manipulations got him into the hole out there," he said, adding that when he confessed, it was "the first time he told the truth about who murdered Rozanne." After that, Oatman said, Andy's attempts to lie and manipulate did him little good.

Swiveling again to face Andy, Oatman implored the jury to convict him.

"This is the man who walked out of that house without a second glance, leaving Rozanne strangling on her own vomit and blood, leaving her there for her little boy to find."

Pointing a vengeful finger at Andy, he added: "It's been eight and a half years that Rozanne has laid in that grave and in that time no killer has been called to account for her death." With a final, cold glare at the rigid Andy, Oatman added that it was time for the jury to rectify the situation.

40

Mitchell and Lesser had decided long before that morning that when the time came for closing arguments, the defense's side would be presented by Lesser, the experienced trial attorney. Clad in a dark blue suit, light blue shirt, and black Western boots, Lesser grabbed three yellow notepads filled with blue-ink scribblings and took Oatman's place in front of the jury. He had been up until after three o'clock that morning working on his presentation and he looked tired. With his hands in his pockets and his suit coat open, he began in a muted but firm voice, building on the precepts he had outlined initially in his opening statement.

Mitchell and Lesser were fully aware of the impact that Andy's confessions had made upon the jury and they had decided that any attempt to try to deny that he had indeed attacked Rozanne would be both silly and suicidal. They also had rejected the option of making an impassioned plea to elicit sympathy for their client, electing to leave that message for the penalty phase of the trial, if it came to that. Instead, Lesser based his argument to acquit Andy on another issue.

"This case has never been about whether Andy Hopper went to 804 Loganwood Drive," he said. "It's about 'the rest of the story.' "

Predictably, his voice increasing in volume as he went along, Lesser hammered at the Thorazine issue, insisting that it was not a minor detail to be ignored by jurors.

"It was there!" he asserted, implying that whoever put it there played a major role in Rozanne's death because, recalling the testimony of the defense medical expert, if it had not been for the Thorazine Rozanne might have survived the gunshot wound.

"Where did that Thorazine come from?" Lesser asked rhetorically, scoffing at the initial prosecution contention that Rozanne took it voluntarily. If she had taken it orally, she would have had to swallow twenty-eight pills to result in the concentration found in her blood, he pointed out, leaving unsaid the question "Who takes twenty-eight pills of anything?"

The effect on her, if she had taken it voluntarily, would have been remarkable, Lesser contended, adding that she would never have been able to perform the activities that witnesses had described her completing on the day she was attacked.

While continuing to use the Thorazine as a basic premise for suspecting the involvement of someone else in addition to Andy, Lesser implied that that other person was Rozanne's estranged husband, Dr. Peter Gailiunas. He reminded the jury that one of Rozanne's neighbors had testified about how Gailiunas had warned her not to tell anyone that she had seen him that day, how his son had also told investigators that his father had been there "before and after Mommy got sick," and how Gailiunas continued doing business with Larry Aylor, the man who was having an affair with his wife.

"Dr. Gailiunas is a very unusual man," Lesser said contemptuously, pointing out how Gailiunas, after talking to his son on the telephone and learning that Rozanne was incapacitated in a mysterious fashion, brought his *mother* along with him when he went into what possibly could have been a dangerous situation. That was not very considerate, he said, "unless he knew what the scene was because he had already been there."

The Dr. Gailiunas the jurors had seen on the witness stand was not the real man, Lesser contended, explaining how jurors had never been able to hear testimony from Larry Aylor in which the homebuilder related how Rozanne had told him that Gailiunas had threatened her with a shotgun and had threatened suicide if his wife persisted in leaving him.

"He was masking his real emotions for you," Lesser asserted. "He masked them with Valium when he testified here in this courtroom."

He said Gailiunas misled them about his lack of knowledge about Thorazine and about the access he would have had to the drug. The prosecution also misled the jury, he asserted, with its weak attempts to explain the presence of the drug.

"But if she didn't give it to herself, and if Andy didn't give it to her, then they tried to tell you it wasn't there. But it *was* there," he repeated. "How did it get there? Where did it come from?" he asked, pausing before adding: "It's the defense theory that it came from Dr. Gailiunas."

Lesser reserved his real scorn, however, for Morris McGowan, assailing the detective for, among other things, failing to take notes throughout the long investigation. "He doesn't take notes because notes can come back to contradict you years later," Lesser asserted.

But mainly Lesser attacked McGowan for his actions during the December 20, 1988, interrogation of Andy, when Andy's repeated requests for an attorney were ignored, and for disregarding Andy's two requests to "go back to his cell to think about" developments during the February 27, 1989, interview minutes before Andy confessed.

"This trial has been the tale of two victims," Lesser argued, claiming that one of the victims was Rozanne. The second victim, he said, surprising those who expected him to say Andy, "was the U.S. Constitution." What the jurors saw evidence of, Lesser bellowed, was "Miranda according to Mo."

Reading excerpts from the transcript of the December 20 interrogation, Lesser derisively accused McGowan of repeatedly trampling on Andy's constitutional right to a have a lawyer present during questioning.

"What happened when Andy asked for a lawyer?" Lesser asked, melodramatically striding across the room to the defense table. Reaching into a paper bag, he produced a bright red can of Coca-Cola and popped the top. "They offered him a Coke!"

Taking a sip from the can, Lesser looked directly at McGowan, who was sitting in the first row of the spectator section.

"What contempt for the Constitution of the United States," he spat. "What contempt! To Mo, our Constitution is a very fluid document that he interprets in his own way. What Mo did is more criminal, I submit to you, than the crime. In this case, the victim is all of us and our rights."

Unhappily, he said, the jurors had little remedy because the judge's charge narrowed their options.

"I wish you had a middle ground," he said, "but you don't. You have a Hobson's choice; it's a real dilemma. But if you enforce the Constitution, maybe there will be no more such violations in Dallas County. I ask you," he concluded, "to enforce the Constitution and find Mr. Hopper not guilty."

When Lesser returned to his chair, it was 11:44. He had consumed eighty-seven of his allotted ninety minutes.

Wrapping up the case for the prosecution was Dan Hagood. The last voice the jurors would hear, except for Judge McDowell's, would be the parade-ground bellow of the the no-nonsense prosecutor.

With a twenty-one-inch television set and a VCR as a background prop, Hagood began by attacking Lesser's "anybody but Andy" defense, ridiculing his opponents' attempts to criticize McGowan, Hemphill, Gilliland, and Gailiunas. "And if you convict Mr. Hopper," he promised, "you will be viewed by him as a bad jury."

As expected, Hagood criticized the defense argument that Thorazine was an important factor in the case.

"It's not a defense to Mr. Hopper's conduct if in fact there was Thorazine in Rozanne's body. Legally," he contended, "Thorazine is a nonissue." But he could not say the same for Andy. "He's the one," Hagood roared, pointing at the defendant, "who pumped a bullet into her brain."

Abruptly changing pace and tone, Hagood asked the jury a rhetorical question. "What would have happened if Little Peter would have waked up and gone into that bedroom?" he asked in a quiet, reasonable tone. Pausing dramatically, he continued: "I don't want to think about that." For emphasis, he added a theatrical shudder.

Turning to the television set, Hagood flipped the on switch of the VCR and Andy appeared on the screen. With his finger over the pause button, Hagood ran a few feet of tape, just enough for the jury to get a look at Andy's semi-relaxed stance.

"Does that look like a man who has had his rights trampled upon?" Hagood asked contemptuously.

He ran a few more feet of tape, pausing again after Andy explained how he had accepted the money from Brian Kreafle, reminding the jurors how the defense had criticized the prosecutors for not calling as witnesses Kreafle and others alleged to have taken part in the conspiracy.

"We're not required by law to bring him in here," Hagood said. "His testimony at this stage is irrelevant."

Hagood hit the play button, running enough of the tape for jurors to witness again Andy's admission to being a heavy user of the drug called crystal.

"What is 'crystal'?" Hagood asked. "It's a drug and Mr. Hopper was a drug user. For the defense to suggest that Mr. Hopper would not know how to inject Thorazine flies in the face of this statement."

Again he ran the tape, letting it go to the end.

"That tape has been saved to show you that Mr. Hopper's rights were not violated," he said disingenuously, not admitting that the tape was played in a final attempt to play on the jurors's emotions.

"He didn't feel his rights were being trampled upon. He lied and lied and he tried to put it off on an innocent man named Chip." But it didn't work, Hagood said. "You ought to exult," he told the jurors, "you ought to rejoice because this man was caught," implying that whatever tactics the investigators used was justified by the end.

"What the defense boils down to is no defense," he said. If there was Thorazine in her body, and Hagood was not going to concede that there was, he had the same question Lesser did: How did it get there?

"It certainly couldn't have been Dr. Gailiunas," he averred, "because Dr. Gailiunas was on the other side of town. So it had to have been put there by Mr. Hopper, by Mrs. Gailiunas herself, or by some mystery man. But even if there is a mystery man out there, folks, Mr. Hopper is still guilty as charged. There is only one human being on this planet who is guilty," Hagood said in summation, "and that is Mr. Hopper. He is as dangerous a human being as you're ever going to see in a courtroom. He has the sadistic capacity to turn *this*," he said, flourishing the portrait of Rozanne, "into *this*," he added, replacing the portrait with a blowup of an autopsy picture of Rozanne showing the bullet wound in the back of her shaved head.

"There," he said dramatically, pointing again at Andy, "is the most dangerous man on this planet."

McDowell glanced the clock. It was 12:56, precisely forty-six minutes since Hagood took the floor. Without hearing further comment from the lawyers, the jury filed out of the room to begin its deliberations.

When the jury left, so did the judge and the lawyers. McDowell retired to his chambers while the prosecutors disappeared into the warren of rooms the district attorney's office commands on the eleventh floor of the new courthouse, directly across the freeway from the well-known Reunion Center. The defense team, whose office was several miles away, nervously paced the hallway or slumped on a sagging couch in a court anteroom. Assistant Jean Bauer and Mitchell smoked and chugged diet soft drinks. Lesser nervously jiggled a handful of worry stones and gulped M&Ms.

When the silver dollar–sized red light on the back wall of the courtroom flashed on at 4:45 P.M., a mere 3 hours and 49 minutes after the jurors left to begin deliberations, the atmosphere became immediately tense. The light signaled that the jury wanted to communicate with the court. Either they had a question for the judge, wanted to examine some of the evidence that had been presented during the trial, or they had a verdict.

A bailiff disappeared through the door and down the hallway. When he returned twenty seconds later, he was solemn.

"They have a verdict," he said.

Lesser, Mitchell, and Bauer were engulfed in gloom. Given the options the jury had, the only thing the defense could pray for was a hung jury. But if the jury was undecided about what to do about Andy, the deliberations would have dragged on for days. Because the verdict was being returned so rapidly, the defense knew instinctively that the jury had found him guilty of capital murder.

Quickly the participants gathered. Hagood, Chapman, and Oatman bustled in, along with a handful of others from the district attorney's office. Rozanne's father, her sister and her husband, having flown back from Massachusetts for the finale, took seats in the second row. Gailiunas's mother was there, as she had been throughout the trial. Andy's parents slid into their customary seats behind the chair occupied by their son. McGowan was there, too, as was Investigator McKenzie, Andy's archenemy.

Andy was escorted into the courtroom from the holding cell where he spent his time smoking and sleeping when his presence was not required before the bench.

Judge McDowell, who had used the interval to dispose of some other cases on his calendar and to visit with the attorneys and spectators who had waited around, donned his robe and slipped into his chair.

At 4:54 P.M., without fanfare, McDowell read the verdict that had been handed to him seconds earlier by the bailiff, who had taken it from the jury foreman.

"Guilty of capital murder," McDowell read solemnly.

There was no commotion in the courtroom, the spectators having been warned by McDowell before the jury was summoned not to react because to do so might send a signal to the jury, which still had to hear more evidence and debate one more time in the punishment phase of the trial.

Go home, Judge McDowell told the jury, advising them to take the next morning off, while he would tend to some of his other duties, and to come back at 1 P.M. prepared to listen to more testimony as the trial progressed to the next phase.

41

With no more than a morning off, a grim group of jurors reassembled in Judge McDowell's courtroom after lunch on March 3 to begin the phase that would determine if Andy spent the rest of his life in prison or was executed.

The precondition for a conviction in the guilt/innocence phase of the trial had been whether Andy had actually committed the murder. But in the punishment phase there were two preconditions: "deliberateness" (which for all practical purposes is synonymous with "intentionality"), and what they called in Texas "probability of future dangerousness." That is, was Andy cursed with such a violent nature that he would be likely to kill again, thereby posing a threat to other prisoners or to society if he were ever released?

In the guilt/innocence phase the prosecution was aided tremendously by Andy's confession. But in the punishment phase the prosecution would be—technically at least—starting from scratch. They would have only the testimony of others to show that Andy was such a dangerous man that the only way they could be sure that he would not kill someone else was to kill him first.

Chapman and Hagood desperately wanted the death sentence. But their job would be tougher this time around because asking jurors to look into a man's psyche and predict what he would do in the future was trickier than proving a past action. The prosecutors ran the risk of having just one juror decide that he or she could not forecast human behavior.

Working against the prosecution in their effort to prove Andy's future dangerousness was the fact that he had no history of violent crime other than the attack on Rozanne. In fact, he had no criminal record at all except for the indecent exposure incident in 1976, a misdemeanor, when he was twenty-one years old. The episode involving the insurance man and his missing wallet occurred in 1984, when Andy was twenty-nine. No one in the courtroom except Andy knew exactly what happened there because no charges were ever filed. Sandwiched between the two incidents was Rozanne's murder.

What Chapman and Hagood would have to prove was that at age thirty-six, almost eight years after his last brush with the law, Andy was a killer incapable of controlling his impulse to murder, that he was, as Hagood had labeled him in his closing statement, "the most dangerous man on the planet."

However, the prosecution was heavily favored by precedent. Of the fifty-eight capital murder convictions sought by the Dallas district attorney's office in the previous seventeen years, prosecutors had been denied only twice. There had been a case in December 1991 when a jury that had already convicted a youth of capital murder for stealing a security guard's gun and shooting him to death was locked 8–4 on whether to sentence him to death. They never were able to make a unanimous decision and the youth got a life sentence. In the only other previous case since 1974, the jury was hung with eleven votes in favor of execution and one against. That defendant also got life.

There was no question that juries across the state, not just in Dallas, had few compunctions about sending convicted murderers to death row. At the time Andy was found guilty, there were three hundred and fifty-five persons, including four women, awaiting execution in Texas, the largest number of any state in the country.

Not all of them would be put to death, of course, since all of their cases are in one stage or another of appeal (in death-sentence cases an appeal is automatic; the jury's verdict *has* to be considered by a higher court). But the odds are that the large majority of those sentenced to die eventually will be wheeled into the lethal-injection chamber. In Texas, only one out of four death sentences is reversed.

In the period since the death penalty was reinstituted and the time Andy was convicted, forty-six prisoners had been executed in Texas, five of them in 1991 and four up to then in 1992, even though the year was not yet two and a half months old. It was the highest rate of execution in the country.

If Mitchell and Lesser hoped to save Andy from the lethal-injection chamber, they would have to convince jurors that Rozanne's murder represented an aberration in Andy's life, that he was not by nature a violent person, and that the chances that he would ever kill again were virtually nonexistent.

Their task was made more difficult by the fact that the attack against Rozanne had been a very brutal one and, by Andy's own admission, well-planned, thus apparently deliberate. And despite any admonitions from the court not to let the details of Rozanne's murder influence the decision on future dangerousness, it would be impossible for jurors simply to disregard the graphic testimony they had heard not many days previously, the vivid autopsy pictures, or Andy's matter-of-fact appearance on the confession tape.

In a typical capital murder case in Dallas, the punishment phase is a relatively straightforward procedure. The prosecution calls witnesses, commonly law enforcement officers, to testify to the defendant's violent nature, while the defense counters with character witnesses in an effort to disprove the accusation that the defendant is inherently and incurably vicious.

Generally, the entire proceeding takes no more than a couple of days. But nothing up to then had been typical about Andy Hopper's case and the punishment phase of his trial would not be any different.

Apparently lacking witnesses to testify about Andy's violent nature (except for the convicted drug dealer James Carver), Chapman and Hagood were forced to fall back on an odd assortment of witnesses, many of whom seemed to be testifying *for* Andy rather than against him. Among the witnesses who were allegedly giving testimony designed to prove Andy's future dangerousness were his ex-wife, Becky, and two women with whom Andy had had affairs, Debbie Hosak Lalor and Stephanie Dyess.

By calling Becky, Chapman wanted to introduce evidence of Andy's quick temper, although her testimony concluded in a poignant scene in which both she and Andy were crying.

Lalor told how she thought Andy had taken advantage of her by sweeping her into bed, although she readily admitted she had been flattered by Andy's offer.

Dyess confessed that she was as much the seducer as the seduced in her affair with Andy. Chapman's reason for calling her seemed to be her rather weak admission that Andy once mentioned bondage during a sexually explicit telephone conversation.

Apartment manager Frances Ferguson told about the indecent-exposure scene, but admitted that Andy never tried to attack her or seemed threatening in any way.

Insurance man Glenn Johnston testified that Andy had threatened his wife and children in an attempt to extort money from him. Andy had admitted taking Johnston's wallet but denied threatening his family.

The only law enforcement officer Chapman could muster to talk against Andy was his old nemesis Detective Ken McKenzie.

But by far the most puzzling witness *against* Andy called by the prosecution was Carl Joplin, Andy's former boss at the Chevrolet dealership. Rather than testifying about faults in Andy's character, Joplin had nothing but praise for his former employee. "I'd hire him tomorrow if he got out," Joplin said.

Then, for a reason clear only to himself, Chapman uncharacteristically created a situation over which he had absolutely no control. Almost as a throwaway line, he offered Joplin the opportunity to say whatever he wanted to the jury about Andy.

"As a matter of fact," Joplin replied with undisguised relish, "there certainly is something I want to say."

For the next five minutes, Chapman, who had been so careful throughout the trial to squelch any mention of Joy Aylor, had to listen to Joplin address that very issue.

"I think Andy's getting railroaded," Joplin said with as much indignation as he could muster. "This is a case where other people are involved and nobody is doing anything about it. They're getting away with it," he said, while Andy was being made a scapegoat. "I'll go to hell believing Andy didn't do it," he concluded.

Mitchell and Lesser could hardly contain themselves, scarcely believing their good fortune. As soon as he got the witness on cross-examination, Lesser moved to broaden the discussion.

"What do you mean 'other people are getting away with it'?" Lesser asked Joplin.

"Objection!" yelled Hagood.

Judge McDowell stared at him in disbelief. "Overruled," he said, pointing out that it was the prosecution who had thrown open the door.

The real villain, Joplin said, mentioning her by name, was Joy Aylor, who was sitting safely in France while Andy was on trial for his life. Even if she were to be returned, Joplin added indignantly, she would never be sentenced to death because the district attorney had already made that promise.

"There are so many people involved," Joplin said, "but the people who pushed this deal are not here to stand trial."

Staring at Lesser, Joplin asked, "Is anybody else in jail?"

Lesser shrugged, unsuccessfully smothering a grin. "I can't answer that," the defense lawyer replied.

"Well, I can," Joplin answered angrily, giving the jury the news that the alleged middlemen in the Rozanne murder plot were walking free and had made "deals with the government" so their punishment, if there were to be any at all, would be minimal. At the same time, he contended, Andy was being tossed to the wolves.

Chapman and Hagood fidgeted nervously, anxious for Joplin to wind down and surrender his seat in the witness box. The defense, on the other hand, hated to see Joplin go, but they knew there was only so much mileage they could get from his testimony. Unhappily for them, a few minutes later, Joplin ran out of steam and Lesser had to dismiss him. It was one of the highlights of the trial for the defense, but it was too little and much too late.

The most damaging testimony, as far as Andy's alleged viciousness went, came from James Carver. But the effect of his words on the jury was mitigated by his background. Being the self-admitted second largest marijuana dealer in the country was not the best credential available if truthfulness were an issue.

The balance of the state's witnesses seemed more like supporters of Andy than detractors. There was a former coworker from Houston, two of Andy's former bosses, and his boyhood friend Randy Cain.

The parade of prosecution witnesses began after lunch on Tuesday, March 3, and ended just before lunch three days later. At that time, honoring a defense request for time to gather witnesses and make last-minute strategy adjustments, Judge McDowell told jurors to take the following week off and report back on Monday, March 16, for the start of the defense's presentation, which was expected to take a week or more.

During the break, Mitchell and Lesser examined and reexamined transcripts of testimony from the prosecution's witnesses up to that point. They concluded that the most damaging thing that had been said about Andy was that he had committed adultery. And that, Mitchell and Lesser decided, was not a crime punishable by death. Not even in Texas.

They were prepared to call as many as sixty witnesses to testify in Andy's behalf and against the state's contention that he would be likely to kill again, including Dr. James P. Grigson, a Dallas psychiatrist often referred to as Dr. Death or Dr. Doom because of his proclivity toward testifying for the prosecution in capital murder trials. Although he occasionally is called by the defense—as he would be in Andy's trial—he usually testifies in favor of the execution of a particular defendant, arguing that in his opinion the accused would be likely to continue to commit murder. Until the fall of 1990, Grigson had testified for the prosecution in 124 capital murder trials. In 115 of those, he convinced jurors that they should assess the death penalty. In this case, however, he was prepared to say that Andy was *not* likely to commit another murder.

Mitchell and Lesser balanced the value of Grigson's testimony, as well as that of the remainder of their potential witnesses, against the testimony of the witnesses Chapman and Hagood were believed to have held in reserve to be called after the defense finished its case. Among those, the defense lawyers suspected, was a woman who they thought was prepared to testify that she had heard Andy claim that he had been involved in a drug-connected killing that had nothing to do with Rozanne. Although Mitchell and Lesser were prepared to refute that, they feared the impact the testimony would make upon the jury even if it was unproven.

The biggest advantage for the prosecution up to then was Andy's confession. Also working in Chapman and Hagood's favor was the apparent mind-set of a jury whose members had taken less than four hours, including time for lunch, to find Andy guilty of capital murder. That rush to verdict was something that caused Mitchell and Lesser considerable distress, but they partially rationalized it by reminding each other how Judge McDowell had not given jurors much of a choice. The fact that the jury convicted Andy, given those options, was not surprising.

Of the things that occurred during the trial that Lesser and Mitchell felt most damaged their case, the failure of Judge McDowell to give jurors another option was paramount, even more harmful than his decision to allow the jury to view Andy's confession. Even after seeing the confession, some jurors may have been inclined, after considering McGowan's testimony and weighing the other issues the defense had fought to raise—Thorazine, the possible role of Dr. Gailiunas, and the hint that Andy may not have acted alone—to vote to convict Andy of a less serious charge if that option had existed.

There was one other thing the defense lawyers considered in devising their final strategy: the actions of Judge McDowell.

Mitchell, the appeals expert, was convinced that McDowell had made enough errors in his rulings, particularly with regard to hearsay and the testimony the jury was not allowed to hear, to insure that a higher court would order another trial. As the prosecution had come into trial confident they had a conviction in their back pocket, the defense went out of it convinced that a higher court was going to overturn *whatever* was decided by the current jury.

After considering the various factors, Mitchell and Lesser decided to again be bold. When they showed up on March 16, rather than calling their first witness, they announced that there would be *no* defense, that they were resting their case without eliciting any testimony.

It was a gamble, a carefully calculated risk. By deciding to rest, they effectively shut off the state from calling its rebuttal witnesses.

Judge McDowell, who was as surprised as anyone else in the courtroom over the sudden turn of events, sent jurors home to pack their suitcases. Come back after lunch, he told them, prepared to listen to final arguments and begin deliberations.

42

As in the guilt/innocence phase, both sides were permitted to make final summations to the jury before the panel began deliberations. According to custom, the prosecution is allowed to speak first, followed by the defense. Then the prosecution gets one more chance.

In this case, Hagood led off for the prosecution, reviewing the evidence for the jury, emphasizing the viciousness of the crime.

"This victim had never done a thing to Mr. Hopper," Hagood said. "She was a complete and total stranger to him. But he was her judge, jury, and executioner for fifteen hundred lousy dollars." And that, he added, should say "volumes" about the defendant.

Three things were important to Andy, Hagood said: "money, self-gratification, and not getting caught." Rozanne was not important to him, the prosecutor contended, nor was her child, who was sleeping in the next room. "Mr. Hopper knows the kid is there, but it doesn't stop him. He lays her down. He strips her and he rapes her," referring to Andy's attempt to rape Rozanne. He wasn't being paid to rape her, Hagood added, but he tried it anyway. "Well, he's done with her. He gets up and calmly cleans himself off because he doesn't want to leave any trace of evidence." Hagood shook his head. "If you talk about deliberate," he told the jury, "this is as deliberate as any crime that's ever been tried."

After the shooting, Hagood contended, Andy showed no signs of remorse. Instead, once he was caught, he tried to blame the crime on an innocent man. "Ask Chip if he thinks Mr. Hopper is a dangerous man. Clearly, you have a very dangerous man here in this room," he said, "and only twelve people—you twelve—can stop him."

Lesser, abandoning his earlier strategy of reminding jurors of the possible complicity of others in Rozanne's death, pleaded for Andy's life, claiming that he basically was a good man whose future had been ruined by drugs, a devout Christian who lost his "moral compass." His mistake, he said, was succumbing to worldly temptations.

"You have to have a moral compass to lose one," Lesser said. "And I submit to you that everything you know about Andy Hopper says he had a moral compass. He was brought up in a good family. He was taken to church. He was going to Bible college. He was good at what he did at work. He got married, had children, and somewhere in the Seventies, Andy Hopper lost his moral compass."

He was not alone, Lesser said. Joy Aylor lost her moral compass, as did Rozanne Gailiunas. "These are tough years; a lot of moral compasses get lost."

But, he said, the loss of a moral compass was not a reason to sentence a man to death. "This is a case," he argued, "where life is the appropriate punishment." Evidence presented by the state, Lesser said, was not sufficient to justify Andy's execution. "It doesn't mean that the crime is any less horrible. It doesn't mean that the suffering of the Gailiunas family and the Agnostinellis is any less. It doesn't mean anything more than our system of justice works."

Chapman, perhaps frustrated by the defense decision not to put on a case, thereby closing off his opportunity to call witnesses who might have given damaging testimony against Andy, for the first time displayed strong emotion before the jury.

"They say you can't fool anybody," he said bitterly. "Well, Andy Hopper fooled everybody. Not one of those people [who testified in Andy's behalf] can conceive of the fact that he committed that crime. It wasn't in his interest for them to know that or to know that there was a different side. It wasn't in his interest for them to know what Andy Hopper was really about."

Chapman scoffed at the defense contention that Andy had never exhibited a tendency toward violence, reminding jurors of the abuses against his wife and others with whom he came in contact, such as Frances Ferguson, the apartment manager in Houston to whom Andy had exposed himself.

"Even back at age twenty-one, you know that he is in a totally sober state . . . and able to get pleasure from another perfectly innocent person's horror. How many people can do that?"

But the incident in Houston, the district attorney contended, just set the stage for what happened in Richardson to Rozanne Gailiunas.

"What is the worst reason in the world to kill somebody?" Chapman asked the jurors. "People kill out of love. They kill out of anger. They kill out of jealousy. They kill during arguments. They kill for greed, a mere fifteen hundred dollars to cash in somebody's life."

While the money may have been the first attraction for Andy, the district attorney argued passionately, it was not Andy's sole motivator. "That's not the real reason that this woman breathes no more. The real reason," Chapman said angrily, "is the thrill of it. He wanted to show himself that he could do it."

And once he had done it, the district attorney added, he believed that he would never be found out. "He's very talented, very intelligent. He committed this crime for the thrill of it with every expectation that he would never be caught."

The district attorney shook his head in disgust. Why did he do it? he asked. "He lost his moral compass," he spat sarcastically. "He had a bad day."

Andy Hopper shot Rozanne because he was a killer, Chapman said, asserting that he was a killer on October 4, 1983, and remained a killer today. "This man is absolutely responsible for what he did," Chapman said, his voice rising. "You will never find a criminal more responsible for their conduct than him. I know that he looks shiny and nice for his friends, but Andy Hopper is human only in court. He's like an alien who could come down to this planet and move about and excel and be well-liked and have no compassion for anyone."

The face that he presented to others, Chapman said, was a false one. The real Andy Hopper was a cold-blooded killer. "The horror that woman suffered, the death that she suffered, was delicious to him. You've got to know that it was. All this suffering," he concluded, "was for his monetary, perverted sexual gratification."

* * *

The case went to the jury at 5:47 that afternoon. Rather than begin deliberations that late in the day, jurors went to their hotel, vowing to start debating Andy's fate early the next morning. By the time the jury retired, the lawyers from both sides appeared exhausted, as they should have been. The trial had been three years in preparation and five weeks in execution. It had been a psychological nightmare for Andy's and Rozanne's families, but it had been a physical as well as psychological ordeal for the lawyers, too.

Since well before the proceeding began on January 28, both prosecutors and defense attorneys had been working seven days a week, fourteen or more hours a day. Prosecutor Jim Oatman's wife told D magazine's Glenna Whitley that her husband had been getting by on three hours of sleep a night for more days than she wanted to remember. The end was almost in sight, but the tension, fueled by exhaustion, was almost unbearable.

Although it was impossible to predict what a jury was going to do, there was a feeling among many of those familiar with the case that Andy's punishment was going to be as quickly decided as his guilt had been. Except the consensus was that the decision was going to be in Andy's favor.

Many observers felt the jury would have difficulty justifying a death sentence based on the testimony of prosecution witnesses if Andy's future dangerousness was a primary consideration, as it was required to be under Texas law.

To get a death sentence, all twelve jurors had to agree. But if one or two jurors held out against it, the result for Andy would be a sentence of life in prison. However, in Texas, as in some other states, life is not *life*. Texas and ten other states are among the thirty-six in the country with death penalty statutes without a corresponding law providing for life in prison without possibility of parole. Sensitive about this perceived deficit, the 1991 Texas legislature adopted a law requiring that anyone sentenced to life in prison for capital murder serve a minimum of thirty-five years before becoming eligible to be released. But Rozanne was murdered in 1983, and Andy would fall under the law that applied at that time. If he got a life sentence, he would be eligible for parole in twenty years. By then, Andy would be in his mid-fifties, his parents would almost certainly be dead, and his two daughters would be in their thirties.

＊　＊　＊

Deliberations began on schedule the following morning, Tuesday, March 17, St. Patrick's Day. The jurors argued, sometimes loudly enough to be audible to courthouse workers traversing the adjacent hallway. When Mitchell and Lesser learned that the jurors could be heard yelling at one another, their spirits soared; the more dissention, the better, as far as they were concerned.

Deliberations continued all that day and into the evening without a decision. That, too, was good news for the defense. As a result, Mitchell and Lesser's hopes were high when jurors finally announced at 3:55 P.M. on Wednesday that they had a verdict. Popular wisdom has it that the longer a jury takes to make a decision, the better it is for the defense. Since this jury had taken almost two full days in deciding Andy's punishment, as opposed to less than four hours in deciding his guilt, Mitchell and Lesser were ready to celebrate.

The time factor had not been overlooked by the prosecution team either. When the lawyers were summoned to hear the jury verdict, Hagood leaned across the aisle and offered his congratulations to Mitchell and Lesser. "It looks like you guys won," he whispered.

The defense hopes collapsed, however, when Mitchell and Lesser heard Judge McDowell, out of the jury's presence, issue a caution. "The jurors have said that they don't want to talk to anybody after this case is over with."

When he said that, Lesser felt like sobbing. "I knew that was bad," the defense lawyer said later. "I knew it was a terrible verdict for us."

True to his expectations, the verdict was against Andy.

In a deathly quiet courtroom, McDowell summoned the jurors and read them the first of the questions they were required to answer.

"Was the conduct of the defendant, George Anderson Hopper, that caused the death of the deceased, Rozanne Gailiunas, committed deliberately and with reasonable expectation that the death of the deceased or another would result?"—legal jargon for "did he intend to kill her?"

Equally as legalistic, the jurors replied: "We, the jury, unanimously find and determine beyond a reasonable doubt that the answer . . . is yes."

The judge then moved rapidly to the second question. "Is there a probability that the defendant, George Anderson Hopper, would commit criminal acts of violence that would constitute a continuing threat to society?"

Again, the jury answered yes.

Temporarily dismissing the jury, Judge McDowell turned to Andy and explained that his sentence could not be finalized until an appeals court could study the verdict, as was required by Texas law in any capital murder case. "But I do sentence you to death," he said.

Looking Andy in the eye, Judge McDowell told him, "Good luck to you, sir, and God bless you."

When the verdict was announced, many of those in the courtroom burst into tears, including Andy's parents and usually stoic court officials.

Before filing out of the courtroom, the jurors huddled quickly and announced a reversal of their earlier decision not to discuss their reasoning in reaching the verdict. They would, they said, meet with one representative from the prosecution and one from the defense.

Chapman went first, closeting himself with the panel shortly after 4 P.M. When he was still inside an hour and a half later, and when Mitchell and Lesser were told that laughter could be heard inside the room, the discouraged defense attorneys packed up their papers and left. Although Lesser later met with several jurors on an individual basis, neither of the defenders ever talked to the panel as a group.

In the long run, it made little difference. Mitchell had already documented, at least in general terms, the outline for an appeal.

In reality, the decision to sentence Andy to death had not been easily reached. One juror told Lesser that the first vote among panel members was 9–3 in favor of execution. If that had held, the jury would have been decreed deadlocked and Andy's sentence would have been life in prison. But the jury foreman, a stocky engineer named Randy Cuevas, argued vigorously for the death sentence, badgering the holdouts to switch their votes, asking them if Andy Hopper was the kind of man they would like to have living in their neighborhood, which he might do one day unless they voted in favor of lethal injection. Even if his release was not likely, Cuevas argued, he would still be a threat because he might kill a fellow prisoner. In the end, Cuevas proved very persuasive.

Unhappily, Mitchell and Lesser learned afterward that the juror who may have been their staunchest ally never got a chance to vote or even debate the case with the others. The woman alternate, who was dismissed when testimony was concluded in the guilt/innocence phase, was particularly interested in the testimony about Thorazine and how it got into Rozanne's system. The woman, at one time, had been under Thorazine therapy herself and she knew firsthand how debilitating the drug could be. As a result, she was highly skeptical of prosecution claims that Rozanne took it voluntarily. However, since jurors were prohibited from discussing the case among themselves until formal deliberations began, she never was able to pass along her experiences and thoughts.

EPILOGUE

▼

Joy Aylor remains imprisoned in France and is fighting extradition to Texas, where she is charged with five offenses: capital murder, solicitation of capital murder, and conspiracy to commit capital murder, all in connection with the death of Rozanne, plus conspiracy to commit capital murder and solicitation of capital murder as a result of the attack on Larry. District Attorney John Vance has agreed not to seek the death penalty on the capital murder charge if the French agree to extradite her. Although a French lower court agreed to send her back, she is appealing the order, a process that could last for two years or more. So far, her requests to be released on bond have been rejected by French officials.

Andy Hopper is in a Texas prison awaiting his fate. Despite his circumstances, his parents told Lesser and Mitchell that he is in good spirits and seems to be adjusting to prison life. Mitchell and Lesser were expected to have his appeal ready by August 1993, but an appeal is a lengthy process that could drag on for as long as ten years.

Mike Wilson was sentenced to twelve years in federal prison and fined $20,000 on charges of conspiring to distribute cocaine. He is not eligible for parole.

Gary and *Buster Matthews* are serving their sentences and will not be eligible for parole in Texas for eight to ten years.

Bill Garland remains free on bond on charges of solicitation of capital murder and conspiracy to commit capital murder. No trial date has been set. The assault charge brought by Carol was reduced to a misdemeanor and then dismissed.

His ex-wife and Joy's sister, *Carol Garland*, remains charged with solicitation of capital murder and conspiracy to commit capital murder in connection with the attack on Larry. No trial date has been set.

Jodie Packer was still listed as a fugitive by the U.S. Attorney's Office. He is being sought on charges of passport fraud, harboring a fugitive, and circumventing federal financial-reporting laws.

Brian Lee Kreafle remains free on bond on charges of solicitation of murder and conspiracy to commit capital murder in connection with the death of Rozanne. No trial date has been set.

Joseph Walter Thomas is free on bond awaiting trial on charges of soliciting the murder of and conspiring to murder Larry. No trial date has been set.

In February 1993, *Brad Davis*, Joy's cousin, was sentenced to thirty days in jail for lying to a grand jury about his role in Joy and Mike's escape. He also was placed on probation for five years for his part in the incident.

Larry Aylor is remarried and living in Virginia. There are no charges against him.

Dr. Peter Gailiunas, Jr. also is remarried and continues to maintain a lucrative medical practice in Dallas. There are no charges against him.

Liz Davis, Joy's younger sister, lives in Dallas and owns a small business. She has dropped the name of her former husband, Goacher.

Morris McGowan remains with the Richardson Police Department. He was promoted to captain soon after Andy Hopper's trial.

Larry Mitchell and *Peter Lesser* continue the appeal for Andy Hopper.

Kevin Chapman left the Dallas County District Attorney's Office in mid-1992 to join his father in his insurance business in Austin. He plans to return as a special prosecutor to handle the case against Joy when she is extradited.

In the meantime, *Daniel Hagood* has taken over as lead attorney in the cases stemming from the murder of Rozanne and the attempted murder of Larry.

Doug Mulder, Joy's attorney, in another highly publicized case, successfully defended a former Methodist minister, Walker Railey, who was accused of trying to kill his wife after having an affair with his bishop's daughter.

AFTERWORD

This story is not as complete as I would have liked it to be. Although much is known about Joy Aylor from the available evidence, from what her family members have said, and from what has been written about her, there are still many unanswered questions about her alleged participation in the series of events that led to Rozanne Gailiunas's murder and the attempt on Larry Aylor's life. These issues will not be definitively resolved until she is returned to Texas and brought to trial.

Unhappily, this does not appear to be imminent. On January 20, 1992, the French prime minister and the minister of justice signed a document ordering her return. But that order can be appealed both before French judicial bodies and the European Commission of Human Rights. The process could take many months. In the meantime, other proceedings which *could* be held in Texas—namely the trials of the other principals charged in the case—are being delayed pending Joy's return. To me, it is a doubly compounded unfortunate circumstance.

In the first place, French courts are, in effect, holding American justice hostage. Secondly, the Dallas County District Attorney's Office seems so obsessed with trying Joy that nothing else appears to matter. The prosecution determination to shut off even the merest mention of Joy's possible involvement in Rozanne's murder during Andy's trial bordered on the fanatical and may be grounds for a reversal in an appeals court.

As much as the district attorney's office would like to compartmentalize the situation, it is much easier said than done. Andy Hopper did not operate in a vacuum. If other events had not preceded Andy's alleged meeting with Brian Kreafle, he might never have been involved. While it would be foolish to contend that he might not have committed some other violent crime, or that someone else might not have been found to kill Rozanne, the fact remains that Andy's involvement stemmed directly from the actions of someone else, allegedly Joy. Without being allowed to see *how* Andy became involved, the jury did not get a clear picture of the dynamics of the situation.

Judge McDowell is unquestionably a skilled and fair-minded jurist, but from where I was sitting he seemed to bend very far backward in favor of the prosecution. From my layman's point of view, considering the sizable amount of information jurors did *not* have about a variety of subjects, including but not restricted to details about Joy's alleged involvement, I wonder how they reached a verdict at all.

As troubling to me as the excision of information about Joy's supposed involvement was the deletion of particulars about the parts in the drama allegedly played by Bill and Carol Garland, among others. For example, perhaps there was something to Carol's hint that her husband and "others" may have been present when Rozanne was killed. No one, least of all the jurors, had a chance to evaluate any statements she may have made in this regard.

I also am intrigued by the Thorazine. I do not subscribe to the prosecution's theory that the presence of the drug in Rozanne's blood can be ascribed to an analytical or mechanical mistake. I believe that Thorazine *was* there. And I further believe that she did not administer it herself, nor did Andy inject it into her. Where it came from, I do not know. And I probably never will.

Then there is the tissue that was shoved down Rozanne's throat. Unlike a drug, which can be detected only by complicated and temperamental laboratory equipment, the fact that the tissue was there is without doubt. There are pictures of it; there is ample testimony attesting to its presence. But, as with the Thorazine, I ask, where did it come from? Andy denies that he put it in Rozanne's mouth. When he has admitted to so much else that he did to her, why he would disavow one more detail?

Also bothering me are some of the maneuvers perpetrated by the district attorney's office and investigators from Richardson. Most important, there is the question of why Andy was not allowed to summon an attorney after his arrest despite his repeated requests. And when the court finally appointed one, she was treated in a very unusual way.

Jan Hemphill had nothing to gain and everything to lose by publicly confessing that she ineffectively represented Andy. I think the jury should have been furnished with this information, should have been told that there was at least a question about what happened in those early stages of building a case against Andy. Also, there is the failure of Richardson police to document the investigation by taking notes.

There is no question, at least in my mind, that the Dallas District Attorney's Office is a smoothly operating, highly efficient machine. Nevertheless, it *is* a machine and sophisticated machines operate with very narrow tolerances. While John Vance's strategy may be effective in the vast majority of cases handled by his assistants, there also may be instances where such tactics work against this country's concept of justice. *Is* the public's interest best served when considerable information is willfully withheld from members of a jury? I suspect not.

Up to a point, I can empathize with the prosecution. This case is *extremely* complicated and involved. Kevin Chapman's desire to keep the state's presentation against Andy as simple, as brief, and as uncluttered as possible is understandable. But, in doing so, he insulted the jury and shortchanged the public. He also may have damaged Andy's right to a fair trial. Did Chapman have so little faith in the intelligence of members of a panel that his own people helped select that he was willing to subvert the judicial process to secure a conviction?

I have a lot of respect and admiration for Chapman. I think his heart is pure. But I also think that the years he spent working on this case, his total immersion in the events surrounding the murder and attempted murder, colored his perceptions. I assume he wanted to keep jurors from becoming confused. But I think he underestimated their ability to sort things out on their own.

One thing that I have not learned, despite my own immersion in the case, is *why* this all happened. Nothing I have seen in the record or heard at Andy's trial has answered that to my satisfaction. The prosecution claims Andy attacked Rozanne because he wanted the money and because he enjoyed committing violence. How much Hagood and Chapman actually believe that, as opposed to how much was said in an attempt to impress the jury, I don't know. I do know that it doesn't impress me a lot; I was not convinced by their argument. I have no clue as to Joy's motivation, if in fact she is guilty, since they would not mention her at all or willingly allow anyone else to do so.

When I asked McGowan why these crimes occurred, he shrugged, explaining that *why* is often the last thing that investigators are searching for. That's an inadequate answer, I feel, perhaps influenced by his own desire to protect the case against Joy.

Carol and Joy, in their conversation in the motel room, implied that Joy launched upon her plot against Larry because she believed he had been having an affair with their younger sister.

Larry himself has a much firmer opinion of why Rozanne was killed and he was ambushed: money. To substantiate his claim, Larry points to how Joy allegedly told him in June 1985 that all their money had been exhausted. Larry believes that Joy stripped their account to help build her escape fund and create a nest egg on which she could live comfortably abroad. As for the attempt on his life, he claims that he had a $250,000 insurance policy naming Joy as beneficiary, plus their not inconsiderable private property, which presumably she and Chris would have inherited. Also, when he was on the stand during Andy's trial, Larry repeated his long-held belief that Dr. Peter Gailiunas was involved in Rozanne's murder. His motive, Larry believes, also was money. If Rozanne had successfully divorced Gailiunas, Larry maintains, she stood to collect almost one third of a million dollars in the subsequent settlement.

The thing that bothers me the most about the situation, I guess, is the possibility that there may never be a final resolution. By running to France, Joy insured that she would never have to face the possibility of being executed for her actions, whatever they were. While Andy was the unknowing instrument in Rozanne's death, Joy may have been the one who set everything in motion. And she apparently will never have to pay the same price as Andy, even though her involvement allegedly was greater, especially when one considers that she also may have plotted the attempted murder of her husband. Seemingly, it was not from lack of trying that the attempt failed. She could not predict that the Matthews brothers were hopeless bunglers.

Troubling, too, are news reports from France indicating that Joy is seeking to be released on bail from her Marseilles jail pending a decision on her extradition. So far, the French courts have refused her request. But if it looks as though the process is going to continue to drag on, a judge could always relent and turn her loose. If that happens, there is no doubt in my mind that she will flee again. Remember that her lover,

Jodie Packer, is still a fugitive, undoubtedly holed up in an out-of-the-way locale hoping for just such an eventuality.

For Larry, that is a nightmare scenario. When Joy was arrested in March 1991, he gave a huge sigh of relief. It was the first time since Rozanne was shot in October 1983 that Larry felt he could breathe easily. Convinced from the day of Rozanne's shooting that it had been a contract job, Larry was certain that he was next. As a result, he always was armed. In his truck, he carried a shotgun behind the seat and a pistol in the glovebox. From the time he moved into an apartment after his divorce from Joy until he married Jan Bell in January 1988, he refused to sleep in his bedroom because there were two large windows over the bed. It would have been too easy for a killer to blast him with a shotgun, he felt. As a result, he'd bed down each night on a sofa in the den. When asked if he felt safer with Joy in jail, his answer was succinct: "Absolutely." Then he added, "But if she's ever freed, I'm a dead man. She's obsessed with destroying me."

Despite all that's happened over the years, especially the death of Chris Aylor—which Larry feels Joy was indirectly responsible for—Larry said he no longer loathes his ex-wife. "I hate what she did, but she's a very sick person. She's also very dangerous. I *know* she's guilty and I'd like to see her get the death sentence."

On the bright side, many of those involved in the succession of tragedies—those who are not in jail or facing criminal charges—have apparently managed to put their lives back together. Little Peter seems well on his way to recovering from the trauma he suffered in 1983. Rozanne's sister and her parents appear to have adjusted to the situation. Andy's ex-wife has begun a new career in a town many miles from Dallas and, according to her, their children have made peace with their father. Andy's parents, largely through their unswerving devotion to their faith, have forgiven their son. And Larry, essentially the sole survivor in a once seemingly solid family of three, has started a successful new life in a distant state with a wife and two teenage children who support him.

CHRONOLOGY OF
MAJOR EVENTS

1968

August 19—One week after her nineteenth birthday, Joy Davis marries Larry Aylor, a $40,000-a-year men's clothing salesman.

1970

May 8—Larry and Joy have a son, Christopher. He will be their only child.

1977

Dr. Peter Gailiunas, Jr., a kidney specialist, marries a nurse he met at a Boston hospital, Rozanne Borghi.

1978

With encouragement from Joy's wealthy father, Larry Aylor opens a homebuilding company. He oversees construction; she designs interiors. The company soon becomes very profitable.

1979

April 19—A son is born to Peter and Rozanne. He is christened Peter Gailiunas III.

1982

The Gailiunases hire Larry to build their $500,000 home in an exclusive Dallas suburb. Within months, Larry and Rozanne are involved in a torrid affair.

1983

June—Larry and Rozanne move out on their respective spouses to better continue their affair.

October 4—Rozanne is found gravely wounded but alive in the bedroom of the small home she shared with her four-and-a-half-year-old son.

October 6—Rozanne, age thirty-three, dies of her injuries.

1984

Larry and Joy attempt a reconciliation.

1986

Late winter—Joy learns that Larry had been having an affair with her younger sister, Liz. A divorce seems imminent.

June 16—In an apparent attempt to discuss their marital difficulties, Joy arranges to meet Larry at a ranch they own in Kaufman County, near Dallas. When Joy does not show up for the meeting, Larry leaves the ranch with a friend to return to Dallas. Driving through a copse of trees near the entrance to the ranch, the two are ambushed by riflemen. Larry's friend is wounded in the elbow, but Larry escapes with minor cuts.

A few days later, Larry learns that Joy has been having an affair with the owner of a Dallas interior-renovation company, Jodie Packer.

August 19—Joy and Larry's divorce becomes final, almost on their eighteenth anniversary.

October 4—Joy's older sister, Carol, secretly marries a man she met through Joy, Bill Garland.

1988

May 26—Acting on information supplied by Carol Garland, Joy's older sister, Joy and Bill Garland, Carol's estranged husband, are arrested as suspects in the murder of Rozanne Gailiunas and the attempted murder of Larry Aylor. Arrests of several others soon follow.

July—An investigative chain leads to a former ministerial student, Andy Hopper, as a suspect in Rozanne's death.

August 1—When investigators seem to be getting close, Hopper flees. He drops out of sight for four and a half months.

August 27—Two bumbling brothers, Buster and Gary Matthews, are arrested as suspects in the rifle attack on Larry.

September 19—Joy is indicted for capital murder, two counts of conspiracy to commit capital murder, and two counts of solicitation of capital murder. If convicted, she could be sentenced to death. Within hours, she is released on bond.

December 20—Andy Hopper is arrested at a friend's house and held for investigation in connection with Rozanne's death.

1989

February 27—As a result of questionable tactics by investigators, Hopper confesses to attacking and shooting Rozanne.

November 30—Carol Garland is indicted for solicitation of murder and conspiracy to commit capital murder in connection with the attack on Larry.

December 26—Joy and Larry's son, Christopher, is fatally injured when a 1987 Corvette Joy gave him for Christmas runs off the road and smashes into another vehicle. He dies of the injuries several hours later. Joy is joined at the hospital by her new lover-to-be, former prosecutor and defense attorney Mike Wilson. Joy and Larry fight bitterly over possession of Christopher's body.

1990

March 21—Mike Wilson is arrested at a north Dallas motel by DEA agents. In his possession is a bag containing twenty pounds of cocaine. Another twenty-six pounds of the drug is found in the room he has just visited.

May 4—Almost two years after she was arrested as a suspect in Rozanne's death and the attempted murder of her then-husband, Joy is ordered to appear in court for a conference on how her trial will be conducted. Her bond earlier had been raised to $140,000.

May 5 or 6—With both their trials looming closer, Joy and Wilson flee to Canada. Joy allegedly has $300,000 in her purse.

June 7—A nervous Joy leaves Wilson in Canada and flies to Mexico using identification issued in the name of Jodie Packer.

June 11—A despondent Wilson, feared by a friend to be suicidal, is tracked down and arrested by Canadian authorities.

August 6—Larry Aylor wins a $31.2 million default judgment in a damage suit against Joy stemming from her alleged attempt to have him killed. Since Joy is a fugitive, Larry's testimony against her is undisputed.

A Dallas woman, responding to media reports on the case, tells police she recognized Joy as a woman with whom she shared a room while attending a Spanish-language school in Cuernavaca, Mexico.

September 17—Joy evades a police trap at the Mexican school. She disappears.

November—Joy's one-time and future lover Jodie Packer allegedly applies for a passport in the name of a long-dead uncle, Donald Averille Airhart.

December—A woman calling herself Elizabeth May Sharp moves into a villa on the French Riviera, near Nice.

1991

March 16—Following an accident in a rental car, Elizabeth Sharp is arrested in France and identified as Joy Aylor. At the police station, she tries to commit suicide.

March 21—The Dallas district attorney says he will abandon plans to seek the death penalty against Joy if the French courts will extradite her to Texas.

April 2—Jodie Packer is arrested at the home of Joy's parents near Austin and charged with passport fraud.

April 30—Mike Wilson is convicted on drug charges.

July 23—Jodie Packer fails to appear in court to answer the charges against him. He is declared a fugitive.

October 15—In response to a suit against Joy, Judge Dee Miller awards Donald J. Kennedy a $20 million default judgment for injuries suffered when the Matthews brothers shot at Larry and hit him instead, wounding him in the elbow.

1992

January 27—Andy Hopper goes on trial before Judge Patrick McDowell on charges of murdering Rozanne.

March 2—A five-woman, seven-man jury convicts Hopper of Rozanne's murder.

March 16—The same jury that found Hopper guilty of murder sentences him to death by lethal injection.

December 18—Jodie Packer is indicted by a federal grand jury on charges of violating federal financial reporting laws while collecting a large amount of cash to help finance Joy's flight.

1993

January 20—French prime minister and minister of justice sign a document ordering Joy's extradition. However, the decision can be appealed.